SOPHIE'S RUIN

A CRIMSON AND SHADOWS NOVEL

V.I. DAVIS

All rights reserved.

No part of this publication may be sold, copied, distributed, reproduced or transmitted in any form or by any means, mechanical or digital, including photocopying and recording or by any information storage and retrieval system without the prior written permission of both the publisher, Oliver Heber Books and the author, V.I. Davis, except in the case of brief quotations embodied in critical articles and reviews.

PUBLISHER'S NOTE: This is a work of fiction. Names, characters, places, and incidents either are the product of the author's imagination or are used fictitiously. Any resemblance to actual persons, living or dead, business establishments, events, or locales is entirely coincidental.

Sophie's Ruin Copyright 2025 © V.I. Davis

Cover art by Dar Albert at Wicked Smart Designs

Published by Oliver-Heber Books

0 9 8 7 6 5 4 3 2 1

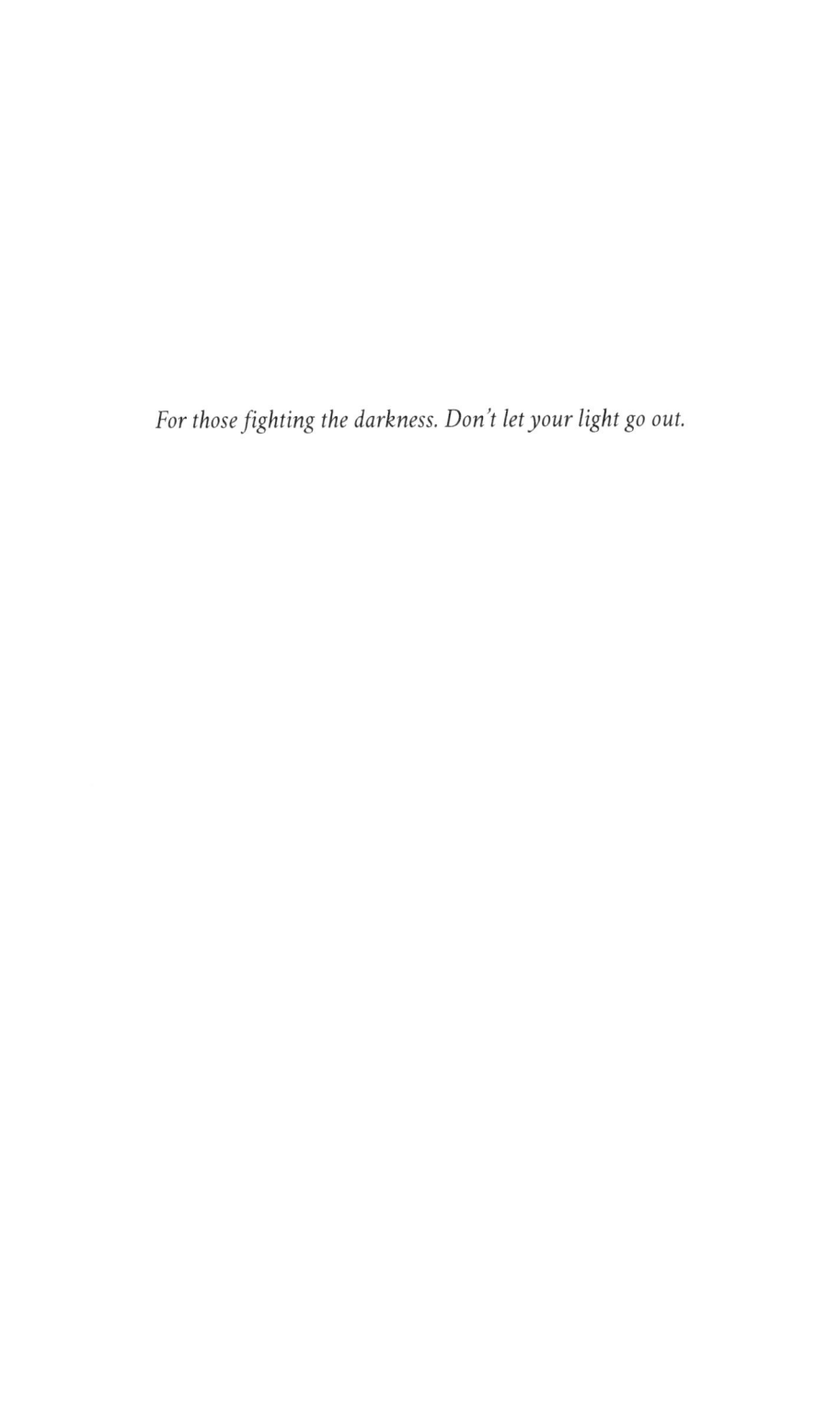

For those fighting the darkness. Don't let your light go out.

To my husband, this book wouldn't have been possible without you.

1

*D*arkness surrounded me. I was standing in the middle of it, completely and utterly alone. The air was still, and no sound disturbed the eerie silence, not even that of my own breathing. My heart stuttered in my chest as terror rose and swelled. I turned around in a circle, but there was no end and no beginning in sight, only the pitch-black. My pulse beat in my ears as my breathing picked up, bursting in and out of me. Before panic could take over entirely, a whisper erupted out of nowhere, skimming the surface of my mind. It echoed inside my head and all around me. Velvety-soft and dripping with allure, the sound was shadows and smoke, probing and prodding, luring me in. My brows knitted—I didn't want to be here, alone, with the darkness whispering things to me. I didn't want to succumb to it, but it was nearly impossible to fight the treacherous pull when my very nature was drawn to it.

"Just a taste." The whisper in my head grew louder, the shadows blooming and swirling.

Suddenly, a hand landed on my shoulder, startling me. The brief burst of panic was quickly replaced by potent relief. Without turning around, I sensed my mother standing behind me, gripping my shoulder to guide me out of the darkness and into the light.

"There is a light inside you," came her measured voice, as a childhood memory invaded my mind. In it, my mother was saying those words to me when I was a little girl.

"As if I'm a star?" I'd asked her then, my high voice full of wonder.

"Yes." She'd smiled at me. "Protect that light, and nurture it so it burns brighter and brighter. Carry it with you always. Even in the darkest hour."

As the memory dissipated, the corners of my mouth lifted, and I spun around, excited to see my mother, relieved to no longer be alone in this dark and quiet place. But it wasn't my mother standing before me when I turned around. It was Henry, and seeing him instead of her did not douse my excitement. Quite the opposite. Happiness flooded me as I stared into his deep-blue eyes. A myriad of emotions churned in them, drawing me in, and I took what felt like my first breath in this unnatural place as if he were the very oxygen I needed. His chiseled face lit up with a brilliant smile as he reached for me to guide me farther away from the darkness and into the light. A charge passed between us when his large hands wrapped around mine. I went to step toward him, but something held me back. It was as if the darkness itself was clinging to me, its inky fingers snagging on my clothes, digging into my skin, and pulling on my hair.

Henry's smile faltered, and his brows pulled together as his grip on my hands tightened. I tried to step toward him again, and this time, I was able to move closer, even though it felt like treading through a pool of black, viscous liquid. Henry's taut features smoothed out, relief radiating from him. Relief flared in my chest as well, and a startled laugh escaped because I couldn't wait to be with him, engulfed in his fresh and woodsy scent. Peace and security awaited me in his embrace. I was so close, yet, for some reason, it felt like an abyss lay between us—an insurmountable distance of darkness and pain, separating us for all eternity. I wouldn't let it. My brows pinched in concentration as I went to take another step. Henry's intense gaze was fastened on mine, and he seemed to have stopped breathing as he watched me.

Only one more step. I knew if I took it, I would be in Henry's arms, and everything would be okay. My life and everything that I was would make sense again. Yet before I could reach him, two black, scaly arms shot out from the darkness behind me, wrapping around my waist like a vise and jerking me back. Despair surged, instant and all-consuming, as I tried to hold on to Henry. Tears rushed to the surface, gliding down my cheeks, because he was slipping through my fingers. I was losing him, losing us, losing myself...A heartbeat later, my hands slipped out of his grip. My curled fingers grasped thin air, and I sucked in a sharp breath a second before the darkness swallowed me whole.

My eyes flew open, and I sucked in a sharp breath, much like I had in my dream before the darkness had consumed me. Except I wasn't in that black void anymore. I was in Henry's bedroom, lying beside him in his bed. My hand was on his hard chest, and I had a feeling that my cheek had rested on it as well, before my head had snapped up when I'd awakened. Releasing a soft exhale, I lowered my head back down to the solid slab of muscle. The steady beating of his heart brought instant comfort, and I closed my eyes, momentarily lost in the familiar rhythm. His heart was strong like he was—strong and relentless. I might have been pulled into the darkness in my dream, but I knew that wouldn't stop Henry from coming for me. He'd fight for me, just like he had when I'd first turned. When I'd become a vampire, the darkness had sunk its claws into me, but Henry had dragged me from the obsidian abyss before I'd plunged into the deep crimson waters of bloodlust, losing my humanity forever. He'd pulled me out, but then why had the darkness returned to haunt me in my dreams?

My forehead creased as I opened my eyes again. Perhaps I was reading too much into my dream. It was possible my subconscious had been playing tricks on me because I was nervous about tonight. In a few hours, Henry and I would meet with the clan leaders to decide the future of the Empire.

Last night, I'd defeated the Dark Witches, using the amulet my ancestors had created to erase them from existence. Josephine's

Tear had the power to eradicate all supernatural forces, but I hadn't used it on the vampires, because I was one of them now. So the vampire clans would remain, even though the humans no longer needed their protection from the Dark Witches.

I'd destroyed our greatest enemy, accomplishing something I'd thought impossible mere hours ago. Why was my chest painfully tight with unease when I should feel lighter than air? Instead of floating, I felt weighted down, the walls of the dark room pressing in on me.

I knew why. Henry and I were prepared to step willingly into the shadows to let the humans have their country back, but I doubted the others were prepared to do the same. My mind flashed back to the moment last night on the border when everyone had realized that I'd defeated the Dark Witches. It hadn't been elation that had splashed across their near-perfect faces; it had been shock and uncertainty. A myriad of questions had burned in the clan leaders' eyes, but before they could voice any of them, Henry had whisked me away from the border after scheduling a meeting for tonight.

Now, I couldn't help but wonder if he'd known the reprieve would be fleeting and had wanted to carve out a few hours of peace before the next storm. A sense of foreboding slithered down my spine at the thought, prickling my skin.

As if he could sense my unease in his sleep, Henry's arm tightened around me, tucking me closer to his unyielding body. Lifting my head from his chest, I looked at his flawless profile, my gaze gliding over the high and broad cheekbones to the well-formed mouth. With his black hair spilling across his forehead and his full lips parted, he looked peaceful and content, breathing softly in his sleep. His expression was almost serene, as if he had everything he needed right here in this room. Seeing him like this helped tamp down my inner turmoil, and I let myself relax into his hold. My gaze roamed over the vast expanse of his chest and the defined lines of his torso. He was truly magnificent, and he was mine. A feeling I couldn't yet put into words swelled in my chest, threatening to overflow and spill into the world around me.

My pulse quickened as an intense desire invaded my senses. Reaching up, I gently brushed my fingertips over Henry's chiseled features before trailing them down his chest to his stomach. When the sculpted muscles tautened under my touch, my eyes darted back to his face to see if I'd successfully coaxed him out of his slumber. He inhaled deeply as he stretched, and my own breathing caught in anticipation of what would come once he was fully awake. A pleasant curling sensation stirred between my thighs, and my lips curved into a sinful smile as my hand dove under the covers to further explore Henry's powerful body. The low, rough sound that rumbled from deep within his throat made my skin flush with awareness.

"Sophie," he growled, opening his eyes to look at me.

"Yes?" I whispered, as I wrapped my hand around his hardness.

"What are you doing?" he rasped, gliding his fingertips up and down my bare back, eliciting a shiver from me. His breath hitched when I began sliding my hand up and down his length, matching the movement of his fingers.

"What does it feel like I'm doing?" I purred, meeting his deep-blue gaze that was turning darker by the second. My heart skipped a beat at what I saw in his eyes, and I felt my cheeks heat at the intensity of his stare. "I think I never want to leave this bed," I added, low and husky.

The heat in his gaze intensified as he swallowed thickly.

"As much as I would love it, you know we can't do that." He tried to be the voice of reason, but his words came out low and rough, his eyes still turning darker with desire.

He was right, of course. Soon we would have to leave this bed and this room. I truly didn't know what the meeting with the clans would bring, and the feeling was more than disconcerting.

It threatened to quell my desire, but I refused to let it, quickly recapturing the feeling.

"Last night, we faced the Dark Witches and prevailed," I told Henry, looking into his eyes. My voice trembled, betraying how much I was still shaken by the fact. "We thought we were going to die..." My breath snagged in my throat as I realized I'd never let that truly sink in. I hadn't known if the amulet would spare my life and Henry's when I'd used it. I'd been prepared to die, and Henry had been prepared to follow me into the void, all for humanity's sake. "But we didn't die," I continued. "We survived, and I want to be alive with you. To enjoy this moment of peace for a little while longer."

Something I couldn't quite decipher flickered across Henry's features at my words. Perhaps the same realization I'd just had hit him, making his already pale skin lose more color and his eyes turn entirely black with molten heat.

Instead of answering me, he threaded his fingers through my hair and guided my mouth to his. I immediately opened up for him, eager to taste him on my tongue, to lose myself in him and in this moment. The kiss was everything I'd wanted and hadn't even realized I'd needed. His tongue rolled over mine painstakingly slowly, as if we had all the time in the world. Each stroke sent sparks of desire through my entire body, all the way to my fingertips and toes, melting away any uncertainty I was feeling about the future. There was no room for it as my blood ignited, and I was on fire, burning only for him. The outside world ceased to exist as we created our own little world inside this room. A world where it was just the two of us, our bodies and our hearts bared, swimming in this feeling of pleasure and bliss that was fusing us irrevocably together.

2

In a few hours, the night had descended. The heavy gray curtains in Henry's bedroom were drawn like always to prevent even a sliver of light from sneaking in during the day. Still, I knew if I opened them, the night would greet me like an old friend, comforting and full of promise. Ever since becoming a vampire, I'd developed this innate sense that told me when dawn was near, urging me to find shelter lest I meet my untimely demise. The same sense also whispered to me like a lover, low and seductive, when the last rays of sunlight disappeared below the horizon, beckoning me outside to frolic in the night. It was as if my body came alive when the blanket of darkness crawled over the city. Every part of me sparked to life like the stars in the night sky until I burned bright like they did, beautiful and otherworldly.

The awakening was happening now as I lay here, restless energy filling my veins. My muscles twitched almost imperceptibly with the need to move, to seize the night. When I lifted my head from Henry's chest, I found him watching me from beneath his thick, dark lashes. The bedroom was pitch-black, but I could see his face clearly because of my vampire eyesight.

"You feel it, don't you?" he asked, reaching up to tuck a strand of hair behind my ear. "The night is calling you."

"Yes," I admitted, bracing my hand on the mattress to sit up. "Should I fear it?" I asked as the gray satin sheet covering us slid down to pool around my hips.

Henry's gaze dropped to my exposed breasts but didn't linger there. His eyes were dark with hunger when he lifted them back to mine, but he didn't pursue the lustful thoughts, focusing on our conversation instead of my naked form.

"Fear it?" he asked, his eyebrows knitting.

"The darkness," I explained.

"The night is not the same as the darkness. There is freedom in it," he said calmly, his features smoothing out again.

"There is freedom in the darkness," I countered, barely above a whisper, as if I were speaking of something forbidden.

"That's what the darkness wants you to believe." Henry's voice was still calm, but tension pinched his features.

"It whispers things…" I continued in a hushed tone.

"All lies," he said vehemently, gently clasping the back of my neck. He was also sitting up now, so our faces were inches apart. "You know the truth." He reached up with his other hand and placed it over my heart, close to where the Tear and the locket holding the portrait of my mother rested. "And if you ever forget, you will always find it in here, in who you are."

"My mother used to say there was a light inside me," I said, remembering my dream.

"She was right. I can see it," Henry replied, one side of his mouth turning up.

Wonder and awe settled into his striking features as he stared at me. He appeared fascinated by me, and being on the receiving end of that look was exciting and terrifying all at the same time. No one had ever looked at me like that before, and I was overcome with emotion as I stared back. I couldn't help but wonder how I'd lived without that look for so long, and a part of me knew that if Henry ever stopped looking at me like that, I'd be devastated.

"You can see it? Truly?" I whispered, in awe of him being in awe of me.

He nodded as his smile grew. "Yes. And if you ever lose sight of it, ask me. I will always be by your side, to help you find it again."

He unclasped the back of my neck and slid his other hand up from where it had been resting over my heart. Gently, he wrapped both hands around my face, cupping my cheeks. The tender way in which he touched me nearly brought tears to my eyes. Henry was a vampire, powerful and deadly. Yet, with me, never-ending tenderness poured out of him. Like a salve, it soothed my skin and filled the cracks in my heart the darkness had created. He would always help me find my light. I didn't doubt it, just like I didn't doubt him.

But what if he's not always by my side? The thought was there one moment and gone the next, like a whisper in the wind. But I heard it, nonetheless.

The feeling of foreboding I'd felt earlier returned, and I shuddered as it washed over me like an icy splash, chilling me to the bone. The dark place inside me stirred again, bleeding into my subconscious like black ink until it oozed out of my pores, dripping on the bed, and staining the sheets. It slithered off the mattress to the stone floor, where it pooled before dashing to the corner of the room. There, it solidified, becoming a tangible and lingering presence. The shadows in that part of the room seemed deeper than the rest, molding into a dark silhouette that just stood there, watching. Waiting. What it was waiting for, I had no idea. Perhaps for Henry to leave my side so it could lash out and choke my light in its black, oily fingers, extinguishing it forever.

"Sophie, are you okay?" Henry's deep voice penetrated the haze of my mind.

Blinking, I realized that I'd lowered his hands from my face.

My fingers were still wrapped around his wrists as I peered into the dark corner of the room. When I refocused on Henry, I found him watching me with a concerned look on his face.

"I'm okay," I told him, letting go of his wrists and reaching for the lamp on the bedside table. When I turned it on, a soft yellow glow cast over the room, banishing most of the shadows. Some still crawled behind Henry's eyes, though, as they roamed over my face.

"I'm okay," I told him again before I clasped his cheeks and kissed him.

I wasn't sure I believed my own words, but feeling Henry's lips on mine helped douse some of my anxiety. An entirely different feeling invaded my blood as he deepened the kiss, fisting his hand in my hair. I wanted to lose myself in him again, to delay the inevitable return to reality we soon would have to face, so I slid my hands over his broad shoulders before dragging my fingertips down his chest to his stomach and lower still until…he stopped me. I whimpered against his mouth as he grabbed my hands to prevent them from diving under the covers. We were both breathless when he broke the kiss and rested his forehead on mine.

"We need to get ready. The clan leaders will be here soon," he said low, his hands pressing mine.

A tiny selfish part of me almost suggested postponing the meeting, but I knew better than to voice that thought aloud. We needed to meet with the clan leaders as soon as possible to try and convince them to slink back into the shadows where they belonged.

"We don't know what's going to happen tonight," I said quietly, my voice dropping almost to a whisper, as if uttering the words would set something into motion. Something terrible.

Still holding my hands, Henry stared at me for a moment. Tension bracketed his mouth and pinched the corners of his eyes, letting me know he felt as uneasy about the upcoming meeting as I did.

"Whatever happens, we will face it together," he finally said, before softly kissing my forehead.

The sweet gesture made my heart squeeze in my chest.

"What if we don't leave this room?" The words tumbled out of my mouth before I could stop them.

Henry's brows pulled together for a moment before he forced them apart.

"The Sophie I know would never back down from a challenge," he said, one side of his mouth lifting. "You defeated the Dark Witches. What is facing a handful of vampires?"

I couldn't bring myself to smile back as I admitted, "For some reason, it feels like they will prove to be a bigger challenge than the witches."

Henry's chest heaved with a harsh exhale as his half-smile faded.

"I fear you might be right, but we can't hide in here forever. We need to meet with the clan leaders to ensure we are all in agreement on what will happen with this country, now that the Dark Witches are no more."

"What if they don't see it the same way we do?" I asked. "That our place is no longer at the top, ruling over the humans?"

A muscle flexed along Henry's jaw as his gaze searched my face.

"I don't know what's going to happen," he said. "All we can do is try to convince them."

Sensing there was no point in delaying the inevitable, I nodded and slowly pulled my hands from his. Longing was etched into his features as he watched me leave the bed, taking the top sheet with me. Was he longing for peace like I was? Longing to stay in this bed and in this room, pretending the outside world didn't exist? Even if he was, he didn't stop me as I wrapped the sheet around my body, clutching it to my chest, and swept from the room.

My unbound hair whooshing around my bare shoulders, I quickly moved through the empty, dimly lit halls of the mansion until I arrived at my bedroom door. The room was dark when I walked in, halting by the vanity as my gaze snagged on the Tear in the mirror's reflection. The crystal in the heart of the amulet pulsed on my chest like a beacon, the pale-blue glow illuminating my face and highlighting my drawn features.

Shaking my head to clear my thoughts, I let go of the sheet, and the satin glided down my body with a faint swish before pooling by my feet. The air caressed my exposed skin as I reached up and unclasped the thin chain holding the Tear and then the one holding the locket with the portrait of my mother. I placed both on the vanity and walked to the bathing chamber, stopping by the bedside table on the way there to flip on the lamplight. After showering, I quickly got dressed, selecting a simple cream tunic and brown pants. I chose comfortable, practical clothing on purpose. Since I truly didn't know what to expect from the meeting tonight, I wanted to be prepared for anything. The pressure on my chest intensified as I stepped into a pair of brown leather boots and returned to the vanity to finish getting ready.

Henry rapped his knuckles on my bedroom door a moment later. I glanced at him when he walked in, quickly drinking in his chiseled form. Dark breeches encased his long legs, and he wore a white shirt that molded to his powerful torso. His blue-black hair was swept back from his face, revealing his strongly defined features that appeared as drawn as mine. The longing I'd seen earlier was still there when our gazes locked, and I knew he could see it reflected in my face before I turned back to the mirror. I pulled the top half of my golden-brown hair up, letting the bottom half flow in soft waves down my back.

"Allow me," Henry said, when I reached for the locket on top of the vanity.

Lowering my hand back down, I gave a small nod, waiting for him to approach me. He did so in two long strides, stopping behind me. When he reached around me to pick up the locket, my breath caught, and I found myself wondering if I ever would not have such a visceral reaction to his proximity. A pleasant tingling sensation erupted over my skin as Henry reached up and brushed my hair to the side, draping it over my right shoulder. His brows pinched in concentration as he laid the locket against my chest and fastened the delicate chain behind my neck. I took a steadying breath, the comforting weight of the necklace grounding me like it always did. In the mirror, Henry's deep-blue gaze lingered on the locket for a few seconds before lifting to my face.

"Eloise would be so proud of you and what you have accomplished. You defeated the Dark Witches," he said, his eyes shining with admiration.

"My grandmother had begun creating the amulet, and my mother finished it. It is their accomplishment, not mine," I said, turning around to face him. "Besides, you helped me find it. You saved me in the Black Forest and then again when the Dark Witches took me."

"True, but you saved everyone else," Henry pointed out, his strong arms encircling my waist. "You saved me," he added low, resting his forehead against mine.

"I did?" I whispered, breathing him in. Somehow, I knew he wasn't just talking about the Dark Witches.

"Of course you did," he said quietly. "Sophie?"

"Yes?"

"Will you keep saving me?"

Forever? I thought I heard him say even though he didn't utter another word.

"We'll keep saving each other," I told him, brushing my lips over his.

We would keep saving each other from the darkness that came with being a vampire. At times, the sinister hunger was hard to ignore, even for Henry. The never-ending thirst was always there, gnawing at our insides. It followed us everywhere, waiting in the shadows like a predator ready to pounce and pull us under, drowning us in bloodlust.

Henry kissed me back deeply but also tenderly—a kiss to seal the promise we'd just made to each other.

"Ready?" he asked when he pulled away.

I wasn't but I nodded anyway. When I did, Henry unwrapped his arms from my waist and took my hand in his, threading his fingers through mine.

"Wait," I stopped him when he went to pull me toward the door.

When Henry gave me a questioning look, I explained, "I want to bring the Tear. I know we no longer need it, but I can't bear the thought of parting with it." The magic of my bloodline was stored in the amulet. Even now, I could feel the Tear's power with each pulse of the pale-blue light.

Henry looked uncertain.

"The clans don't know the amulet can also destroy vampires, and we need to keep it that way. I don't want you to become a target," he cautioned.

With a nod of understanding, I grabbed the Tear off the vanity and shoved it in my pant pocket.

Hand in hand, we walked out of my room and headed down the long hallway illuminated by wall sconces. The mansion was eerily quiet since all the human servants were still up north, where we'd sent them in preparation for war.

"I miss her," I said as if to myself while we walked.

"I do, too," Henry replied, lost in thought. I didn't need to tell him I meant Rory. "I wish she were still alive so she could experience it—this new world where the humans no longer have to serve the clans." A soft smile pulled at his lips, making me wonder if he were imagining her in this new world, free, unburdened, and happy. There was no doubt in my mind that she would know how to live this new life to the fullest, with undiluted curiosity and joy.

"I saw her when we were at the border," I confessed.

My words snapped Henry out of his reverie, and his head swung to me.

"You saw her? Like a vision?" he asked, his face taking on a contemplative expression.

"Yes. She appeared in my mind." I tried to explain the best I could what I'd experienced that night. "One moment I was at the border, trying to figure out how to use the Tear. Then, the next thing I knew, I was at the Mayfair Park with Rory. It was broad daylight—"

"It was daylight?" Henry interjected, seemingly more amazed by that little tidbit of information than by the fact that I'd seen Rory.

"Yes," I replied, feeling a pang in my chest. I didn't miss the daylight as much as I'd thought I would, but I knew Henry was starved for it. Perhaps I would be, too, after two hundred years. "That was how I knew what I was seeing wasn't real. That, and seeing Rory, of course, because she was alive and not…dead." The night of her death flashed through my mind, provoking an involuntary shudder. Henry squeezed my hand in quiet support.

"So, you got to experience daylight again," he said, as another soft smile graced his lips. "And you saw Rory…how was she?"

"She was…happy and hopeful. I latched on to her hope, using it to channel the magic of the Tear."

Henry seemed to think it over for a few moments as we reached the foyer, stopping before the double front doors.

"If she was happy in your vision, then perhaps she already knows true freedom," he finally said, his smile growing.

"I think she knew that freedom even before she was truly free. She knew how to find joy in life despite her circumstances," I said quietly, my own lips curving up.

"We can all learn from her." Henry squeezed my hand again.

"Is that what we're going to tell the clans?" I asked him, my smile fading. "That they can still find happiness despite living in the shadows?"

"Whatever you decide to say, you'd better make it convincing," Isabelle chimed in, arriving in the foyer with a stir of air.

Her black, thickly curled hair swooshed around her heart-shaped face as she stopped before Henry and me. She, too, had opted for a tunic and pants instead of one of her usual revealing gowns. My brows knitted as I took in her outfit. I wondered if she'd also chosen to dress comfortably in case the meeting didn't go as planned and we had to fight.

Or flee, a whisper of thought in my mind.

No, I will not flee. I squared my shoulders and lifted my chin. I'd come too far to cower before the clan leaders. They were greater in number, but we were greater in spirit. They would not prevail. They couldn't; I would not allow it.

A knock on the front door snapped me from my thoughts—the clan leaders were here. Henry's hand tightened around mine, and I glanced at him while Isabelle strode to the entrance. His deep-blue eyes were fastened on me.

Together, I read in them as he gave a small nod.

3

Camilla Devillier strolled inside the mansion first, her high heels clicking on the polished stone floor. She looked stunning in a pale-blue gown that hugged her lithe form and matched the color of her eyes, which were like two chips of ice when they landed on Henry and me. With hair so fair it was almost white, the Lady of the North was winter personified, and the temperature seemed to drop as if she'd brought some of the chill of her region with her. Moving with sinuous grace, she glided through the foyer as if she owned the place. Her perfume-infused presence instantly set me on edge, and all my muscles tensed as I became on high alert.

"Henry," Camilla purred in her husky voice, stopping before us. Her red-painted lips curved into a smile, showing the hints of her fangs, as her gaze slid to me. "Sophie." She inclined her head in greeting.

Her glacial eyes dropped to my chest, and she scowled, making me wonder if she was disappointed at not finding the Tear there. My brows pulled together as I watched her, unease growing and spreading. I glanced at Henry, but he seemed relaxed next to me as he greeted the Lady of the North. He trusted Camilla because she was an old friend, and I hoped his trust wasn't misplaced. Chances were, Camilla was the least of our worries tonight, but I wasn't ready to lower my guard around her yet.

My gaze snapped from Henry and darted behind Camilla when Benjamin Moreau walked in, his musky scent filling the foyer. I couldn't stop a low, feral growl from escaping as my upper lip curled in a snarl. I loathed the male with everything that I was, and wished I'd killed him when I'd killed Stern. He had no respect for human life, and saw people as nothing more than livestock, which existed purely for his enjoyment. Perhaps now, with the Dark Witches no longer a threat, the other clan leaders wouldn't care if I drove a stake through his heart, ending his vile existence.

As if he knew what I was thinking, Moreau gave an answering snarl when our gazes locked. Hatred flashed in his brown eyes, and I glared right back, refusing to back down.

"Moreau," Henry said with bone-chilling menace, drawing the male's attention to him.

The Lord of the West dragged his gaze away from me and focused on Henry.

"You need to keep her on a leash," he hissed, baring his fangs.

My upper lip peeled back, revealing my own sharp canines, but Henry pressed my hand—a silent request to control my temper.

"Watch your mouth, or it will be you who ends up on a leash…tied to a pole outside at sunrise," he said darkly, his eyes blazing with fury.

Moreau's already pale face became leached of all color as he curled into himself. The Lord of the West was wider than Henry, but the latter was taller, towering over him with a hostile look of superiority. There was no doubt in my mind that if the two got into a fight, Henry would prevail. Moreau seemed to know it, too, because he averted his gaze and clamped his mouth shut, hiding his fangs. I let my upper lip relax over my fangs as well, just as the clan leaders of the Midlands stepped through the doors.

Like their neighboring regions that occupied the middle of the Empire, the three vampires couldn't be more different. Emeric Laurent—an older vampire with silver hair and tired eyes—was the clan leader in the mountainous region closest to the West. The land next to his was ruled by the Bouvier clan, with Lena Bouvier as their leader. The petite female with wavy copper locks and creamy skin must have been very young when she'd turned, because she looked no older than sixteen and had an air of innocence and naivety about her. I knew the looks were deceiving, though—Lena was wiser than she appeared. It was because of that wisdom that she was entrusted with running her clan. The last of the three, Yvonne Durand, was the clan leader in the region closest to our Eastern region. She was a tall, slim female with a golden-brown complexion and wide-set, amber eyes.

After Yvonne had entered the foyer, I went to turn my attention away from the door, not expecting anyone else, but stopped when one more vampire strolled in after her. My stomach dropped as I took in the jet-black hair, the narrow face with features so sharp they could cut glass, and the eerily dark eyes.

"Beatrice Stern," Camilla introduced the female, unable to hide the depraved excitement in her voice. I felt her eyes on me, watching closely for my reaction.

"So, you are the one who killed my brother," Beatrice said coldly, stopping before me.

If her resemblance to Everett was any indication, she was related to him by blood instead of considering him her sibling in the familial bond sort of way customary for clan vampires. The sheet of glossy, chin-length hair shifted, gleaming in the light of the chandelier, as Beatrice angled her head, studying me with those cavernous eyes that were so much like her brother's. She'd seen me before now, of course, the other night at the border, but she hadn't gotten a chance to confront me then. It seemed she was doing so now, and I wondered how far she was willing to take it. The darkness within me stirred as if in anticipation.

Henry became a wall of hard, coiled muscle next to me, emitting a low growl that threatened bloodshed if something were to happen to me. When he moved to block me from Beatrice's view, I stepped around him, refusing to let him be my shield—I didn't need his protection and could take care of myself.

"Yes, I killed him," I replied, holding Beatrice's fathomless gaze. "And I'd do it again. He was a monster."

The female smirked. "We are all monsters. And if you think you are different, then you are delusional. You will see. Perhaps sooner than you realize."

My scalp prickled. "What is that supposed to mean?"

"Nothing," Camilla interjected, shooting Beatrice a look of warning. "Shall we begin our meeting?" She gestured toward the study.

No one moved as a tense silence ensued. Everyone's eyes were on Beatrice and me, waiting to see what would happen next. We were squared off against each other like two predators poised to lash out at any moment. It never came to that, though, because Henry decided to de-escalate the situation. He relaxed next to me, loosening his iron grip on my hand.

"We will begin the meeting as soon as Celeste arrives," he said, louder than necessary in an attempt to snap Beatrice and me out of our stare-down.

"Celeste?" Camilla arched one perfectly trimmed brow. "Isn't she one of the White Witches?"

Henry nodded. "White Witches deserve a seat at the table as we discuss the future of the Empire."

"Do they, though?" Camilla asked. "They have been in hiding since the Red War. Now, a century later, you want them to have a say in what happens to this country?"

I tore my gaze away from Beatrice and glanced at Henry, wondering if he was thinking the same thing I was—we were already being challenged, and the meeting had not even begun yet.

His features remained impassive as he replied, "Yes. They might have descendants among the human population. Those like Sophie, who carry magic in their blood but don't know about their heritage."

"Why do we care?" Beatrice snarled. So, she was like her brother not only in appearance but also in her superiority complex and blatant disregard for anyone she perceived as inferior.

"Because we do," Henry insisted. "The world is changing. Things will be different now."

"We will see about that," Moreau said under his breath.

"What did you say?" I narrowed my eyes at him.

Before he could answer, a knock on the door announced Celeste's arrival. The witch walked in a moment later, her blue cloak flowing around her as she moved.

"Celeste," Henry greeted her with a warm smile. "Thank you for coming."

A curt nod was the witch's only reply as she scanned all the vampires in the foyer, her lips pressed in a thin line. She appeared uneasy about being here, and I didn't blame her—she was outnumbered.

"Great, now that we are all here, shall we?" Camilla snapped, turning on her heels toward the study.

Henry's jaws clenched as his hand tightened around mine again. We exchanged a glance and a silent message: the Lady of the North was acting like she was in charge. We needed to take back control and quickly if we still hoped to convince the clans to agree with our line of thinking. Henry gave a small nod to let me know that we were on the same page before the two of us strode after Camilla. Everyone else followed, and soon, the ten of us filled the brightly lit study. I immediately wished we had remained in the foyer because no one sat down. Everyone was still standing, now in closer proximity to each other, as palpable tension saturated the air.

Henry and I stood by the credenza, flanked by Isabelle and Celeste. The witch stood by my side, her expression stoic, while Isabelle had picked a spot by Henry, looking wary. My gaze stretched to the painting of the battle of New Haven on the wall behind the oversized desk. I hoped that the bloody violence depicted on the canvas would not spill from it, unfolding right here in this room. Silence reigned for a few minutes until Henry rolled his shoulders, preparing for a difficult conversation.

"We are gathered here tonight to discuss the future of this country," he began speaking, his deep voice carrying through the room. "With Dark Witches no longer a threat, humans do not need the clans for protection."

"How do we know that Dark Witches are no longer a threat?" Yvonne asked, the glow of the lamps dancing in her golden eyes.

"I destroyed them," I spoke up. "You were all on the border when it happened. You witnessed it."

"We saw you wipe out the forces closing in on New Haven," Lena interjected. "How do we know that there aren't any of them left in the Black Forest and beyond?" she asked, concern pinching her delicate features.

My brows flew up in shock. I couldn't believe the clan leaders were doubting that Dark Witches were no more.

"I erased Dark Witches from existence. They're all gone. I'm sure of it," I said, keeping my voice steady. I refused to let my emotions rise to the surface and sweep me under.

"But what guarantee do we have?" Emeric chimed in.

I couldn't help but feel like this was a planned interrogation. The clan leaders must have worked together to prepare for this meeting. It quickly became clear that it was Henry and I versus them. I wasn't even sure Isabelle was on our side as she stood there, her big brown eyes darting between us and the clan leaders.

"Celeste, you live in the Black Forest. Have you seen any signs that any of the Dark Witches remained?" I turned to the White Witch. The possibility that not all of the Dark Witches had been eradicated had not occurred to me until now. A niggle of doubt crept in, but I quickly squashed it. My mother's note about the Tear had claimed it could destroy all supernatural forces, and I had to believe that. A moment later, Celeste confirmed what I already knew in my heart.

"No, the Dark Witches are gone. There is no doubt about it," she gave a curt response.

"Provided you did destroy them all...How did you do it exactly?" Camilla asked, scanning me from head to toe. Her sharp gaze was too inquisitive, too perceptive. She knew I had a weapon in my possession and was trying to learn how powerful it truly was.

"It doesn't matter," Henry interjected, his tone final to curb further questions. "What matters is that the Dark Witches are gone, whether you like it or not. We cannot hold the threat of them over the humans any longer. We need to spread the good news and bring back home those we sent up north for safety. The human governors can take over running their respective regions until people hold an election to decide how they want this country to be ruled."

Henry's words ricocheted off the study walls, sounding loud as if he'd shouted them. They'd made the new world without the Dark Witches a reality—one the clan leaders were not prepared to accept.

A heavy silence settled over the room, oppressive and foreboding. The tiny hairs on my arms rose as if the air itself became charged. Something was brewing in the quiet that stretched. I could see it in the taut faces and hard eyes, in the jaw muscles that flexed, and lips that quivered as if trying not to curl in a snarl to reveal gleaming sharp fangs. My own lips twitched, and my fingertips burned where I was trying to prevent my nails from elongating into deadly sharp claws.

I couldn't take a breath in as I stood there, waiting…hoping, my chest tight. Henry had laid out the plan before the clan leaders. Now, it was up to them if they would go along with it.

4

My breathing quickened as my anxiety climbed. When I'd found my mother's note about the Tear, I'd known that had been a moment of great significance. I had the same feeling now. Whatever happened here tonight would determine the future of this country—mine and Henry's future. Just when my anxiety was about to reach its peak, Camilla broke the tense silence, and with one word, she shattered my heart and crushed any scraps of hope I'd managed to gather.

"No," was all she said in the otherwise quiet room.

My gaze shot to Henry, and I found him looking appalled. He blinked slowly as if he couldn't quite believe this was happening.

"No?" he asked low.

"The humans will never learn that the Dark Witches were defeated. We will tell them that when the Dark Witches attacked, we were able to push them out past the border and drive them back to the Black Forest. People will return to their regions, but they will return to the same life they knew before—one of subservience to us, the superior species," Camilla declared as bile rose in my throat, threatening to choke me. She was speaking with a level of authority that only meant one thing...the other clan leaders were all in on the plan; she had their full support.

I glanced at Celeste and found impossible sadness carved into her weathered features. She didn't look shocked, though, as if she hadn't expected anything different from the entitled monsters crowding this room.

Turning back to Camilla, I somehow found my voice, but it came out broken and defeated. "But the human guards who stayed behind...they know the truth." As soon as I'd uttered the words, I regretted them, fighting the urge to clamp my hand over my mouth. Camilla's crimson lips stretched in a sinister smile—I hadn't said anything she hadn't already considered. My stomach knotted with dread.

"We will take care of them," she said without hesitation. "Just like we will take care of anyone who stands in our way." She gave me a pointed look.

Henry and I—we stood in their way.

No, no, no! A cry of despair sounded in my head. This was not what I had fought for; sacrificed for. What Josephine, Celine, and my mother had lost their lives for.

The pressure burned behind my eyes as tears threatened. I wouldn't let them fall. I couldn't let the clan leaders win.

My gaze darted to Henry at the same time he looked at me.

Don't do anything rash, his eyes pleaded.

I felt the amulet's pull from where it pulsed in my pocket. I could use the Tear to destroy the vampires—to finish what I'd set out to do when I'd first arrived at the estate. Would the amulet let me destroy the very species I was now a part of? It followed my will, but did I have it in me to wish for my own demise? For Henry's death?

I wasn't prepared to find out, I realized with a sinking heart. Sacrificing for humanity had not been an impossible choice before, because I hadn't had that much to lose. But now that I had Henry... The selfish part of me reared her head, refusing to give him up, to lose us and our future. We deserved to live. Humans deserved to have their world back, but we also deserved a place in it.

"What's going on here?!" Waylon exclaimed as he burst into the room. I was so shell-shocked by Camilla's proclamation that I hadn't even heard him walk into the mansion and approach the study.

My brows shot up in surprise at the same time my stomach dropped.

"What are you doing here?" I demanded, as fear spiked. Camilla was planning to kill the border guards who knew the truth, and Waylon had just made it that much easier for her by showing up uninvited.

"Interrupting a very important meeting by the looks of it," Waylon snapped, quickly taking in everyone in the room. His forest-green eyes narrowed when he noticed Celeste. "You are deciding the future of this country, aren't you? And you didn't think a human should be a part of this conversation?" he seethed, his blazing gaze locking on me.

"Waylon," Henry warned in a raised voice.

"You said you'd still be you after you turned," Waylon continued, looking at me, "but you're one of them now." His face contorted in a mix of rage and disgust. "Let me guess, even with the Dark Witches now destroyed, you vampires won't give us back our country?"

"This country has not been yours for a hundred years, boy," Moreau spat, his fangs flashing. "It belongs to us. Humans belong to us. We rule this world."

All color drained from Waylon's face at Moreau's words, but his eyes never left mine.

How could you?! Betrayal burned in them, red-hot and scathing.

I thought I was going to be sick.

"The amulet. Do you still have it?" Waylon asked urgently, as his gaze dropped to my chest. When he didn't find the Tear there, his feverish eyes returned to my face. "You can put an end to this. To all of this."

Henry went incredibly still next to me, his breath catching. I stopped breathing, too, as all the eyes in the room locked on me.

"What is he talking about?" Camilla demanded.

"Let's not lose our heads," Henry said, moving in front of me to block me from Camilla's view.

"Sophie, please," Waylon begged, stepping closer to me. "Use the amulet to destroy them. It's the only way."

Time screeched to a halt as the world stopped along with my heart. If there had been any doubt in the clan leaders' minds about what Waylon was implying, his last words had made everything clear—the amulet that had erased the Dark Witches from existence could also destroy vampires.

Camilla was the first one to bare her fangs with a hiss as she crouched down and unsheathed her razor-sharp claws. The other clan leaders rapidly followed. Henry became an impenetrable wall in front of me as his muscles tensed. His nails turned into claws, and he bent his knees, leaning forward with a vicious snarl. A similar sound escaped Isabelle as she assumed a fighting position next to him. Waylon stopped his approach toward me, his wide eyes flooding with sheer terror.

"Where is the amulet?" Camilla asked, her voice low and guttural.

"Run," Henry ordered over his shoulder without looking at me, his eyes trained on the vampires before him.

"No," I said, defiantly lifting my chin.

Adrenaline rushed through my veins, coiling my muscles as I prepared to fight. When I tried to step out from behind him, he threw his arm out to stop me.

"Get out of here. Now!" he growled, hoping to jolt me into action.

"No," I repeated, not rattled by his tone. My voice was full of resolve as I said, "I won't leave you."

I knew we were outnumbered, but the wild, beastly side of me rose to the challenge, ferocious and bloodthirsty. Besides, we had Celeste on our side, her curled fingers spewing crackling white lightning of her magic.

"Get her!" Camilla barked an order, and all the clan leaders snapped into action.

Still partly hidden behind Henry, I crouched down and bared my fangs, my claws gleaming, as the clan leaders dashed through the room with supernatural speed, converging on us.

"Celeste!" Henry roared, snatching Moreau by the throat out of thin air before he could get to me.

The next thing happened too fast, but also as if in slow motion. The magic at Celeste's fingertips disappeared as if snuffed out by the wind. The witch grabbed my arm at the same time Waylon lunged at me, fisting the hem of my tunic.

"You are my heart," Henry said with one quick glance in my direction.

His stormy blue eyes were the last thing I saw before everything went black.

HENRY

Just like that, she was gone, taking my heart with her. At least she was safe—as safe as she could be. When I'd yelled Celeste's name, I hadn't known what would happen. I knew the witch was powerful, and I'd wanted her to do something, anything, to get Sophie out of here. She had, and now it was time to fight.

The momentary distraction to say goodbye to Sophie had cost me, allowing Moreau to take a swipe at me, leaving deep gashes in my chest. I didn't feel the pain, though, trusting my vampire body to patch itself up. With a roar, I tossed Moreau away from me, and he crashed into the nearby wall. In the blink of an eye, he was back on his feet, lunging at me. I retreated. We began to dart around the room, colliding to exchange blows in a blur of claws and fangs. We weren't the only ones. The study had become a battlefield, much like the one depicted on the large canvas, which took up most of the wall behind my desk.

Six against two. Isabelle and I would not win this fight. I needed her out of here.

"Get out!" I shouted, finding her wild black eyes in the moving shadows.

"And miss all the fun?" She gave a savage smile as she jumped back from Yvonne, barely escaping the swipe of her claws. My heart twisted with dread as I took her in. Ragged wounds covered her body, blood seeping out of some, gushing out of others.

"Watch out!" I shouted a warning, but it was too late.

Lena rushed her, her mouth stretching wide before it clamped down around her neck. A strangled cry left Isabelle as she clawed at the vampire, shredding her flesh. She managed to fight her off, but not before Lena tore out a chunk of her throat.

"Isabelle!" I stepped toward her but didn't make it far.

Moreau appeared before me, slashing at my chest again. With a roar of fury and pain, I went for his throat, but Emeric and Beatrice stopped me, grabbing my forearms. Moreau's clawed hand balled into a fist a moment before he slammed it into my midsection. A grunt escaped as air whooshed out of my lungs.

The world flipped as Beatrice and Emeric brought me down on my back. The stone cracked under my weight and my eyes watered from the impact because it wasn't just the floor that had cracked but also my ribs. Without wasting any time, Moreau jumped on top of me, looking deranged as he lifted his clawed hand high above his head, ready to deliver the fatal blow. The bastard was reveling in the moment, salivating at the thought that he was about kill me.

My long life didn't flash before my eyes. Only the past few

weeks did. The time Sophie had been in it. I had been ready to follow her into the void before when we had thought the Tear would destroy us. Now, I would slip into the nothingness without her. A smidgen of sorrow filled my heart, but I pushed it out. I should feel joy, not sorrow, because she would live, and I would wait for her in the void for as long as I had to. It might take millennia, but the wait would be worth it if I got to reunite with her in the end.

Moreau's claws and fangs gleamed in the lamplight. I thrashed and bucked under him, trying to throw him off, but Emeric's and Beatrice's hold on me was strong, and I was weak because I'd lost too much blood. Isabelle couldn't help me either—she was pinned to the wall by Yvonne and Lena. Any second now, Moreau would rip out my heart. No matter—my heart was not here; it was wherever Sophie had gone.

"Stop," came Camilla's husky voice.

Moreau stilled above me. I stilled, too, turning my head to look at the female.

"Stop?!" Moreau snarled.

"Yes." Camilla's lips curved upward. Somehow, her smile was more menacing than Moreau's gleaming claws. "We can't kill him. We need him," she explained calmly.

My heart sank.

I bucked under Moreau again, throwing all the strength I could muster into it, but he didn't budge. Emeric and Beatrice tightened their hold on my forearms, their claws digging into my flesh. I stopped thrashing and locked eyes with Isabelle.

Run, I implored her without saying a word.

Despair and heartbreak flashed in her eyes, but she gave a small nod. Using the distraction Camilla had inadvertently provided to her advantage, she twisted out of Yvonne's and Lena's hold and fled the room. The two females snarled in frustration, preparing to follow, but Camilla stopped them by blocking the study door.

"Let her go," she ordered low. "We need her to escape and find Sophie so she can tell her."

"Tell her what?" Yvonne growled.

Before Camilla could answer, Moreau shifted above me, snapping my attention to him. With a smirk that twisted my insides, he retracted his claws and curled his hand into a fist above his head.

"That we have him," I heard Camilla say a moment before Moreau slammed his meaty fist into my face, plunging my world into darkness.

5

SOPHIE

I landed on my hands and knees, my stomach churning. Waylon crumpled to the ground next to me, quickly rolling to the side to vomit in the grass. Celeste was the only one still standing, but even she bent at the waist and braced her hands on her knees, breathing hard.

"What did you do?" I rasped, in between waves of nausea, my eyes trained on the ground below me.

My vision swam, blurring the individual blades of grass and insects crawling between them. I knew we weren't in the study anymore as I inhaled the fresh air, willing the queasiness in my stomach to subside. Once it had, I swiftly rose to my feet, looking frantically around. Disbelief surged through me as my heart dropped like a stone to the pit of my stomach—I was in the Black Forest. A wall of trees encircled the clearing where I stood. Celeste's weathered cottage sat under a beam of silvery moonlight a few feet behind me.

"What did you do?!" I whirled on the witch, my eyes wide.

"I brought us here using my magic," she answered, straightening from her waist.

A gust of cool wind whipped through the clearing, stirring her long white hair, and billowing her cloak.

"Take me back!" I snarled, getting in her face.

Her features were impassive as she stared back at me, her luminous blue eyes so bright they seemed to glow.

"I will not," she declared calmly. "I couldn't even if I wanted to. Bringing us here nearly depleted my magic. Bringing even one person with you is difficult. I didn't realize that he latched on to you until it was too late." She nodded at Waylon, who'd stopped vomiting but still looked sickly pale, slowly rising from the ground on shaking legs.

I knew what the witch had said should rattle me—she had the ability to move through space in the blink of an eye, faster even than a vampire. My skin still tingled from the effects of her magic. Did all White Witches possess that ability? Did I?

I couldn't bring myself to care at the moment. All I cared about was getting back to the mansion, to Henry. He was fighting for his life right now. My mind quickly conjured up an image of the battle that was undoubtedly unfolding in the study. He needed me. I needed him, too. The look he'd given me before Celeste had brought me here could not have been the last time I'd seen his face.

With a snarl of determination, I spun away from the witch, facing the direction of where New Haven lay miles away. All my muscles tensed as I prepared to cross that distance with supernatural speed.

"Don't be foolish," Celeste warned from behind me.

"You're the foolish one—they'll track my scent," I threw over my shoulder as I stepped back with my right foot before bending my knees and leaning forward.

"No, they won't," Celeste said calmly. She was too calm, and that got my attention. Confused, I straightened from my pre-sprint position and turned back around to look at her. "There is a powerful protection spell on the area around the cottage that masks smells and sounds. It also veils my house, making it invisible to the naked eye. Only someone who has been here before would be able to find us."

Henry, the thought immediately popped into my head. *He's been here before. He'll find us...if he survives.*

Despair rose and spread, coating my insides with ice. I winced in pain as shards of it pierced my heart.

"I have to go back," I said, but my voice shook.

I'd wanted to sound firm, but the words had come out as a plea, as if I were asking for Celeste's permission. I didn't need it, of course, but what I *did* need was for her to stop me from making the wrong move. Deep down, I knew I shouldn't return to the mansion.

"Henry was trying to protect you," the witch said, looking into my eyes as if to make sure her words were sinking in. "Do not go back and undo what he did."

"But who is going to protect *him*?" I argued as tears threatened.

"Isabelle is with him," Celeste pointed out. "Besides, it's not him they want, it's you. You and the Tear. Together, you two are the ultimate weapon."

"She's right," Waylon chimed in from my right. He'd gotten some color back in his face but sweat still dotted his brow. "Sophie, do you have the amulet?" He was looking at me as if I was his only hope. And I supposed, at the moment, I was.

"I do have it," I admitted, taking a step back to put some distance between us. The look in his eyes was almost maniacal, and I didn't trust him not to lunge at me again.

"Then use it," Waylon said vehemently, stepping toward me. "Put an end to all this. You're the only one who can."

"No." I scowled at him as my hand spasmed by my right thigh, where the Tear seemed to burn through the fabric of my pants.

Waylon noticed the barely-there twitch of my fingers, and his gaze dropped to my thigh, the maniacal gleam in his eyes burning brighter. "I will find another way to put an end to this," I said quickly, taking another step back.

Waylon cared about me, always had, but did he care enough to spare my life if the alternative was saving his people? A few weeks ago, I wouldn't have faulted him for sacrificing one for the benefit of many. I'd been a different person then.

Waylon's frenzied gaze lifted from my thigh, fastening on mine.

Don't make me take it from you, his eyes pleaded.

My jaw ached from how hard I was clenching it, trying to suppress my nature and not flash my fangs. I didn't want to provoke Waylon, because if I did and he lashed out, the wild side of me would break free and hurt him…savagely. The predator within was prowling just below the surface of my skin, waiting for what would happen next. I was brimming with primal violence on the brink of being unleashed. Suddenly, the predator stopped prowling and sniffed the air. My nostrils flared as I smelled it. Blood.

Heart pounding, I turned toward the dark woods surrounding the clearing and held my breath. I peered into the tall and twisted shapes making up the tree line as I waited, praying to see an outline of the familiar silhouette, a shadow of the powerful body I'd only begun to explore, but that was as dear to me as my own. When the scent of the one who was bleeding intensified, carried to me by the breeze, relief sparked in my chest, but it was mixed with heart-wrenching disappointment. The scent wasn't the one I'd hoped for. It wasn't him. I'd known it all along. When I'd first smelled the blood, I knew it wasn't the sweet essence of him, but I'd still allowed myself to hope, if only for a moment.

A dark shape separated from the trees, and I narrowed my eyes, zeroing in on the one who'd stepped out of the woods. I smelled Isabelle, I was sure of it, but she wasn't alone, and she wasn't walking. She was being carried by a hooded figure. The scent of the one carrying her was familiar somehow, but I couldn't place it. Muscles tensing, I moved my right foot back, preparing to run to Isabelle. I didn't know if the one carrying her was friend or foe, and I wasn't going to wait any longer to find out.

"Wait," Celeste stopped me with a hand on my arm.

I glanced at her before refocusing on the hooded figure. A man, judging by his gait and musky scent. His face was cast in shadows as he made his way toward us until he was close enough for me to peer under the hood. My eyes widened in shock as I took in the shaggy blond hair and light stubble. Pale-blue eyes locked on mine, but they didn't dance anymore like they'd used to.

"Wren," I breathed, staggering back a step.

The young man quickly closed the distance between us with Isabelle limp and boneless in his arms. When he approached, the coppery smell of her blood enveloped me as I quickly scanned her injuries. Countless cuts and lacerations covered her body, and a ragged wound gaped on the side of her neck as if someone had tried to rip out her throat. A shudder rolled through me at the grisly sight.

"I found her not far from here. She's in really bad shape," Wren told Celeste.

"Were you followed?" I asked, not looking at him. I couldn't force my gaze away from Isabelle's mutilated body.

"No," Wren replied. "No one will be able to track us here."

I finally tore my eyes away from Isabelle and looked at him.

"I carry a hex bag in my pocket to cover up my scent and protect me when I'm moving about the Black Forest," he explained when I arched a brow.

"I need one of those," Waylon said, drawing my attention to him. "I can use it to return to New Haven. I have to warn the others about what the clans are planning."

"You can't return," I heard myself say. My voice sounded foreign to my ears. It was cold and detached. "The clans will catch you and use you to find me."

"I won't tell them anything. I'd rather lose my life than—"

"You won't get a choice," I cut him off. "Some of the vampires can compel. Bend your will to theirs. They will get the information out of you."

In fact, the clan leaders could simply compel the guards to hide the truth about what had truly happened on the border, but I doubted they would choose such a humane approach.

Waylon paled, swallowing hard.

"I have to warn the others," he insisted. "The clans want to hide the truth about the Dark Witches, to keep up this farce that we need their protection. The guards from the border are the only ones who know what really happened. The clan leaders will come for them–"

"I know," I said low, my voice hollow.

Waylon's face became leached of all color. I knew what I was asking of him was too much—an impossible decision. But I couldn't let him return to New Haven and undo what Henry had done to protect me and the amulet.

The air became thick with misery and anguish as Waylon and I stared at each other in silence. A few minutes ago, I'd wondered what he was prepared to do for his people. Now, I was wondering how far I was willing to go to not let him leave this clearing. Judging by his expression, he was wondering the same thing.

His gaze flicked over me, sharp and assessing. A muscle flexed along his jaw as he calculated his odds. They weren't good. Waylon was a skilled fighter, but even he couldn't go up against a vampire, especially one anticipating an attack. Another second passed in tense silence as Waylon and I stood squared off against each other. Finally, his eyes shuttered and he released a jagged breath, giving in. My coiled muscles relaxed just a fraction because I wouldn't have to hurt my long-time friend. If I could still call him that after tonight.

Isabelle whimpered softly in Wren's arms, snapping my attention to her. I knew the weak sound couldn't possibly be a true representation of the agony raging inside her.

"Is there anything you can do for her?" Wren asked urgently, turning to Celeste.

My brows lifted at the genuine look of concern on his face.

"No." The witch gave a small shake of her head. "She needs blood."

Wren's boyish features hardened with determination.

"Out of my way," he said firmly, his eyes trained on the cottage behind us.

Waylon and I stepped farther apart from each other to give Wren a wider berth to pass between us. Our eyes locked for a second, but Waylon quickly averted his gaze as if he couldn't bear to look at me. No matter. His palpable hatred toward me was the least of my concerns.

"What are you doing?" I demanded, turning after Wren.

"Saving her life," he threw over his shoulder as he strode toward the cottage.

The low-rise steps of the porch creaked as he quickly climbed them, stopping before the worn front door. He glanced at me and jerked his chin in a silent request to open it for him. Once I had, he carried Isabelle inside and laid her on the threadbare rug in the middle of the living room. Her blood quickly soaked the thin and tattered fabric, staining the wooden floor underneath.

I halted on the other side of the threshold as I watched Wren shrug off his cloak and drop to his knees by Isabelle's side. He retrieved a pocketknife and sliced open his wrist before promptly bringing it to her mouth, his blood mixing with the dried blood around her lips.

"Drink," he pleaded low. Isabelle lay unmoving on the floor, her mangled body bathed in the glow of the oil lamps. "Damn it,

Isabelle, drink!" Wren shouted as if the raised volume of his voice would make her obey his command.

Nothing happened for several long minutes as I listened to the sluggish beating of Isabelle's heart. It was growing weaker, fainter by the second, slowing down until I held my breath, fearing the next beat would never come.

Suddenly, Isabelle's chest rose sharply, and her eyes flew open, pitch-black and unseeing. Her hands snapped up, grabbing Wren's wrist, and she began drinking deeply, savagely. A harsh grunt left Wren as he clenched his teeth, breathing through the pain while Isabelle fed as if her life depended on it. And in that moment, it did.

"Don't let her take too much," I said to Wren before I turned around and stepped outside, closing the door softly behind me.

6

A breath of relief left me when I saw Waylon was still here. I'd feared he'd taken off toward New Haven while I'd been distracted. I'd hoped he wasn't foolish enough to brave the Black Forest alone, but he was desperate, and desperate people did foolish things. I knew because I was desperate, too.

Angling my head, I listened to Isabelle's heartbeat inside the cottage. It was growing stronger by the second, her breathing becoming more even. She was going to be okay. She had to be—I needed to know what had happened at the mansion after Celeste had snatched me away. What had happened to him... A ragged exhale escaped as my eyes pricked with tears. Briefly squeezing them shut, I pinched the bridge of my nose with my thumb and index finger. I couldn't give in to panic. Not until I knew how dire the situation truly was. Swallowing the lump in my throat, I opened my eyes and took a steadying breath.

Waylon paced the front porch, the warped wooden boards groaning under his heavy footsteps. Celeste sat in an old wooden chair in the corner, her eyes closed, and her weathered face relaxed. She appeared asleep, but I knew better than to think that she was—she was listening to the world around her. I had to fight the urge to shake her and ask if she knew what had happened to Henry.

"What's going on in there?" Waylon asked, stopping his pacing. He jerked his chin toward the closed door behind me.

It seemed we were putting what had happened earlier aside for now. Fine by me. We would just add what had transpired to the many things that had been left unspoken between us ever since I'd turned.

"Wren is giving Isabelle his blood," I said, and Waylon's brows shot up in shock. "Willingly," I added quickly.

The thought of Wren doing that for Isabelle brought a scowl to my face because I didn't trust his motives. I had good reasons not to trust him. Two weeks ago, he'd kidnapped me and brought me to the Black Forest to deliver me to the Dark Witches.

"Do you need to feed?" Waylon asked, snapping me out of my thoughts.

Now it was my turn to be shocked.

"Are you offering?" I asked, pinning him with a stare.

He paled and swallowed thickly but didn't avert his gaze.

"Yes," he replied.

The tendons in his neck stood out as all his muscles tensed. The smell of his sweat and fear permeated the air.

"Why would you do that?" I asked, folding my arms over my chest.

He clearly didn't want to do it. In light of recent events, I realized that I didn't trust his motives, either.

With a heavy sigh, he dragged a hand through his short, light-brown hair. "I feel like what happened was my fault."

"It was," I said without hesitation. "It's because of you that we're stuck here, and Henry's life is now in danger."

If he's still alive, an echo of thought in my mind. *He is!* I shouted in my head, refusing to believe the alternative.

"And his life wouldn't be in danger otherwise?" Waylon challenged. "The clans are not going to give up control over the Empire. You and Henry stand in their way."

"You said I'm just like the rest of them," I bit out.

"Words spoken out of rage," he admitted, as his forest-green eyes softened just a fraction. "I know you're different. You've given up so much for the humans."

"And now you want me to give up my life?"

"You were willing to do it before."

"But now I have something worth living for."

"And you didn't before?" He tilted his head, looking at me incredulously.

"Of course I did, but–"

"But now you have Henry," he finished for me.

I hoped I still had him. Would I know if he'd met his demise? Would I have felt it in my heart if he'd been killed?

I should have told him, I thought, as the last look he'd given me flashed through my mind. *But I didn't, and now it might be too late.*

Despair surged, threatening to sweep me under, but before it could, I heard shuffling footsteps coming from inside the house. Spinning around from Waylon, I yanked open the front door to find Isabelle on the other side. Our gazes locked just as she started to crumple to the ground. I caught her before she could collapse.

"Henry?" I asked, staring into her wide eyes, which were still mostly black with hunger.

I knew my own eyes were pleading with her to tell me what I wanted to hear…*needed* to hear.

"He lives," she rasped, clutching my forearms for support. "But they have him. The clans took him."

A strangled cry tore from my throat as my legs buckled, and I went down to my knees, dragging Isabelle with me. When Waylon rushed to our side, I shook my head, refusing his help. I needed this, and Isabelle did, too. We latched on to each other, sharing in our anguish about Henry and the dread and uncertainty about our future. It seemed holding on to each other was the only thing preventing us from falling apart. I began to tremble as tears spilled, running down my face. They were tears of relief because Henry was alive, but they were also tears of sorrow because the clans had him. They'd taken him to lure me out, I was sure of it. I had something they wanted, so they'd taken something I wanted—some*one* I couldn't live without.

"I should have told him," I whispered, as a ragged sob escaped me.

Understanding washed over Isabelle's blood-covered face.

"I think he knows," she said low, her dark gaze flicking over my features. "Find solace in that."

I gave a small shake of my head. "Even if he knows, I should have told him. He deserved to hear it from me."

"Then tell him when you see him again," Isabelle whispered, her eyes soft.

She'd never looked at me like that before, with empathy and compassion.

"We have to go after him," I declared, as I rose to my feet, bringing Isabelle with me.

She swayed where she stood but managed to stay up.

"You can't," Celeste said, rising from the chair she'd been occupying.

"What?" I swung my head to look at her.

"You are part White Witch, Sophie. Listen to the world around you. What is it saying?"

"I don't care what it's saying," I snarled. "I'm going after Henry."

"That's not what you're supposed to do, and you know it," Celeste said calmly.

"She's right," Isabelle chimed in.

My head snapped back to her, and the look I gave her must have been scathing because she staggered back away from me. She grasped the doorframe for support, but held my gaze.

"Henry is my brother, and I love him. I want to save him just as much as you do, but we have to be smart about this. It's us against the clans. The odds are not in our favor."

I knew she was right. Celeste hadn't been wrong, either. The world was whispering things to me at that very moment, urging me not to leave this place. The voices in my head were becoming louder, more demanding. I gritted my teeth and shut them all out. They died just as quickly as they had appeared.

Still, I couldn't ignore the message the world was trying to send, even though it went against everything I felt in my heart. There was a pull, a tug in my blood, in my very bones that urged me to go to Henry, to find him. The pull that I knew wouldn't abate until I held him in my arms again, breathing the same air as he, listening to his heartbeat. Strong and relentless. I recalled the steadfast rhythm I would recognize anywhere as if it were my own. Henry was strong and relentless. Unyielding. He would not break. I had to believe that, if only to keep my sanity. He would survive, because as much as I wanted to live for him, he wanted to live for me, *with* me, in this brave new world.

"You're right. The odds are not in our favor," I finally conceded.

Isabelle's grip on the doorframe was still tight, but the tense muscles of her neck and shoulders relaxed just a fraction.

"What are we going to do?" she asked.

"We're going to even the odds." I turned to Celeste. "I want to learn my magic."

The witch's shrewd eyes narrowed as she appraised me as if measuring my worth. I stood unmoving, waiting for her perusal to be over. I wasn't sure what she was looking for, but she must have found it because she gave a curt nod.

"Very well. I will teach you. We will begin soon, but right now, the dawn is near. We all should go inside and get some rest."

She was right yet again—I could feel the sunrise creeping up on these woods. A pins-and-needles sensation pricked my skin and drove me to find shelter from the first rays of the new day.

Isabelle must have felt it, too, because she let go of the doorframe and retreated back inside the house, leaving a trail of blood in her wake from the deep lacerations covering her body. I looked down at myself, realizing for the first time that my tunic and pants were also covered in her blood from when we'd held on to each other.

"Is she going to be okay?" Waylon asked, drawing my attention to him.

"Yes, but she needs to feed more," I replied.

I hoped that Wren was still up to the task of giving Isabelle what she so desperately needed. I could hear his labored breathing coming from inside the house. He hadn't followed Isabelle out on the porch earlier, staying behind to recover from her feeding on him.

"And you?" Waylon asked, his voice strained.

The smell of his fear returned, strong and overwhelming.

"I don't need to feed if that's what you're asking. I'd fed before the Dark Witches attacked, and I can go days without needing blood unless I'm injured."

A breath of relief left Waylon as his taut features smoothed out just a little. He reached up and clasped the back of his neck with a heavy sigh.

"I'm sorry about Henry," he said low.

He didn't add that everything would be okay, and I found myself wishing that he would. This moment was one of those rare instances I wanted to be lied to, if only to make the situation more bearable.

"I'm sorry you can't go back and warn the others," I told him, my voice hoarse.

I'd meant what I'd said. I couldn't go to Henry, and Waylon couldn't go to his people. Staying here instead of rushing back to the Empire was torture, and we were both suffering.

Waylon nodded but didn't say anything else before he walked inside the house. Celeste followed him in, leaving me alone on the porch. With a rough exhale, I turned around and faced the woods, lifting my eyes to the night sky.

"I will come for you," I said to Henry, hoping he could hear me somehow across the distance that lay between us.

The dream I'd had right before I'd awakened tonight resurfaced in my mind. In it, a dark abyss of pain and suffering separated Henry and me. Little had I known the dream had been prophetic. Tears welled, and I blinked rapidly to keep them at bay. Inhaling deeply, I uttered the three words I should have said to Henry when I'd had the chance. After all, I'd felt them in my heart for a while now, even if I hadn't realized it. I hoped the air would carry the words to Henry until I could say them to his face.

"Have hope," I added.

I wasn't sure if the last two words were meant for him or me.

They were for both of us, I decided, as I turned around and walked inside the cottage.

HENRY

Sophie's voice beckoned me to the surface of the obsidian waters I was submerged in. Slowly, I swam toward it, anticipation building the higher I rose in this bottomless ocean of pain. I knew she shouldn't be here. I had sent her away so she could be safe. Why had she returned? It didn't matter. I knew she shouldn't be here, but a small, selfish part of me rejoiced that she had come back. I couldn't wait to see her face and breathe her in, if only for the last time.

Heart-wrenching regret surged, threatening to suffocate me before I made it to the surface. I had just found Sophie. My life was finally complete with her by my side, but soon, it might get cut short just as I had truly started living. My eyes pricked with tears, but still, I pushed through, rising higher and higher until I broke through the glossy black surface.

Sophie wasn't there when I came to with a sharp gasp. But Moreau was, glaring down at me, his fangs glistening in the yellow glow. Candlelight. Where was I? My gaze stretched past Moreau to the cavernous ceiling, then lowered to the rows of skulls sitting on the shelves carved into the stone wall. I had been in this place before—Stern's lair. They must have brought me here while I had been unconscious.

I was lying on my back, my shredded shirt providing little barrier between me and the cool, rough ground. My nostrils flared as I smelled the other vampires in the room. The other clan leaders were all here. My captors. I will fucking kill them.

A menacing snarl escaped as my lips peeled back to expose my fangs. I prepared to kick up, the stiff muscles of my torso tensing, but before I could, Moreau slammed his booted foot into my chest, keeping me down.

"Not so fast," he growled.

With an answering growl, I wrapped both hands around his foot, intending to throw him off, but I didn't get a chance to follow through because someone kicked me in the ribs. Pain exploded as another kick came to the head. Everything in me screamed to fight back, but I was weak—weaker than I had expected. I had forgotten the beating my body had already been through. I needed blood to recover. My stomach twisted at the thought as hunger spiked. It seemed that once I had acknowledged my thirst, given life to it, it seized control, lashing at my insides.

A strangled sound left me as my body spasmed. My stomach cramped, and I wanted to curl into myself. Doing so would also help withstand the kicking better, but Moreau's foot on my chest was pushing me down, driving me into the floor. The beating continued for a while until it eventually stopped when I'd become a bloody, battered mess on the floor. Moreau's foot was no longer on my chest. He didn't need to keep me down. I couldn't get up even if I tried.

The clan leaders surrounded me, peering down at me. Blinding hatred blurred their features as I stared up at the perfect faces. Fucking monsters. I couldn't stand looking at them, so I let my gaze slide to my left, to the small wooden table sitting there. Something metal lay atop it, I could smell it even past the metallic scent of my blood, but I wasn't sure what it was. I solved that mystery a moment later when Moreau reached for the table and picked up a sharp sickle blade. My stomach twisted again but now for a different reason.

"This is going to be fun," Moreau drawled, with a deranged expression on his rough-hewn face.

I closed my eyes and swallowed hard, mentally preparing myself for what was to come. This was going to be worse than I'd thought. They couldn't kill me yet because I was bait for Sophie, but that didn't mean they couldn't make me suffer. When I opened my eyes again, Moreau's features were mottled in a savage smile.

"Does anyone else want to join me?" he asked the others in the room.

My gaze darted to the other clan leaders. Beatrice Stern looked like she was on the verge of saying yes, her fathomless eyes lighting up with wicked excitement. She was so much like her brother, a monster through and through.

"Maybe later," she said. "I need to feed first." She turned and left the room.

Lena and Yvonne also declined before leaving.

"You're going to enjoy this, aren't you?" Emeric asked Moreau, his face set in a strange expression. He looked like he couldn't decide if he wanted to be impressed or disturbed.

"I am," Moreau drew the word out, his tone chilling my blood. "Very much so."

Deciding on disturbed, Emeric just shook his head, his brows knitting before he strolled out.

Camilla was the only one left in the cavernous room besides Moreau and me. She eyed the Lord of the West as if she wasn't sure she should be leaving him alone with me. A tiny spark of hope flared in my chest. Perhaps I would be spared from what Moreau was planning to do to me. Silence stretched for a few seconds as Camilla stood unmoving, staring at Moreau. He stared back, a challenge in his feverish brown eyes. My heart stuttered as I waited for my fate to be sealed, and stopped when Camilla turned to leave.

"Don't kill him," she threw over her shoulder before she walked out.

Moreau looked unhinged when he turned toward me, the sickle blade gleaming in his hand.

"You're mine now," he snarled, seconds before my screams filled the cave.

7

SOPHIE

I was in the dark place again, the eerie quiet chilling my skin. Frantically, I looked around, searching for Henry or my mother, but they weren't here to guide me into the light. It was just me and the darkness.

"You're mine now," *it whispered maliciously from the shadows.*

A cold feeling invaded my chest, and I shivered, wrapping my arms around myself.

"No," *I said into the pitch-black, but my voice came out weak and unsteady.*

"There is no one here to save you," *another slithering whisper of smoke and shadows.*

"I don't need anyone to save me. I can save myself," *I said louder, but my voice still shook as trepidation curled down my spine.*

"You couldn't even save* him. *The one who'd pulled you out before."*

"I will save him. I will do anything for him," *I declared, lowering my hands and squaring my shoulders.*

"Anything?" the darkness whispered, and the hunger in the question twisted my stomach with dread.

"Anything," I said with resolve, my fingers curling into fists at my sides.

The darkness came alive then, pulsing all around me. The shadows rushed toward me, enveloping me in their dark embrace. They climbed into my ears, nostrils, and mouth, filling me as if I were an empty vessel, until I was choking on the thick black smoke, gasping for air.

I bolted upright from where I'd been asleep on the floor, my breathing coming in short, rapid pants. My heart hammered against my ribs, and I placed a hand over it, willing it and my breathing to slow as I looked at the old, faded sofa next to me. Isabelle lay on top of it, her breathing soft and even as she slept. Wren had given her more blood and had helped her clean up before we'd all hunkered down in the living room for the day. I'd cleaned up, too, borrowing a faded tunic and black pants from Celeste to change into.

The lone oil lamp on the small rustic table by the sofa bathed Isabelle's features in a soft, warm glow. All her wounds had healed, fading to raised pink welts, but she was still weak. That was why she hadn't even stirred when I'd awakened. Exhausted, she was not on high alert, sleeping right through it.

"Sophie?" came Wren's voice from my left, snapping my attention to him.

He'd claimed a spot on the floor next to me last night, refusing to leave Isabelle's side.

"Are you alright?" the young man asked, using his forearm to prop himself up off the floor.

"Yes. Just a bad dream," I murmured, as I scooted closer to the wall and rested my back against it.

Wren sat up fully then and scooted back as well, leaning against the wall next to me. Uncomfortable silence ensued as I let my gaze travel over the small room. The plain blue curtains were drawn closed to prevent the bright daylight reigning outside from spilling inside the dimly lit house. A lumpy armchair sat by the opposite end of the sofa, and Waylon was asleep in it, breathing shallowly. He didn't look peaceful in his slumber, the muscles of his face twitching slightly, his brows moving and knitting at times. I wondered what nightmares were haunting his dreams. Then I remembered my own nightmare, and a shudder rolled through me at the thought.

"Are you sure you're alright?" Wren asked, and I nodded.

My gaze dropped to the spot on the floor in front of the sofa. We'd thrown out the thin, blood-soaked rug that had covered it before, but a faint smell of Isabelle's blood that had seeped into the wood still lingered in the air. I tilted my head to the side, studying the floorboards. They reminded me of the floorboards in my mother's old study, and a shuddering breath left me as I remembered the day I'd found the note about the Tear. So much had changed since then. I'd changed. I was no longer human, but I'd still kept my humanity. Thanks to Henry. He was my compass, my anchor, my guiding light, even in the darkest hour. I missed him like I'd never missed anyone in my life. I missed my mother, of course, but the feeling wasn't the same. It couldn't compare. The way I missed Henry…I felt it in my heart and in my bones as if it weren't just blood I needed to keep me alive, but also him.

I should have told him, I thought again, as tears threatened.

"How did you survive?" I asked Wren, trying to distract myself from my dreary thoughts. When I turned to look at him, I found him watching Isabelle with a mix of concern and affection on his handsome face. "You care about her?" I asked, my gaze flicking over his taut features.

"I do," he said with a heavy sigh, focusing on me. "Not everything that happened at the mansion was a lie."

"Just most things," I scoffed.

"Look." He dragged a hand through his tousled hair. "I'm sorry about what happened, about what I did. But you have to understand, I had no choice."

"There is always a choice," I countered.

"Oh, really?" Wren smirked bitterly. "Okay, then you have a choice, too. You can choose to use the amulet to destroy the vampires, but you're not going to do it, are you?"

"We're talking about you, not me."

"I was simply trying to prove a point. You might have had the right to rebuke me for my decision in the past...before you turned. But you don't have the right to do so now. Not when you're putting yourself first, choosing your own happiness over humanity's freedom."

I flinched at his words as anger rose, swift and overwhelming.

"Have I not already done enough? Sacrificed enough?" I whispered harshly, the words leaving my mouth before I could stop them.

Wren's eyes widened at my outburst as if he'd never expected it from me. I hadn't expected it either, but now that the words were out, they hung in the quiet room like a heavy weight. I knew I should feel regret for uttering them, but I couldn't bring myself to do it. I *had* sacrificed enough, and I wasn't going to sacrifice Henry and our future together. I deserved it. I deserved the happiness Wren had mentioned, throwing it in my face as if to shame me.

"How did you survive?" I asked again, changing the subject.

"You mean after you stabbed me with your dagger?" Wren arched a brow.

I just stared at him, refusing to engage. Surely, I didn't need to remind him that I'd stabbed him after he'd brought me to the Black Forest, doing the Dark Witches' bidding.

Sensing that he wouldn't get a rise out of me, Wren finally said, "The White Witches found me bleeding out on the forest floor. They took me in and nursed me back to health. They also lifted the spell binding me to the Dark Witches' will. I was finally free." He got choked up on the last word, his eyes glimmering with tears. "They let me stay here with them, and two weeks later, you defeated the Dark Witches."

"I didn't see you at the border when the White Witches joined our fight," I pointed out, thinking back to that night.

"I stayed behind," Wren murmured low.

Of course he had.

"Like a coward," I bit out.

Wren exploded, whispering harshly, "Yes, like a coward. I knew you'd say that. You'd never understand. You don't know what I've been through."

"I've been through worse. I almost died–"

"But you didn't! Instead, you were granted eternal life."

"I didn't want it!" I seethed, raising my voice almost to a shout.

Wren opened his mouth but clamped it shut when Isabelle stirred on the sofa—we were being too loud.

"You might not have wanted it then," Wren said low, his anger visibly deflating. "But tell me…now that you have eternity, would you go back and make a different choice?"

Though the question caught me by surprise, the answer came quickly and without hesitation.

"No," I said vehemently, trying to keep my voice down. "I wouldn't choose differently."

Choosing differently would mean not choosing Henry. And I would always choose him.

Wren's gaze darted to Isabelle as I uttered the words. Shadows crept across his features, and I wondered if the question had been more about him than me. He'd wanted to know if turning into a vampire was worth it in the end. It was worth it to me because I had Henry. Would it be worth it to him if he wanted to be with Isabelle? He was the only one who could answer that for himself.

As if sensing Wren's gaze on her, Isabelle woke up, slowly blinking open her eyes. They were a beautiful, deep-brown hue now, not black with hunger, when she looked in our direction.

Her skin was also back to a rich-brown shade instead of the sickly, ashen tawny.

Wren shifted from his spot by the wall, moving closer to the sofa.

"How are you feeling?" he asked Isabelle, stroking her hair.

"Much better," she replied. "Thanks to you."

One side of Wren's mouth turned up, and Isabelle gave a small, answering smile.

The interaction was intimate, tugging at my heart because it made me think of Henry. A bitter taste pooled in the back of my mouth as I tried to imagine where he was and what he was going through. The clans would keep him alive because they wanted me and the Tear, but they wouldn't be kind to him. There was no doubt in my mind they would unleash pain and misery on him. He was probably suffering at this very moment, while I lounged here on the floor.

Anxious and frustrated, I swiftly rose to my feet and left the living room, quickly crossing the dark and narrow hallway leading to the kitchen. I stopped in the doorway, my gaze fixed on the closed green curtains draped over the small kitchen window. My chest tight, and my muscles tense, I counted down the seconds until sunset. Closing my eyes, I imagined the daylight receding, gradually surrendering to the darkness.

When I felt the last sun rays disappear below the horizon, a soft exhale left me, as if the night made breathing easier somehow. The pressure on my chest alleviated just a fraction. My muscles were still tense, but it was now restless energy, not anxiety, coiling them tight. In a matter of seconds, I felt stronger, faster. My body came alive like it always did at sunset, my blood singing for the freedom of the night.

A soft smile tugging at my lips, I approached the window and pulled open the curtains, peering into the darkness outside. When I noticed my own fuzzy reflection in the glass, the corners of my mouth pulled down as last night flashed through my mind.

I'd been so close to the world I wanted. How had it all gone so terribly wrong? I couldn't believe I was here, and Henry was…I swallowed to relieve the tightness in my throat.

Reaching inside my pants pocket, I pulled out the Tear and looked at it. The crystal in the middle pulsed, casting a pale-blue glow around the dark kitchen. The amulet had freed us from the Dark Witches, but now it felt like a cursed object in my hand because it was causing suffering—Henry's and mine. What if I destroyed it? My brows knitted at the thought. Destroying the amulet wouldn't save us, I realized with a heavy heart. Even without the Tear, Henry and I stood between the clans and the current world order they were so desperate to keep. The only way to ensure our safety was to defeat the clans.

An impossible task, the world whispered.

I dismissed the warning with a shake of my head. My grandmother had begun creating the amulet that could destroy supernatural forces, and my mother had finished it. The magic of my bloodline was strong. I had to believe it was powerful enough for me to be able to face the clans and prevail.

"Good evening," Celeste's gentle lilt pulled me from my thoughts. "Would you like some tea?"

She lit the oil lamp on the kitchen table and began rummaging around.

"I want to learn my magic," I said, instead of responding to her question. "As soon as possible."

When I turned around from the window, Celeste was putting a kettle on the hearth.

Those luminous blue eyes of hers fastened on me.

"Patience," she said calmly, and the sound of her measured voice made me clench my teeth so hard that my jaw ached. "It will be a process and will take some time."

Time was the one thing I didn't have to spare. Henry was suffering. I wasn't foolish enough to hope otherwise. The longer I delayed coming for him, the longer he was in the clan leaders' claws. I was at Celeste's mercy, though, and lashing out at her would be unwise. I needed her help to learn my magic if I hoped to stand a chance against the clans.

So I took a breath and asked, making sure my voice didn't betray my ever-increasing dread and anxiety, "Where do we begin?"

8

"We begin with the fundamentals," Celeste said, before taking a sip of her tea.

We were sitting across from each other at the kitchen table.

A steaming cup sat before me as well, but I was too on edge to even think about taking a sip. The herbal aroma was soothing, but it did little to help calm my nerves. My knee bounced under the table as I watched Celeste swallow her tea and lower her cup back down.

"There is energy around us, ebbing and flowing like a current," she finally said. "Do you feel it?"

My knee stopped bouncing, and I closed my eyes, taking a deep breath. Slowly, I let the air empty out of my lungs as I attempted to listen to the world around me. My vampire ears instantly picked up on many noises—Isabelle and Wren talking softly in the living room, Waylon stirring from his sleep, the wick burning in the oil lamp on the kitchen table, Celeste's steady heartbeat. It was a cacophony of sounds, jarring and chaotic.

"I don't feel it," I said, opening my eyes and looking at the witch.

"You are not focusing on the right things," she stated, matter of fact, as she brought her cup to her lips for another sip.

"The problem is...I can't focus. There is too much chaos around me." *And in my heart*, I didn't add.

"You need to shut it all out and find your center."

Shut it all out. Right. I could do that. It had been one of the first things I'd learned after becoming a vampire—the ability to tone down my heightened senses.

Placing my hands on top of my thighs, I sat up straighter in the rickety old chair and closed my eyes again. Sounds rushed in, loud and overwhelming. I let them wash over me and fade away until they were nothing more than a steady hum.

Find my center, I repeated Celeste's instruction in my head.

My center was in my chest, near my heart that ached for Henry. The second I thought about him, silence slammed down on me as if someone had covered my ears. All sounds died, and the quiet stretched, growing taut like a bowstring until tiny vibrations tickled my eardrums. Whispers erupted, coming from all around me at once. They were elusive, like smoke and shadows, and I couldn't make out what the voices were saying. Out of nowhere, a blood-curdling cry pierced my ears. It was a sound of agony...and it belonged to Henry.

My eyes flew open as I gasped for air, scrambling out of the chair and overturning it in the process. I staggered back from the table, my heart pounding in my chest.

"What happened?" Celeste asked urgently, rising to her feet.

"I heard him. I heard Henry. They're torturing him," I rasped, tears streaming down my face.

Celeste's features crumpled as deep sadness invaded her gaze, dimming her lustrous eyes.

"I'm sorry to hear that," she said low.

"How is it possible? How was I able to hear him?" I asked, reaching up with trembling hands to brush the tears from my cheeks.

"The energy around us…imagine it as threads, connecting people and places, carrying information through the world," the witch explained.

"Can I use the threads to communicate with him?" I asked, latching on to the idea. I needed to tell him, to give him strength to wait for me, and let him know that I would come for him.

"You can't," Celeste replied, and my heart dropped to the pit of my stomach. "He doesn't have magic in his blood. He will not hear your message."

Tears threatened again as I ducked my chin in disappointment before another thought crossed my mind. My head snapped up, hope flaring in my chest.

"Can I use the threads to find him? To find where they're keeping him?" I asked, and held my breath.

Celeste tilted her head to the side. Her white hair gleamed in the light of the lamp as she thought it over.

"Perhaps," she finally said, and my heart sped up at the possibility. "But even if you find out where they are keeping him, there is nothing you can do for him now. You need to awaken your magic and grow strong enough to face the clans."

"I know," I assured her as I picked up the chair I'd overturned and put it by the table. Even if I couldn't go to Henry now, knowing that I could use the threads to find him later—when I was ready—made it easier to breathe. "I want to try again," I said, gripping the back of the chair.

My fingers dug into the wood as I closed my eyes and took a deep breath.

*Find my center…*I hesitated. *What if I hear Henry again?*

Under any other circumstances, I would give anything to hear his voice, but he was suffering, and I…I didn't think I had it in me to hear the sound of his anguish and not break down. Especially because there was nothing I could do to help him at the moment.

With a shuddering breath, I opened my eyes and looked at

Celeste. Her lips were pressed in a thin line as if she knew what I was thinking.

"Come with me," she said, reaching for the colorful woven shawl hanging on the back of her chair. She draped it over her shoulders and came around the table.

"Where are we going?" I asked.

"I want to show you something." Celeste extended her hands toward me as if expecting me to take them. "We will move through space using my magic like we did yesterday."

I nodded, placing my hands in hers. I hoped the journey this time would be less unpleasant than the last.

Celeste's magic poured out of her, and my skin prickled a moment before the world went black like it had when she'd whisked me away from the mansion. This time, I paid attention to the sensation, aware of the pull of magic on my limbs. It felt like being sucked into a void, floating weightless for a moment, before being thrust back into the world full of colors and sounds. A harsh exhale escaped me when the soles of my feet connected with solid ground. I swayed where I stood, but Celeste steadied me by clasping my shoulders.

"Where are we?" I asked her as I waited for my head to stop spinning.

"We are not far from my cottage. In a place that has been our safe haven for the last century." She made sure I was steady on my feet before she let go of me.

"A White Witches settlement," I breathed, slowly looking around.

Small wooden cabins with thatched roofs and stone chimneys jutting from their sides clustered all around me. They looked different from the cold, stone buildings of New Haven, appearing whimsical and cozy. The whole atmosphere was different in this place, where the air itself seemed to be charged with magic. Its concentration made my skin hum and my fingertips tingle. The feeling wasn't unpleasant, as warmth invaded my chest and settled in my heart. In a strange new way, I felt like I belonged here. This place felt like home, and I wondered if that was because of my witch blood. Like called to like, and it seemed the magic here recognized me as one of its own, welcoming me into its warm embrace.

Slowly, I turned around, taking it all in. The cabins sat in a circle, spreading outward, and in the middle of the settlement, a big bonfire burned, with people clamoring around it. Some were dancing while others were playing string instruments, sending twangy, bright melodies into the night. A pleasant smell of roasting meat and potatoes, and fermented honey wafted through the air. There were a lot more people here than the mere fifty who'd shown up to join the clans to fight in the war. There were men and children, too, their joyous laughter adding to the lively hum of the large group.

"They are celebrating you defeating the Dark Witches," Celeste explained unprompted.

"There are so many of them," I said. "Of us," I quickly corrected myself.

I was a White Witch like them, though that part of me was more muted than the rest. I liked to think that the human part was the most dominant one, but I couldn't deny that the vampire part had been growing stronger. I feared it might soon take over if I didn't have Henry by my side to remind me of who I was—to remind me of the light he'd promised to keep burning inside me.

"We didn't want to send everyone to the border when the war was upon us. We needed people to stay behind to care for our young. Our men stayed behind as well. White Witches usually bear daughters, so we protect our men to carry on our bloodlines."

My brows lifted at her words. There was so much I didn't know about my people.

"How have you been able to stay hidden for all this time?"

"There are powerful magical wards veiling this place, much like the ones around my cottage."

"They are powerful enough to hide an entire village?" I looked at her in disbelief.

Celeste's features were aglow from the dancing flames of the bonfire. We stood a short distance away from it, but no one seemed to be paying attention to us, reveling in their celebration.

"It's not an easy task to accomplish on such a scale," she admitted. "We all contribute to it, constantly pouring our magic into the wards."

"Have the White Witches ever considered coming out of hiding to settle in the Empire? You could have been hidden behind the border, out of the Dark Witches' reach."

"We have always feared that instead of offering their protection, the vampire clans would choose to destroy us, not wanting to risk us turning dark and joining the ranks of Xanthus's followers. We were safer here, in the Black Forest, than inside the Empire's guarded walls."

My heart squeezed in my chest at her words. For a hundred years, the White Witches, much like humans, had been trapped between two supernatural evils. They hadn't trusted the clans enough to seek refuge in the Empire. They'd chosen to dwell in these woods instead, sharing them with other supernatural creatures who were all out for blood.

"The Black Forest…has it always been this dark and unnatural place?" I asked, barely suppressing a shudder. I remembered my encounter with a giant wolf in these woods all too well.

"No, it was a thriving and beautiful place when the White Witches first settled here centuries ago. It wasn't known as the Black Forest back then. When the White Witches began turning dark, their black magic bled into the woods, poisoning the land and trees, morphing forest creatures into monsters."

I found it hard to imagine these woods as anything different than this dreadful place full of twisting, slithering shadows, all primed to snuff out any sliver of light.

"Will the forest go back to how it was now that the Dark Witches are gone?" I asked, hopeful.

Celeste's words had made me realize that the woods and the creatures dwelling within were not malevolent in and of themselves. They were victims, just like everyone else who'd suffered at the hands of the Dark Witches.

"Perhaps, but it will take time. It takes a lot longer to restore something to its former glory than to ruin it in the first place."

9

Xanthus—he was the one who'd ruined this place. He was the root cause of it all.

"Where did he come from? Xanthus?" I asked in a hushed tone.

It felt wrong to utter his name aloud as if doing so would conjure him. An image of a horned monster with scaly black skin, dark, bottomless eyes, and rows of sharp teeth filled my mind as I recalled the mural I'd seen on the ceiling at the Dark Witches' temple. I wasn't able to suppress a shudder this time as it rolled through me.

Celeste didn't answer for a long time as she stood there, watching the fire. I wondered if she hesitated because it was painful to talk about the White Witches' downfall.

The downfall of a few of them does not make them all evil, Henry's words floated up in my mind. He'd said them to me back when I'd still been human, trying to convince me that not all vampires were monsters. It was hard to imagine any of the people here as Dark Witches. Yet, the past couldn't be erased or ignored. White Whites were susceptible to Xanthus, and just because the Dark Witches had been destroyed did not mean that the Dark god was not still out there, lurking in the shadows, waiting to turn more White Witches into his followers.

"There are other realms alongside this one," Celeste finally said, not looking at me. "Where a constant battle between good and evil rages. Sometimes, it spills into this world. Where there is light, there must also be darkness. Usually, they are in delicate balance, but Xanthus wanted to tilt the scale, so he found a White warlock to corrupt. The warlock's mind was already warped by jealousy and envy. He was susceptible to Xanthus's influence because he always felt at a disadvantage, since female witches are usually stronger magic wielders. Xanthus promised him more power, and the warlock began using his magic for evil, nefarious acts. Over time, his magic turned black, feeding on his dark, depraved soul. Eventually, the darkness consumed him, turning him into the first Dark Warlock."

The story was a startling revelation. It was common knowledge that Xanthus had corrupted the White Witches, but I hadn't known all the details, just like I hadn't realized that it had been a warlock, not a witch that had surrendered to Xanthus first.

"I thought that black magic came from Xanthus…but it comes from us?" I asked, unable to hide the shock from my voice.

Celeste finally tore her gaze away from the bonfire and turned to look at me. Her cerulean eyes fastened on mine as if she wanted to make sure I was listening and paying attention.

"Magic in and of itself is neither good nor bad. It feeds off the host's energy. Whether it's light or dark is determined by the one who wields it."

A feeling of foreboding invaded my chest as I remembered my dreams about the quiet place and my conversations with the darkness that dwelled there.

Perhaps I shouldn't be learning my magic right now, a thought flashed through my mind, but I dismissed it. Learning my magic was the only way to get Henry back.

"I understand," I told Celeste, feeling a surge of resolve.

"Good," she said, but her eyes narrowed just a fraction, as if she didn't quite believe me. Her gaze lingered on me a moment longer before it returned to the crowd by the fire, gliding over the sea of faces as if she were looking for someone. She must have found whom she was looking for because she turned back to me and said, "I need to speak with a friend. You should walk around, soak up some of the magic in this place. I brought you here for a reason. I thought it would be good for you to meet your people and get closer to your roots."

"Thank you for bringing me here," I told her, and I meant it. "I needed to see this."

My people had not all been eradicated, and there were a lot more of them than I'd realized. There were children here, and laughter. There was hope, and it filled my heart with joy, momentarily pushing the dreadful feelings aside. I knew they wouldn't stay away for long. They would spread again soon, weighing my heart like a stone, but for now, I wanted to allow myself a moment of peace.

When Celeste left my side, quickly getting lost in the throng of people, I began a leisurely stroll around the bonfire, keeping my distance as I watched the celebration from a few feet away—an observer, not a participant. I couldn't celebrate defeating the Dark Witches because it hadn't been a true victory. One enemy had been destroyed, but the threat from the clans still remained.

The Tear pulsed in my pocket at the thought as if reminding me, *I'm still here if you need me.*

I don't need you, I wanted to say. *I need Henry.*

Suddenly, the sounds of the celebration became too much, the conversations too loud, and the music too harsh. It felt wrong being so close to happiness and joy while Henry was far away and suffering. Scowling, I put a few more feet between myself and those gathered around the bonfire. The added distance helped, and my scowl smoothed out as I resumed my stroll, looking at the cabins as I walked past them. They were all constructed in a similar manner—a slightly raised front porch, a narrow door with a small window by it—but each one had something unique about it, as if the inhabitants had wanted to add their own special touch to the simple facade. Planters teeming with colorful flowers lined the front of one house, while a wreath made of twigs decorated the door of another.

A smile tugged at my lips as I walked, soaking up the magic of this place as Celeste had suggested. My steps slowed when I noticed a young woman sitting on the porch of the cabin coming up in my path. Hunched over slightly, she was perched on one of the wooden steps, an oil lamp sitting next to her. Her gaze was cast down, and I stopped in my tracks when I noticed a book in her lap.

Such a simple pleasure in such a complicated world. Reading had been something I'd shared with my mother. Then, Rory and I had bonded over our love for books. My mother and Rory were both dead, and it had felt wrong to enjoy reading with them gone, so I hadn't picked up a book since Rory's death.

The woman on the steps must have felt my gaze on her because she lifted her eyes from the pages and looked in my direction.

"Hello," she said, one side of her mouth turning up.

She was around the same age as me, maybe a year younger. Her green eyes were sparkling and bright, and a thick braid of fiery red hair was slung over her shoulder.

"Hello," I found myself saying in response.

My feet moved as if of their own accord as I approached the girl, drawn to the book in her lap.

"I'm Amelie. You must be from New Haven." She smiled at me.

"Yes, I'm Sophie," I introduced myself when I stopped before her.

Her eyes widened.

"As in Sophie Devereaux? You're the one who defeated the

Dark Witches?" Her voice was full of wonder as she stared up at me from where she was sitting.

I quickly looked around us to make sure no one had overheard her. I didn't want the attention. That was why I hadn't asked Celeste to introduce me to her friend or anyone else in the village.

Amelie seemed to pick up on my unease and didn't say anything else on the matter. Instead, she moved the oil lamp, setting it on the porch behind her.

"Would you like to join me?" She patted the spot next to her on the step.

I hesitated for a moment, but then my gaze snagged on the book again, and I couldn't resist. Perching next to Amelie, I took a closer look at the tome in her lap.

"It's printed," I observed, as if to myself. I would have expected a hand-written book, considering the simpler, more primitive living conditions here in the woods.

"Yes," Amelie replied, her expression open and warm. "This particular book is rather old, from the time before we went into hiding."

My brows flew up in surprise.

"It's still in such a good condition," I observed.

Amelie let out a soft laugh at my bewilderment.

"It's been preserved with magic." Her gaze dropped to the book, and she lovingly brushed her fingers over the pages. "Some words are a bit archaic, but they're words nonetheless, so I cherish them. Do you like to read?" Her eyes were curious when she lifted them back up to my face.

"I do. I did…before everything…" I trailed off, my brows pinching.

Understanding crept into Amelie's eyes. Understanding, not pity, for which I was grateful.

"I've heard about your mother…and the ones before her," she said quietly. "You've had to sacrifice so much. You all did."

Her soft tone almost brought tears to my eyes. She was intuitive and sweet like Rory, and I had to fight the urge to tell her about the situation with the clans and the sacrifice others, like Waylon, were expecting from me now. I thought if I did, she'd understand why I was hesitating, why, for the first time ever, I wanted to live for myself instead of living, or rather dying, for others.

"Take it," Amelie said a heartbeat later, closing the book and handing it to me.

"What?" I asked, caught off guard.

A small smile graced her lips.

"I often find solace in books. Perhaps you can find a bit of comfort in this one."

My eyes pricked with tears as I stared at her, seeing Rory.

"You remind me of someone," I said, my voice hoarse with emotion.

"A friend?" she asked, and I nodded. "Does she like to read?"

"She did," I said past the lump in my throat.

Amelie's soft smile faded, another wave of understanding washing over her delicate features.

"I see. You know...when I think about my people—our people," she quickly corrected herself. "The ones that we lost...I like to imagine that they are in a better place, surrounded by people they love and things they enjoy. I think your friend is there, too, reading all her favorite books."

A startled laugh burst out of me as I quickly wiped away the tear that had escaped. "I think you're right."

10

A warm breeze whispered through the meadow, stirring my unbound hair, the soft strands tickling my shoulders and my back. I was sitting cross-legged on a blue-and-white blanket, my hands folded in my lap, and my face turned up to the clear, cerulean sky. Even with my eyes closed, I knew that colors surrounded me. Everything was bright—the sun, the sky, the grass. Even the dress I was wearing had splashes of yellow and pink.

My ears vibrated with sound, picking up on the swishing of grass and rustling of flower petals. Animals scampered around as the humming of insects and the trilling of birds filled the air. Inhaling deeply, I soaked up the heady, sweet aroma of the wild grasses mixed with the soothing floral notes and the smell of the warm earth underneath. The most alluring scent, however, the fresh and woodsy one, was coming from my right. With a soft exhale of contentment, I opened my eyes and looked at Henry lying on the blanket beside me.

Watching me from beneath his thick, black lashes, he looked carefree, his arms folded behind his head and his long legs stretched out before him, crossed at the ankles. Barefoot, he was wearing casual brown pants and a white shirt that was unbuttoned at the top, revealing a part of his chest. My fingertips itched with the need to touch it. Every-

thing about him was relaxed; even his hair, which he usually slicked back from his face, was tousled, brushing the top of his forehead.

"Enjoying the sunshine?" he drawled, not taking his eyes off me.

His gaze roamed over my face, taking in every tiny detail as if he were trying to get it etched into his memory.

"I am. Enjoying the view?" I teased, arching a brow.

"I am," he replied, one side of his mouth turning up. "You are always breathtakingly beautiful, but especially here and now when you look so...peaceful. It fills my heart with joy."

"I do like it here," I said, looking around the open, bright-green field spotted with wildflowers.

"I like it anywhere as long as I'm with you." Henry's smile grew as he sat up, bringing his face closer to mine.

Sunlight danced on his striking features, glancing off the calm blue waters of his eyes. There was something different about him, and it took me a moment to figure out what it was. His skin was sun-kissed, not pale. It was a faint golden hue, and my breath caught as I stared at him.

"What is it?" he asked, his smile burning brighter.

"You're beautiful," I breathed, reaching up to trace his cheekbone with my fingertips.

"I'm yours," was all he said, as he turned his face into my palm and placed a soft kiss there.

The sweet gesture did something to me, and when he turned his face to look at me again, I clasped the back of his neck and pulled his mouth to mine. His lips parted, and a low, rough sound left him as he kissed me back, his fingers sinking into my hair. The taste of him lit up my senses, instantly driving me wild. I lifted my other hand to where his shirt parted and raked my nails down his chest, eliciting another rough growl from him that heated my blood.

He lessened the pressure of the kiss, nipping on my lower lip before skimming his mouth down my neck to where my pulse thrummed just below the surface of my skin. The scrape of his fangs over the sensitive spot dragged a breathy moan from me, making me desperate for him as a wave of sharp, acute desire rolled through me. I pushed on his chest to bring him to the ground so I could straddle him, but he resisted, lowering me down instead.

When my back hit the blanket, he hovered over me, his eyes now black and consumed by hunger—not hunger for blood, but for me. My breathing quickened as I stared up at him, my heart swelling with emotion. I ached for him, and I knew he ached for me, too. I could feel it where he was settled between my thighs. He rolled his hips, and we both groaned, his hardness pressing into my softness. I couldn't wait to have him, to feel him inside me, but I needed to do something first. I needed to tell him. He had to know.

"Henry, I—"

My eyes flew open as I woke with a jolt, my gaze fixing on the exposed wooden beams of the ceiling.

Just a dream, I thought with a sinking heart.

Potent sadness and disappointment washed over me, pressing me deeper into the mattress, threatening to crush me under their weight. Swallowing thickly, I lifted a trembling hand to my mouth, brushing my fingertips over my lips, which still tingled from Henry's kisses. My breasts felt heavy and sensitive, and a dull ache still throbbed between my thighs from what I'd experienced in the dream. If only the bucolic meadow had been real… but that idyllic setting was not my reality. In this reality, Henry was captured and tortured, and I couldn't do anything about it.

Not yet, I thought with a surge of determination.

When I sat up in the bed, the book Amelie had given me slid off my chest. I must have fallen asleep reading it last night. The young witch had been right—the text was archaic, and I had difficulty interpreting it at times, but the outdated words were still a gift, and it was still a book, which was a beauty in and of itself. The story was one of love and hope, and my lips curved up when I thought about how Rory would have enjoyed it.

My smile fell as my mind went back to the dream. Henry and I had been basking in the sun in it. What a cruel joke—my mind showing me things that could never be. I couldn't bring myself to be upset about it, though. Not when I'd gotten to spend some time with Henry, to feel his lips on mine. The experience had only been in my imagination, but it would have to do until I could hold him in my arms again and make the dream a reality.

Setting Amelie's book to the side, I looked around the small room bathed in the warm glow of the oil lamp sitting on top of the rustic bedside table. I'd claimed the only spare bedroom at Celeste's house for myself after Waylon and the others had decided to stay in the village. A couple of the White Witches had opened their homes to them for however long we'd have to stay. I'd remained here, wanting to be close to Celeste since she was going to train me how to use my magic.

This wasn't the first time I'd stayed in this room, of course. Henry had brought me here after he'd saved me from the Dark Witches two weeks ago. My heart squeezed at the memory as my gaze landed on the nearby chair. Henry had sat in it when I'd regained consciousness that night. He'd saved me then; it was my turn to save him now.

Clenching my jaw with resolve, I left the bed and quickly washed up, using the pail of water I'd fetched into the room last night. The cold liquid prickled my skin, but I welcomed the sensation, letting it douse the remnants of desire sparked by the dream. I dried off the best I could using a thin, scratchy towel, and picked a purple tunic and black pants from the stack of clothes sitting on the chair. They'd been donated to me by a few of the witches. The clothes' material was rough, irritating my sensitive vampire skin, but I knew better than to complain. Celeste and the others had taken us in, and I was grateful for that. I just hoped we wouldn't have to stay long. The locket with my mother's portrait rested on top of the folded clothes, and I lifted it up and put it around my neck, tucking it under the collar.

Anxiety surfaced as I stepped into my boots and reached up to tie my hair at the nape of my neck, using a thin leather strip. I couldn't wait to work on my magic. Yesterday had been a failed attempt but I hoped to make up for it today. My gaze flicked to the table by the bed, to the Tear sitting atop it. The pale-blue crystal still glowed in the heart of the amulet, reflecting in the dull glass of the oil lamp beside it. My head tilted to the side as I stared at the pulsing light, lost in thought. My ancestors had created the amulet. Did I possess the power to forge magical objects? That was a question for Celeste, so I darted to the table and grabbed the amulet before sweeping from the room.

11

A pleasant herbal aroma climbed up my nostrils as soon as I left the bedroom, and I followed it to the kitchen, where I found Celeste sipping tea at the table.

"Good evening," the witch greeted me, setting down her cup.

"Evening," I murmured, as I approached the table and took a seat across from her.

Resting my forearms on the flat wooden surface, I cradled the amulet in my hands. My gaze cast down, I got momentarily distracted by the pulsing blue light.

"Is there anything you want to ask me?" Celeste prompted, drawing my attention to her. When I looked up from the Tear, her sharp blue eyes watched me as she waited. My brows flew up—she'd known I'd come here in search of an answer. The world must have whispered it to her, carrying the news through one of the invisible threads.

"Yes," I told her. "My grandmother and my mother forged the Tear." I waved the amulet in front of Celeste before putting it in my pocket for safekeeping. "Do you think I could create an enchanted object?"

"Perhaps one day, but you have a long road ahead of you before then," Celeste gave a practiced answer.

My forehead creased. "I need a shortcut, don't you think? The longer I delay going after Henry, the more torture he endures."

"His suffering is unfortunate, but you cannot rush this," the witch explained calmly. "They will not kill him because they need him alive to lure you out."

They would not kill him, but they would make sure he wished he were dead, I wanted to say but saw no point.

The way Celeste had spoken the words, matter-of-fact and detached, let me know there was no appealing to her softer side. I wondered if she even had one. Was that why she lived alone, separated from the village? She'd never mentioned any family or anyone she was close to. Perhaps she chose not to grow close to anyone on purpose because having loved ones or people dear to you was a weakness in this world where evil roamed so freely. Still, I had the urge to shake her to rattle the stoic facade, but I didn't, reminding myself that I needed her guidance. So, I balled my hands into fists in my lap under the table and took a steadying breath.

"I'm ready to begin my training. What's the lesson for today?"

"You still need to work on establishing your connection to the world. Once you accomplish that, you will be able to tap into the energy around you and manipulate it."

My ears perked up at her words. "Manipulate how? Will I be able to use it for fighting?"

"Yes, but that shouldn't be your main focus."

"It is my main focus. I need to learn my magic so I can fight for Henry."

"That cannot be the only reason. The magic in your blood is your legacy. You need to learn how to honor it."

"I will honor it. I just don't have years to learn it," I bit out.

"It will take as long as it takes. You are only at the beginning of your journey, and it is not something you can force."

My nails dug into the palms of my hands from how hard I was clenching my fists, trying to keep my composure. I wanted to force it, and I wanted to force Celeste to approach the situation with the same urgency I did, but the witch seemed unyielding.

"Alright," I tried to say calmly, but the word came out as a growl. Celeste arched a brow, the look on her face warning me not to challenge her on this. I cleared my throat and tried again, "What should I work on tonight?" This time, my tone was more measured.

"You need to get to know your magic. It is a part of you, but it has been dormant for all your life. Think of it as trying to unlock it. Your powers are asleep. You need to wake them up and bring them forth."

"I thought I needed to learn how to tap into the world around me?" I asked, uncurling my fists, and scrubbing my face with my hands in frustration.

"The two are not mutually exclusive," Celeste replied.

When I stared at her, waiting for more instruction, she gave none before lifting her cup to her mouth to finish her tea. I imagined reaching across the table and swatting it out of her hand.

"You should go for a walk in the woods. Being close to nature helps," she said, eyeing me over the rim of her cup.

"The woods?" I stared at her in dismay. "Are you suggesting a stroll in the Black Forest?"

"You are a vampire. I trust you can take care of yourself," she said nonchalantly. "But you can also take this." She reached across the table to hand me a small brown pouch. "A hex bag to protect you in the woods."

My eyes grew bigger at her words as something occurred to me.

"You're not coming with me?" I asked in disbelief.

"This is something you must do on your own. This journey is between you and your magic."

Of course, it is.

"Very well," I said, squaring my shoulders and lifting my chin. "I'll see you later."

If it was between me and my magic, then maybe I could speed things up. Celeste not coming with me was a good thing because then she wouldn't be there to hold me back.

Rising from my seat at the table, I crossed the short hallway to the living room and then stepped outside into the cool night air. It washed over me like a caress, and I inhaled deeply, breathing it in. The primal side of me reared her head, beckoned by the darkness, and my blood began to hum, answering the call.

My muscles tensed with the need to dash into the woods, to join the other wild creatures roaming there and go on a hunt. My fangs throbbed with the need to sink them into something, and my stomach hollowed out as hunger surged. I quickly tamped it down. I needed the witch inside of me to rise to the surface tonight, not the vampire. I patted my pockets, feeling the amulet in one and the hex bag in the other and set off toward the tree line with supernatural speed.

The dark woods rushed by as I ran through them, carefully avoiding gnarled roots and twisted branches. When my ears popped and magic snapped around me as if I'd broken through some kind of a barrier, I knew I must have left the warded area surrounding Celeste's cottage. The intense pins-and-needles sensation stopped me in my tracks, and I shook out my limbs and rolled my neck before resuming my journey.

I didn't know where I was going until I heard it. Water. A gentle whisper of a shallow stream flowing over stones tickled my ears, and I adjusted my course, heading in the direction of the sound. I halted when I reached a small creek, the bottom part of my tied hair swooshing around me to catch up from the movement. The Forest creatures that had kept their distance until now because I'd been sprinting too fast, slithered in the shadows all around me, watching me with glowing red eyes and snapping at me with gleaming sharp teeth. They didn't advance, though, as if

I had my own warded barrier around me. The hex bag must be working.

Suppressing a shudder, I turned from the woods and approached the creek, stopping by one of the trees. The skinny trunk sat at an angle, its roots trying desperately to hold on to the abrupt and rocky bank. The low-hanging branches reminded me of slim, knotted fingers as they drooped over the water, skimming the silvery currents sparkling in the glow of the moon.

As good place as any to tap into my magic, I thought, planting my feet firmly into the ground and closing my eyes.

Sounds and scents assaulted my senses, but I pushed them aside, focusing instead on the rushing of blood in my veins. I tried to find the magic within. Power coursed through me; it was only a matter of distinguishing and plucking it out of my essence. Vampire, human, and witch were all intertwined inside me, and I needed to learn to single out the part of me I needed the most so I could use it to my advantage.

Easier said than done.

I stood unmoving by the creek for quite some time, my eyes closed and my breathing even. I couldn't feel it. I couldn't feel the magic in my blood or discern the energy around me, let alone tap into it. With a rough exhale, I opened my eyes and dragged a hand down my face. Failing. I was failing at the time when Henry needed me the most.

The sound of a twig snapping alerted me to the presence behind me. Whirling around, I crouched down and bared my fangs with a hiss.

"Whoa!" the young man in front of me exclaimed, raising his hands in surrender. "I'm not a danger to you. I live in the village."

Slowly, I straightened from my crouch and retracted the claws that had snapped out at the sound of a threat.

The man before me instantly relaxed, lowering his hands and extending one of them to me.

"I'm Damien," he introduced himself in a smooth, rich voice.

"Sophie." I shook his hand, noticing his flinch at my cool touch even though he'd tried to hide it. "I didn't see you at the bonfire," I told him, taking in his pale blond, almost white hair and dark eyes that were a striking contrast to his alabaster skin.

"I was too drunk on mead and passed out early at my friend's house," the man said, embarrassment coloring his cheeks a bright red shade. "Don't tell my mother," he added hastily. "I know I'm a grown man, but she doesn't like it when I drink." I opened my mouth to tell him I didn't know his mother when he continued, "My mother Agatha is good friends with Celeste, so please don't tell her either. In fact, I wouldn't tell her about our meeting at all. She has given strict orders to leave you alone."

My brows pinched in confusion. "Leave me alone? Why?"

Damien shrugged. "Something about letting you come into your own power. Celeste wants you to forge your own path without anyone giving you direction."

"I don't have time to forge my own path." I blew out a breath of frustration. "I just need answers."

"Well, did Celeste explain anything to you about our magic?" Damien asked, angling his head with a look of curiosity on his narrow and angular face. The straight fringe of his hair shifted to one side when he did so.

"She didn't give me much to go on," I told him. "She said my magic is a part of me, but it has been dormant, so I need to bring it forth."

"And did she tell you how to accomplish that?"

"Well, no, not exactly. She said being close to nature helps. That's how I ended up here," I said with a sweeping arm gesture.

"I see," Damien replied. He quickly glanced behind his shoulder as if he wanted to make sure we were alone. When he turned back to me, a mischievous look settled into his features. "Tying your magic to your emotions helps sometimes when you're first starting out," he said quietly, as if sharing a secret.

"What do you mean?" I tilted my head to the side.

SOPHIE'S RUIN

"You feel frustrated about not being able to awaken your powers, right? Channel that frustration to bring your magic forth."

A memory invaded my mind about how I'd defeated the Dark Witches. I had channeled the power of love to activate the Tear. Perhaps I could do something similar to stir my magic awake.

Closing my eyes again, I took a deep breath and thought about Henry, about how he made me feel and how my very bones ached, missing his closeness. The feeling that came forth was not the one I'd hoped for when I'd closed my eyes. I'd planned on channeling joy, happiness, and the one feeling that was the strongest and the purest of them all, but instead, despair rose, swelling in my chest. Refusing to wallow in it, I weaponized it instead.

My brows pinched in concentration as I let the dreadful feeling ignite my blood until it was boiling with fury. The clan leaders' flawless faces flashed through my mind. They would pay. I didn't know how yet, but they would suffer for what they'd done, for what they were currently doing to Henry. I gasped as potent power surged through my veins at the thought. It rippled through me, spilling outward, making the air around me charged with magic. My eyes flew open as I lifted my hand to my face and rolled my magic between my fingers. The power shimmered with a faint blue light, captivating and beautiful.

Damien was smiling when my wide-eyed gaze darted to him.

"How does it feel?" he asked.

"It feels...like lightning in my veins." I tried to convey what I was feeling.

"Incredible, isn't it?" the young man said, turning to leave.

"Wait," I called after him, and my magic dissipated the moment I stopped concentrating. "You'll have to show me more."

"Oh, I don't think that's a good idea. Celeste was very clear about letting you find your own way. I just pointed you in the right direction. Eventually, you'll come into your own power, figuring out what works and what doesn't."

"I already told you, time is not on my side," I bit out, my tone harsher than I'd wanted it to be. Damien recoiled, clearly taken aback. I let the muscles of my face smooth out as I tried again, "I just need your help. Please."

His dark gaze flickered over my features as if assessing how desperate I truly was. Silence stretched for a few seconds until he gave in with a heavy sigh.

"Alright, meet me here tomorrow night."

He turned away then, and I watched him disappear into the woods. The corners of my mouth lifted as I recalled the rush of power I'd felt at my fingertips a few moments ago. Hope flared in my chest—I was one step closer to getting Henry back.

12

HENRY

I'm getting out of here, was my first thought when I regained consciousness.

He's not here, was the second, as I held my breath, listening.

Moreau must have left after I had passed out from the pain. After all, he only wanted to torture me while I was conscious so he could revel in my screams of agony that inevitably escaped. I had cursed my vampire body endless times during the last two nights. It was nearly indestructible, which meant I could endure a lot more than a mere human…and endure I had—pain, misery, the sight of my own entrails, and Moreau's face sprayed with my blood. He was a sick fuck. I needed to get out of here. I was weak, but I was only going to get weaker. At least my body was still healing itself, drawing from its reserves, but they were quickly depleting; I could feel it. It was now or never.

From my last time here, I knew that there were two ways out of Stern's lair. One lay to the right of where I was sprawled on the hard ground, and one to the left. The one on the right led to a steep stairwell that ascended into Stern's study. The one on the left led to the tunnels that connected different regions of the Empire. Stern's Ravagers, the feral vampires he'd sired in an attempt to build his own personal army, had used those tunnels to prowl about the country before I had killed them all.

Slowly, I turned my head to the left and focused on the shadowy opening in the cave wall. Only a few feet separated me from my escape route, but right now, the short distance seemed insurmountable. I willed my weak muscles to move, but they didn't budge, too drained from all the torture and the blood loss. Gritting my teeth, I tried again, imagining myself slowly lifting off the rough cave floor. The mental exercise worked, and with a grunt, I was able to peel my bare back off the ground and roll to my left side. Now came the hard part—I needed to get up.

Propping my right hand on the ground, I pushed up, trying and failing to stifle a loud groan as I sat up. Half-way there. Moving slower than I ever had before, I got on all fours and then eventually rose to my full height. My breath sawed in my throat and sweat beaded on my forehead as I stood in the middle of the candlelit cave, my gaze fixed on the shadowy exit—my target. I didn't dare take my eyes away from it because I knew if I did, I would collapse back to the hard floor. Taking a deep breath, as deep as my mutilated body allowed, I braced myself and took a step toward the exit. My knees buckled, but I didn't go down, grabbing the nearby wooden table for support—the same table that housed the torture instruments Moreau had been using on me. The blades of various shapes and sizes were covered in my blood, old and new, and seeing them only strengthened my resolve to flee this place.

Fastening my gaze back on the exit, I let go of the table and took a few more steps. My movements became surer the longer I stayed up on my feet and the closer I got to my escape. A ragged exhale left me when I reached the exit. I stepped inside the tunnel and was plunged into darkness, my vampire eyes adjusting slower than usual because of the condition I was in. Still, I knew I shouldn't stop moving, so I placed my hand on the rough tunnel wall and kept walking, the sound of my shuffling steps filling the narrow space. Once my vision had finally adjusted and I could see more clearly, my steps became more confident. I let go of the stone wall and picked up my speed, thinking about how I was heading toward my freedom, toward Sophie.

The thought of her spurred me further into action. It gave me strength to push myself, and the next thing I knew, I was running, my steps echoing in the pitch-black. They were heavy and not feline-light as usual, because I was weighted down by what I had been through in the past two nights. I was not moving as quickly as I would have liked. I had cursed my vampire body during the torture sessions, but now I wished I could take it all back—I needed my vampire speed. I tried to summon it, but it wouldn't come. So I kept running at human speed, only putting a short distance between me and Stern's lair even after several long minutes.

Too focused on putting one foot in front of the other and on my labored breathing, I didn't even hear his approach. I didn't know Moreau was right behind me until he snatched me by the back of my neck, yanking me out of my run. Something inside me snapped when I felt his claws digging into my skin—I wasn't going back there; this would end here and now. Only one of us would leave these tunnels alive.

Moreau's eyes widened as I whirled on him and attacked swiftly and viciously. I went for his throat, sinking my fangs as deep as they could go before I tore at the skin and flesh. Blood filled my mouth, warm and thick, and I almost moaned at the taste. It wasn't as rich and sweet as human blood, but at the moment, it was the sweetest nectar to my beaten body.

Focus, I ordered myself. I needed to finish this and escape.

With a snarl, I jerked my head back from Moreau's throat, taking a chunk of it with me. A wet, ripping sound echoed in the tunnel a second before Moreau roared in pain. He crumpled before me, clasping his ravaged neck with his hand. Blood gushed out of the wound, and I wanted to bathe in it, just like he had been bathing in my blood for the past two nights. I wanted to, but I knew I wouldn't do it because I wasn't like him. I was a vampire, but I was not a monster. I spat the piece of flesh I had bitten off Moreau to the side, and it landed on the ground with a wet smack. Moreau shook before me as I towered over him, feeling...pity. Pity that I didn't have time to drag this out, to torture him as he had tortured me.

Not a monster, I reminded myself. It was easy to forget after what I had been through.

"You're lucky I'm not like you," I spat, my voice rough and gravelly as it bounced off the tunnel walls. "Because your death will be swift."

A gurgling sound escaped Moreau as blood bubbled up and spilled out of his mouth, flowing like a crimson river down his chin, neck, and chest. I stepped closer to him to deliver the final blow, but before I could finish him, the others arrived, and the moment they did, I knew it was over.

Shadowy figures of the clan leaders moving imperceptibly fast filled the tunnel. Emeric and Lena dragged Moreau away from me a second before Camilla appeared before me. Her face contorted in rage, but she didn't say anything as she wrapped her clawed hand around my throat and threw me to the side with such force that the tunnel wall shuddered when I collided with it. The outer edges of my vision dimmed as I slid down it to the hard ground.

I failed, was my last thought before everything went dark.

13

SOPHIE

"I really shouldn't be helping you," Damien said, glancing behind his shoulder at the woods he'd just emerged from.

"No one will find out you're helping me. Celeste didn't even ask if I'd made any progress last night."

"Probably because she didn't expect you to make progress so quickly, but I felt your power. The magic in your blood is strong. The way it was rolling off you...that was quite impressive." He chuckled low, his eyes full of wonder as they settled on me. The dark, almost black depths reminded me of Stern, but there was no malice in them, only curiosity.

I squared my shoulders, standing tall under his admiring gaze. While Celeste was trying to stifle me, Damien recognized my potential and was willing to help me grow stronger. Hope that had flared in my chest after our interaction last night began to burn brighter.

"I want to learn more," I told him, my tone eager. "What's the next step?"

The young man just stared at me for a few minutes without saying a word. My stomach dropped—was he questioning his decision to help me? I wasn't sure what I would do if he decided that going against Celeste's wishes was too much of a risk and changed his mind. I was not above begging him not to abandon me. So much hinged on me learning my magic. Henry's life depended on it.

After another beat of silence, Damien finally spoke, choosing his words carefully, "Once you bring your magic forth, you can manipulate it."

A soft sigh of relief left me—he was still going to help. With a nod, I closed my eyes and focused on my breathing. At once, my mind went to Henry, and I felt my power surge to life, lighting up my veins. I stared at his beautiful face as if he were standing right in front of me. He stared back, his eyes like blue waters, drawing me in until I was swimming in them. I knew this wasn't real, but I wanted it to be real so much that it hurt.

Suddenly, Henry's features contorted in pain, and he let out a scream of agony, the sound piercing my ears and my heart. I might have been screaming with him as power swelled inside my chest, crackling down my arms until it concentrated in my hands. I had to save him. I would stop at nothing, even if I had to kill them all—the ones who had torn us apart.

Now, it wasn't just magic burning in my blood but also fury, white-hot and blinding, painting my vision with red. Just like I would paint the walls red with the clan leaders' blood when I found out where they were keeping him. Breathing through my volatile emotions, I opened my eyes and looked down at my magic-wreathed hands. The rippling blue flames were darker than the night before, but burned brighter as if infused with more power. I was getting stronger; I could feel it.

"You're a natural," Damien said, when I lifted my gaze to his.

He was wearing a strange expression on his face—a mix of awe and something else I couldn't quite decipher. "Try to wield the power at your fingertips."

"Wield it how? What can I do with it?" I asked, looking down again and flexing my fingers. The flames flickered with the movement but didn't go out. My lips curved into a smile as I watched my magic burn, mesmerized by its quiet power and haunting beauty.

"Whatever you want," Damien said in a hushed tone.

A short burst of laughter escaped me. Celeste would have advised me to start small, to take my time and not force it. Damien wasn't imposing any restrictions, trusting me to trust myself. Excitement buzzed in my veins as I turned toward the shallow stream glistening in the pale white moonlight. Letting my instincts take over, just as I'd done when I'd activated the Tear, I allowed my magic to guide me, but I was also in control. It was a give and take, a push and pull, my powers and I working together toward one goal. Right now, the goal was to move the water in the creek. Soon, it would be freeing Henry and ending his captors' miserable, worthless lives.

My upper lip curled in a snarl at the thought, and my fingers elongated into claws as I stretched my arms out in front of me, imagining that I was reaching into the stream. Gritting my teeth in concentration, I slowly turned my palms up as if holding an invisible weight. My eyes widened as the water in the creek followed my intent. A churning orb of dripping liquid separated from the stream, rising above the gurgling surface. The air became strangely charged as blue flames erupted around the sphere, enveloping it until tiny sparks of lighting crackled all around it.

A sheen of sweat broke across my forehead as I tugged on the magic in my body, pulling it like threads from my fingertips and toes and gathering it inside my chest, in my very center. In a few seconds, my power was concentrated in the middle of my chest, churning and crackling like the spewing orb hovering above the stream. All my muscles tensed as I focused on the ball of water, and a heartbeat later, released my power with a low grunt. My magic exploded out of me, its force launching the water sphere into the woods on the other side of the creek. It crashed into the trees with a thunder-like sound, incinerating them in the process.

I sucked in a sharp breath as a heady rush of power flooded my veins. The exhilarating feeling was intoxicating, and I closed my eyes, reveling in it. Tilting my face up, I basked in the power and in the moonlight. I'd never felt so alive and so much in my element. Here, at nighttime, using my magic—I'd been born for this. There was freedom in the darkness, and there was freedom in the magic. When the two combined, I felt limitless. As a master of both, I could be unstoppable.

"That felt amazing," I said, still with my back to Damien. "I can't wait to find out what else I can do."

"Who are you talking to?" came Celeste's voice from behind me.

When I spun around, Damien was no longer there. He must have disappeared when the witch had shown up, using his magic to move through space.

How convenient, I thought, taking a mental note to ask him about how that worked when we resumed our training tomorrow night. At least, I hoped Damien would still show up tomorrow.

"No one," I finally responded, focusing on Celeste. The witch eyed me suspiciously as she ducked her chin. "What are you doing here?" I asked, and immediately regretted it. The question sounded accusatory as if I had something to hide.

"I wanted to check on your progress..." Celeste trailed off, her gaze stretching behind me to the burnt woods on the other side of the creek. Her eyes widened in shock as she took in the damage. So, the witch could be rattled after all. "How did you do that?" she asked low, returning her gaze to my face. Her eyes flicked over my features as if looking for something. "You are not supposed to be progressing so quickly."

"Why not?" I challenged. "You know how motivated I am to learn my magic."

"You want to use it for fighting," Celeste pointed out before pressing her lips together in disapproval.

"Because I have something to fight for!" My voice rang out in the night.

My temper rose and my magic rapidly followed, brimming under the surface of my skin, right at my fingertips.

A muscle ticked in the witch's cheek as she clenched her jaw. Her hands balled into fists at her sides, the knuckles whitening.

I felt all color drain from my face. I knew that if Celeste and I went against each other, the witch would prevail, at least in magic. I could prevail with my vampire part, but I didn't want to hurt her. So I tried to force my magic down. Surprisingly, it resisted, spiking back up as if unwilling to be tamed. Pushing harder, I managed to suppress it, dispersing it through my body until it was nothing more than a steady hum in my blood. It was no surprise I had prevailed. Magic might be fickle, but I was no stranger to suppressing my true nature. The faint current of my powers ran through my veins alongside the insidious thirst that could never be truly quenched and would accompany me until the end of my nights.

"I'm sorry," I said, keeping my voice even as I looked at Celeste. "I didn't mean to lash out. It's just…I can't wait to get Henry back and put an end to this."

Celeste's bright blue eyes softened just a fraction. My neck and back relaxed—the apology seemed to be enough to placate her. The witch was still on my side, and I needed to keep it that way, if only for her to leave me be and not interfere with the progress I'd been making.

"You need to be smart about this," Celeste said calmly, uncurling her fists. "Magic is a powerful force. It is not something to be meddled with without proper motivation or preparation. You are just starting to come into your power. You need to take it slow. I know the timing is not ideal, but don't rush it. Trust me on this."

Trust her…Henry was placing his trust in me to rescue him… or perhaps he wasn't. Perhaps he expected me to use the Tear to end vampires once and for all. He carried this weight—this guilt—with him, trying to atone for the mistakes in his past. And wouldn't that be the ultimate act of atonement? To rid this world of his kind so humans had nothing to fear.

He probably wanted me to use the amulet to obliterate the vampires, leaving only humans and White Witches. I knew him better than to think he wished for death, but I could see him resigning himself to that fate. All for the greater good of humanity. Well, if he had, then he would be disappointed in me because I was no longer the selfless martyr. Perhaps that part of me had died when I'd turned. Henry had pulled me out of bloodlust, but maybe that part of me had remained behind, claimed by the never-ending darkness. Henry might be disappointed in me, but at least he would be alive. He deserved to be. Even if he didn't always believe it himself.

"I understand," I finally acknowledged Celeste's warning.

I didn't say I would heed it, and the witch eyed me warily as if not trusting I'd truly heard her words of caution. She opened her mouth to say something else, but I interjected, changing the subject.

"How did you find me?" I asked, shaking the remnants of my magic from my arms.

My fingertips tingled as if the power begged to be expelled and unleashed, but I ignored the feeling, opening and closing my fists until I didn't feel the needling sensation anymore.

"The hex bag I gave you. It also has a tracking spell on it," the witch replied.

My brows knitted. I didn't like being tracked, but I knew

better than to voice my displeasure aloud. Celeste had probably put a tracking spell on it in case something happened to me when I ventured into the Black Forest on my own.

"I'm going into the village. You should come with me. Amelie was asking about you," Celeste said.

I stifled a sigh. I didn't want to go into the village. I wanted to stay here and keep practicing my magic. But I doubted Celeste would let me out of her sight after the little demonstration she'd witnessed from me earlier. I just hoped I would still be able to practice by myself from now on without her hovering over my shoulder. I also hoped Celeste's unexpected arrival hadn't spooked Damien, deterring him from ever helping me again.

"Alright. I'll go. Perhaps I could try using my magic to move through space like you do?" I asked, hopeful. Maybe Celeste wouldn't have a problem with guiding me through it.

"We call it glimmering, and it requires much practice and energy. Again, don't get ahead of yourself," the witch said sternly.

I clenched my teeth to stop myself from muttering a curse at her stubbornness. Damien had said the magic in my blood was strong. Could she not sense it? I wished she would trust in my abilities.

I will advance quickly, I vowed to myself. *The witch will regret underestimating me.*

"I'll run then," I told her, wanting some time and space to clear my head.

To my surprise, Celeste didn't offer to take me to the village with her, and I wondered if it was because my growing power was making her uneasy. The witch didn't say anything else as she gave a curt nod and disappeared into thin air. The spot where she'd stood shimmered with soft, wavering light, and my head tilted to the side as I watched it dissipate. I supposed "glimmering" was more than a fitting term for that act of magic. If only Celeste had been willing to teach me how to glimmer… No matter, I would learn one way or another. In the meantime, I still had to rely on my supernatural speed.

My muscles tensed as I shifted my weight and leaned forward. A heartbeat later, I was flying through the dark forest, reveling in the freedom of the night. This was where I belonged—in the wilderness with other nocturnal creatures. My heart was full, but also empty, because Henry wasn't by my side. I hoped I would dream about him when I went to sleep tonight. Maybe we would get to finish what we'd started in my dream the other night. It wouldn't come close to the real thing, to the feeling of his body on mine, but it would still provide temporary release. My eyes pricked with tears as I suddenly felt sorry for myself because I was hoping for glimpses of Henry in my dreams. I would get him back soon—I had to, and nothing and no one would stand in my way.

14

The village was bustling with activity when I arrived, which took me by surprise. I'd thought the other night had been the exception because of the celebration, but seeing people milling around now, despite it being late evening, proved it was the norm. The crowded street was illuminated by dozens of lanterns sprinkled throughout the settlement, and various sounds and smells floated through the air.

My gaze glided over the throng of people, looking for Damien, but his tall, thin frame and blond head were nowhere to be seen. After a few seconds of not finding him, I decided to look for Celeste instead. The witch smelled like herbs and tea leaves to me, and my nostrils flared as I tried to pluck her scent from the others. After I'd identified it, I followed it to one of the cabins—the same one I'd come across the other night. Amelie had been sitting on these very steps, and judging by her floral scent that permeated the air on the porch, she hadn't simply chosen this spot to be closer to the celebration; she lived here.

I knocked on the simple wooden door and waited, catching another familiar scent—Waylon was inside the house. Was he staying here? Two nights ago, when he'd left Celeste's cottage, I hadn't followed him into the village, trusting Isabelle to keep an eye on him. I knew that one of the witches had agreed to take him in, but I didn't know which one.

An older witch opened the door a few seconds later.

"You must be Sophie," she said, beaming at me. "We have been expecting you. I'm Genevieve, Amelie's mom. Please, come in. Join us for some tea."

She stepped to the side and extended her arm in a welcoming gesture. I quickly took in her unbound, flaming-red hair and open, round face. Amelie was a spitting image of her mother, down to the copper freckles covering her nose and the apples of her cheeks. My heart squeezed as I lingered on the threshold, momentarily lost in thought about my own mother. Our resemblance had been uncanny as well, and based on what I'd been able to do by the creek earlier, it appeared I had not only inherited her looks but also her magical prowess.

"Sophie?" Genevieve asked, her soft voice gently pulling me from my thoughts.

She was looking at me expectantly, and after another beat of silence, I stepped inside and followed her deeper into the small but cozy house. My vampire ears picked up on lively banter and laughter drifting from the direction we were heading. When we walked into the cramped kitchen, Waylon and Amelie promptly stepped away from each other, putting as much distance between them as the tight space allowed. Waylon was trying and failing at hiding a grin, and Amelie's cheeks were flushed when they both whipped their heads to the kitchen's entrance.

"Sophie!" Amelie exclaimed, clearly happy to see me. "Would you like some tea?" she asked in a soft voice, which was so much like her mother's.

"Yes, please." I smiled at her. "Where is Celeste?" I asked.

The witch been here earlier—her scent still lingered in the air.

"She left to visit Agatha," Genevieve replied while setting out four simple teacups on the table.

My heart thumped over in my chest. Did Celeste somehow suspect that Agatha's son had been helping me develop my magic? I quickly dismissed the thought. I hadn't been followed the last two nights, I was sure of it. She had no way of knowing… unless the hex bag had not only a tracking spell on it but also a spying one. I pulled the pouch out of my pocket and eyed it suspiciously.

"Sophie, can we talk in private for a moment?" Waylon asked, tension bracketing his mouth. Gone was the mischievous, carefree grin from a few minutes ago. Now, Waylon's face was all hard lines and wariness.

"Sure," I replied, as I shoved the hex bag back into my pocket and walked out of the kitchen.

Waylon followed me back to the front door, and we stepped outside, stopping on the other side of the threshold.

"So, you and Amelie?" I asked without further ado.

Waylon's brows slammed down as he shifted from foot to foot.

"Her family took me in…they had an extra room," he said, clasping the back of his neck, looking uncomfortable with this conversation. "It's not just her and Genevieve, of course. There is a man of the house—Alaric, Genevieve's husband and Amelie's father," he added, looking down and to the side as if lost in thought.

He must have borrowed the loose white shirt and buckskin breeches he was wearing from the warlock. It was strange seeing Waylon in anything but the guard leathers, but the simple clothing suited him. Amelie suited him as well.

"Amelie seems very genuine and sweet," I said, and Waylon's forest-green eyes shot to mine.

"I don't need your approval," he grumbled, his fair brows knitting.

"I know. Just like I didn't need yours," I said simply.

I hadn't asked for his approval before deciding to become a

vampire. Waylon was a lifelong friend and had been more in the past, but only one person's opinion had mattered to me back then—my father's. A pang pierced my heart at the thought. The last time I'd seen him, he'd been setting off toward the Northern region while we'd been preparing for war. He would have still been traveling when I'd defeated the Dark Witches. Had the clans begun spreading the lie that they'd pushed the Dark Witches back to the Black Forest? Had my father turned around when he'd heard it?

I wanted to see him, but fear took root in my chest. What if the clans decided to use him in addition to Henry to lure me out? I swallowed thickly. The clans didn't know who my father was, and without knowing his whereabouts, all I could do was hope they wouldn't find out. I hoped to see my father again soon, but I also felt like I couldn't face him right now. Because if I did... would he be disappointed in me because I wasn't putting humanity before myself this time? Or would he understand, just like he'd understood my decision to turn?

"Where did you go?" Waylon asked, snapping me out of my thoughts.

I blinked several times and refocused on him.

"I was just thinking about my father," I admitted.

A muscle flexed along Waylon's jaw as his eyes searched my face. His gaze grew distant for a moment, and I knew that while I was thinking about one human—my father—he was thinking about the entire human population of the Empire.

"When do you think we can go back?" he asked low, his eyes returning to me.

His tone told me he wanted to press for answers but was choosing not to. He needed me, and he didn't want to push me.

"I've been making progress with my magic, but it's only been three nights." I forced the words out, even though I hated them.

It had been three nights of Henry being tortured and starved. From Isabelle, I knew he'd been injured during the altercation in the study before he'd been taken. The clan leaders would withhold blood from him so he wouldn't heal. Without blood, he would remain weak and wouldn't be able to put up a fight and escape. My magic bubbled up in my veins at the thought.

"I know how determined you are, Sophie. Once you set your mind to something, there is no stopping you," Waylon said, and while the words were meant to be encouraging, they set me on edge. It was as if by saying them, he had picked up a large stone and sat it on my shoulders, adding to the weight that was already pressing down on me.

"I'm doing everything I can," I bit out. "You know I want to leave as soon as possible, but Celeste…she's holding me back."

"Why would she do that?" he asked, his brows pinching in confusion.

"She wants me to get to know my magic and not force it. She's underestimating me."

Waylon seemed to think it over. "I don't know, Sophie. She's old and wise. I doubt she would be giving you that advice if she didn't have a very good reason."

"There is no reason good enough to hold me back. Especially not now," I said vehemently.

Waylon's eyes widened, and he opened his mouth to say something else, but clamped it shut when Amelie cracked open the front door and poked her head out.

"Tea is ready," she announced with a small smile.

Her lips turned down as her gaze darted between Waylon and me.

"Is everything okay?" she asked, opening the door wider and stepping onto the porch.

"Did Celeste give instructions not to help me with my magic?" I asked the girl.

"She did," she admitted, and I shot Waylon a pointed look—*see*.

"But I'm sure it's for your own good," Amelie added, her brows knitting. "Celeste only has your best interest at heart."

When I scoffed and averted my gaze, it landed on the busy street.

"It's late. Why is everyone still out and about?" I asked, curious.

"The Dark Witches were most active at night, so we adopted the same lifestyle to be better protected from them. We didn't want them to catch us unawares if they ever broke through the protective barrier surrounding the village," Amelie explained. "Some of us are still active during the day, of course, to keep watch and to tend to our gardens."

"Smart," I murmured to myself, still looking at the people going about their day, or rather, night.

Some were carrying pails of water from the well at the other end of the village, while others were trading root vegetables and herbs. A group of women sat on the porch steps of one of the cabins, mending clothes together, while their children played, their laughter spilling into the night. The sounds of hammering and wood-chopping echoed through the settlement from where a few men were fixing one of the houses.

Absentmindedly, I let my gaze glide over all the activity until it snagged on Isabelle and Wren. They appeared to be out for an evening stroll, looking relaxed next to each other as they walked at a leisurely pace. Isabelle was so immersed in her conversation with Wren that it took a few minutes before she picked up on my scent. When she did, her head swung in my direction, and she placed a hand on Wren's arm to stop him in his tracks. He followed her gaze, and together, they adjusted their course and began making their way toward the cabin. Jealousy spiked as I watched them, my brows pinching in a frown. I wished it was Henry and me walking around the village. I knew he would have been overjoyed to see the settlement and all its people. Pushing the unpleasant feeling aside, I willed my frown to smooth out as Isabelle and Wren approached where I was standing.

"Sophie, how are you?" Isabelle asked, her brown eyes fastening on me.

There was genuine concern in her voice, and I almost laughed at how far we'd come. Ever since I'd turned, she'd been tolerant of me at best. Now, she was beginning to treat me more like a sister, everything happening with the clans bringing us closer together.

"I'm okay," I lied. "How are you?"

My gaze flicked over her features. She looked well in a navy dress with her black curls left down to frame her face. It seemed the beating she'd taken three nights ago was now a distant memory. Wren looked well, too, standing next to her. I quickly appraised the young man. His pale-blue eyes shone, and a healthy pink hue colored his cheeks—Isabelle had been giving him her blood. It wasn't the only thing she'd been giving him—I could smell her on him, and him on her, their scents intermingled. My longing for Henry intensified.

"I'm doing okay," Isabelle said, forcing a smile. It came out more like a grimace and didn't reach her eyes. "I'm worried about Henry," she admitted, the corners of her mouth turning down. "How is the magic training going? Will we be able to go after him soon?"

Waylon cast his gaze down at her words, looking as if he wanted to be anywhere else but here for this conversation.

I gritted my teeth at the question. Everyone was waiting on me before we could act. My chest constricted with pressure as the weight on my shoulders became heavier, almost impossible to bear.

"It's only been three nights." I repeated the same words I'd said to Waylon. They came out as a hiss, but Isabelle seemed unaffected by my menacing tone.

"Is there anything we can do to help?" she asked.

Can you speed it up? the question truly meant. She knew there wasn't anything in their power to help me.

"No, this task lies solely on me. I know that. You know that. Everyone knows that. So why can't you all just trust that I'm doing the best I can? I know what's at stake. It's my skin stretching tauter over my bones the longer I'm away from Henry. The desperate desire to put an end to this burns brighter in me than in all of you. And I *will* put an end to this, mark my words."

Isabelle's eyes widened at my outburst, the whites strikingly contrasting her rich-brown skin. Wren scowled, placing a hand on her lower back.

"I know, I just… You are not alone in this," Isabelle said softly, compassion infusing each word.

This new side of her set me on edge. It felt as if we'd switched places because she was demonstrating more humanity at the moment than me.

"I *am* alone in this," I told her. "I am alone unless Henry is by my side. And he *will* be by my side soon. I won't have it any other way."

The words sounded like a vow, ringing out in the cool night air as I turned and walked inside the house.

15

I was lying on my back on the blue-and-white blanket, bathed in the warm sunlight. A sigh of contentment left me as I closed my eyes and let myself sink past the fabric into the soft grass and the hard earth underneath. Small rodents scurried in the tangled undergrowth, while tiny insects burrowed into the ground, and birds fluttered in the tree branches above. The cacophony of sounds had harmony in it—endless and beautiful, and the world around me was how it was meant to be—bursting with life. I inhaled deeply, drawing the bountiful energy in. It settled deep inside my chest, grounding me, making me whole. I thought I was beginning to understand what it truly meant to be a White Witch, to embrace that side of me in its entirety.

"Sophie?" came Henry's deep voice from my right, and my eyes fluttered open as my skin prickled with awareness. It was a pleasant feeling, one of acute excitement and anticipation. Feeling my cheeks flush, I turned my head and smiled softly.

"I was hoping to see you," I breathed, my gaze gliding over the features that were painfully beautiful yet harsh and unyielding at times.

Right now, Henry's face was relaxed, his eyes hooded as he stared at me from beneath his long lashes.

"I was hoping to see you, too," he said low, reaching with his right hand to brush a strand of hair from my cheek.

My throat dried when his fingertips skimmed my cheekbone. The feather-light touch sent a jolt through me. At once, I became very aware that this was a dream, and I didn't have a second to spare. I wanted to wring out every drop of pleasure from my time with Henry—I wanted to drown in it.

Moving in a flash, I straddled him, my flowery dress riding up my hips. Henry laughed, the sound nice and deep, as he hardened underneath me. Bracing my hands on his chest, I swiveled my hips, eliciting a groan from both of us. I bent down to kiss him, but before I could claim his mouth, he sat up and clasped the back of my neck.

Holding me in place, he rested his forehead on mine and whispered, "As much as I love how eager you are..." He paused, pulling away to peer at my face. "Tell me something first. How are you?"

The question caught me off guard, tamping down some of the burning desire. My heart sank just as the world around me dimmed, the sunlight receding and the temperature dropping. The darkness was closing in—I was running out of time.

Instead of answering Henry, I sealed my lips to his. He didn't resist, opening up for me, our tongues mingling. The taste of him invaded my senses, and I sank my fingers into his hair, tugging on the silky strands. Henry let go of my neck, his hands diving under the skirts of my dress. His fingers dug into my thighs as he ground me against him. A gasp escaped, making me break the kiss to gulp a mouthful of air. Henry took the opportunity to trail kisses down my neck before I clasped his chin and guided his mouth back to mine. I kissed him deeply, greedily, as I slid his unbuttoned shirt off his broad shoulders.

The world had gotten even darker around us, but that only spurred my desire. The strokes of my tongue against his became fiercer and more demanding. When I grazed a fang over his lower lip, he shuddered, as a low growl rumbled from deep within his throat. The rough sound sent a pulse of potent lust through me, making me feral for him. I *pushed on his chest, trying to bring him down, but like the last time, he resisted, lowering me to the blanket instead.*

His mouth left mine, and he began kissing down my neck to my chest, pausing by my breasts to drag one sharp fang over my sensitive nipple straining through the thin fabric of my dress. My back arched off the ground as another wave of raw desire rolled through me. A breathy moan escaped when he closed his mouth around the hardened tip and sucked long and deep. I felt each maddening pull between my thighs as I writhed underneath him. He didn't stop there. Releasing the tingling peak, he kept moving lower down my body, sliding my undergarments off in the process. My breath caught when he settled with his head between my thighs, his hands fisted in my skirts.

Darkness surrounded us now, our blue-and-white blanket the only bright spot in the pitch black. The churning shadows were beginning to encroach on our little island, licking the edges of the fabric. Panic set in as I looked frantically around, but then my gaze returned to Henry. When I saw his eyes, black with an insatiable hunger for me, desire overrode everything else, crashing into me like a powerful tide. I didn't care about the darkness then. It could swallow me whole for all I cared, as long as I was with Henry. My gaze dropped to his mouth, and I watched him wet his lips as if in anticipation.

All my senses became hyperaware—I couldn't wait to feel his tongue on the throbbing point between my thighs. I knew that just one graze of his fang down there would undo me. He knew it, too, his lips stretching in a decadently sinful smile. His dark lashes swept down, hiding the predatory gleam in his eyes as he lowered his head. My muscles tensed, and my breathing quickened. Waiting for him to do something, anything, was the sweetest torture. I almost whimpered when I felt his breath on me, on my very core. The first glide of his tongue sent a surge of lightning through my veins, jerking me awake.

I bolted upright in the bed, gasping with pleasure. My eyes darted around the room until I realized where I was—back at the witch's cottage. Squeezing my thighs together, I threw myself against the mattress, turning my face into the flat pillow to muffle my scream of frustration. My dreams had become a blessing and curse. I couldn't say I didn't want them, because I would take any glimpse of Henry I could get, but waking up before being able to expel the pent-up desire for him made me want to weep. I managed to keep the tears at bay as I flopped on my back and stared at the ceiling, waiting for the brimming arousal to subside. After a few minutes, when it was still there, humming just below the surface of my skin, I slid my hand under the covers and took care of the throbbing ache while fantasizing about Henry.

Once my heartbeat and my breathing evened out, I threw the covers off me and got out of bed. Like the night before, I quickly washed up and pulled a pair of pants and a tunic out of the pile of clothing on the chair. Tonight's garments were a warm green hue, almost matching my hazel eyes. After getting dressed, I braided my hair, hung the locket with my mother's portrait around my neck, and put the Tear in my pocket. When I reached for the hex bag on the bedside table, I hesitated, my brows pinching in a scowl. Celeste had told me yesterday that she wanted to be present tonight when I practiced my magic.

She only wants to be there so she can hold me back, I thought, my scowl intensifying. I couldn't let that happen. Going into the Black Forest without the hex bag was risky, but I was a predator now, much like the beasts that dwelled in those woods. I could take care of myself. Closing my outstretched hand into a fist, I dropped it and turned away from the table, leaving the hex bag behind.

Breathing shallowly to make less noise, I slowly opened my bedroom door, careful not to make it creak. Shadows filled the short hallway, the only light a faint glow coming from the direction of the kitchen. I could hear Celeste rummaging around in there, making her customary evening tea. Leaving the bedroom, I moved through the house on soft feet, avoiding any objects with feline grace. My vampire abilities helped me to stay undetected as I slipped out the front door and set off toward the woods.

The Black Forest felt different tonight, more awake and... hungry. When I stepped into the woods, the Forest creatures swarmed, no longer kept at bay by the hex bag I'd left behind. I bared my fangs and let out a low, menacing hiss when they converged on me. They hissed back, but scuttled away, scurrying back into the shadows. Crouched down, my claws drawn, I spun in a circle, waiting to see if any of them would be bold enough to attack. They kept their distance—it seemed I'd established my dominance.

No sooner had the thought crossed my mind than a giant wolf leaped out of the shadows from my right. The red glowing eyes and glistening teeth barely registered before the beast barreled into me, knocking me off my feet. The air whooshed out of my lungs as we landed on the ground and rolled, the force of the impact propelling us into a nearby tree. The sound was deafening as we collided with the wide, thick trunk, demolishing it in the process. With a snarl, I kicked the wolf off me and jumped to my feet. The creature flipped in the air and landed on all fours, crouching low to the ground with an answering snarl. I crouched down, too, and we squared off against each other as wooden fragments rained down all around us.

The slick black fur gleamed in the moonlight as the wolf prowled before me, hulking muscles bunching and flexing. I stood frozen, tracking its every movement. My mind flashed back to when I'd encountered one of these beasts before. The creature had almost killed me then, but Henry had saved me. He wouldn't be able to come to my rescue now.

My breathing quickened as terror spiked. I shuddered when the wolf let out a blood-curdling growl and snapped its teeth, advancing closer. My knees weakened as I began to tremble. On shaking legs, I went to retreat, but then I remembered something —I was a vampire now and could hold my own against the beast.

A dark, guttural sound erupted, and my skin prickled before I realized that it was coming from me. I felt the other parts of me recede until the vampire side took over, and I became a predator—a killer through and through. The next thing I knew, my muscles coiled, and I was moving—rushing toward the wolf. There was no doubt, no fear. The vampire me had come for blood—she'd come to fight, and she was getting what she'd come for. When I leaped into the air, the wolf did the same, and a heartbeat later, we collided, becoming a blur of fangs and claws as our growls and snarls filled the air, echoing through the Forest.

The wolf was fast, but I was faster, avoiding the swipes of razor-sharp claws and the snaps of deadly teeth. Hot saliva splashed on my face when the beast went for my throat, but I ducked, avoiding its gaping maw, and slashed my claws across its midsection. The wolf roared in pain and tried to retreat, but I kept going after it, slashing and biting, tearing at its flesh with my teeth—the creature had brought this upon itself…it had attacked me first.

Unexpectedly, the wolf stopped trying to escape and went for another attack. When it threw itself at me, I wrapped my arms around its torso and squeezed. I kept applying pressure as the beast thrashed in my hold until a loud crack sounded, and another roar of anguish pierced the night. When the wolf went limp in my arms, I relaxed my hold, and it crumpled to the ground in a massive, bloody heap. Breath wheezed out of it, its chest rising and falling shallowly because of the ribs I'd broken. I towered over the beast, my vampire side urging me to finish this, to deliver the killing blow.

Silence settled over the woods as I lowered my gaze to the ground, to the wolf lying by my feet. Broken and helpless, it seemed smaller now, as if it had shrunk down in size. The glow of the red eyes was dimming by the second as the creature stared up at me, whimpering softly. I wasn't sure if it was begging for mercy or asking me to put it out of its misery.

It's neither of those things, my vampire side growled in dismay. *It's just a mindless beast, finish it.*

With a snarl, I drew my clawed hand back, excitement buzzing in my veins.

16

Just a mindless beast... Something Celeste had said the other night floated up from the recesses of my mind.

When the White Witches began turning dark, their black magic bled into the woods, poisoning the land and trees, morphing forest creatures into monsters.

Had the wolf always been this thing of nightmares? Or had it turned into a monster when the Dark Witches' magic had poisoned these woods? I didn't know the answer to that, and I suddenly felt conflicted, the human side of me peeking through.

What if you and the beast are more alike than you realize? What if the creature also has to constantly fight the darkness within? my human side whispered.

Slowly, I retracted my claws and lowered my hand. Lifting my gaze from the wolf, I looked around, noticing the oily black scales and disjointed limbs of the forest creatures slithering through the trees. Hundreds of glowing eyes watched me from deep within the shadows, waiting to see what I would do next. I could feel their anticipation and hunger for blood. The air was thick with it, just like it was thick with the smell of rot and decay. What a putrid, miserable place...

I looked down at the wolf again. Even if I spared its life, the forest creatures would tear it apart the moment I'd left its side. It was injured, and the Forest preyed on the weak. Would killing it be more of an act of mercy than letting it live? Once again, I felt conflicted. The wolf moved by my feet, startling me. I took a step back as it rose off the ground, standing on four legs that trembled but didn't give out. Blood dripped from its mouth as the red glow in its eyes intensified. I expected it to come at me, but it turned toward the woods instead and let out a menacing growl. I supposed that was its way of showing me it still stood a chance against the creatures of the Forest.

My mind made up, I turned away from the wolf and assumed a pre-sprint position.

"Good luck," I threw over my shoulder at the beast before I began running, flying through the woods.

I wasn't sure where I was going. I couldn't go back to my spot by the creek because Celeste knew about it now. So I ran until I came across a clearing. The Forest creatures swarmed again when I stopped in the middle of it, but I wasn't afraid of them. I'd fought a giant wolf and prevailed, and I doubted there was anything bigger or more vicious than it in these woods. Except me. I wondered if, no matter how powerful one became, there was always a more superior creature, a bigger predator, or in my case, a group of them, like the clans.

No. I scowled, rolling my neck and shaking out my arms, preparing for another fight.

I would become the biggest, baddest predator there was. Never again would anyone be able to take something that was mine away from me. My magic surged to life at the thought, sparks flying from my fingertips. I inhaled deeply as the power swelled, filling me until I was brimming with it. Ducking my chin, I looked around the clearing at the creatures scuttling closer. As if sensing my power, they stopped their approach and backed away, retreating deeper into the impenetrable darkness of the forest.

I cocked my head, my forehead creasing. Was my power that terrifying to them? Should *I* be terrified of it? I quickly dismissed the thought. It was *my* power. I was its master, not the other way around. I would not cower before it. And if others bowed down before it—good. I wanted them to be terrified of me.

Still, disappointment washed over me that the forest creatures had retreated—I'd been looking forward to practicing my magic on them. Now, I would need to find a different target. I looked around the clearing, my gaze searching until it snagged on a small boulder several feet away. I concentrated on the gray stone, imagining it was the head of one of the clan leaders. Thrusting my hand toward it, I threw my magic out, and it crackled through the clearing like lighting, blasting into the boulder. My jaw clenched as I channeled my powers, applying great pressure onto the stone. Seconds ticked by with the boulder just lying there, seemingly unaffected by my magic. Frustration rose, but before I could give in to it, the stone groaned, and a crack appeared in the rough gray surface. Excitement replaced the feeling of frustration as I increased the pressure on the stone until it exploded with a loud boom that echoed through the clearing. My lips turned up in a triumphant smile, because I would crush the clan leader's skull just like I'd just crushed that boulder. The outpour of power had made me feel drained, but my veins still buzzed with restless energy as if my magic urged me to do more—to push myself further.

I took another sweeping look around the clearing, searching for the next challenge. When my gaze landed on some gnarled tree roots protruding from the ground, I narrowed my eyes and cast my power out. Drawing on the magic in my chest, I willed the roots to move, to lift from the soil. For several long minutes, they didn't budge. I gritted my teeth, concentrating harder until sweat beaded on my forehead. The roots creaked, aglow with the blue-black flames of my magic, and the ground shook as I pushed with all my might.

"Come on," I bit out, tugging on the roots with my powers.

It felt impossible, as if the earth itself was hanging on to them, until it suddenly gave way. With a grunt, I ripped the roots from the ground and launched them toward the dark woods. Damien ducked out of the way, barely avoiding the projectile, when he separated from the tree line.

"Still channeling that frustration, I see," the young man chuckled as he came closer.

He had no idea, I thought, wiping the sweat from my brow.

"What happened to you?" Damien asked, stopping before me.

His dark gaze flicked over me, and his eyes widened before they returned to my face. Only then did I realize that I was covered in blood, mine and the wolf's. I looked down at myself, at the cuts and bruises peeking through my tattered clothes. They were not healing as quickly as I would have liked. I would need to feed soon. With the realization, came a feeling of discontent. I could drink animal blood, and while it would sustain me for a short while, that was not the blood I needed. I needed human blood. My stomach knotted with unease. I'd never fed from a human before, only resorting to drinking the blood stored in the cellar at the Duval Estate or tasting Henry's blood when we would... I closed my eyes and took a breath.

"A giant wolf attacked me," I explained, opening my eyes again.

"What? I thought you had a hex bag. The forest creatures are supposed to stay away—"

"I didn't bring it," I interjected. "I didn't want to make it easier for Celeste to track me. How did you find me?"

"Well, I knew I shouldn't go back to our usual meeting spot, so I wandered around the forest for a while, listening to the world around me. Eventually, the threads led me to you."

"I'm glad they did," I told him. "I want to ask you something. Glimmering. How does it work?"

Damien's lips pressed into a thin line at my question.

"Uh, listen, Sophie. I know you're doing remarkably well with your magic, but glimmering is quite advanced. It usually takes years of practice. I'm a quick learner myself, but it even took me a while before I mastered it."

"Are you telling me to take it slow?" I narrowed my eyes at him.

"No, no." Damien lifted his hands in defense. "I'm just saying you should know your limits."

"I need to push myself so I can learn my limits," I bit out.

"Glimmering is not the best way to learn what those limits are."

"Why not? What can go wrong?"

Damien stared at me as if I'd lost my mind.

"You can launch yourself into a different realm or get stranded in the void."

My heart dropped to the bottom of my stomach.

"So, things can go very, very wrong," I said shakily before I cleared my throat and infused my voice with resolve. "Still, I'm willing to take the risk." Being able to glimmer would provide yet another advantage when I went after Henry, and it would be yet another weapon in my arsenal if I wanted to become the biggest and the baddest.

"You're a vampire, Sophie. You already can move with supernatural speed," Damien pointed out. If he were trying to talk me out of it, his attempt was half-hearted, as if he knew I couldn't be swayed.

"Being able to disappear from somewhere and reappear somewhere else entirely in a heartbeat is not the same as my vampire ability to run fast. It's on a whole different level."

"Yes, the level that might still be too advanced for you,"

Damien said in a measured tone. "For now," he added hastily when I scowled.

"There is only one way to find out," I drawled, my lips stretching into a daring smile.

Damien scanned me from head to toe as if taking a second look at me.

"I suppose I shouldn't be surprised that you don't back down from a challenge. You did defeat the Dark Witches, after all."

"I did. And soon, I will defeat the clans."

"Defeat the clans? I thought the goal was to save your lover?" His white brows lifted in question.

"I will save him, and then I will make them pay," I growled.

Damien's eyes shone with approval, and his lips twitched as if he were fighting a smile.

"Very well... To glimmer, you need to visualize in your mind the place you want to go. Then, you gather up your magic until it's concentrated in your center." He touched the center of his chest. "When ready, you send your magic first, like a beam of light piercing through the void and emerging on the other side, in the place where you're trying to go. Imagine your power like a bridge connecting where you are to where you want to be. To use that bridge, you need to enter the beam of light, which is your magic, and exit it when you arrive."

"It sounds...complicated," I admitted, as anxiety spiked. I wouldn't let it take over. I needed a clear head if I hoped to pull this off.

Releasing a long exhale, I closed my eyes and let my mind go quiet. I needed to begin with something simple. Perhaps I could glimmer from where I stood to the tree line where Damien had emerged from. It wasn't that far. I could do it. I pulled the magic from my limbs, willing it to travel from my fingertips, toes, and even the ends of my hair, to the center of my chest.

As Damien had instructed, I imagined my power like a beam of light and then flung it across the clearing, connecting the patch of land where I stood to the dark and twisted trunks of the tree line. Now came the tricky part. I stepped into the beam of light, imagining myself growing smaller until I was no bigger than a gnat. I waited for the light to suck me in and spit me out by the tree line, but nothing happened. After a few minutes, when I didn't feel any different, I cracked open one eye and confirmed what I already knew—I was still in the same spot, with Damien watching me intently.

Opening my eyes fully, I let out a growl of frustration. Damien sighed softly—a mix of relief and disappointment. He was relieved I hadn't proved him wrong, but also disappointed, all for the same reason.

"I told you it takes years," he said, folding his arms over his chest.

"Then I will find a way to turn years into days," I responded with determination.

17

When I closed my eyes at the break of dawn, I didn't dream about Henry. Instead, I was in the dark place again, with shadows whispering things to me. Strangely enough, I was no longer afraid of them. My breathing and heartbeat were even as I sat down cross-legged in the pool of darkness, closing my eyes and resting my hands on my knees. Somehow, I knew I was dreaming, so I just sat there quietly, waiting to wake up. The darkness lapped at my skin and tugged on my hair, and I let it, barely noticing the icy-hot touch. At one point, I opened my eyes and ran my hand through the wispy black tendrils that surrounded me. They wrapped around my fingers, tickling my skin, and a faint smile graced my lips.

"You're not scary at all," I said, my voice echoing in the large, open space. "Perhaps you're just misunderstood…"

As if in response, the smoke slithered up my arm, perching on my shoulder. It caressed my cheek, and I turned my face into its gentle touch, closing my eyes with a soft exhale. My mind became empty as I sat there, wrapped in the darkness's embrace. I didn't think about Henry, my mother, or the fate of the world. I simply existed, unburdened and free. I wasn't sure how much time had passed as I floated in the nothingness, but the next thing I knew I felt myself beginning to wake up.

"I have to go," I told the darkness, opening my eyes again. "I have to keep working on my magic so I can rescue Henry."

As soon as I'd uttered the words, the thoughts of him rushed back in, pushing me to my feet.

"I'll be back," I promised the darkness. I knew sooner rather than later I would return to this place where there was no end and no beginning. The thought didn't terrify me anymore. On the contrary, excitement sparked in my chest...excitement and anticipation.

"Until next time," I whispered, as I felt myself beginning to float up.

My heels separated from the floor first, then the balls of my feet, then my toes. Oily, tar-like substance dripped from them as I floated up, higher and higher, until I broke through the surface of my dream, taking some of the darkness with me.

I didn't bolt upright in the bed like I'd done in the past few nights. My breathing was steady when I opened my eyes. The darkness didn't terrify me anymore. I understood it better now, and it had felt wrong leaving it behind in my dream. It understood me, too. I'd felt...at home when I'd been surrounded by it. That couldn't be right, I thought to myself as I scowled. My home was where Henry was. Nothing else could provide the same sense of security. Or could it?

Shaking my head to clear my thoughts, I left the bed and got ready. Once I was dressed in black leggings and a simple white tunic, I tied my hair at the nape of my neck and put the Tear in my pocket. Ready to leave, I stepped closer to the bedroom door, but froze when I smelled Celeste on the other side. A frustrated sigh left me as I yanked open the door, glaring at the witch. She glared right back, her face set in determination.

"You are not going to sneak out this time," she said coldly, her tone final.

"I wouldn't need to sneak out if you didn't feel the need to hold me back," I bit out, my voice as cold as ice to match hers.

"I am not holding you back. I only implore you to take it slow. To approach the magic with the care and respect it deserves."

"It's my magic, so I get to decide how to handle it."

"You have so much to learn."

"Then teach me!" I raised my voice at the witch.

Celeste opened her mouth to reply, but clamped it shut as her gaze drew distant. I knew that look.

"What is it?" I asked, trying to glean the answer from her face. Her warm, beige skin paled as her lips pressed together.

"Nothing," she finally said after a few seconds' delay.

Lies.

"You're lying. The world whispered something to you. What was it?"

"It was nothing. Nothing that is in your power to change at the moment."

My heart sank as a cold feeling invaded my chest. Telling myself to breathe through the increasing sense of unease, I closed my eyes and tapped into the world around me, picturing a myriad of shimmering strings carrying pulses of information in short, rapid bursts. As I opened my senses, voices rushed in, flooding my head with sounds. My brows pinched in concentration as I began wading through the bits and pieces of information that the voices were whispering, talking over each other.

She's here...the clans...right on the border, I heard the words rising and falling like a tide, growing louder at times before fading into the jarring chaos of noise.

Over the next few seconds, the whispering intensified, growing louder and louder, until it reached its peak, and the voices shouted all at once, *He's here!*

My eyes flew open, my chest rising and falling rapidly.

"Sophie—" Celeste warned, but I was already gone, flying through the forest.

I skidded to a halt in the tree line facing the stone wall of the border with the Empire.

"Stop," came Celeste's voice from behind me a second before her hand landed on my shoulder, her fingers digging into my skin and bone.

I froze, my eyes trained on the border, where Camilla paced the top of the stone wall with feline grace. The twin chips of ice that were her eyes glided over the tree line, and my breath caught when she looked right at where Celeste and I stood.

"She can't see or hear us," the witch said as Camilla's gaze slid past us. "And she can't smell us. I have cast a masking spell, but I need to be touching you in order for it to project onto you."

"Okay," I said low, my gaze tracking Camilla's every movement.

The Lady of the North stopped her pacing and planted her hands on the stone ledge.

"Are you out there, Sophie?" she called out, leaning slightly over the edge. "Come out, come out, wherever you are," she taunted with a chilling smile, showing the gleaming tips of her fangs. "It's been nights, Sophie," she said, taking her hands off the ledge and inspecting her pointed nails. "I'd have expected you to come for him by now." She paused, her gaze flicking back to the woods. "You know, we almost killed him."

When a growl rumbled from deep within my throat, Celeste's grip on me tightened.

"I am willing to bet he sometimes wishes he'd died that night. Death would have been easier than enduring everything we have put him through. It's only been four nights, but we have ensured it felt like an eternity to him. An eternity of pain and suffering."

My body was frigid cold and didn't feel like my own. I was floating above it, watching the entire exchange from afar.

I didn't move, didn't breathe as Camilla continued, "How long are you going to let him suffer?" she called out into the pitch-black darkness of the woods, where I stood frozen, blending in with the shadows.

I imagined myself a part of the landscape, imagined the darkness wrapping around me like a blanket, dulling the pain Camilla's words caused. They were lashing at me like whips, breaking my skin until I was bleeding on the dark forest floor. Or at least that was what it felt like.

Camilla's smile disappeared as her features became all sharp angles and hard lines.

"Bring him out," she barked an order over her shoulder without taking her eyes off the woods.

I closed my eyes and tried to force down the lump that had formed in my throat. It didn't budge, clogging my airway. I choked on it, wanting to claw at my neck, but I couldn't move as I listened to the commotion on the border. His scent reached me first, nearly knocking me off my feet. It had been here all along; I'd just been too shocked and blinded by my rage to notice it. Blood. I smelled his blood, the scent so potent that it overpowered the fresh and woodsy notes of him. In a heartbeat, I knew why when I opened my eyes. There was no point in keeping them closed—I couldn't hide from what was unfolding right before me on the border.

I shattered into a million tiny pieces when my gaze landed on Henry being dragged out from behind Camilla by Moreau and Beatrice Stern. He was covered in blood. His blood, I knew from the smell. It matted his hair and ran down his bare chest, trickling from open wounds and lacerations. His pants were soaked with it. He wasn't healing. As I'd suspected, they'd been withholding blood from him so he would be too weak to fight or escape.

My vampire ears picked up on his ragged breathing and the sluggish beating of his heart. My own heart lurched in my chest as if trying to rip out of my rib cage and launch itself toward the border to reunite with Henry. My muscles tensed as I prepared to run, to close the distance between us. In the back of my mind, I knew it wouldn't be smart, but I didn't care. I couldn't stand here and do nothing. I refused to spend another second separated from him.

"Don't do anything foolish," Celeste warned from behind me.

Snarling at her over my shoulder, I went to rip myself out of her grip. Except, my body didn't obey. All my muscles locked up. I couldn't move.

"It has to be done," Celeste said low from behind me.

The bitch was freezing me in space, preventing me from going to Henry. I thrashed in the hold of her magic, or at least I thought I did. The fight was happening on the inside. On the outside, I was just standing still, my muscles stiff.

Moreau and Beatrice threw Henry to the ground, and he landed with a grunt in a heap by Camilla's feet. She bent down and picked something up off the ground next to him. Terror choked me when I saw it was a metal chain attached to a metal collar around Henry's neck. They'd leashed him like a fucking dog!

"How about now, Sophie?!" Camilla shouted into the night, her words a question and a challenge. "Will you surrender?"

A loud hiss erupted from me as I curled my fingers into fists, my elongated claws piercing my palms. My blood began trickling on the ground as I stood there, unable to move a muscle. I cursed Celeste under my breath, but I was also thankful for the spell she'd put on me, because at that moment, I would surrender. I would do anything to end Henry's suffering.

Camilla's upper lip curled, and she yanked at the chain attached to Henry's neck, snapping his head back. He snarled in defiance, but Camilla slammed her booted foot into the middle of his back, pushing him to the ground. Pain laced up *my* back as if it were me in Henry's place. My neck burned as if the collar was encircling my throat, not his.

"No?" Camilla challenged again, scanning the woods.

I dug my claws in deeper, focusing on the pain instead of the border. Then I focused on Henry's features, blood-smeared and covered in blue and purple splotches. His eyes were dark and wild, his gaze unseeing as he stared into the space before him. I latched on to his face, trying to communicate with him across the distance. To let him know I was here, that I hadn't abandoned him, and he wasn't alone. Or perhaps he was better off not knowing I was here, because I could do nothing to help him right now. His clumped lashes swept down, shielding his eyes, and when they lifted again, his gaze was bluer and more focused. He stared at the spot where I was standing in the woods as if he knew I was here.

"You are my heart," he rasped, barely above a whisper.

The wind carried the words to me, and it felt like my legs would go out from under me, but Celeste's spell held me upright.

Did he know I was here? Could he sense it somehow?

Camilla's head jerked in my direction.

"Is she here?!" she demanded in a raised voice.

"We're leaving," Celeste said urgently behind me.

"No," I ground out, tears welling and gliding down my cheeks.

My vision blurred, and I blinked rapidly to clear it, but before I could see Henry's face again, I felt the pull of Celeste's magic. A second later, she glimmered from the tree line, bringing me with her. We appeared in the heart of the Black Forest, and when she finally released her hold on me, my knees buckled, and I crumpled to the hard ground, sobbing.

"Take me back," I begged, my voice hoarse.

"No." The witch's tone was unyielding.

"We have to save him."

"You aren't strong enough."

"But you are," I wept, clutching the hem of her cloak. "You're strong, and so are the others in the village. We can go after him."

"I will not wage a war against the clans." Celeste brushed me off, yanking her cloak out of my hands. "Pull yourself together," she instructed sternly.

I wasn't ready to give up just yet.

"You don't think you can prevail?" I challenged the witch.

"I am not willing to find out. It's not worth the risk."

He's not worth the risk, I heard the meaning behind her words. And perhaps he wasn't, not to her. But to me, he was everything. And I could do nothing.

I wasn't sure what happened next. All the feelings I'd kept bottled up the last four nights rushed to the surface of my skin. I couldn't contain them anymore, and I didn't want to. My blood boiled, making it feel like I was being ripped apart. A keening scream tore from my throat as my magic exploded out of me, rippling like a wave through the woods around me. With a curse, Celeste threw her arms up, crossing them in front of her to create a shield. Her magic enveloped her in a protective barrier, molding to her body.

My outburst was powerful but fleeting, and when it was over, an unearthly silence followed, eerie and jarring all at the same time. A few seconds passed when nothing happened. Then, things began dropping all around me. Birds plummeted from the night sky like stones while other forest creatures fell out of trees, hitting the ground with dull thuds. The rain of death seemed to last an eternity until all sounds ceased again. My breath sawed in my throat as I sat on the ground, surrounded by dead things.

Celeste's eyes were wide when she reined in her magic, lowered her arms, and took a few steps back to put some distance between us. She swallowed audibly, her face as white as her hair.

"Listen to me very carefully, Sophie," she said in a hushed tone as if she didn't want the night to overhear.

"No," I interjected, rising to my feet. "I'm done listening to you."

"Sophie—"

"Stay away from me!" I shouted before I set off into a run, leaving the witch behind.

18

HENRY

So much pain. For the past four nights, I had been drowning in it. Tonight, had felt like coming up for air. She'd been there, in the Black Forest; I could feel it. Her proximity had helped alleviate the pain, but it had also made my chest strain with burning longing. The entire time on the border, my body had been pulled to the tree line to reunite with her, my heart beating within her. So close, yet out of my reach.

A part of me wished she hadn't been there, seeing me leashed like an animal, powerless and weak. I wanted to be strong for her. I didn't want her to worry about me, to feel like she had to do something. She didn't need to do anything for me except survive and stay out of the clans' clutches. They wanted her and the Tear, so they were making her choose between me and her people, the humans. I knew they were still her people. She was a vampire now, but humanity still burned bright inside her. It was one of the things that drew me to her —that light. Beautiful and powerful, it helped banish the shadows of my past. I couldn't walk in daylight, but as long as I had Sophie in my life, I had my own personal sunshine. Turning her was still one of the worst things I had ever done, but I couldn't deny that a tiny, selfish part of me was glad she had decided to become a vampire, because that meant we would never have to part. Or so I had thought.

The stir of air by the entrance to the cave snapped me out of my thoughts a moment before Moreau strolled in, a smell of wild excitement rolling off him. I supposed I shouldn't be surprised he took such perverse pleasure in torturing me. He had always hated me; now, even more so after I had almost killed him two nights ago. One side of my mouth turned up at the thought.

"What are you smirking at?" Moreau snarled, as he approached where I was slumped on the floor by the wall.

"Just thinking about how close I came to killing you," I snarled back.

The feverish craze in Moreau's eyes dimmed just a fraction. The other side of my mouth turned up when the smell of excitement around him became tinged with fear.

"Yes, that was unfortunate." He rubbed his neck.

My smile fell—there were no remnants of the savage wound I had inflicted because he'd fed and healed. My stomach spasmed at the thought, making me grunt in pain. Four nights without a drop of blood, not counting Moreau's blood when I'd torn out a piece of his throat. Four nights that had felt like an eternity. I needed to feed. Desperately. Without blood, my flesh was drying out, turning me into a husk. I swore sometimes I could hear my skin stretching over my bones in the rare moments I was alone in this gods-forsaken place.

It was ironic that Stern's lair was now my holding cell. The last time I'd stepped foot in here, I'd been with Sophie, and we had found the Tear in one of the chests. We had found hope. Now, all I felt was despair. In my weakest moments, I wished Sophie would use the Tear to destroy us all, because then the pain would be over. The merciless hunger would finally cease. But every time I thought about it, my chest constricted until my lungs were being crushed, and I couldn't breathe. If Sophie used the Tear, would she perish like the rest of us? Or would the amulet spare her life since she was the one wielding it? With everything that I was, I hoped it would, because I wanted her to live, even if she was the only vampire left in this world.

"Let's get to it, shall we?" Moreau drawled, pulling me from my thoughts.

He moved to the wooden table and began sorting through the torture instruments lying atop it. My breathing picked up as my muscles tensed. I was never prepared for the torture, even though I knew it was coming. Every time, dread surged, threatening to suffocate me. It was as if my body begged me to do something, anything to prevent what was coming, to save it from all the suffering it would have to endure again. The suffering *I* would have to endure again.

Seconds stretched as Moreau was trying to decide on his weapon of choice for tonight. By this point, I was well familiar with all the torture instruments he had laid out before him and even had some I preferred over the others. A soft exhale escaped when Moreau picked up the serrated knife. His gaze shot to me—he'd heard my subtle breath of relief.

Shit.

He smirked and lowered the knife back down. My stomach dropped when he selected the sickle blade instead. It was the worst of them all. The curved blade was perfect for tearing skin, ripping flesh, and hooking organs.

Satisfied with his selection, Moreau stepped closer to me, the sickle blade in his hand and a deranged expression on his face. With a vicious growl, I lashed out, baring my fangs…only to be yanked back by the chains that now bound me.

Moreau laughed, the creepy sound echoing in the cavernous space.

"The chains came in handy, don't you think?" he asked, angling his head.

They sure had. The clan leaders hadn't even needed to install them. They had already been attached to one of the walls. Stern must have used them on his Ravagers, to restrain the feral vampires when he'd first turned them, so he could train them into submission just enough to make them do his bidding, never fully guiding them out of bloodlust.

The thick metal cuffs attached to the chains encircled my wrists and ankles, restricting my movements. I had woken up in them after losing consciousness in the tunnels after my failed escape attempt. I hated the fucking things, but I hated the collar around my neck the most. The clan leaders had disconnected that chain from the wall earlier so they could drag me to the border to taunt Sophie, but it had gone back into the wall when we'd returned.

"The collar is a nice touch, wouldn't you agree?" Moreau asked, as if reading my thoughts. "It's funny how mere nights ago you threatened to leash me, and now you are the one on a leash."

Mere nights ago, I had thought that Sophie and I were about to start a new life together, but then I had been diminished to this —a prisoner, chained to a wall. Fury simmered in my blood, but I refused to engage with Moreau. I didn't want to give him the satisfaction of seeing that his words had gotten to me.

When I didn't acknowledge what he'd said, he continued, "You know," he drawled, turning the sickle blade in his hand as if studying it. "I truly thought that bitch would come for you." His dark brown eyes met mine. "She was there, wasn't she? In the Black Forest. Yet, she didn't turn herself in. Even after seeing the condition you were in. Does it make you wonder if she truly cares about you?"

"No, it doesn't," I said, my tone final. I hadn't for a second doubted Sophie's feelings for me. Moreau's words were not getting to me, but this conversation was. He was just dragging this out, while I sat here and waited for the torture to begin. He was letting the dread build up, demonstrating that he was the one in control. There was only one way for me to gain back a sliver of it, so, as much as I hated it, I opened my mouth and said, "Get on with it."

Moreau laughed again, and I loathed the sound with every fiber of my being. "You don't have to tell me twice."

As he pulled his arm back to deliver the first blow, I let myself slip into a state of near unconsciousness where I was in my body but also separated from it. I let myself retreat inside my mind as my physical form took the beating. Drifting into the past, I thought about Sophie. Memories of her were the only way for me to get through this...

"The Candidates are here," Isabelle said, angling her head to better hear what was happening on the side of the study door.

Excitement laced every word as she dragged her fangs over her lower lip. I scowled at her reaction. She had always embraced her bloodthirsty side more than I ever had mine, but such a display of depraved anticipation disturbed me. After Vincent's death, she had been drifting closer to the darkness and farther away from the light, and I had no idea what I could do to stop it.

"Vincent would not have approved of you getting such enjoyment from the Selection," I pointed out, my scowl intensifying.

Isabelle's gaze fastened on me, her big brown eyes darker with hunger.

"Vincent is dead because he went to try and rescue Eloise from the Dark Witches. He sacrificed himself for a human. It's only fair they sacrifice something in return." Isabelle shrugged with cold indifference. "Besides, don't tell me you haven't been enjoying Eleanor. She is such an eager little vassal." Her crimson-painted lips stretched into a smile, revealing the hints of her fangs.

"Too eager." I blew a breath of frustration.

"So she tried to stake you." Another shrug. "Makes things more exciting if you ask me."

"That's not the type of excitement I need in my life," I grumbled. "Vassals are usually eager to leave the estate when their year is up. She wants to stay. 'If I can't have you, then no one else will,' she told me when she tried to kill me."

"You shouldn't have let her get so close. She is infatuated with you, Henry," Isabelle pointed out.

Gritting my teeth, I rubbed my chin, momentarily lost in thought.

"I never meant for Eleanor to become this attached to me," I said, as if to myself. "I will need to be more careful next time."

"Speaking of next time." Isabelle rose to her feet. "Shall we?"

My jaw hurt from how hard I was clenching it, my fangs grinding on my bottom teeth. I hated the Selection, always had, but I was in no power to do anything about it. Vincent had kept the clans under control as much as he could, and I tried to do the same after I'd become the new leader of the Duval clan, but there was only so much I could do. I was their equal, not their superior. Vincent had held certain authority because he'd been the oldest vampire among the clans. I didn't have that advantage and couldn't exert the same influence.

"You can look at least a little bit excited about this," Isabelle said, strolling to the door.

"There is nothing to be excited about, Isabelle. We don't even need vassals. The humans already donate blood to keep our cellars well-stocked."

I rose from the chair behind my desk and joined her by the door.

"True, but we both know it's not the same. Oh, the thrill of biting into a human, of having fresh, warm blood spill into your mouth..." Isabelle moaned, closing her eyes. When she opened them again, they were almost entirely black. "Tasting that essence, that vitality on your tongue... There is nothing like it. It's what gives us life, Henry. You can't change your nature, so you might as well enjoy it."

I swallowed, shifting from foot to foot. She was right—I couldn't change that I was a vampire—but enjoying that aspect of it just felt... wrong. Always had and always would. Still, I couldn't fight my nature, as excitement invaded my veins at Isabelle's words. Rolling my shoulders, I tamped it down as much as I could.

"Let's get this over with," I said grimly, reaching for the handle and opening the door.

Isabelle's eyes were bright as she walked past me into the foyer.

I stepped out of the study next, halting right on the other side of the door. She was here. Her light floral scent hit me first, nearly knocking me off my feet. I'd recognize it anywhere. It had stayed with me after the Selection last year. My mind even played tricks on me sometimes, making me think I picked up on it when I was at the border where she couldn't possibly be. I didn't know why her scent had stayed with me. Perhaps because she smelled like a meadow on a bright sunny day, only more subtle, more delicate. At least, I thought she did. I wasn't sure I still remembered what a meadow would smell like during daylight, after all that time living in the shadows. I must still remember, though, because a picture of one appeared in my mind just now when her scent hit my nostrils.

Sophie Devereaux. I had been drawn to her last time, every instinct in me screaming to choose her as my vassal. I had resisted because I knew Vincent wouldn't have approved of me choosing Eloise's daughter. I had resisted then, and now she was back to taunt me again. Why had she returned? She had been terrified last year; I had smelled her fear, so what had driven her to volunteer to participate in the Selection again? I was about to find out. My legs moved as if of their own accord as I began gliding down the first row of the Candidates, each step bringing me closer to her.

"Sophie?" I asked, stopping before her.

Her floral scent enveloped me, and I was instantly in a meadow, basking in the warm sun.

"My Lord." She gave a small, innocent smile, gazing up at me from beneath her lashes.

Her eyes were a stunning hazel color with a warm green hue like her mother's. She also had the same shade of hair—a glossy golden brown—and the same smattering of freckles on the bridge of her nose. I had *always thought Eloise was beautiful, but I had never been drawn to her like I was to the woman before me. My throat dried as we stared at each other. The difference between the Selection last year and this time was astounding. Then, she had been a frightened little bird. Now, she stood with confidence, her delicate features set with resolve. Her eyes were almost feverish, and that made me wary. No human in their right mind would return for the Selection a second year in a row. Something was off about Sophie, but I didn't know what it was.*

Not a mystery for you to solve, *I told myself, dragging my gaze away from her to focus on the young woman to her left. When I did, Sophie grabbed my hand, her warm touch sending a charge through me at the contact. My gaze darted back to her, and she dropped my hand as if startled by the coolness of my skin. Her eyes wide and her lips parted, she looked like she wasn't sure what she was doing. Then she bit down on her lower lip, drawing my attention to her mouth.*

I knew I should look away, but I couldn't stop my gaze from gliding down the column of her neck. Her hair was pulled up, giving me an unobscured view of where her pulse thrummed under her smooth, supple skin. My mouth watered as the hum of the blood flowing through her veins filled my ears. Her floral scent surrounded me, and for a second, I was gone again, no longer in the foyer of the mansion. I was in a meadow drenched in sunlight with Sophie in my arms. I held her as I was drinking from her neck... I knew my eyes were nearly black when I blinked a few times to bring myself back to the present. If the hunger in them terrified Sophie like it had last year, she didn't show it. Her quickening pulse betrayed her emotions, but it was unease, not pure terror, that I smelled on her this time. Interesting.

"I choose you as my vassal." The words left me, rough and thick.

I told myself I was choosing her because she might shed some light on Vincent's disappearance, but I knew deep down that wasn't the only reason. I craved her, and instead of fighting the urge like I should, I was giving into it. It seemed from the very beginning, when it came to Sophie, my will was not entirely my own, and I was completely and utterly at her mercy.

19

SOPHIE

I was dreaming about Henry again. Only this time, it didn't feel like a dream, but rather a vision, as if I'd projected myself to the place where he was, floating like an apparition above his crumpled form on the floor. He was tucked against a rough rock wall, lying unmoving and still. Too still, I feared, my heart thumping heavily in my chest. Refusing to give in to panic, I held my breath and listened. Potent relief washed over me when I heard his labored breathing and the strained beating of his heart. He was alive.

Barely, I realized, quickly assessing his condition. Deep gashes ran down his broad back, and smaller cuts and lacerations covered the rest of his body. I'd seen his abused state when I'd watched from afar at the border, but up close, it was a truly gory sight. It filled me with so much rage that my entire body shook. Then I noticed the chains. Thick, metal ones, binding him to the wall, and the collar...the collar was still there, around his fucking neck.

Red-hot fury surged, begging to be released and unleashed on all those who'd hurt him, were still hurting him, judging by the array of torture instruments on the nearby table. Serrated blades designed to tear through skin and muscle lay covered in blood, both fresh and dried. His blood, I knew, my nostrils flaring. This place reeked of it. It also reeked of misery and anguish. I swore I could hear Henry's cries of agony echoing off the cavernous walls as if the sound had forever seeped into the rough surface.

Cavernous walls...I know this place, I thought, looking around.

Stern's lair. They'd brought him here of all places?! Another wave of wild, violent rage rolled through me, curling my hands into fists. Breathing through the volatile emotion, I focused on Henry's form underneath.

"Henry?" I said, my phantom voice ringing out in the candlelit cave. I didn't expect an answer, but he flinched at my words—a small, barely-there motion. "Can you hear me?" I rasped past the lump in my throat. My chest was so tight I couldn't take a full breath in.

Blood seeped out of the gashes on Henry's back as he pushed himself up off the floor, groaning in pain. He slumped against the wall, and his head fell back as he stared up at the ceiling. His deep-blue eyes fastened on me, and my heart skipped a beat as I stared down at him, wondering if he could see me.

"You know what they say," he ground out, and I held my breath, hoping he was talking to me. "Like father like son." He coughed, and some blood bubbled up, spilling out of his mouth. "Was that how you felt before you died? You were so close to ushering in a new world, but then you went to the Dark Witches, thinking they had Eloise, and they killed you," Henry paused and swallowed. He was talking to Vincent, not me. My heart sank with disappointment. "I was close, too," he continued, looking right through me. "Sometimes I think this is the end I deserve. For everything I have done. I never deserved her. I only thought I did. I hoped..." he trailed off as a single tear rolled down his cheek, mixing with the blood covering his face.

I began crying, too, my tears evaporating in this strange state I was in before they could land on Henry sitting beneath me. He looked so very human in this weakened state—more man than vampire—and a ragged sob escaped me because I wanted to reach for him, to cradle him in my arms and take him as far away from this place as I could.

"To whom are you speaking?" came Camilla's husky voice, as she stepped inside the cave.

I instinctively bared my fangs in a hiss, forgetting that I wasn't truly here. I was just a phantom, an observer unable to do anything about what was unfolding before me. Camilla strolled to where Henry sat by the wall, the ivory silk of her gown clinging to her legs like liquid. She stopped before him, waiting for him to acknowledge her. When he didn't, she kicked him in the stomach, and he grunted in pain.

"I asked a question," she snarled, grabbing the chain attached to the collar around Henry's neck. She yanked on it sharply, snapping his head to the side.

A growl escaped me—I will shove that collar down Camilla's fucking throat. I will make her choke on it.

"Vincent," Henry said, in between the wet, wheezing sounds coming from his bruised chest.

"Ah, yes. My dear old friend," Camilla crooned as she let go of the chain and inspected her pointed nails.

"So, all those years of friendship. Just a lie?" Henry asked, each word a struggle.

Camilla smirked as she looked back at him. "Vincent was the oldest and the strongest of us. Friendship with him gave me an advantage. I always like to be on the winning side."

Henry smirked in response. "You are not on the winning side now."

"Says the one bleeding out on the floor," Camilla hissed.

"It doesn't matter what happens to me. It only matters what Sophie does, and I hope she uses the amulet to wipe the vampires out of this world."

My heart seized in my chest at his words. I'd suspected that Henry might feel that way before, and now I had the confirmation. Briefly closing my eyes, I let the words wash over me before dissipating into thin air. I didn't let them sink in—I couldn't. If that was truly what Henry desired, I couldn't give him what he wanted.

"You know what I think?" Camilla purred, dropping to her haunches by Henry's side. *The hem of her gown dipped in the pool of his blood, the fine fabric quickly absorbing the crimson. "I think if Sophie was going to use the amulet to destroy us, she would have done so already."* Her ice-blue gaze roamed over Henry's face as she continued, *"I heard what you told her before the witch spirited her away from the study.* You are my heart. *How romantic."* She cringed in disgust. *"Your words made me realize something, though. Sophie might be a vampire, but her heart is still human, and it beats for you."*

"Don't underestimate her dedication to her people," Henry bit out through his blood-stained teeth.

"You mean the humans?" Camilla smirked. *"She might have been devoted to them in the past, but I think she is now devoted to only one creature above all else."* She paused, bringing her lips to his right ear. *"You,"* she whispered, seductively low.

Henry's eyes fluttered closed as he suddenly looked defeated. Was it because he knew she was right? I knew she was, and I wasn't ashamed of it. I didn't feel regret about my feelings for him, only resolve.

"So, you see." Camilla's red-hued lips stretched in a malicious smile. *"She will come for you. It's only a matter of time."*

She reached up and dragged her index finger through one of the lacerations on Henry's chest, eliciting a hiss from him. Rising to her feet with preternatural ease, she brought the finger to her mouth and sucked off the blood. Then she was gone, the stir of air rippling the flames in the dozens of candles illuminating the cave.

I woke up with a gasp, my eyes darting around the dark house. If one could still call it that. The doors and windows were missing, and while the walls still stood, they were rotten and on the brink of collapse. I'd half-expected them to crumble down on me while I'd slept. The only reason I'd still stayed was because I knew that, as a vampire, I would survive if that happened, and because I had nowhere else to go. After I'd left Celeste in the woods, I'd run until I'd found the decrepit structure Henry and I had sheltered in when we'd been stranded in the Black Forest before.

Three days I'd been here, refusing to go back to Celeste's cottage. On the first day, I'd barely gotten any sleep as I'd watched the sun rays crawl over the warped wooden floor, hoping they would stop before they could reach where I was tucked away in the corner in the heart of the house. On the second day, I'd been able to sleep once I'd made sure the daylight wouldn't reach me once the sun rose. Tonight, on my third day here, I'd finally seen Henry in my dream.

Not a dream—a vision, I corrected myself, my brows knitting.

Everything that I'd seen had truly transpired; I was sure of it. It seemed I'd finally established my connection to the world around me and had been able to tap into the constant current of information. I'd been able to grasp the thread connected to Henry, and it had led me to Stern's lair in the Southern region, where Henry was being kept...in the pool of his own blood, chained to the wall next to the table holding the rusted instruments being used to make him bleed and suffer. My stomach churned, and I rested my head against the wall, breathing through the nausea.

"I'm coming for you," I rasped, talking to Henry.

Tonight was the night. It had to be. I'd been practicing my magic every night since I'd gotten here. My powers had grown stronger over the past three days, though the art of glimmering still eluded me. Damien hadn't found me during all that time. Celeste hadn't come for me, either, which was very unsettling. She had to know where I was. After all, her connection to the threads was much stronger than mine. She hadn't come to collect me because she was planning something. That was the only explanation for why she'd left me alone.

I knew I was making it easy for her to find me by staying in the same spot, but I hadn't wanted to risk not being able to find another shelter in the woods before sunrise. Besides, I couldn't hide forever. My hope was that I would become strong enough and go after Henry before Celeste or anyone else could stop me. Thirst was also becoming a problem, but I'd been brushing it aside. Henry was experiencing it, too, and the increasingly growing gnawing ache in my gut was nothing compared to what he was going through. He was suffering, so I would suffer, too. I refused to let hunger deter me from my mission.

I scrubbed my face to wake myself up fully and rose to my feet, my muscles sore from sleeping sitting up on the floor, my back against the rough wall. I cracked my neck and rolled my shoulders in preparation for another night of practicing my magic. My power answered my call almost instantly now, especially if I channeled my loathing for the clans to bring it forth. It lit up my veins with liquid lightning, making me feel exhilarated and alive, and giving me a rush I could only compare to what I experienced when drinking blood or being in Henry's arms as he made love to me. My pulse quickened at the thought. I couldn't wait to practice my magic, to feel that rush again until I could feel the other kind—the one elicited by Henry.

Buzzing with excitement, I quickly crossed the run-down house and stepped outside. My muscles tensed as I halted right on the other side of the threshold. Celeste had finally come for me…and she wasn't alone. Isabelle and Wren were here, and Waylon, too—an intervention, then. I balled my hands into fists at my sides and lifted my chin, preparing for what was to come. Would they use force or try talking to me first? Whatever they did, I would not go down without a fight.

"Sophie, we need to talk," Isabelle said, separating from the tree line and stepping toward the house. Dressed in black, she blended in with the night, which was darker than usual because of the heavy rain clouds obscuring the moon.

"If you've come to tell me to take it slow, save your breath," I told her, surprised to find my voice steady even as my temper rose.

"Henry is my brother. You know I want to save him," she replied, coming closer.

"Then let me do what I need to do to get stronger."

I stepped away from the house to meet her halfway. It was my way of showing her that I didn't consider her an enemy. Not yet.

"Sophie, please," Isabelle said, her eyes pleading as I stopped before her. "Celeste told us what happened in the woods. Your power is—"

"Growing," I interjected. "And it's scaring her." I jerked my chin at Celeste, who'd also entered the clearing, stopping a few feet away from Isabelle.

"Your power is wreathed in shadows," the witch declared, her voice ringing out in the darkness. Thunder rumbled deep in the forest behind her after she'd uttered the words. "I know you feel it, too."

"What I feel is power. Raw and beautiful. It will help me fight the clans and save Henry."

"But at what cost?" Celeste challenged, taking a step toward me.

"Whatever it takes. No price is too high."

"You're a fool," the witch said, advancing more in my direction.

Out of the corner of my eye, I saw Waylon and Wren step out of the woods as well. They were all closing in on me, trying to trap me like a wild animal.

I will show them wild, I thought, as another roll of thunder sounded, now closer to us.

"No, you're a fool if you think that you can stop me," I hissed, baring my fangs.

Isabelle hissed, too, crouching before me, her white teeth and claws a startling contrast against her dark skin and clothing.

"Ladies," Wren said in a warning tone, as he slowly approached where Isabelle and I were facing off against each other. "Let's not get carried away."

He didn't want Isabelle to get hurt, I could hear it in his voice. He cared about her just like I cared about Henry. He, of all people, should understand why I was doing this.

"Sophie, I know you'd do anything for those you care about, but we care about *you*. That's why we're trying to help," came Waylon's measured voice from my left.

He stood a few feet away, his muscles tense and his forest-green eyes trained on me.

"You can help by staying out of my way," I growled as I glanced at him.

"We can't do that," Celeste interjected, throwing her hands out to cast a spell.

Everything slowed as I watched her power ripple through the air toward me. I knew if it reached me, I would be immobilized like I'd been the other night in the woods by the border. Panic set in as I drew on my own magic, quickly gathering it in my chest, in my very center, like Damien had taught me. I imagined my power as a beam of light and flung it into Stern's lair, to where Henry was, but before I could step onto it, the magic bridge I'd created dissipated into swirling black smoke.

Your power is wreathed in shadows, Celeste's earlier words floated up in my mind. Perhaps it wasn't light that I needed to glimmer. Maybe I could use shadows to get to where I wanted to go. Embracing the darkness like an old friend, I let it gather me up in its wispy tendrils and take me out of the Forest. The world faded to black for a moment, and when the light returned, I was in Stern's lair, standing next to Henry's limp form on the floor.

20

HENRY

*M*oreau had paid me a visit not long after Camilla had left. He had chosen the serrated knife that time, and I'd had to suffer through yet another torture session. After he had left, satisfied with the damage he'd done, I had begun slipping in and out of consciousness. Each time I retreated into my mind, it was harder to bring myself back to reality. Here, pain and despair awaited me. There, I could be with Sophie, reliving our brief time together as memories flashed through my mind…

"Good evening," Sophie's voice pulled me from my slumber.

I blinked open my eyes and found her watching me from where she sat on top of my bed, hugging her knees to her chest.

"Good evening," I replied, as I ran a hand down my face to wake myself up.

I couldn't believe I had fallen asleep. The last three nights must have taken more out of me than I'd thought. At least Sophie was more lucid now, having overcome the bloodlust last night. Had I dropped my guard any time before then, she would have ripped out my throat and escaped, I was sure of it. Now, she seemed in control of the darkness, albeit sitting unnaturally still and rigid, not used to this new body of hers. She was wearing one of my tunics and seeing her in my clothes was strangely intimate. I had wanted to borrow Isabelle's clothes, but Sophie had been desperate to shed her blood-covered dress. She had also made me change the sheets after she'd spilled blood on them.

"*How did you sleep?*" *I asked her, letting my gaze roam over her features.*

Her tousled hair spilled over her shoulders, and I could see her creamy skin where the tunic didn't quite cover her legs. Gods, she was beautiful.

"*I was dreaming about you...*" *she started, but trailed off, her brows knitting.*

I didn't need to ask what kind of dream it had been. There was no mistaking the notes of remaining desire I could detect in her scent. My throat dried when I picked up on it, and I shifted in my chair as arousal spiked. I immediately tried to tamp it down, hoping Sophie's heightened senses weren't keen enough yet to detect it. She looked concerned about the dream, and I didn't want to make it worse. If anything, I wanted to put her at ease.

"*You were dreaming about me because I'm the one who turned you,*" *I explained.* "*There is a special bond between a vampire and their sire. Perhaps that's how our bond is manifesting. The dreams don't mean anything. They will pass.*"

My brows pulled together as I felt a niggle of disappointment at my own words. I caught myself wishing the dreams wouldn't pass, but wishing for that was selfish of me. Sophie's life and everything she knew had just changed. She was frightened and confused, and I would not add to that state of confusion. I was here to help her, not make it worse. So she would never know about the thought I'd just had, just like she would never know I had seen her in my dreams. She didn't need to know, because as I'd told her, the dreams would pass, even if I didn't want them to.

Sophie's frown deepened at my words, and she opened her mouth to say something, but I interjected, desperate to change the subject.

"How are you feeling?" I asked, watching her closely.

She looked as if she wanted to go back to the previous conversation, but then decided not to.

"I'm hungry," *she said simply, and I knew she was—her eyes were black, not the beautiful hazel hue I was so fond of.*

My gaze darted to the empty cooler on the floor by the chair I was occupying. I had meant to get more blood before I had fallen asleep.

"I will bring you some blood," *I said, rising from the chair.*

"Can I come with you?" *Sophie asked softly.*

I froze where I stood, staring at her as silence stretched. The question had caught me off guard—I hadn't expected her to ask to leave this room so soon. She was a new vampire, and bloodlust could strike at any moment. If it did, and she somehow escaped from the mansion...I knew she wouldn't forgive herself if she hurt innocent people. My unease about the request must have been written on my face because Sophie's delicate features crumpled as tears glistened in her eyes. I was instantly overcome with the urge to gather her in my arms to comfort her, but I fought it, keeping my distance.

"I don't think it's a good idea," *I finally voiced what she had already gleaned from my face.*

"I understand," *she rasped, hanging her head.* "If you think I'm not ready, then I trust your judgment," *she added low.*

I felt conflicted. She trusted my judgment, but I trusted my instincts, and right now, they were telling me that I needed to believe in her. She needed me to believe in her so she could believe in herself. I suddenly realized that I would always do anything in my power to give her whatever it was she needed. It was a shocking revelation I decided not to dwell on at the moment.

My mind made up, I extended my hand to her and said, "Come with me."

Her head snapped up, disbelief flaring in her eyes.

"Really?"

"Yes." I gave her a small, reassuring smile. "You are in control."

She appeared to be in control. She had done remarkably well fighting the bloodlust. It had taken me weeks to overcome it when I'd turned. It had taken her three nights. I was amazed by her, and I had a feeling it was only the beginning of all the marvelous things she would do.

Hesitantly, Sophie reached out and placed her hand in mine. As soon as I wrapped my fingers around hers, regret surged, powerful and overwhelming, because we were the same temperature now. At least she hadn't lost her floral scent when she'd turned. It was still there, though it was headier than before. The smell of wildflowers was now laced with more lush, decadent notes. It was intoxicating, and I tried as much as I could not to focus on it.

I had spent the last three nights trying not to focus on a lot of things, like how much I liked holding her in my arms, or how much I had wanted to go through with what she'd tried to initiate when she'd first come to after I'd turned her. When her eyes had snapped open, and she'd straddled me, raking her nails down my chest...I had felt my self-control slipping. It had taken everything in my power to not give in to the maddening rush of desire. But she hadn't been herself then, lost in the frenzy of bloodlust, and I had refused to take advantage of her in that state. I'd be lying if I said the thought hadn't crossed my mind several times since then. Being locked up in this room with her had been the sweetest torture—her smell and everything about her taunting me, tantalizing and sinful.

Perhaps I needed to leave this room as much as Sophie did. I could ask for Isabelle's help to keep an eye on her, so I could get some distance from her to clear my head. The thought terrified me more than I was willing to admit, because I didn't want to be apart from her. Not now. Not ever.

"Henry?" Sophie's voice snapped me from my thoughts.

"Sorry." I cleared my throat. "Are you ready?"

She nodded and rose from the bed. When she stepped closer to me, I picked up on our scents, which were intertwined because she was wearing my clothes, and the smell went straight to my head as my breathing hitched.

"Don't let go," *she begged, when I went to pull my hand away.*

Her eyes were pleading when my gaze darted to hers.

"I won't," *I assured her, as my hold on her hand tightened.*

Together, we walked to the door.

"Wait," *Sophie said when I reached for the handle.* "Are you sure this is a good idea?" *she asked, turning to me.*

Her eyes were filled with fear. Not fear for herself but for others. She was terrified of leaving this room and succumbing to the bloodlust that would drive her to escape the house and go on a hunt for any human she could sink her fangs into. Seeing that fear only reinforced my belief that she was ready, because that fear was her humanity shining brightly inside her.

"I'm sure," *I told her, gently cupping her cheek.*

Reaching up, she placed her hand over mine and turned her face into my palm. Breathing had already been difficult, and now my chest was constricted so tight that the next inhalation never came. She truly had no idea what she was doing to me. Being so close to her, touching her... Gods, I wanted to haul her to me and claim her mouth and then her body. Her delicate nostrils flared before she looked at me again, her lips parting slightly. Could she pick up on my scent that undoubtedly betrayed my thoughts?

"Your eyes..." *she said, her voice a bit huskier than before.*

Of course. My scent wasn't the only thing that could betray my intentions.

"I'm hungry," *I said, my voice low and thick. It wasn't exactly a lie. I was hungry, just not for blood.* "Shall we?" *I asked, dropping my hand from her cheek.*

*A strange expression settled over her features, a mix of disappointment and relief. Seeing the conflicting emotions on her face only confirmed my decision not to pursue my selfish desires. Sophie needed to gain purchase on her new reality, to learn who she was now before she could figure out what she wanted...*whom *she wanted.*

She stared at me a moment longer, and I found myself wishing she did or said something to give me an excuse to touch her again, though I knew that once I started touching her, I would never be able to stop.

I imagined the look on my face mirrored hers—a mix of disappointment and relief—when she simply nodded and turned to the door. Pulling myself together, I grabbed the handle and walked out of the room. Sophie hesitantly followed, stepping into her new life as a vampire.

I pried my lashes apart for a moment, but all that greeted me was pain, so I let my eyes drift closed again as I went back to her...

Our swords clashed with a loud clink, and Sophie grinned, her smile beautiful and savage. I still regretted turning her; I always would, carrying that guilt with me for the rest of my eternal nights, but I couldn't deny that the creature before me was stunning. She had been breathtaking as a human, but as a vampire, she was truly magnificent. Once she had gotten used to her new body and had learned to control her heightened senses, it seemed as though she had been born for this. Not the blood-drinking part—she still recoiled from that, and I hoped she always would, but everything else that came with being a vampire. It was important for her to be in control of her life, and now she was, more so than ever.

Sophie jumped back with feline grace and then attacked again, delivering a blow I easily deflected. As a new vampire, she was not a match for me yet, but I knew it was only a matter of time—time we didn't truly have, with the threat of the Dark Witches looming over us.

Sophie came at me again, and this time, I didn't simply block the attack. I retaliated, swiping with my sword. With a startled gasp, she danced out of the way and thrust her blade out, aiming at my midsection. I moved back with vampire speed to avoid being stabbed before I caught the hand holding the sword and squeezed. Her weapon clattered to the floor as I hauled her to my chest, wrapping my arm around her waist. Our faces were inches apart, and we both froze, breathing shallowly. My gaze dropped to her mouth for a second before I forced it back up. I knew I needed to put distance between us, but I found I couldn't move.

"The dreams," Sophie rasped, looking into my eyes. "They haven't stopped."

She was bringing this up now? When our bodies were near flush with each other?

My mind flashed back to my own dreams, where I had been swimming between her thighs. She was right—the dreams, they hadn't stopped. If anything, they had been growing in their intensity, driving me mad with desire—desire I knew she could smell on me now, her nostrils flaring. Even if my scent didn't betray me, I knew my eyes did. Her eyes were turning darker, too, and it excited me as much as it terrified me. I had caught her looking at me like that on more than one occasion during the past two weeks, but I still wasn't convinced her desire for me wasn't just a byproduct of me turning her.

My blood had made her into a vampire. Perhaps it had also made her believe that she felt things for me...things she couldn't possibly feel, I tried to tell myself. Still, every night in the past two weeks, I had woken with a sense of dread, fearing that tonight would be the night when she no longer looked at me like she wanted me. But the way she was looking at me now told me that tonight was not the night. But tomorrow could be. She needed more time to acclimate to her new life, to figure out what she truly wanted. I told myself I was only looking out for her, but the truth was, I was terrified of opening myself up to her because I knew that once I gave her my heart, there would be no going back.

My eyes flew open, and I groaned as pain rushed in, merciless and overwhelming. I didn't want pain, I only wanted her...

I stood before her bedroom door, cursing myself for how foolish I had been for the past two weeks. I should have told her. I should have acted on my feelings, but I hadn't, and now it was too late. Celeste had just told us that the attack was imminent. Dark Witches were coming. What was I doing here? I wanted to tell her, but what was the point? We might die tonight, so did she really need to know? A rough exhale left me as I rested my forehead on the door. She yanked it open a second later, peering at me from inside her bedroom.

"Sophie," *I breathed, as our gazes locked.*

A myriad of unspoken things hung in the air between us.

I'm not worthy of you, *I wanted to tell her. But if you'll have me...please have me, I wanted to beg, as the desperate need I felt for her nearly drove me to my knees.*

"I want you," *she uttered, and my heart stopped.*

A second passed. Another. Then a beat sounded—my heart had restarted, but it was no longer in my chest. It was inside Sophie, beating within her.

I didn't realize that I had moved until my mouth crashed into hers. No more holding back. No more wondering if she truly wanted me. She had just told me that she did. The raw need in her eyes had confirmed it for me, also. Her scent, lush and smoky with potent desire, enveloped me as I kissed her...her scent...her scent was here, in this place where my physical body was...

"Sophie?" I rasped as I forced myself to open my eyes. "Am I dreaming?"

21

SOPHIE

The air in the cave chilled my skin. Not the air, the sight before me. Camilla must have changed her mind about not torturing Henry. Not Camilla, Moreau, I realized, detecting his musky scent. My gaze darted to the torture instruments on the wooden table. As I'd suspected, they now had a fresh coat of Henry's blood on them. Breath snagged in my throat as my gaze slid back to him, to his large and powerful body. It was now one giant wound, throbbing and seeping blood. The damage they'd done was unbelievable. All in a span of several nights. Monsters. They'd unleashed their worst on him. I would unleash my worst on them.

"Sophie?" Henry ground out, his nostrils flaring as he pried his lashes apart. His bloody, cracked lips barely moved. "Am I dreaming?"

A choked sound escaped me when he asked the question, and I began to shake as tears filled my eyes. I lifted them to the rough stone ceiling to stop myself from crying. Henry was weak right now, so I needed to be strong. I needed to be strong for both of us. Taking a steadying breath, I slowly released the air out of my lungs before returning my gaze to him. He watched me from beneath his lashes, his expression guarded, as if he wasn't sure I was real. I needed to prove to him that I was.

On weak legs, I stepped closer to him and lowered to my knees by his side. My hand trembled as I reached up, unsure of where to touch him to avoid causing him pain. My gaze flicked over his blood-smeared face for a few seconds until I finally dared to press my fingertips to a tiny spot on his cheek that was free of cuts and bruises. He flinched at the feather-light touch but didn't pull away. A shudder rolled through him when I brought my face closer to his and gently brushed my lips over his brow.

"I'm here," I whispered against his temple. "I'm really here. You're not dreaming. I've come for you. We're leaving this place."

Henry went very still and seemed to have stopped breathing as his eyes fluttered closed. He looked almost peaceful as if he were asleep or...dead. I knew he wasn't—I could hear his heartbeat, but it was faint, not the thundering and strong sound I was used to. Panic flared in my chest, snapping me into action. Pulling away slightly, I bared my fangs and bit into my wrist before pressing it to Henry's mouth.

"Drink," I urged him, cradling the back of his head.

When the first drop of my blood touched his lips, Henry's eyes flew open, the blue in them instantly receding to black. His fangs pierced my skin above the bite marks I'd created as he latched on to my wrist and began drinking deeply and greedily.

Desire pulsed between my thighs with each long, staggering pull, but I ignored it, which wasn't that difficult to do given the situation we were in. While Henry drank, gulping down my essence, I tried to devise a plan to get us out of Stern's lair. I'd been able to glimmer here, becoming one with smoke and shadows. Perhaps I could glimmer both of us out to safety.

You can launch yourself into a different realm or get stranded in the void, Damien's words flashed through my mind. It was too risky. I'd been able to bring myself here, but I wasn't sure I was strong enough to glimmer both of us out.

Panic rose as I took a sweeping look around the cave. To the right lay a way out of this place through Stern's library. That was how Henry and I had gotten in when we'd come here in search of the Tear. I knew we couldn't use that route to escape now, because the mansion was teeming with clan vampires. There was another way out, though—my gaze darted to the left of the cave—through the tunnels the Ravagers had used to get in and out of this place.

My mind made up, I returned my gaze to Henry. His eyes had drifted closed again as he drank, restoring his strength with each drop of my blood. A breath of relief left me when I noticed the bleeding from the cuts covering his body had slowed, and some of the bruising had faded. Still, I knew he would be in no condition to help me once we stepped outside this room. We would use the tunnels to escape, but the journey to safety would be difficult and long, which meant I needed to preserve my strength.

"That's enough for now," I said gently, trying to pry my wrist from Henry's mouth.

His eyes snapped open, entirely black and unseeing, and he growled, refusing to give up the blood. I winced in pain because his fangs were tearing the skin where he was latched on. Quickly deciding on a different approach, I stopped trying to pull my wrist away and lowered my face closer to his.

"Please. Let go," I whispered, hoping he could hear me through the roar of bloodlust in his ears. He was not that different from a Ravager right now, in this state where his nature drove him to feed, to take everything from me to replenish his own depleted resources.

My voice must have penetrated the haze of his mind because Henry blinked, and a thin strip of blue appeared in his eyes. It gradually took over, crowding out the black. When his gaze focused on me, his eyes were pleading.

It's not enough, his look conveyed.

"I know, I know," I whispered, fighting back tears. "But I need my strength so I can get us out of here. Please. You need to let go."

Seconds ticked by as we stared at each other. His draws on my wrist slowed, but he wasn't ready to let go. Not yet. There was a war inside him. He was trying to fight the bloodlust. I could see it in his eyes—black was bleeding into the blue again, trying to take over, but the blue was pushing back because Henry was pushing back, trying to subdue the bloodlust. My heart pounded in the silence as I hoped he would prevail. I wasn't sure what I would do if he didn't. I would have to rip my wrist out of his jaw and break his neck to render him unconscious. Then, I could free him from the chains and carry him out of this place. But I hoped I wouldn't need to resort to that.

A few more seconds passed as I held my breath and waited. The warring hues in Henry's eyes swirled a moment longer until the blue pushed out the black entirely. A ragged exhale escaped me as I dove into the deep-blue waters of his gaze. I wanted to swim in them forever, but that would have to wait until we'd made it to safety. Henry's jaw unclenched and once he'd let go of my wrist, I quickly wiped the blood from the already healing bite marks on my tunic.

"I'm going to take off the collar," I said low, my gaze fastened on Henry's.

He gave a small nod, and I swiftly broke the metal band wrapped around his neck. I wanted to fling the fucking thing away from us with such force that it would embed into one of the cavernous walls, but I knew better than to make noise because it would alert the vampires in the mansion above us to my presence. So, I placed the broken collar on the ground beside me as gently as I could before returning my gaze to Henry's face.

"Now, I'll free you from the chains," I told him, feeling the need to explain what I was doing. He seemed in control, but I knew that bloodlust could surge back at any moment, and I didn't want to provoke him.

When he nodded again, I snapped the bands encircling his wrists and then the ones around his ankles. The metal clanked as the chains dropped to the ground, and I winced, hoping we weren't being too loud. Rising to my feet, I glanced at the exit leading to Stern's library. My ears perked up as I listened for any sign that we'd been overheard. When I heard none, I turned back to Henry.

"Can you walk?" I asked, bending down to help him up.

With a groan, he braced his hands on my shoulders and pushed himself up to his feet. My stomach roiled when the blood he'd been sitting in made a sickening, squelching sound as he got up. Henry let go of me and took a few deep, labored breaths, swaying on his feet. When he went to crumple to the ground, I held him up by propping him on my shoulder and wrapping my arm around his torso. I was a bit lightheaded myself from the blood he'd taken, and my stomach cramped as thirst lashed out. Sucking in a sharp breath, I waited for the wave of hunger to subside. I should have fed nights ago. Now, my stubbornness could cost us.

"Sophie," Henry rasped, snapping me out of my frantic thoughts. "You're really here."

He lifted one trembling hand to my face and cupped my cheek. Then he crushed his mouth to mine, the kiss raw and desperate. I tasted blood on his lips, his and mine. The kiss was intense but also fleeting; we couldn't afford anything more at the moment.

"Where are the others?" Henry asked when he pulled away.

"I came alone," I told him.

"What?" He stared at me with wide eyes.

"It'll be okay," I assured him, as I called upon my magic.

It slithered down my right arm like a snake made of dark shadows. Henry recoiled from me, staggering back a step. When his knees buckled, he braced his hand on the nearby wall for support.

"It's okay," I told him, as my other arm also became wreathed in shadows. "I've been learning my magic."

"Your magic?" Henry stared at me in disbelief. "But it's—"

Before he could finish his thought, darting shadows filled the cave as the clan leaders arrived. I cursed, angry with myself for having missed their approach.

"Well, well. What do we have here?" Camilla crooned as she strode in, flanked by Moreau and Beatrice Stern.

Emeric, Lena, and Yvonne rushed past me to block the other exit out of the cave.

I cursed again, my gaze darting between the two groups. Then, I felt my magic pulsing at my fingertips. My power rolled through me, calming my nerves.

You needn't be afraid, it whispered in my head. *They should be afraid of you.*

Squaring my shoulders, I turned to Camilla and lifted my chin.

"I've come to take back what's mine," I declared, my voice ringing out in the cavern.

"Is that so?" she hissed, crouching and unsheathing her claws.

The other clan leaders did the same. They all looked vicious, but I had something other than fangs and claws to fight with this time—something more powerful and deadly.

Thrusting my right arm out, I unleashed my magic, and it cracked like a whip on the hard ground, rolling toward Camilla. Before it could reach her, she darted out of the way just as Moreau and Beatrice scattered to the opposite sides of the room. In the blink of an eye, Camilla appeared closer to me on my left, and I thrust my left arm out, releasing the shadows toward her. Once again she dodged my magic, this time reappearing right in front of me. Before I could react, her arm shot out, and her clawed hand closed around my throat, cutting off air.

"Where is the amulet?" Camilla growled as she tore at the collar of my tunic with her other hand, her claws flaying my skin. When all she found was my locket, she ripped it off my neck and tossed it aside. "Where is it?!" she snarled, inches away from my face.

Suddenly, her glacial eyes widened, pain mixed with rage mottling her features. With a roar, she let go of my throat and spun around. The torture instruments I'd seen on the table earlier were now protruding from her back, and Henry stood in front of her, breathing shallowly. He didn't stay standing for long before Moreau tackled him, driving him to the ground and burying him under his weight. I moved to get Moreau off Henry at the same time Beatrice rushed to Camilla. While she was yanking the torture blades out of her back, I jumped on Moreau's back, my claws drawn, and my fangs bared. I reached around to slash his throat, but he grabbed me by the scruff of the neck and threw me over his head. Bones cracked, and teeth rattled as I collided with the rock wall before crumpling down to the ground.

Henry's roar of fury filled the cave as he bucked under Moreau, trying to throw him off to come to my aid.

Get up, I ordered myself, scrambling to my hands and knees.

My vision swam for a second until it became razor sharp and focused on Henry. Moreau was pressing his knee into his chest to keep him down, and the sight fueled my rage, giving me the push I'd needed. With a snarl, I jumped to my feet and stepped toward them. The sound of wood splintering stopped me in my tracks, and I spun around to see Camilla had broken the table that had housed the torture instruments.

"Where is the amulet?" she demanded, strolling over to where Moreau was holding Henry down. I tracked her every movement, my gaze zeroed in on the thin piece of wood in her hand. "Tell me, or I swear to gods I will drive this stake into his heart." Camilla jerked her chin toward Henry.

A shuddering breath left me as my gaze darted to him buried several inches into the ground under Moreau. The outer edges of my vision dimmed until all I could see was him—my lover, my friend, my savior. It was my turn to save him now.

Don't do it, his eyes pleaded as our gazes locked. *Don't give them the Tear.*

The amulet pulsed in my right pants pocket, burning right through the fabric and scorching my skin. A cursed object, indeed. All this pain and suffering was because of it. My hand twitched by my right side, but I curled it into a fist. The pain and suffering wouldn't be over even if I gave up the Tear. It wouldn't be over until the clans were no more.

At once, I knew exactly what I needed to do, and it didn't scare me anymore. Not like it had in the past. Closing my eyes, I retreated inside my mind, where I stood before a vast obsidian door with a key in my hand. All was quiet around me and the air was still, but I knew that the silence was deceiving. Great power churned behind the door, waiting to be unleashed and set free. It begged me to let it out, so, after a heartbeat, I did. I lifted the key to the door and unlocked it, releasing the darkness within. When it spilled like a tidal wave, rushing out after being kept at bay, I let it take over. I welcomed the shadows as they wrapped around me, enveloping me until I became one with them—a whisper of swirling darkness and smoke.

I glimmered, disappearing into the void that strangely felt like home now, only to reappear a moment later in front of Camilla. Her eyes widened in shock, but she didn't have time to react as my shadows swept her up. Following my will, my magic threw her against the wall with such force that the sound of her bones shattering tore through the cave. I didn't stop there. Darting toward her with supernatural speed, I drove the stake she'd threatened Henry with through her heart before she had the chance to slide to the ground. Her mouth opened wide, but no sound came out as she began decaying, her flesh drying out on her broken bones. I stared into her dead eyes, unflinching, until nothing was left of her but dust.

When she was gone, I spun around, still holding the stake in my hand. Moreau cursed as he jumped off Henry and darted toward the exit leading to Stern's study. Disappearing into the void again, I reappeared in front of him, blocking his escape. My claws gleamed in the candlelight as I slashed them across Moreau's midsection. He roared in pain, but the sound quickly turned garbled as I tore out his throat with my teeth. I spat out the chunk of his flesh and drove the stake through his heart, reveling in his death as I had in Camilla's. After Moreau had shriveled up and disintegrated to nothing, I faced Beatrice and found her shaking before me. Slowly, she backed away from me, putting distance between us until her back hit the wall, and she had nowhere else to go. Glimmering again, I appeared right in front of her a second before I painted the wall behind her red with her blood. Her death was just as swift but no less gruesome than Camilla's and Moreau's.

As I stood in the middle of the cave with my enemies' blood dripping from my chin and claws, the darkness inside me rejoiced, and I let out a vicious growl, whirling around on the remaining three clan leaders. Their already pale faces turned white as they stared back at me. Lena moved first, but instead of coming at me as I'd expected, she spun around and disappeared into the dark tunnels behind her. Emeric and Yvonne exchanged a terrified look before they also turned around and fled. With a snarl, I stepped back with my right foot, preparing to go after them, but halted when I heard Henry groan in pain. My gaze shot to him, to where he was still embedded in the ground, his heartbeat sluggish and stuttering.

He needed me, but I felt torn. The darkness inside urged me to go after the clan leaders. Bloodthirsty and driven by revenge, it pulled me toward the tunnels. But another side of me, the human side, urged me to tend to Henry. I'd come here for him; revenge could wait. Gritting my teeth, I reined in the darkness and sheathed my claws. With one last wistful look toward the tunnels, I turned away from them and approached where Henry lay. As gently as I could, I gathered him in my arms and glimmered us out of Stern's lair, acutely aware that I would never truly leave this place. It would stay with me forever, carved into a part of my mind like my own personal cave. A cave I would visit sometimes to cry about what had been done to Henry or to revel in what I'd done to those who'd caused him pain.

22

I took us to the Duval Estate, straight to the cellar where I hoped crates with blood awaited us. A breath of relief whooshed out of me when I saw my hope hadn't been misplaced—the clans hadn't raided the cellar and taken all the blood. After carefully laying Henry on the stone floor in the middle of the dimly lit room, I dragged one of the crates closer and lowered to the floor next to him, folding my legs under me to prop his head on my knees. The heavy lid creaked in the quiet space as I opened the chest and retrieved a blood bag before tearing it open with my teeth and pouring its contents into Henry's mouth. He was nearly unconscious as his throat worked on a swallow, but then his hand shot up, closing around the bag. He ripped it out of my hand and began drinking greedily, gulping down the deep-red liquid.

Exhaustion washed over me with the realization that he was going to be okay. I wanted to sag all the way down to the floor with relief, but willed myself to stay upright as I reached back into the chest and pulled out a bag for myself. When I sank my fangs into it, blood poured into my mouth, rich and sweet, and I moaned at the exquisite taste. My veins lit up with liquid fire as the blood began coursing through me, traveling to each part of my body, healing cracked bones and torn tissue.

Henry drained his bag first, throwing it to the side with a snarl. When he did, I gave him another bag and also retrieved one for myself. We fed for what felt like hours until eventually, Henry rolled to the side and vomited some of the blood. He'd taken too much too fast after not feeding for days.

"I think you've had enough for now," I said gently, brushing his matted hair from his damp forehead. He didn't protest as he lay on my lap, trembling slightly. My gaze roamed over his body as I assessed the damage. Feeding had kick-started the healing process, but it was difficult to judge how well it was going because he was covered in blood. "We should go upstairs and clean you up. Can you walk?" I asked, my tone urgent. I couldn't wait another second to wash away the horrors of the past few nights from his skin.

Henry nodded, planting his left hand on the floor. He pushed up to a seating position first, before slowly rising to his feet. I stood up as well, wrapping my arm around his waist for support. When I did, he winced in pain, which let me know the healing process had only just begun. Slowly, we made our way out of the cellar and climbed the narrow stone steps to the foyer.

"Wait," I stopped Henry with a hand on his chest as I strained my ears, listening for any sign we might not be alone on the estate.

I wasn't worried about the clans coming for us—I could take care of them, but I hoped they would stay away for a while. I also hoped that Isabelle and the others had not come for me. I wanted to be left alone with Henry. I'd just gotten him back, and we deserved some time together. Silence stretched, as my ears picked up on the creaks of the empty house and the drumming of the rain outside.

A sigh of relief left me when I'd made sure we were alone, and

I nodded at Henry before steering him in the direction of the grand staircase.

He was silent on the way to his bedroom on the second floor, but his hold on me was strong, as if he feared that if he'd let go, I would slip out of his arms and disappear. My grip was also tight on him because I needed to feel he was real and that this wasn't some twisted, delusional dream. When we reached his bedroom, I pushed open the door and we walked in, heading to the bathing chamber. Bright light flooded the space, glancing off the marble shower and the porcelain soaking tub when I flipped on the switch.

"Wait here," I told Henry, leaving him propped on the vanity as I walked over to the shower and turned it on.

The soft hum of water filled the quiet as I thrust my hand into the stream, holding it there until I adjusted the temperature and made sure it was not scalding hot. When I turned around, Henry was watching me intently as if he were scared to take his eyes off me.

"You need to shower," I said as I approached, stopping before him.

Slowly, I reached out and undid the buttons on his pants before tugging them down his hips. The blood-soaked garment dropped to the floor, and Henry stepped out of it, his chest heaving with a shuddering breath of relief. Wrapping my arm around his waist again, I led him to the shower. His steps were steadier now, but he still let me help him, which I appreciated because I still needed to be touching him to make sure he was real. I had to let go of him, though, when we reached the shower so he could step inside. He eased under the stream, hissing when the water hit cuts and bruises. Bracing his hands on the shower wall, he hung his head, letting the water plaster his hair to his face as it washed away the blood. It glided down his body like a river of crimson, pooling on the marble floor under his feet before swirling and disappearing down the drain.

I wished the water could wash away everything that had transpired, but I knew that what had happened to Henry would cling to his skin like a sticky residue for years to come. I wished I could take it all away, all the pain and suffering. Henry was strong; the tortures hadn't broken him. The aftermath of what had happened wouldn't break him either. Still, I wished I could bear the brunt of it, sparing him from it all. He was strong, but I wished he didn't have to be. I wanted to be strong for both of us. Perhaps I was still a martyr, willing to suffer only for him.

"Get in," he said softly, pulling me from my thoughts.

Relief crashed into me at the request, nearly knocking me off my feet. I'd planned on getting in when I'd first turned on the shower, but then had thought better of it, wondering if I should give him some space. Now he was asking me to join him, and I almost wept with joy. I would have given him space if he'd needed it, but it would have been torture because I didn't need any space from him. We'd never be separated again if I could help it.

Henry lifted his face up into the stream and scrubbed it with his hands while I peeled my bloodstained clothes off my body. I stepped into the shower behind him and reached for the soap sitting on the shallow shelf carved into the marble wall. Gripping the lavender-scented bar with one hand, I reached up with my other hand and pressed my fingertips to Henry's back to let him know I was about to wash him. He tensed but didn't object as I began gliding the soap over his body, gently washing away blood and grime. I started with his neck and shoulders, which were taut and hard as stone but eventually relaxed as I massaged them lightly, carefully avoiding the tender welts and pink skin where the injuries were healing.

Working my way down, I washed the broad expanse of his back before moving lower, all the way to the soles of his feet. When I popped up in front of him, he braced his hands on the wall again, caging me in. My heart skipped a beat because I was now inches away from his face, which was still covered in small cuts but was no longer covered in blood, revealing the chiseled features underneath. Deep-blue eyes were fastened on me, as one side of Henry's mouth turned up.

"Hi," he said low.

I felt one corner of my lips turn up in response.

"Hi," I breathed, getting lost in the depths of his gaze.

I wanted to close the distance between us and kiss every inch of his face, but I told myself to focus and finish washing him. Lowering my gaze to his throat, I ran my soapy hand over the column of his neck before sliding it to his chest. The sculpted muscles flexed as I washed his torso before moving lower. My throat dried at what I found below his navel, and my gaze darted back to Henry's face. His eyes closed and his lips parted, he looked enraptured as I washed him. Still watching him closely, I wrapped my fingers around his hardness and glided my hand up and down his length, eliciting a full-body shudder and a harsh groan from him.

A low sound broke past my lips as arousal flooded me, pooling in my core. I remembered all too well what it felt like to have the thick hardness deep inside me, stretching me, bringing me to the edge. My restraint was slipping; I could feel it, but I refused to give in to the burning need in my blood. This was about Henry, not me, and he didn't stop me as I kept moving lower down his body, washing his legs to the tips of his toes. When I rose back up, Henry's eyes were still closed as he rested his forehead against mine, swallowing thickly.

"I need to wash your hair," I told him, my voice low and husky.

He pulled away then and opened his eyes. They were darker now, sending a shiver of anticipation through me. His hungry gaze stayed on me as he slowly lowered to his knees and clasped my hips. Desire pulsed between my thighs as I felt his breath on my flushed skin. I wanted to give in to it so badly, but I resisted. I would follow Henry's lead and feed his desires, not my own. His dark lashes swept down as he lowered his head—a cue for me to wash his hair. I lathered up the silky strands, massaging his scalp until a sigh of contentment left him.

"You can get up and wash the soap out," I instructed, ignoring the dryness in my throat.

Henry obeyed, but not before planting a soft kiss below my belly button. I sucked in air as another wave of raw lust rolled through me. I knew he could smell my desire, but he seemed impervious to it save for his eyes, which were almost entirely black when he rose to his feet. He proceeded to rinse the soap out of his hair, while I quickly washed myself.

When the streams gliding down our bodies ran clear and not red anymore, Henry turned the water off and stepped out of the shower while I remained behind, wringing out my hair. He handed me a towel, a predatory gleam invading his gaze as it roamed over my naked form. Our eyes locked, and it felt like I'd forgotten how to breathe until Henry eventually looked away, grabbing a towel for himself from the nearby cabinet. I watched his muscles bunch and shift as he dried himself off, dabbing the towel over the healing wounds before draping it around his hips. I wrapped my own towel around myself and followed him out of the bathroom, my damp feet pattering on the cool stone floor.

Henry headed for the dresser, his large frame bathed in the soft yellow glow of the lamp on the bedside table. My brows pinched as I followed after him, telling myself not to be disappointed that he was going to get dressed. He was undoubtedly exhausted after everything he'd been through. It was selfish of me to expect anything... Henry stopped abruptly by the foot of the bed and turned around to face me. I halted before him, clutching the towel to my chest.

The air between us became charged as we stared at each other, unmoving, barely breathing. My gaze fastened on him, I could see the bruises on his face fading away, the cuts healing, his strongly defined features slowly returning to near-flawless perfection. The rest of his body was trying to catch up, I noticed, lowering my gaze to his hard chest, but the lacerations there were deeper, taking longer to heal. I took a breath, swallowing to relieve the tightness in my throat. My fingers itched to reach for Henry, to pull him to me. My lips tingled, yearning for his kisses, but I held myself back. He'd been through so much. I would wait for him to come to me. I would not be selfish and take. I would only give. When he was ready for it.

"You need to rest," I said, but the words came out more as a question than a statement, and I chided myself in my head. I really didn't want to push him.

"I need *you*," Henry rasped, raw emotion in his broken voice.

My legs became weak with relief. He wanted me. Now. I didn't have to wait any longer to feel his body on mine.

"Anything you need, I'm yours," I told him, looking into his dark eyes. I knew the same molten heat had also invaded my gaze.

A harsh exhale of relief left him, as if he'd needed the confirmation.

"Anything?" he asked, low and thick.

"Anything," I breathed, unwrapping the towel from around my chest and letting it drop to the floor.

Any blue remaining in his eyes instantly gave way to black. His hungry gaze became all-consuming as he slowly drank in my naked body. I shivered at the intensity of his stare, feeling every part of me coming alive with sparks of desire. They skittered over my skin like tiny bursts of lightning, making it flush and sensitive. My pulse quickened, my breathing coming in short, rapid pants, as Henry's eyes lifted back to my face. His gaze was raw and pleading. I'd wanted him to come to me and now he had, asking me to make the next move without saying anything at all.

I stepped into him, his fresh and woodsy scent enveloping me. It went straight to my head, driving me wild. I'd gotten him back.

He was right here in front of me. Waiting for me to touch him. So I did. Lifting my hand up, I gently pressed my fingertips to his chest. He shuddered, covering my hand with his to press my palm more flat against his skin. His other hand went up and he dragged his fingers down my cheek, his eyes following the movement.

"I prayed that I would get to touch you again," he said low, his voice hoarse. "To hold you in my arms."

"You didn't think I'd come for you?" I asked, my brows knitting in confusion.

"I thought that even if you did, it would be too late," he said, the last part barely above a whisper as if he didn't want to admit it aloud.

"I would always come for you," I told him fiercely. "It would never be too late. I would drag you from the edge of the void if I had to."

Henry's eyes widened at my words, and instead of responding, he clasped the back of my head and sealed his lips to mine. There was no build-up to the kiss. Our mouths collided, desperate and seeking. I opened up for him, and he delved deep, our fangs clashing and our tongues mingling. He let go of my hand on his chest and wrapped his arm around my waist to bring me flush with him. I gasped into his mouth at the feel of his body on mine, skin to skin. He tried to turn me toward the bed, but I resisted. There was a question in his eyes when I broke the kiss and pulled away.

Looking up at him from beneath my lashes, I gave him a sultry smile before I brushed my lips over the firm line of his jaw. He shivered at the soft contact and became incredibly still as I unwrapped the towel from around his hips, letting it drop to the floor. I began trailing kisses down his neck, nipping at the spot where his pulse thrummed just below his skin. His breathing hitched, but I didn't linger, kissing down his chest to his torso and lower still. I heard him swallow thickly when I dropped to my knees and planted a kiss on his thigh, close to where he throbbed for me. The sight of him, long and thick, made my mouth water and set all my senses on fire.

I looked up at him then, and the way he stared down at me sent a bolt of desire straight through me. I might be the one on my knees, but he was the one entirely at my mercy, and knowing that only intensified the potent lust. My eyes fastened on his face, I wrapped my hand around him and began moving it up and down his length. His head fell back, and a rough sound left him, a low growl that sent another pulse of arousal through me, making me squeeze my thighs at the curling sensation. The sound of him coming undone before me was like a drug, and I wanted to hear it again, willing to do anything for it.

Opening my mouth, I wrapped my lips around the thick hardness and began moving on him together with my hand. I was rewarded with that primal growl again as his fingers threaded through my hair, gently urging me to go faster, to take him in deeper. I was more than happy to comply, and for a few minutes, the sounds of me pleasuring him and his harsh breathing filled the quiet bedroom. I was prepared to go until I tasted his release on my tongue, but to my surprise, he tugged on my hair, pulling me off him.

23

"Come here," Henry said, his voice lush and smoky.

When I rose to my feet, he captured my mouth, kissing me until we were both breathless. He broke the kiss first, tugging on my lower lip with his fangs as he pulled away. I let him turn my back toward the bed and lower me to the soft mattress. His dark eyes locked on mine, he prowled up my body, muscles shifting and flexing, and a soft gasp escaped me when he settled between my thighs. I welcomed the weight—it felt like coming home.

"Tell me how much you missed me," Henry rasped, hovering over me.

Before I could respond, he reached up and began gliding his fingertips down my chest, leaving a trail of fire in their wake.

"I missed you with everything that I am. I felt it in my bones. I had dreams about you. About this." My breath caught as he ran a thumb over my nipple.

"About this?" he asked, as he lowered his head to my breast and swirled his tongue over the hardened peak.

"Yes," I gasped, my eyes drifting closed.

"And this?" He grazed a fang over the nipple.

My back arched as I breathed, "Yes."

"What about this?" His hand dove between my thighs, his finger parting the soft flesh there.

A throaty moan was my only reply as my hips rolled into his touch.

"Fuck," he growled, his finger sinking in deeper.

His mouth returned to my breasts as he slowly worked another finger in, stretching me in the most decadent way. Ripples of acute pleasure darted through me as he began gliding his fingers in and out while teasing the sensitive bundle of nerves with his thumb. Panting, I moved on his hand, meeting each plunge of his fingers. I quickly got lost in the pleasure as the tension inside me built, but what Henry was doing wasn't enough, not tonight. I needed to feel him inside me, *all* of him, and I didn't want to wait.

"You know what else I dreamed about?" I asked, opening my eyes to look at him. He lifted his head from my breasts, his gaze hooded and dazed. His lips parted, revealing the hints of his fangs. "This." I reached up and wrapped my hand around his thickness.

Henry groaned as his hand stilled between my thighs. Slowly, he withdrew his fingers, slick with my desire, and brought them to his lips. The sight of him sucking them clean sent another rush of damp heat to my core, and I whimpered as my hold on him tightened.

"I will always give you what you want." His words were a dark, sensual promise. "Anything you want," he added, a second before he thrust in, slamming in to the hilt.

My head fell back against the mattress, my mouth parting in a silent scream as Henry moaned against my neck. I'd been wrong before—*this* was home, with him buried deep inside me. Clasping his shoulders, I wrapped my legs around his hips, urging him to move, to give me what I wanted. What I *needed*. With a low growl, he complied. He began sliding in and out of me, one hand fisting in my hair while the other one gripped the underside of my thigh. The world faded away as all my senses zeroed in on the feeling of him moving inside me, hitting the spot where the pressure built, curling tighter and tighter.

My body began to tremble, on the brink of release, but I refused to give in to it, trying to prolong the pleasure. Henry trembled, too, snarling as his thrusts became wild and erratic. I was teetering on the edge, barely holding on, when he pulled on my hair, exposing my neck. He struck fast, his fangs piercing my skin, and I cried out as powerful release crashed into me, pleasure rippling wave after wave. With one last deep thrust, Henry roared against my neck as he came, in between taking draws of my blood. I felt weightless, my body floating as sparks of pleasure slowly flickered out, my limbs becoming limp and boneless as I sank into the mattress. Henry's draws on my neck slowed, and he ran his tongue over the puncture wounds that were already healing, before lifting his gaze to mine.

My breath caught because there was so much in his intense stare. Raw vulnerability invaded his eyes, which were gradually turning bluer. Passion and yearning and…love. My heart swelled in my chest, making it difficult to breathe. I was drowning in what I was feeling, wondering how I would ever be able to put what he meant to me into words. My eyes pricked with tears as the emotion overwhelmed me. Henry was everything to me, and I'd almost lost him. A cold feeling crept into my chest at the thought, wedging itself next to my bursting heart. My gaze dropped to Henry's chest, where the wounds were still healing, turning to angry-looking welts. Would they turn to scar tissue? Could vampires have scars? Even if they didn't, there would be scars on the inside because of what the clans had done, the suffering they'd put him through.

"We have to make them pay," I said low, as ice filled my veins.

"What?" Henry's brows knitted as he peered down at my face.

"We need to make them pay," I repeated, looking up at him.

My voice sounded strange to my ears as the ice in my veins spread to my entire body, making it cold and heavy. I shivered as the darkness draped over my heart, craving retribution. The oily feeling was nothing new. It had stayed away while Henry and I had showered and made love, but it was back now, hungry and demanding. It urged me to get out of bed and go on a hunt for the remaining clan leaders, to spill their blood and break their bones.

"Revenge? Is that truly what's on your mind right now?" Henry asked, staring at me in disbelief.

"How can it not be when I'm looking at the remnants of the savage wounds on your chest?" I asked, my voice rising.

"Then you should focus on my face instead. What do you see in my eyes?" he demanded.

Heart pounding, I refocused on the emotions shining in his gaze. What I saw almost crowded out the darkness, but the oily feeling remained, pushing back, growing roots, and establishing its presence. I tried to pull the black drape off my heart, but it clung to it, wrapping around it, sealing on tight.

When I didn't respond, Henry stared at me for a moment longer as if not recognizing who was in front of him before he shifted off me and left the bed. Immediately missing his weight on me, I brought my thighs together and lifted my burning eyes to the ceiling to keep the tears at bay. I was still cold, but now it wasn't just from the darkness but also from missing Henry's closeness. How had we ended up like this? We'd gone from being as close as we could possibly be to having this abyss between us. The bed I was lying on felt like an island, and I was completely and utterly alone on it. Henry was still in the room, pulling on some clean clothes he'd retrieved from the dresser, but it felt like he was hundreds of miles away.

Refusing to linger on this lonely island, wallowing in my misery, I drew in a shallow breath and got out of bed. Moving with supernatural speed, I grabbed the Tear from the pocket of my pants lying in a heap on the floor in the bathroom and swept from the room. Henry didn't try to stop me, and I wasn't sure if I was relieved or disappointed. I dashed through the empty house until I reached my bedroom, where I quickly got dressed in black pants and a matching tunic, before hanging the amulet around my neck. A knock sounded a moment later.

"Can we talk?" Henry asked when he walked in.

I stilled before the vanity, my features turning harsh in the mirror. They softened slightly when I glanced at him and saw the raw vulnerability return to his face.

"Sophie," he said low, closing the distance between us. I turned from the mirror, and he stopped before me, lifting his hands to cup my face. The gesture was sweet and tender, thawing some of the ice that had coated my insides. "I love you."

Everything stopped as if Henry had frozen time with those three little words. He had uttered them so simply, as if saying them was the easiest thing in the world. And perhaps it was for him. But not for me.

I love you, too, danced on the tip of my tongue. Yet, I didn't open my mouth to let the words out. I just stared at Henry, his deep-blue eyes drawing me in. I wanted to drown in them, in him. But I couldn't. Not until the clans had paid for what they'd put us through. I *did* love Henry with everything that I was, and it was because I loved him that I couldn't let what the clans had done go unpunished.

Henry's eyes shuttered as the silence between us stretched. He wanted me to tell him—to say the words he'd just told me, but I couldn't. Not yet. For I knew if I said them, I wouldn't want to follow through with my revenge. I would want to stay by his side, right here in this room, wrapped up in our love and in him.

Those stormy blue eyes searched my face as his dark brows wrinkled. "What happened to you while I was gone?"

"Gone?" An unexpected laugh burst out of me, but there was no humor to the sound. "You say it like you went on a trip. Henry, you were tortured and starved. You weren't *gone*. You were held captive at the clans' mercy."

"It's over now," he said vehemently, his eyes fastened on mine. "I'm back here. With you."

"But the others are still on the loose. We have to hunt them down and make them pay," I said just as vehemently.

Henry recoiled from me. His hands dropped from my face before he dragged them through his tousled hair.

"I don't want to make them pay. I just want to stay here. With you. Sophie, I just told you I loved you. I am in love with you. Isn't that enough?"

"No." The word was out before I could stop it.

Henry bristled as if I'd delivered a physical blow. At once, I wished my magic could turn back time so I could go back to a few seconds ago and undo the damage I'd done.

"No?" he whispered, his expression one of impossible sadness and loss.

And we had lost something, hadn't we? From now on, our relationship would be defined by before and after. *Before* Henry had confessed his feelings to me, and I'd told him they were not enough, and *after* our beautiful bond had become irrevocably tarnished. I wished I could go back and change the past, but I couldn't; I could only move forward.

"Nothing will ever be enough until we make them pay," I said with a surge of determination.

Henry's eyes glistened as his throat worked on a swallow. "There is no *we*, Sophie. You're on your own."

Now it was my turn to bristle. "You're not coming with me?"

Henry shook his head instead of replying.

Shocked, I stared at him. He stared back as neither of us spoke for a few seconds.

"I don't want you to go," he finally said, breaking the tense silence. Hope flared in his eyes as he reached up and gently pressed his fingertips to my cheek. "Don't go," he added softly, resting his forehead on mine. "Stay with me. Please."

Please. The word nearly undid me. Closing my eyes, I took a breath, wanting to give in. The muscles of my neck and back relaxed at Henry's proximity as I breathed him in. Perhaps he was right. We were back together now. He was safe.

Safe? the darkness whispered. *How can he be safe when they are still out there?*

My heart sped up in my chest as my eyes flew open. I stepped away from Henry, and his fingers, which had been brushing my cheek, curled into a fist around thin air. His blue eyes dulled, and he looked defeated, his mouth wan and his face ashen.

"I have to go," I told him, my voice cold and detached. "And if you're not going to help me, I know someone who will."

That got Henry's attention, and his head snapped up, his eyes boring into me.

"Who?"

"I'll be back as soon as it's over," I told him, as I called upon the magic in my blood.

"Wait, who is going to help you? Answer me, Sophie!"

Sensing that I was about to make my escape, Henry lunged for me, but it was too late. My entire body tingled, wreathed in obsidian flames as my magic pulled me from the bedroom. I felt weightless for a moment, floating in the void, before I came out on the other side—in the Black Forest. Glimmering had come easier this time, but I was still unsteady on my feet after they'd hit the solid ground in the woods. Bracing my hands on my knees, I focused on my breathing as I tried to tame my frantic thoughts along with my racing heart.

How could Henry not want retribution for what the clans had done to him?

I don't want to make them pay. I just want to stay here. With you. His words floated up in my mind.

He loved me...I closed my eyes, my heart sinking. I loved him, too. I hadn't said it back, but actions spoke louder than words. I would prove my love to him by making the clan leaders pay. I'd claimed him as my own, and I would stop at nothing to protect what was mine.

24

HENRY

She disappeared, wreathed in smoke and shadows. When my fingers closed around thin air after I'd lunged for her, I roared in frustration and smashed my fist into the vanity, splintering the mahogany wood.

Breathe, I ordered myself as I dragged a hand through my hair. My eyes burned, so I squeezed them shut. We had been separated for only a few nights, but it had felt like an eternity. Not only because of the torture I had endured, but because I had been away from her. Tonight, we had reunited, but now she was gone again. I opened my eyes, staring into the space before me, my chest painfully tight. I had told her I loved her…she hadn't said it back. I knew her feelings for me ran deep. I could see it in her eyes. I could see it on her face, but I still wanted to hear her say it. The three little words. It was selfish of me to want her to say them. Gods, it was selfish of me to even want her to love me because I didn't deserve it. Would she still love me if she knew about my past? About the monstrous things I'd done?

A ragged breath escaped as I shook my head to clear my thoughts. I needed to focus if I wanted to help Sophie. And she needed my help even if she didn't realize it. Her magic...it was not like the magic of the other White Witches. I knew little about their powers, but I could tell that hers was different. It hadn't been white lighting running down her arms when she'd called upon her magic in Stern's lair—it had been dark shadows slithering like snakes.

A shudder rolled through me at the thought. Whatever her magic was, I had no doubt it was the reason Sophie was not acting like herself. Her thirst for justice had always been strong, but it wasn't justice she was after now, it was vengeance. She was out for blood, and that wasn't the Sophie I knew and loved. That Sophie would have stayed with me. That Sophie would have told me she loved me. I clenched my jaw and headed for the door—I would bring that Sophie back.

The fresh smell of rain hung heavy in the air when I stepped outside, and I inhaled deeply, grateful that my ribs had healed enough to allow the movement. Being out here and being free felt surreal. I couldn't believe Sophie had rescued me. I couldn't believe she had thought I was worthy of saving.

Don't go there, I told myself as I rolled my shoulders. She had saved me, and now I would save her, even if I had to save her from herself.

Stepping back with my right foot, I set off to a sprint, running toward the Black Forest. When I entered the dark woods, the forest creatures swarmed, but I kept moving, unbothered by their presence. I was the Alpha in these woods. I knew it, and they knew it, too. The wet soil squelched under my booted feet as I ran, and my shirt quickly got drenched from the water stored in the tree canopy when I disturbed it rushing by.

Celeste's rustic cottage appeared sooner than I had expected. The witch was outside, and so were Isabelle, Waylon, and...Wren. My upper lip curled in a snarl as I headed straight for the fucker.

Sophie had almost died twice because of him. I thought she'd killed him. I didn't know how he had survived, but he wouldn't stay alive for long because I would tear him to shreds. A vicious growl escaped at the thought as I kept running toward him. He stood with his back to me, and I was almost on him when he whirled around, his pale-blue eyes wide in panic and shock. Suddenly, Isabelle's face replaced his in my line of vision, and I skidded to a halt before her.

"Move," I snarled at her.

In the back of my mind, I knew this wasn't the reunion we both deserved, but I didn't care at the moment. I only cared about getting to Wren.

"No," Isabelle declared, squaring off against me.

When I growled at her, she growled back. Why was she protecting him? She was acting as if she were protecting something that was…hers. My nostrils flared as I detected their intermingled scents. Disbelief surged through me as I stared at her with wide eyes. Her eyes were pleading as she stared back, but her jaw was set in determination. She would fight me if it came to it, but she hoped it wouldn't, her look conveyed. Gods. Of all people, why did it have to be Wren? It truly didn't matter, I realized, as my fury deflated. I couldn't rip out Wren's heart like I wanted to, because then I would be ripping out Isabelle's heart, too, and I would never forgive myself if I hurt her. Erasing the snarl from my face, I sheathed my claws. Isabelle did the same, relief washing over her features.

"Henry," she breathed, closing the distance between us.

She wrapped her arms around me, squeezing tight, and I embraced her back, resting my chin on top of her head. We stayed like that for a few minutes until Isabelle pulled away.

"You're alive," she stated the obvious. "And well," she added, her gaze quickly scanning me from head to toe.

"I am," I assured her. "Sophie rescued me."

That got Celeste's attention.

"Where *is* Sophie?" the witch asked, stepping closer to me.

"She's...gone." I swallowed to relieve the tightness in my throat.

"What do you mean 'gone'?" Waylon chimed in, his gaze stretching behind me as if he were expecting to see Sophie standing there.

"She rescued me from the clan leaders' captivity, but some of them got away. She went after them. She wants revenge." The last three words were difficult to get out because they were not my Sophie.

"She truly rescued you all by herself?" Isabelle's delicate brows climbed her forehead.

"She did, but I think something's wrong."

"Something *is* wrong," Celeste said grimly.

"It's her magic, isn't it?" I asked, looking at the witch, and she nodded. "What happened while I was gone?" I demanded, looking between Celeste, Isabelle, and Waylon. I didn't dare look at Wren lest my fury return in full force.

"What happened was...she went a little insane with worry when the clans took you. She became obsessed with getting you back," Isabelle explained, but I knew there had to be more to it.

"She wanted me to come with her to hunt down the remaining clan leaders, and when I refused, she said someone else would help her. Do you know who she was talking about?"

Isabelle shook her head, but Celeste's eyes narrowed.

"I thought I caught her talking to someone in the woods the other night, but I didn't see who it was," the witch said.

"Someone from the village?" Isabelle gave Waylon a questioning look.

"Not Amelie. She's been spending all her free time with me," he replied. His face took on a strange expression as he shifted from foot to foot.

"Wait, what village?" I asked Isabelle, as her words finally sank in.

Her gaze found mine again, and she smiled, her face lighting up with warmth and excitement.

"The White Witches settlement. Henry, there are so many of them. It's truly amazing. I can't wait for you to see it."

I stared at her in disbelief. I'd thought most of the White Witches had been eradicated or turned Dark during the Red War. Their tragic fate had always weighed heavily on me because I wished there had been something I could have done to prevent it. Learning that there were a lot more of them than I had realized alleviated the weight just a fraction.

"There is an entire village?" I looked at Celeste and she nodded, pride and joy shining on her aged face. "I can't wait to see it," I told her. "But first, I need to find Sophie."

Understanding settled into her features as they became hard with determination.

"I will listen to the world and see if it whispers about her whereabouts. I'm afraid she is not only a danger to others but also to herself. Her magic is—"

"Dark," I interjected. "I've seen it firsthand."

How did you let that happen? I wanted to shake the witch.

The question was on the tip of my tongue, but I didn't voice it. I needed Celeste's help to find Sophie, so I couldn't confront her like I wanted to. Her lips pressed into a thin line as if she knew what I was thinking, but she didn't say anything else before she turned around and walked inside the house. I took a step to follow after her, but Isabelle's hand landed on my arm.

"It's good to have you back," she said, her voice shaking with emotion.

When I looked at her, her eyes were glimmering with tears. I couldn't bring myself to say anything in return. I wanted to tell her it was good to be back, but I couldn't force the words out because my feeling of elation was tamped down by one of dread. I couldn't help but feel like my freedom had come at a price, and Sophie was currently paying it. What that price was, I wasn't sure, but a cold, heavy feeling of foreboding crept into my chest and settled there.

"You said some of the clan leaders escaped," Waylon said, drawing my attention to him.

"Yes, Emeric, Lena, and Yvonne are still on the loose."

"What about Camilla, Moreau, and Beatrice Stern?" Isabelle asked.

"Dead. Sophie killed them." My heart squeezed when I uttered the words. The three clan leaders had deserved to die, but I wished I had been strong enough to kill them, so Sophie wouldn't have had to do it. I didn't want blood on her hands—it didn't matter whose blood it was.

"I'm going back to New Haven then," Waylon proclaimed, his voice ringing out in the clearing. "I need to see if any of the border guards are still alive and spread the word that the Dark Witches were defeated."

"We will go with you," Isabelle said, glancing at Wren, who nodded in agreement. My brows knitted—I truly didn't like seeing her with him. "Unless you need help?" She looked back at me.

"No, go. Celeste will help me," I assured her, even though there was this feeling in my gut telling me that helping Sophie was something I had to do on my own. "Be careful."

"You, too," Isabelle said, still gripping my arm as if she was afraid of letting go.

A moment later, she did let go of me, and I headed toward the house, passing Waylon on the way there.

"Bring her back," he said, as I walked by.

"I will," I told him, hoping I wasn't making a promise I wouldn't be able to keep.

25

SOPHIE

I will hunt every last one of them like the savage animals that they are, I thought with a snarl as I walked through the Black Forest without a destination in mind. At least, it had stopped raining.

"Sophie?" came a male voice from behind me.

I spun around and faced the woods just as Damien stepped out of them. He was garbed in a black cloak, the darkness of his clothing highlighting his white hair and pale skin. With eyes fathomless and black, he looked much like a vampire, and I saw red for a second before I breathed through the blinding rage, telling myself to calm down.

"How did you know I was here?" I asked when he approached.

"I heard a whisper in the wind. Did you summon me?"

I thought about it for a moment. "I did want to see you."

"Then you must have projected it into the world around you." His bottomless gaze flicked over me. "Something's different about you," he observed.

I lifted my chin. "I saved my lover."

"Alone?" His brows shot up.

I shrugged. "I had my magic." *And the darkness.* "So, no. I wasn't truly alone."

Damien appraised me from head to toe. The look he gave me was one of impressed appreciation. He suddenly struck me as someone who was drawn to power and wanted to be in the orbit of the one wielding it.

"Tell me what happened," he asked in a hushed tone.

I told him everything in every gory detail. He didn't recoil from any of it. If anything, he seemed to be feeding off the pain and suffering I described. The look on his face was one of depraved pleasure as I talked about killing Camilla, Moreau, and Beatrice.

"The other three clan leaders...they escaped," I finished the story as rage surged again. I couldn't believe I'd let them get away.

"I see," Damien said low, his eyes dimming as if he were disappointed the bloody retelling had come to an end. "What do you want to do now?" he asked, and seemed to have stopped breathing, waiting for my answer.

"I want to find them and make them pay," I told him vehemently. "I need your help hunting them down."

Damien's face lit up at my words as his mouth curved into a sinister smile. Malevolent energy emanated from him, and I knew it should raise the tiny hairs on my body, but I was unaffected. I'd been growing closer to the darkness, getting more comfortable with it. Dark things didn't affect me anymore like they'd used to. I knew Damien's reaction should bother me, but I couldn't bring myself to care. I only cared about revenge, and Damien could help me get it.

"So, what do you say?" I asked him.

"Well, Sophie...to accomplish what you want, you need

powerful magic, and powerful magic rarely comes without a price—"

"I'll do whatever it takes," I interjected. I would not stop now. And I wouldn't be stopped, either.

"Whatever it takes..." Damien murmured, his gaze dropping to the Tear on my chest. "You know a thing or two about sacrifices, don't you." A statement, not a question.

"I do," I said, as a cold feeling of foreboding flared in my chest. I ignored it. "So, what sacrifice will I have to make this time?"

"We'll get to that," Damien said, with another chilling smile.

I couldn't help but feel like I was exactly where he wanted me to be. He was looking at me like a spider who'd trapped a fly in its web. What his agenda was, I had no idea, but as long as I was getting what I wanted, I didn't care.

"First, you need to use your magic to track the other clan leaders. Whom do you want to hunt down first?" Damien asked.

It really didn't matter; they would all die in the end.

"Emeric." I blurted out the first name that came to mind.

"Very well," Damien drawled darkly. "Close your eyes and concentrate. Now that you know how to glimmer...very impressive, by the way. This is very similar. Picture the vampire you want to find and cast your magic out, but instead of focusing on one place, cast it wide like a net. Imagine its tendrils reaching far and wide, looking for the one you want to find."

With a nod, I closed my eyes and called upon my magic. It flared to life, slithering through my veins. The rush I felt was both powerful and overwhelming in the most beautiful way. Concentrating, I pulled on the dark, pulsing strings of my power, gathering them in my center. I imagined holding the shadowy threads in my hands like a net a moment before I cast them out.

Like trails of dark blood, they began spreading outward...on the hunt for my next victim. As the black rivers of my magic poured out into my surroundings, I felt the darkness inside me sink in deeper. It burrowed into my flesh and settled in my heart, but I wasn't concerned. I knew it was a give-and-take. The darkness gave me power, and I had to give something in return. Perhaps that was the sacrifice Damien had mentioned. Even if it was, I was prepared to pay the price if it meant keeping Henry safe.

My eyes moved under my eyelids as the tendrils of my magic searched, pushing and prodding, sniffing and tasting, looking for Emeric. Suddenly, I gasped, and my eyes flew open—they'd found him. I knew where he was.

"He's hiding out in the Maivayan Mountains," I declared.

"Excellent." Damien's glossy black eyes shone brighter. "Are you ready?"

"Yes," I said, as my pulse quickened in anticipation.

My mouth watered as if I could taste the blood I was going to spill. I closed my eyes and felt my skin tingle and hum as the shadows of my magic began churning around me, about to take me to my destination. Before they could, though, Celeste's voice reached me from my right.

"Sophie?" she said urgently, and my eyes snapped open. The space in front of me was empty; Damien was no longer standing there.

"To whom were you speaking?" Celeste asked.

I turned to the witch and found her watching me, her luminous blue eyes narrowed in suspicion.

"Damien," I told her. I didn't see a reason to lie anymore. "Agatha's son. He's been helping me with my magic. Doing what you've failed to do—helping me grow stronger."

Celeste's warm complexion became leached of all color in the light of the moon.

"Agatha doesn't have a son," she said. "And there is no one by that name in the village."

A strange feeling washed over me at her words. I knew what she'd said was the truth. Deep down, I'd known it all along. Terror didn't seize me like it should. Instead, I felt numb. What

Celeste had revealed would not change what I was going to do next. I wouldn't let it. I would have my revenge, consequences be damned.

"How long have you been communicating with this…being?" Celeste asked in a hollow voice.

"A few days. He was willing to help me when you weren't."

"Help you? Sophie, whatever he said…whatever he promised you—"

"He didn't promise me anything. He simply told me how to tap into my magic, using my emotions."

"Emotions? We don't use our emotions because doing so makes magic unpredictable."

"Even if it does, it's better than no magic at all."

"You're wrong…what emotions did he tell you to channel to bring your magic forth?"

Her bright blue eyes narrowed to thin slits, but the question was not truly a question—she already knew the answer.

"It doesn't matter. What matters is, it worked. I was able to save Henry."

"But at what cost?"

"Do you still not understand? The price doesn't matter. I would do anything for him."

"You are blinded by your love for him."

"No, I see more clearly now. My ancestors suffered so much and for what? I rid the world of the Dark Witches, but the humans are still not free. I will free them when I destroy the clans."

"Don't masquerade your thirst for revenge as a noble cause."

"Why can't it be both?"

"Because only one will set you free. The other one will make you a prisoner to the darkness."

"What do you know about the darkness, witch?" I challenged.

"Enough to know it's tempting you. Don't give in to it, Sophie. Because if you do, there will be no going back."

"See, that's the problem with you, Celeste. You always tell me what I *shouldn't* do. Always imposing limits."

"Limits are what keep this world in balance."

"Limits almost cost Henry his life! I almost lost him!" I shouted.

"But you didn't. Though now, you are at risk of losing your soul." Celeste said. Her voice was still measured in spite of my outburst.

"I'm a vampire. Who knows if I still have my soul," I pointed out.

"Don't be so eager to condemn yourself."

"You're the one condemning me."

"No, I'm the one trying to save you from yourself."

"I don't need saving!" I threw the words in her face as I summoned my shadows.

"Sophie, wait!" Celeste lunged for me. She grabbed my tunic, but I shook her off and glimmered out, leaving her behind in the woods.

When I appeared on the tallest peak in the Maivayan Mountains, my skin instantly prickled with awareness. The sunrise was approaching; I could feel it. My breath caught as I took in the view below me, my gaze gliding over the tapestry of valleys and peaks bathed in the glow of the moon. The light from the stars sluiced over the steep slopes and sharp, jagged ridges. I lifted my eyes to the night sky. It stretched indefinitely, making me feel infinite as I stood on the peak, barely feeling the harsh wind whipping around me.

My gaze trained on the horizon, I thought about Henry. I wondered how he would feel if he could watch the dawn from this height. It had to be devastatingly beautiful from this vantage point as the sun crested the horizon, open and unobscured. I wished that Henry could experience it. What I wouldn't give to see his face bathed in the first rays of a new day. But while my new powers made me feel limitless, some things were still out of my reach.

"Beautiful, isn't it?" I heard Damien say to my left.

"You lied to me." I glanced at him.

"About some things, yes. I didn't lie about your power. You feel it, don't you?"

"I do."

"And now you know who I am."

"I do."

"Does it scare you?"

I thought it over for a moment.

"No. I'm learning that nothing really scares me anymore," I said, rolling the shadowy tendrils of my magic over my knuckles.

"Ah, but that's not entirely true, is it? You're scared of losing Henry." Potent fear pierced my heart at his words.

"I won't lose him." My brows pinched. "No one will ever get close to him to make that even a possibility."

"And what are you prepared to do to ensure that?"

"Anything." There was no hesitation, only resolve. Celeste thought my love for Henry blinded me, but she was wrong. I'd never been so sure about my purpose before. Even when I'd thought that saving humanity was the most important mission of my life, I'd been wrong. Fighting for Henry and our future together was the only thing that truly mattered.

"Excellent." The word left Damien in a strange mix between a hiss and a whisper. "Let's get started. You know where he is?"

I nodded. "He's hiding in a cave on the right side of the mountain."

"He's not alone," Damien said, and my brows shot up. That was news to me.

"He brought his clan with him?"

Damien nodded. "All five of them."

Emeric's wife and daughters. I'd met them all before. A part of me wished he hadn't brought them here, because by doing so, he'd sentenced them to death, but another part—the bloodthirsty one—rejoiced that he had. There was duality inside of me —a human heart against a vampire's viciousness. The battle of warring emotions ensued but didn't last long as the vampire side prevailed, squelching the human one. Damien watched me closely, as if waiting to see if what he'd told me about Emeric's family being here would change my mind.

I squared my shoulders and lifted my chin. "What are we waiting for?"

26

I'd thought Damien would follow me to the cave, but he didn't, and I was glad for it—this was something I needed to do on my own.

The cavernous space was bigger and wider than I'd expected. It was no ordinary cave—it was a shelter. Perhaps Emeric had always had it, or perhaps he'd had it prepared right before the impending war with the Dark Witches, anticipating that he might have to go into hiding. I couldn't help but wonder if he'd planned to abandon the fight once he saw we were losing. Fucking coward. The spineless bastard deserved to die.

"You," Emeric breathed, his eyes widening in panic when I stepped out of the shadows in the middle of the cave illuminated by lanterns. "Flee. Now!" He shouted for his family to run.

"Not so fast," I said calmly, when the five of them rushed for the exit.

The rough walls shuddered as I unleashed my power, collapsing some of the rock to seal the vampires away from their freedom. They collided with the jagged stone, trying to break free, but their supernatural strength was no match for my powers, which blocked the only exit like a barrier.

Emeric stood unmoving before me while his family darted around the cave, trying to find another way out. They thrashed in the confined space for several long minutes as Emeric and I stared at each other. I knew they wouldn't be able to escape. He knew it, too. Despair mixed with resignation settled into his perfect features. He didn't beg me to spare their lives, and I wondered if he could see it in my face—that begging was pointless, and I would show no mercy. A few seconds passed before his wife and daughters stopped searching for a way out of the cave that would soon become their grave. The smell of their blood from where they'd cut themselves on the sharp rock permeated the air. Heady notes of fear were mixed in the scent, and I inhaled deeply, reveling in it.

"Mercy," came a quiet, weeping voice from behind Emeric.

My gaze tore from his and stretched behind him to his youngest daughter, Julia. She sat on the cave floor, huddled together with her mother and sisters, who were all wailing as if they were in mourning. And perhaps they were—they were mourning their eternal lives that would soon be cut short. By me.

"Mercy?" I curled my lip in a sneer.

"You have to understand. It was all Camilla," Emeric said vehemently, snapping my attention back to him.

"You were on the border when she had Henry on a leash like a fucking dog, and you did nothing!" I shouted, my voice echoing off the cave walls.

Emeric flinched but held my gaze.

"If you do this," he said quietly. "You will be no better than her, than me, than all of us."

A menacing laughter escaped me. "You're right. I'm not better than you, and for the first time ever, I don't want to be. To fight monsters like you, I have to become a monster myself." Tears gathered in Emeric's eyes as the wailing behind him grew louder. I stepped closer to him, bringing my face inches away from his as

I whispered, "You and your family will die, and it will be all your fault. Just remember, you turned me into this."

Emeric's throat bobbed as he swallowed when I pulled away. The tears spilled, gliding down his pale cheeks. Without taking my eyes off him, I lifted my hand and used my magic to move the stones blocking the cave's exit as if they weighed nothing. Emeric's gaze darted to the opening before snapping back to me. My lips curved into a savage smile as I wrapped him in the tendrils of my power and flung him out of the cave. Moving my hands like a puppeteer to manipulate the strings of my magic, I slammed Emeric against the outside of the cave, his back to the jagged, rough surface. Black spikes shot out from the rock, spearing through his legs and arms and pinning him to the slope of the mountain. A strangled cry left him before everything went quiet. He was still alive, but he wouldn't be for long.

A hushed silence settled over the place as Emeric's family watched me with wide eyes. I stared back, still wearing a deranged smile on my face. It turned into a grin when the first rays of sunlight spilled over the horizon, and Emeric's screams of agony filled the cave. Still smiling, I closed my eyes and let the sound wash over me. In a strange, cathartic way, it replaced the sounds I'd heard Henry make when he'd been held captive and tortured by the clan leaders. Emeric's screams didn't erase those memories completely—nothing ever would—but hearing them did make breathing easier somehow.

Emeric's death was over all too soon, and the darkness within me was not satiated. It demanded more blood, urging me to slaughter his family in the most horrific way. I fought the twisted desire, resisting the darkness as something inside me was holding me back from surrendering to it completely. The darkness tried to overpower me again, and when it did, my feet moved as if of their own accord to step toward Emeric's family, who were still huddled together, watching me, waiting for their death to come.

My fingers elongated into claws, but before I could begin

ripping them to shreds, Henry's face appeared in my mind. I froze as I stared at him. He stared back, begging me to leave this place without going through with what the darkness drove me to do. A battle ensued inside me as I felt conflicted. The darkness pushed but I pushed back, my gaze latched on to Henry's face in my mind. I didn't know which side of me I wanted to prevail. The pressure inside me built until I couldn't take it anymore. With a snarl, I shoved the darkness aside and glimmered out, but not before collapsing the cave and burying Emeric's family underneath.

My shadows took me to my childhood home, to the corner in my mother's study, where I knew the sunlight wouldn't reach me. Damien hadn't followed me here, either, for which I was grateful—darkness didn't scare me anymore, but it didn't mean I wanted to bring it here, to this place where I'd been a child, innocent and sweet, before I'd turned into…this. I tucked into the corner, sitting on the floor with my knees close to my chest and my back propped against the hard wall. The sunlight drifted through the small window above my mother's desk, bathing a part of the room in a soft, warm glow. I glared at the sun rays, my lips peeled back in a snarl.

How could I truly become the most powerful being if I had to hide in the shadows, curled into a ball, trying to occupy as little space as possible? I hissed at the sunlight as if the vicious sound would chase it away. Pathetic. No wonder the clans had refused to slink back into the shadows after I'd defeated the Dark Witches. They wanted to keep ruling this world, prowling around freely like the apex predators that they were. My brows pulled together at the thought. Was I beginning to think like the monsters I was trying to destroy?

I knew the realization should disturb me, but it was hard to care when exhaustion pulled at my limbs, making my eyelids heavy. I knew this should also bother me—the fact that I was so relaxed and drifting off to sleep right after the heinous acts I'd just committed. But I couldn't bring myself to care. All I wanted to do was fall asleep because the darkness awaited me in my dreams, and I couldn't wait to reunite with it. I knew it was waiting for me with open arms, ready to wrap me in its embrace. I was ready to be enveloped in it, so, with a sigh of contentment, I closed my eyes and went to sleep.

HENRY

"Where is she?" I growled when Celeste reappeared in the kitchen.

"I couldn't convince her to see reason," the witch replied.

"You should have taken me with you!" I raised my voice, failing to keep my frustration in check.

When Celeste had picked up on Sophie's location, she had disappeared in the blink of an eye. Glimmering, they called it. A magic trick I was growing increasingly annoyed with. My supernatural speed was no match for the witches' ability to warp from one place to the next.

"I didn't bring you with me because Sophie is dangerous."

"She is not a danger to me."

"You don't understand. You have only glimpsed a fraction of her power. Her magic is deadly."

"The more reason for me to find her and bring her home. Do you know where she is?"

Celeste didn't respond for a few seconds as if contemplating if she wanted to disclose that information.

"I have a way of tracking her," she finally said. "I will gather a few witches from the village to help me trap her."

"Trap her? She's not a fucking animal!" I seethed.

"I know she's not, but she is not herself."

"Just tell me where she is so I can go to her," I asked with a breath of frustration.

"I would advise against it—"

"I don't fucking care what you advise!" I didn't realize I'd moved until my face was mere inches from the witch's, my fingers digging into her flesh where I was clasping her bony shoulders.

"Control your temper," Celeste said low. Her voice wavered slightly, letting me know my outburst had rattled her stony facade. "I will tell you where she is, but there is nothing you can do at the moment. The sun is rising."

My skin prickled at her words as the muscles along my shoulders tensed. I didn't need to glance at the small kitchen window to know she was right. Swiftly, I let go of her and retreated into the shadowy hallway separating the kitchen from the living room. Without saying a word, Celeste turned and walked to the window, pulling the faded green curtains closed.

"Let's get some rest," she said when she faced me again. "We will devise a plan of action in the evening."

"Tell me where she is," I said low. "Please."

Celeste's shrewd cerulean eyes flickered over my face.

"She's at her father's home in New Haven," she said. "Don't do anything foolish."

I didn't respond before I turned around and walked off, knowing full well I couldn't make that promise.

27

SOPHIE

*M*y eyes flew open—he was here.
How did he find me?

My muscles locked up as I met Henry's deep-blue gaze. He was sitting on his haunches, peering down at me where I was slumped against the wall on the floor. The night had descended, and moonlight had replaced the sunlight seeping through the window. The silvery sheen caressed one side of Henry's face, highlighting his harsh, unyielding features. Tension bracketed his mouth, and shadows crawled behind his eyes. Not the shadows I'd been growing close with. They were shadows of concern and apprehension. I didn't want him to be concerned for me. He didn't need to be concerned about anything in his life anymore. I would ensure that nothing and no one ever touched him again.

"How did you find me?" I asked, severing the tense silence between us.

"I will always find you. Even if you don't realize you're lost,"

Henry replied softly. Despite his quiet tone, determination dripped from every word as if he was making an unbreakable vow.

"I'm not lost, but found. All the pieces of who I am finally fit together," I told him, hoping he'd understand.

Concern in his stormy blue eyes intensified.

"But this is not who you are. There is light inside of you, remember?"

"What good is that light? It did nothing to fend off the shadows. I was only able to come for you when I embraced the inner darkness. It helped me save you and bring you home."

"You would have found another way. That way just seemed easier. But that's what the darkness wants you to believe. That things are easier with it by your side. But nothing worth having should come easily."

"Why not? Don't we deserve it? After everything we've been through?"

Henry pulled away slightly, his already pale face growing ashen. He was looking at me like he had back at the estate after we'd made love, like he didn't recognize who was in front of him. The look hurt me. How could he look at me like that? Didn't he know that everything I had done was for him?

"It's the hard times that make us who we are," he finally said, his voice hoarse.

I shook my head. "Not anymore. I refuse to accept that when there is another way."

"Sophie, the darkness is not the way."

His words did something to me, stroking something in me that raised my hackles. It was as if the darkness reared its head and hissed at what he was suggesting.

"You need to leave," I snarled, not recognizing my own voice. The sound was rough and guttural, coming from deep within my throat. Before, I'd wanted to never be apart from Henry, but now

I couldn't stand being near him because he was trying to hold me back like Celeste had done.

"I'm not leaving here without you," he said fiercely, his features becoming even more unyielding in the moonlight.

"Then I'll go," I told him, rising from my spot on the floor.

"Where will you go?" he asked, rising to his full height and towering over me. "What happened yesterday after you left me?"

I flinched at his words because they made it sound like I'd abandoned him.

"I didn't *leave* you," I bit out. "I will come back to you once this is over."

"What *is* this exactly? A quest for revenge?"

"You can call it what you want."

"Then I will call it what it is—madness… Sophie, you're not yourself—"

"Stop saying that," I hissed, throwing him a scathing look. "Stop saying I'm not myself. I'm the only one who knows who I truly am."

Shock splashed across his face before deep sorrow settled into his features.

"I'm sorry," he rasped.

"What?" I asked in confusion.

"I'm sorry I had to leave your side."

A strangled sound left me.

"You're apologizing for leaving my side? You didn't choose that, Henry. You were torn away from me and tortured. You can't apologize for that."

"Circumstances do not matter. I'm still sorry I couldn't be there when you needed me the most."

"I need you now. I needed you yesterday when I—" The air got snagged in my throat.

Henry's eyes narrowed. "When you what? Sophie, what did you do?" he asked, stepping closer and caging me in.

"I did what had to be done." I lifted my chin. "I avenged your pain and suffering."

Henry swallowed thickly. "What did you do?" he asked again as his nostrils flared. "Emeric," he said low, picking up on the vampire's faint scent on me. "Is he—"

"Dead. He burned with the rising sun, pinned to the slope of the mountain in his region. The same mountain I brought down on the rest of his clan who were with him."

Henry sucked in a sharp breath, staggering back as if my words had scorched him.

"You killed them all?" he asked quietly, as if it pained him to say it aloud.

"I did." Emeric's family might still be alive, but they were as good as dead, trapped under the rubble with no way to feed or escape. "And I'd do it again. I *will* do it again when I find the remaining clan leaders."

"You're—"

"A monster. I know. But if you think that scares me, you're mistaken."

"It should scare you. It should terrify you."

"You know what I'm terrified of? Losing you."

"I don't want to lose you, either, but it feels like that is what's happening right now. I'm losing you to the darkness."

Oh, how mistaken he was.

"Do not be afraid," I said, reaching up to cup his face. He flinched at my touch as if it burned him, and my heart twisted at his reaction. "I'll be back when I'm done killing the ones who hurt you."

"Let me help you," he begged, his eyes pleading.

Excitement flared in my chest. "Help me? Do you want to help me hunt them down?"

"No. I want you to stay here with me so I can help you fight the darkness."

"Fight the darkness? I no longer fight the darkness. It fights *with* me, helping me defeat our enemies. We are on the same side."

"No, that's just what the darkness wants you to believe."

"And I believe it. I do," I told him, lowering my hands from his cheeks.

He moved then, clasping the back of my neck and my waist, resting his forehead against mine.

"Please, let me help you. If you want me to beg on my knees, I will. I don't want to lose you."

"You won't," I assured him before I kissed him.

He kissed me back deeply, hungrily, and I melted into him, my hands fisting in his shirt. A whimpering sound escaped when he bit my lower lip, drawing blood. The sweet taste mixed with the rich and smoky flavor of him invaded my senses, setting them on fire. I became desperate for him, every stroke of my tongue a plea and a demand. He pushed me back against the wall and lifted me up so I could wrap my legs around his lower back. A harsh groan left him when he rocked his hips into me, and I gasped against his lips as desire pulsed between my thighs.

Was he as desperate for me as I was for him? I thought he looked at me differently now, but perhaps the primal, wild part of him was drawn to my dark side, excited by the violent acts I'd committed. Unless…he was just trying to distract me; to keep me here, wrapped up in him for as long as he could. A part of me wanted to give in, to lose myself in him, but the burning desire in my blood quickly turned to ice. Right now, my thirst for revenge was stronger than my hunger for Henry. I abruptly broke the kiss, dropping my feet to the floor and shoving at his hard chest to put some distance between us. His black eyes were wide as he stared at me, breathing heavily.

"We'll be back together soon," I promised, glimmering out before I could change my mind and stay in his arms forever.

. . .

"I've been waiting for you," Damien said, when I appeared in the central region of the country, known as the Lowlands.

It was Lena's domain and consisted mostly of vast and flat patches of land. We stood in the middle of one right now. The plain stretched for miles, the endless green interrupted by only a few trees.

"There was an unexpected distraction," I said, wincing at my own words.

Henry was so much more than a distraction...but right now, he was a distraction from my mission. My mind was a bit hazy from what he and I had just shared. Absentmindedly, I lifted my hand up to my face and ran my fingertips over my lower lip, where the bite mark he'd given me was healing.

"Are you still distracted now?" Damien asked, watching me closely.

My gaze snapped to his black, cavernous eyes.

"No," I assured him, telling myself to focus. "Do you know where she is?" I asked, taking a sweeping look around the moonlight-drenched field.

In a rush to leave Henry before my feelings for him could overpower my need for revenge, I'd cast my magic out, searching for Lena, but the spell had not been as clean and precise as the one I'd used to locate Emeric. My shadows had brought me here, and while I could sense I was in the general vicinity of my next victim, I couldn't pinpoint exactly where she was.

"She's right under our feet," Damien said in a hushed tone.

My brows climbed my forehead as I looked down. An underground shelter? The question was on the tip of my tongue, but I stopped myself from asking. I needed to learn to read the threads instead of relying on Damien to give me answers. Closing my eyes, I took a deep breath, focusing on the world around me. As always, sounds rushed in, chaotic and disorientating, making it difficult to concentrate. I pushed through the noise, and sooner than I'd expected, a web of shimmering strings appeared in my mind. Tiny, pulsating bursts of light flickered along them, and I began picking out individual strands, following where they led.

Several failed attempts later, I picked out a thread that arced down, disappearing into the ground close to where I stood. Tilting my head to the side, I latched on to the thread and imagined myself seeping into the ground along with it. Down and down we went until we reached a crypt-like chamber. So Emeric hadn't been the only one preparing a shelter before the war. My lip curled in disgust. I no longer thought of the clan vampires as apex predators. They were more like insects, hiding in caves and underground.

Lena sat on the stone bench in the middle of the crypt, her copper hair glowing in the light of the oil lamp. Her gaze was cast down to her lap, where a small portrait of the rest of her clan rested on top of her emerald skirts. She appeared to be waiting for me, and I wasn't sure if the portrait was a ploy to appeal to my softer, human side or if she simply wanted to spend the last minutes of her life with her family, without actually bringing them here.

Disappointment washed over me when I saw she was alone, because that meant only her blood would be spilled tonight. I recoiled at the thought as soon as it entered my mind. I shouldn't feel disappointment, only relief, but the depraved, twisted part of me wanted there to be more victims. Suddenly, I felt a pang in my chest and a tug on my heart, pulling me to go back to Henry, because he could shelter me from such disturbing thoughts. As if sensing my hesitation, the darkness slithered over my shoulders, wrapping me in its protective shroud until I wasn't scared of my thoughts anymore. My thirst for blood was not something to fear, it whispered. It was a part of me, of my vampire nature.

Perhaps I'd suppressed it for too long. Doing so had made me appear weak, allowing the clan leaders to swoop in and take advantage. Maybe if I would have let the monster out sooner, all that had transpired could have been avoided. There was no point in dwelling on the past, though. I had to focus on the future—a future where all my enemies were eradicated and turned to dust.

I quickly followed the thread back to the surface and rallied my magic. Raw power surged, thrumming through my veins. Shadows thickened all around me, pouring out of me and blanketing the ground. The earth began to shake beneath my feet. Lena had made this too easy, really. She'd practically dug out her own grave. Opening my eyes, I looked at Damien standing beside me. His eyes were closed, his chin lifted. He looked enraptured as if he were feeding from the darkness that now surrounded us, soaking it in until it slithered just below the surface of his skin. When he opened his eyes and looked at me, they were entirely black, like two glossy, obsidian pools.

"Finish this," he hissed. "Rain death and destruction on your enemy."

Lips stretching into a sinister smile, I did what he'd instructed. My magic blasted from me, collapsing the ground underneath. Lena's muffled screams tore through the night as the twisted shadows of my magic lashed at her skin and broke her bones, grinding them until nothing was left of them but dust. I glimmered out, jumping into the void, to reappear a few miles away from where a deep, bowl-shaped cavity had appeared on the site of the collapse. Damien glimmered in next to me a moment later.

"Where to next?" he asked.

His features sharpened, making him look almost reptilian, and I half-expected a forked tongue to dart out of his mouth.

"Yvonne's domain. She's the last one left," I told him, feeling a pang of disappointment that my quest for revenge would soon be over.

But can it truly be over while the others live? the darkness whispered.

It was right. The rest of the clans were still out there, and they all deserved to die for what their leaders had done.

Yes, the darkness whispered in my ear, low and seductive.

Smiling, I turned my face into its shadowy caress.

"Are you ready?" Damien asked, and I nodded.

I'd been born for this. Who would have known that spreading death would make me feel so alive?

HENRY

She'd wanted to stay; I could feel it, but the darkness had pulled her back, dragging her right out of my arms. I was losing her. She was slipping through my fingers. No matter how hard I tried to hold on, I couldn't make her see reason. I couldn't make her choose me over the darkness. My heart shattered at the thought. Perhaps I had overestimated her love for me.

No, I quickly squashed the thought.

I believed in our love and in her. She was lost, but she would find herself again, and I would help her. Even if I had to forfeit my own life. She was mine, and I would not give up on her. The darkness was strong, but our love was stronger. I had to believe that.

"Where is she?" I demanded, as I stormed into the cottage.

Celeste wasn't alone. A young witch with thick red hair stood up from the sofa when I walked in. Her bright green eyes widened as she took me in.

"I'm not telling you," Celeste said, also rising to her feet from the sofa.

"Damn it, witch, I need to know!" I demanded again, my deep voice booming in the small living room.

"Why? So you can go after her alone again? We were supposed to devise a plan—"

"I have a plan. It is to save Sophie."

"Seeing how you have returned without her, your plan is not working," Celeste pointed out.

"It *will* work. I just need to talk to her again. I'm the only one who can make her see reason."

"And what if you don't?" Celeste challenged.

"I will not even consider that possibility," I bit out.

"Well, you should. Sometimes, they are too far gone and cannot be saved."

They? My brows knitted in confusion.

"She will never be too far gone. I will *always* bring her back."

Celeste shook her head, her expression grim.

"You are as blinded by your love for her as she is by her love for you."

My frown deepened. What Celeste was saying sounded a lot like she wanted me to give up on Sophie, and I would never give up on her.

"Just tell me where she is. Please."

"No," the witch said, unyielding. "Amelie and I are going to the village to gather a few more witches, and then we are going after Sophie. If we are able to bring her here, you will get a chance to try and convince her to see reason and accept our help."

"She will not come willingly."

"I know, that's why I'm going to bring others with me."

"So you can force her into submission?!" I raised my voice as my heart sank. I couldn't bear the thought of them hurting Sophie…or worse.

"We'll do what's necessary."

"No! Just…" I ran my hands through my hair in frustration. "Let me try one more time."

"We can't afford for you to try again. Her power is dark and dangerous. It has to be contained before it's too late. The longer we wait, the more powerful she will become."

"At least let me come with you," I begged.

"No. Wait here and hope that we can bring her back," Celeste said, her tone final.

She looked at the young witch then and nodded—a cue for them to leave. I stood frozen in place, feeling utterly powerless as Celeste disappeared from the living room. The other witch remained behind, and when our gazes locked, her emerald eyes were full of sympathy and understanding.

"She's on the Durand Estate," she whispered quickly before she glimmered out.

28

SOPHIE

The Tear pulsed on my chest, casting a pale-blue glow into the night around me as I stood before the Durand Estate, the mansion ominous and dark. My shadows had brought me here. Yvonne had not hunkered down somewhere as Emeric and Lena had done. She was waiting for me inside her clan home, and I couldn't decide if I found that admirable or extremely foolish.

"She didn't run and hide," I said, more to myself than to Damien standing beside me.

He smirked. "She knew there was nowhere for her to go where your magic couldn't reach." His pitch-black gaze focused on me. "How does it feel to be so feared? As a vampire, you were impossibly strong and fast, but with black magic flowing through your veins, you're virtually unstoppable."

I did feel unstoppable, but I also felt…cold and detached. The feeling reminded me of when I'd projected myself into Stern's lair in my dream. I'd floated like an apparition outside of my own body then, and it felt like I was doing so now. I was simply an observer, watching myself carry out my revenge with cold indifference and without emotional attachment. I still felt things...like loathing and fury directed toward the clans, but I was losing sight of why I was waging this war. I knew I couldn't stop, though—the darkness wouldn't let me.

"Sophie?" Damien asked, drawing my attention to him. "Are you ready to finish this?"

"Finish it? Oh, this is not the end. I'm only getting started." The words escaped, and I had no idea where they'd come from. My voice was eerie and dark, like smoke and shadows.

Damien threw his head back and laughed, the menacing sound ringing out in the night.

"You *are* just getting started," he said, when he looked at me again. "You're the beginning, Sophie. Together, we will show the others the ultimate power they can achieve if only they give in."

"Give in?" I asked, confused.

"To the darkness. As you have," he explained, matter of fact.

The light inside me sputtered at his words.

That's strange, I thought, my brows knitting.

I hadn't realized that light still burned. A part of me wanted to put my hands protectively around it and nurture it back to full strength, but that part was tiny and weak. It was buried deep inside and easy to ignore. The bigger, stronger part of me wanted to let the light go out. After all, Henry was the keeper of the light, and he wasn't here. If he was really that concerned about me, he would have found me again by now. The tiny, weak part of me hoped that he still would, but the bigger part wanted him to stay away.

The darkness feared him, I realized. Was it afraid he could still pull me from its embrace? Because he couldn't, I was sure of it. I just hoped he would eventually learn to love that side of me. After all, I'd changed for him...to better protect him from the dangers of this world. Speaking of...

My eyes narrowed, and my ears perked up as I listened for any sound coming from the mansion. All was quiet, but the silence felt unnatural. It reminded me of the Black Forest, where predators roamed in the hushed stillness, veiled by the darkness.

A heartbeat later, they came out of nowhere, converging on me much like the forest creatures had done the first time I'd faced them without the hex bag in my pocket. Ravagers. About a dozen or so. At the first sight of them, Damien glimmered out, leaving me alone and surrounded. I wasn't scared, though—my shadows were ready. They rushed out from all around me, splintering in different directions to fend off the feral vampires when they attacked.

Some of the Ravagers darted toward me, while others scuttled closer, crouching low to the ground. A few launched themselves at me, their fangs and claws gleaming, as they flew through the air. The black vines of my magic were there to defend me. They speared the Ravagers in the air and twisted around the ones on the ground, tearing the limbs and breaking the bones. I didn't need to lift a finger as I stood unmoving in the middle of the courtyard in front of the mansion. Death reigned all around me, and I was its Queen. After my shadows had snuffed out the last cry of agony, an unearthly silence settled over the place.

Several moments passed as I waited for what would happen next. If Yvonne had known better than to run and hide, surely she hadn't thought that little diversion would stop me. The sound of a door opening snapped my attention to the mansion's grand entrance. Yvonne emerged from the darkness of the house a moment later. The whites of her wide-set eyes stood out against the blackness of the night and the golden-brown tone of her skin. Her face was a sickly pallor, her thickly curled hair disheveled as if she'd run her hands through it too many times.

"We need to talk," she said, her amber eyes fastening on me. Her low and husky voice wavered.

"Talk?" I smirked. "Let me guess, you're going to blame everything on Camilla?"

"No." Yvonne shook her head. "It was her plan, yes, but I helped her carry it out. We all did." She paused, and swallowed audibly. I heard her heart speed up in her chest as her breathing hitched. In the next moment, I knew why. "I am willing to pay for my actions. But the rest of the clan doesn't have to. Spare them, I beg you."

My gaze stretched to the dark house behind Yvonne before returning to her.

"I have to admit I admire your courage. You're the only one who had the guts to face me like this."

Yvonne's face paled even more in the moonlight. Silence stretched for a few seconds until she found her voice again.

"Does my courage buy my clan's freedom?" she asked, lifting her chin.

"Freedom? No. But they can have a head start if they choose to flee." I raised my voice for the next part so the ones inside the house could hear me. "They should do so now because once I'm finished with you, I'll be going after them."

Shadows erupted from the mansion at my words. Not shadows—vampires—moving with supernatural speed. They fled through the windows and side and back doors. The exodus was over quickly, and a shuddering exhale left Yvonne when the last of her clan had fled the estate. Her eyes glimmered with tears as she lifted them up to the night sky. I followed her gaze, momentarily lost in the star-studded canvas.

"It's a beautiful night to die," I said, lowering my gaze to Yvonne's face.

My right arm shot out in front of me, and the shadowy vines of my magic darted out, quickly crossing the distance between us. They wrapped around Yvonne's throat, and a strangled sound left her as she gripped the torc of churning shadows around her neck. Her bulging eyes settled on me as she thrashed in my magic's hold. She might have accepted her fate when she'd turned herself in, but the survival instinct was impossible to ignore. It still urged her to fight for her life, so she did, even though it was futile. The fingers on my right hand curled, and the vines followed my will, twisting tighter around Yvonne's neck. She clawed at the shadows, her razor-sharp talons slicing through the black tendrils and flaying her skin. Blood gushed out of the open wounds, its sweet scent filling the air. I ducked my chin and bared my fangs as my vampire side reared her head at the tantalizing smell.

"Stop!" came Henry's voice from behind me.

It echoed in the courtyard, interrupting the hushed quiet. The grip of my magic still tight on Yvonne's throat, I glanced over my shoulder. Henry stood a few feet away, his chest rising and falling rapidly. He must have run here.

How did he find me again? Suddenly, I felt the weight of the hex bag in my left pants pocket. My mind flashed back to the last time I'd seen Celeste. The witch had lunged for me before I'd glimmered out. She must have dropped the hex bag in my pocket. How had I not felt its weight until now?

You wanted him to find you, a tiny voice whispered in my head, but the darkness quickly silenced it.

"Stop?!" I threw over my shoulder at Henry. "Why would you ask me to stop? How can you not want to inflict the same pain and suffering they inflicted on you?" The words came out rough and guttural. I could have sworn it was the darkness forcing them out of me.

"Believe me, I do," he rasped, stepping closer to me. "And I am honored that you want to fight for me so fiercely. But if we give in to this urge to do to them as they did to us, what makes us better than them?"

"Maybe we're not," I said, and Henry's face fell, shock splashing across his features. "We're vampires, Henry. We're monsters, just like the rest of them. We just hide it better."

"How can you say that? Are you even hearing yourself?" he asked low, his voice hoarse. "This..." His deep-blue gaze flicked over me. "This is not you."

Those words again. I hated them.

"Is it not? Because I feel more myself now than I ever had before. Perhaps this has been me all along. It's time I stopped fighting my true nature."

"This is not your true nature, and if you will not fight for who you truly are, then I will."

"I will not let you stand in my way," I hissed, narrowing my eyes at him.

"Then, you will have to fight me, but I will fight for you. I will not lose you."

"Lose me?" I angled my head, my brows drawing together.

"To the darkness. It's consuming you. Can't you feel it? I will not let you succumb to it. The light inside you...it's still there. I can see it. Even if you can't see it for yourself."

My upper lip curled as I said, my voice dripping with disdain, "That light was extinguished when the clans captured you. And to be honest, I don't mind. It would be a hindrance to what I need to do. I don't need the light. I only need the darkness. Perhaps you're right, and it's trying to consume me, but I won't let it. I'm in control."

Henry's taut features softened just a fraction as a mix of horror and pity washed over his face. "But darling, you are not in control. Not anymore."

Yvonne made a choking noise in front of me, snapping my attention back to her. Henry was wrong—I felt in control as I held her worthless life in my hand.

"Let her go," Henry ordered, coming to stand by my side.

Reluctantly, I dragged my gaze to him.

"Or what? You're going to make me?" I smirked.

He wouldn't hurt me, I knew that without a doubt. I still expected him to try to take me down, though. I was prepared for that. I wasn't prepared for what he did next. His touch was like a brand on my cold skin when he reached up and cupped my cheek.

"I love you," he said softly but with resolve.

The quiet words rolled through the courtyard like thunder, loud and clear.

The darkness inside me shuddered...before it lashed out.

I threw a punch with my right arm, but Henry blocked it. I wasn't worried about losing my grip on Yvonne—my shadows still encircled her throat, much like the collar they'd put on Henry when they'd held him captive. Pulling my arm back, I went to kick out, but Henry darted out of my reach. We began a dance, moving like smoke and shadows through the courtyard—two supernatural creatures colliding, stirring the cool night air. Henry was holding back, and it infuriated me, as I fought with everything I had, slashing my claws and snapping my fangs.

Frustration spiked. As a vampire, Henry was older and stronger than me, and it showed. He kept caging me in, hauling me to his powerful body, or pinning me down to the ground, all in an attempt to get in my face and talk to me, to make me hear reason. He was doing so right now, his face mere inches from mine. I was pinned to the ground, and he was kneeling beside me, his broad hand on my neck to hold me in place as gently as he could. His blue-black gaze flicked over me, taking in all the nicks and bruises from us exchanging blows. His expression turned pained before his gaze returned to my face. It was clear he hated hurting me. I hated being so weak that he *could* hurt me. I needed my magic. I hadn't used it until now because it was still preoccupied with Yvonne, holding her in its tight grip.

You also didn't want to hurt him, the tiny voice was back inside my head.

I snarled, thrashing under Henry's hold.

"Sophie, please," he bit out, anguish in his voice. "You have to stop. I don't want to hurt you."

"Hurt me?" I snarled. "I'm going to hurt you!"

I summoned my shadows. Like whips, they snapped from Yvonne and began hurling toward me. As soon as they let go, Yvonne crumpled to the ground, fighting for breath, blood dripping from the wounds she'd inflicted on herself.

The shadows wrapped around Henry, and I watched his eyes widen in shock a second before he was dragged to the side and slammed into the ground. Once his hand had left my throat, I swiftly jumped to my feet. Henry didn't stay down for long, popping back up and rushing toward me. He jerked to a stop inches away from me, his lips parting as a low, wheezing sound escaped. Our eyes locked and held, and there was so much in his gaze. Shock, dismay, longing, love…sorrow. Slowly, his gaze lowered, and I followed it down to his chest, to where my claws had sunk in so deep that my fingers were buried in his rib cage. His heart beat against my palm as if my fingers were wrapped around the organ. They weren't, but I held his life in my hand, nonetheless. Black magic slithered down my arm, pumping into Henry's body, boiling the blood in his veins and shattering his bones.

Suddenly, the veil of darkness lifted, and I realized what I was doing. I was hurting him. I was…killing him. With a sharp gasp, I pulled my hand back, my fingers leaving his chest with a sickening sound. Henry gasped, too, and went to drop to the ground, but I held him up, bringing him flush with me, the blood from his wound soaking into my tunic. His face was so close that we shared a breath.

"No, no, no," I whispered over and over again, as if the word were a chant, an incantation to turn back time, to undo what I'd done.

My shadows swirled around me, but they were no help—they couldn't take me back. Tears welled and spilled, burning as they rushed down my face. I wondered if they were black like tar. Black like my magic…like my soul.

"It will be okay," Henry whispered, blood bubbling up and spilling from his mouth, painting his perfect lips crimson.

It felt like I was bleeding with him. I was drowning in blood, choking on it, as my heart ruptured into a million pieces. Terror seized me as I stared into his dulling blue eyes, seeing my own demise. Life was bleeding out of him, and without him, I would cease to exist.

"I love you," Henry said, barely above a whisper, or maybe I only thought he did.

A keening, mournful sound tore from my throat as I slid to the ground with him a dead weight in my arms.

Darkness surrounded me. I was standing in the middle of it, completely and utterly alone. Only this time, it wasn't a dream. It was my reality.

29

"We can be together now," the darkness whispered. "Without him standing in our way."

A piercing sob escaped as I looked down at Henry. He lay unmoving in my arms, his beautiful blue eyes open but unseeing. So much blood. His blood was soaking my clothes and seeping into my skin. I knew I would never be able to wash it away. It would forever stain my body and my soul. I trembled as I stared down at him and wept, my tears landing on his perfect face. He hadn't decayed like the others, and I didn't know if it was a blessing or a curse. It was a blessing because he hadn't turned to dust, drifting through my fingers. I could still hold him in my arms. But it was also a curse, all for the same reason, because he was still here as if there was something I could do to bring him back. I knew I couldn't—his heart wasn't beating. It had stopped —*I'd* stopped it with my terrible magic.

When the darkness wrapped around my shoulders in an attempt to comfort me, I flinched away and shouted in a raw voice, "Get away from me! I don't want to be with you! I only want to be with him!"

The darkness recoiled at my outburst but didn't leave, lingering nearby.

"The heartbreak you're feeling right now is temporary," it whispered. "It will pass, but the power I offer you will last forever if only you give in."

"Forever?" I rasped, and the darkness whispered back a confirmation. "Forever means nothing if Henry is not by my side. I don't want forever without him."

"Foolish girl," the darkness seethed. "You don't understand your potential. You're stronger than most."

"You're wrong. I'm weak. I'm weak without him."

I *was* weak, wasn't I? I'd let the darkness warp my mind. I'd lost sight of who I was, and that had cost Henry his life, because he'd fought for me even when I hadn't been worth fighting for.

Perhaps I should give in and let the darkness swallow me whole. After all, there was nothing left for me in this world if Henry was no longer in it. Maybe if I gave in, the darkness would take away the pain. It would consume my soul, and without it, I wouldn't feel like my heart had been carved out of my chest. I would feel very little, if anything at all.

"Yes, give in," the darkness hissed, inching closer to where I was sitting on the ground, clutching Henry's body to mine.

I curled into him, trying to hide from the darkness, looking for his protection even though he could no longer offer it. Shadows swarmed around me, heavy and dark. Squeezing my eyes shut, I buried my head in Henry's chest, right above the gnarly wound I'd inflicted.

"Leave him. Come with me," came the darkness's eerie whisper in my ear.

Leave him? I would not leave him. I would remain here with him until the sun rose and turned us both to dust. We would go into the void together, where I would beg for his forgiveness. I would beg for eternity if I had to.

The shadows around me thickened, churning faster, creating

a vortex. They were trying to urge me to move, to let go of Henry's body. The merciless wind lashed at me, tearing at my clothes and whipping my hair. It felt like being in the middle of a storm. I sat unmoving, curled into Henry, my head on his hard chest. Focusing on his scent, I breathed him in and let the roaring sounds around me fade into the background. I created a cocoon around us in my mind, an impenetrable shield that protected us from the storm raging on the outside.

I wasn't sure how much time had passed as I sat there, holding Henry and listening to my own breathing and the beating of my heart. I didn't care, either. The sun would rise soon and put me out of my misery. Its warm rays would burn my skin and disintegrate my flesh and bones. I would welcome death because that was the only end I deserved after what I'd done.

Thump.

My breath snagged in my throat. I went incredibly still as I listened, shutting out the sound of my own heart. The thump I'd just heard...I was desperate to hear it again. I would do anything to hear it again, but silence reigned.

Must have been my imagination. I let the air whoosh out of my lungs. My mind was playing tricks on me.

Thump.

My eyes flew open, and I lifted my head from Henry's chest. Thick shadows still churned around us, but the wind had died down. The darkness had changed its tactic. It was being gentle now, licking my skin and caressing my hair. I ignored it, as all my attention zeroed in on Henry. His eyes were still glassy and unseeing, and I couldn't bear the sight of his empty gaze. With a shaking hand, I reached up and lowered his eyelids. Doing so brought some relief, because now I could pretend he was simply asleep and not...dead. A whimpering sound escaped as another wave of tears swept me under.

Violent sobs racked me for a few minutes until I got ahold of myself, taking a few steadying breaths. Trembling slightly, I lowered my head to Henry's chest again. His skin was cooler than usual when I placed my cheek on the spot above the wound. Closing my eyes, I stilled and listened as I prayed. I wasn't sure I believed in any gods, but at that moment, I prayed to all of them. I begged them to bring him back to me. Silence stretched, and I'd never loathed quiet so much in my life. My own heart beat loud in my chest, and I hated the sound. Mine was not the heartbeat I wanted to hear. I wished I could rip my heart out of my chest and give it to Henry so he could live. He deserved to live more than I did.

Thump.

A strangled cry erupted from me.

Henry's heart was strong and relentless like he was. Strong and relentless and...beating.

I lifted my head from his chest and opened my eyes.

"Stay away from me!" I hissed at the darkness, staring into the pitch-black shadows that surrounded us.

"Your soul is mine!" the darkness hissed back like a serpent.

"It's not, nor will it ever be! My soul belongs to him! I belong to him, *with* him, and he belongs with me!"

"You need me..."

"I don't need you! I have everything I need right here in my arms."

I gathered Henry closer to me and squeezed my eyes shut, as I imagined where I wanted to go—the cellar at the Duval Estate. My magic poured from my pores, enveloping Henry and me. The darkness hissed and screeched, sensing I was about to escape. It latched on to me as hundreds of tiny sharp hooks burrowed into my skin and pulled on my hair, preventing me from glimmering out. A shout tore from my throat as I fought against the darkness, thrashing in its hold.

There is a light inside you. My mother's words invaded my mind.

I can see it, came Henry's voice from another memory.

The light…it still burned inside me. It could help free me from the darkness's hold. All I had to do was let it out. Gritting my teeth, I imagined feeding that light like a fire, blowing on the flames until they burned brighter and brighter. Warmth flared in my chest, radiating outward, and the darkness shrieked, recoiling from me as if burned by the light. Its blood-curdling screech was the last thing I heard before I glimmered to the Duval Estate.

When I appeared in the softly lit cellar, Isabelle was there, and her brown eyes widened as they locked on Henry's limp form in my arms.

"Is he…" she gasped.

"No, but he needs blood," I told her, lowering him to the stone floor.

My mind flashed back to the other night when I'd done the same after rescuing him from the clans. Then, he'd needed blood because of the torture he'd endured from Moreau. This time, I was the monster who'd caused his pain and suffering.

Isabelle rushed to the crates of blood and dragged one closer to Henry. She then lowered to her knees by his side and pulled a blood bag out of the crate.

"I can't hear his heartbeat," she said, her voice shaking.

Her eyes were filled with tears when her gaze shot to mine.

"His heart is beating, just barely," I replied, my own voice strained.

Without another word, Isabelle ripped open the bag and brought it to Henry's parted lips. When she tried to pour some of the blood into his mouth, it bubbled up and spilled out because he wasn't swallowing it.

"Please," Isabelle whispered. "Please, drink. Please," she chanted the word like a prayer.

She looked so small and fragile, like a little girl on the verge of losing her big brother.

"What happened?" she asked, lifting her red-rimmed eyes back to mine.

"I...I..." I stuttered as tiny tremors shook my body. "He was trying to stop me from killing Yvonne, and I—"

"You did this to him?!" Isabelle snarled.

Gone was the little girl I'd glimpsed a moment ago, as red-hot fury flashed in her eyes. She lunged at me, her clawed hands wrapping around my throat, but froze when a strangled noise left Henry. We both looked down just in time to see his chest heave on a sharp inhale as he swallowed the blood that had pooled in his mouth.

In the blink of an eye, Isabelle let go of me and bent down to her brother.

"Here," she said gently, as she cradled his head and gave him more blood.

"What's going on down here?" came Wren's voice as he walked into the cellar.

He froze right on the other side of the threshold. Pale-blue eyes darted to Henry before fastening on me.

"What happened?" he asked low.

"*She* did this to him!" Isabelle growled over her shoulder, and I flinched.

Henry coughed, choking on the blood and I involuntarily reached for him.

"Don't," Isabelle snarled at me. "Don't touch him. Get out!"

I curled my fingers into a fist and lowered my hand.

"Get out!" Isabelle screamed, jarring me into action.

With preternatural ease, I jumped to my feet and swept from the room, passing shocked Wren on the way out.

Powerful magic blasted into me the moment I stepped into the hall. With a sharp cry, I went down on one knee, bracing my hand on the floor for support. White Witches surrounded me, with Celeste standing closest to me, her arm lifted as magic poured out of her open hand.

"Please," I managed to get out through gritted teeth.

My breathing was coming in short, rapid pants as Celeste's magic bore down on me, constricting my chest and pressing me lower to the ground.

"Celeste—" Amelie said meekly, stepping closer to the witch.

"Don't," Celeste warned her. "Her magic is dark. We need to detain her."

"I left the darkness behind," I bit out, straining against Celeste's powers.

"Am I supposed to believe that?" she challenged.

"Yes," I rasped. "I hurt Henry—" My voice broke as tears surged and spilled.

Celeste's eyes widened as Amelie paled next to her.

"Let her go," the young witch said. "She's clearly distraught."

"She's dangerous," Celeste insisted.

"I don't think she is. Not anymore," Amelie said, as she stepped closer to me and lowered to her knees.

I felt the pressure of Celeste's magic gradually alleviate until it disappeared entirely. The crushing weight was still there, though, pushing me to the ground. It was the weight of what I'd done to Henry.

Amelie's features were blurry through my tears as she stared at me with empathy on her freckled face.

"Are you okay?" she asked low.

I shook my head "no" and crumpled to the ground, where I curled into a ball and wept.

30

I watched him breathe shallowly. In and out. In and out. My chest rose and fell, matching the rhythm. I couldn't get enough air into my lungs. Good—I didn't deserve it. I didn't deserve to breathe the same air as he. Nor did I deserve to be here. In Henry's bedroom, with him lying still on his bed. I'd almost killed him...

A ragged sob escaped, and I clamped my hand over my mouth, my entire body shaking.

Isabelle shot me an annoyed look from where she sat by Henry's bed.

"Pull yourself together. He's alive. He's healing."

He *was* healing, thanks to her. She'd made sure he'd gotten enough blood in his system to speed up his stuttering heart to a steady rhythm. She'd also cleaned him up and put him in his bed. While she'd nursed Henry, Amelie had nursed me. She'd helped me get up off the floor, shower, and change. She'd also brewed some herbs to help soothe my nerves. The concoction was supposed to help me sleep, but it hadn't worked so far. So, I'd stumbled on weak legs to Henry's bedroom. To my surprise, Isabelle had let me in and let me stay.

"I should leave," I rasped, wiping away the tears that had never stopped streaming down my face.

I sat on a chair by the wall as far away from Henry's bed as I could possibly get without leaving the bedroom.

"Don't be ridiculous. He'd want you here," Isabelle said in a clipped tone.

"Would he? Still want me here? After what I'd done—"

"Yes," she cut me off. "He would. I have no doubt in my mind. He loves you, Sophie. Deeply, madly. Everyone can see it."

"I love him, too," I said in a hoarse voice. It felt wrong saying the words after what I'd done.

"I know. Everyone can see that, too. And it was because of that love that you went unhinged," she said simply. "Look, I'm not going to excuse your behavior, but I know one thing for certain—what happened is not going to change Henry's feelings for you."

"It's not?" I asked, my voice dropping to a whisper.

"No. Don't be silly. Now, I am still very much furious with you. I wanted to rip out your throat in the cellar…" Her big eyes fastened on me. Staring back, I swallowed thickly. "But I knew if I killed you, I would incur his wrath after he'd healed."

Without saying another word, she turned back to Henry, and we sat in silence for a few minutes as the tears gliding down my cheeks slowed. I hoped Isabelle was right, and that what I'd done wouldn't change Henry's feelings for me. When I'd almost killed him, something inside me had snapped, like a lid shutting closed on a chest, locking the darkness away. There was no room for it inside me anymore. There was no room for anything but despair and utter desolation because I'd thought I'd lost him. It was because of the darkness that I'd hurt him. The shadows were not my allies. They were evil—the darkest, vilest type. I couldn't believe I hadn't seen that before. I'd been blind, but I could see clearly now. I just prayed it wasn't too late.

The bedroom door creaked open, pulling me from my

thoughts, and a second later, Wren walked in. His pale-blue eyes immediately locked on Isabelle.

"Do you need anything?" he asked her. When she gave a small shake of her head, his gaze slid to Henry, and his jaw tightened.

Slowly, he turned his head to look at me.

"How are you holding up? Do you need anything?" he asked low.

"A way to turn back time," I said quietly.

Wren's gaze softened.

"I know a thing or two about wishing you could change the past," he told me with a wistful smile. And I supposed he *did* know. I'd been so eager to condemn him in the past. Now, I was the one who deserved condemnation. Yet, he was choosing a different way—compassion. "We can't go back and change the past. We can only hope for redemption."

I stared at him, speechless. It seemed he didn't expect me to say anything anyway, because with one last glance at Isabelle, he slipped out of the bedroom.

Isabelle's gaze lingered on the door long after it had closed behind Wren.

"You and Wren..." I started, if only to distract myself from the thoughts of what might happen when Henry woke up.

"Are doomed," Isabelle interjected, her gaze fixing on me.

"What?" My brows wrinkled.

"Rule number one of being a vampire. Don't get close to anyone, because time will take them away," Isabelle said, matter-of-fact.

I stared at her in disbelief. Was that why she was so cold? She couldn't get hurt if she never let anyone get close.

She rolled her eyes. "I know you think that I'm heartless."

"I don't—"

She arched a brow with a skeptical look.

"Well, not anymore," I told her. "Things have changed between us," I said hesitantly, looking for confirmation from her.

We'd begun growing closer when Henry had been taken by the clans. I hoped that what I'd done would not undo the progress we'd made in our friendship.

"They have," she agreed, after a beat of silence, and I let out a breath of relief. "You saved Henry, and I am grateful for that. You went deranged and then almost killed him after you'd saved him, but I suppose we all make mistakes." Her gaze returned to the bedroom door, and I knew she wasn't just talking about me but also about Wren.

"So, you and Wren?" I prompted again.

"Are temporary." She cast her gaze to the ground.

"You don't have to be," I said softly. "Wren had asked me before if turning into a vampire was worth it."

Isabelle's gaze shot back up to mine.

"Why would he ask you that?" she asked quietly, and held her breath as if she already knew the answer.

"Why do you think?" I gave her a pointed look.

A hint of a smile pulled at her lips as her gaze drew distant. I wondered if she was imagining her life with Wren—her very long, eternal life.

Suddenly, the corners of her mouth turned down, and her forehead creased.

"No. I will not turn him if his only reason for wanting to become a vampire is to be with me."

"Why not?" I challenged, a moment before understanding dawned on me. "Unless you don't believe in you and Wren. You don't want to shackle him to you for all eternity."

"Eternity is a long time to be with someone," she countered.

"It is," I agreed.

"Yet, you are sure you want to spend it with my brother," she said, her eyes searching my face. If she was looking for any hint of hesitation, she wouldn't find it.

"I am."

"How do you know?" Now, her look was incredulous. *How would I know?* The question was implied.

"I just know." I shrugged.

Isabelle lifted one brow, silently demanding more of an explanation.

"Because eternity means nothing if I'm not with him," I said with a heavy sigh. "Because even if I die tomorrow, I would die happy and with no regrets, knowing that I'd spent the time I had by his side, loving him…" My voice broke—I'd never told him. He'd told me he loved me, and I'd told him it wasn't enough.

"He will be okay," Isabelle said, her eyes flicking over my features.

Her gaze returned to Henry, and I could see the love for her brother shining through on her heart-shaped face.

"You've never told me how you joined the clan," I prompted, curious about how she'd become one of the Duvals.

"I haven't, have I?" Isabelle said, looking back at me. "To be fair, we weren't speaking much until only a few nights ago," she pointed out.

"Why is that?" I asked, seeing no reason to tiptoe around the subject. "I knew you didn't like me when I was Henry's vassal, but I hoped it would change when he turned me. But it didn't. You shut me out."

"I did, and if you expect an apology, you will not get it."

"I don't want an apology, just an explanation."

Isabelle swallowed.

"After you were turned, Henry was spending all of his time with you…"

"I was a new vampire, I needed guidance…"

"I know, but I was jealous…and scared."

"Scared?"

"I could see the way Henry was looking at you. The way he was acting around you. In you, he had found his mate. Someone to share his everlasting nights with. I knew because I'd seen that before…Vincent and Rosalind had been like that before she died. When you were around them, it always felt like they were one, moving in unison. They existed for each other. They were just gracious enough to welcome others into their circle. And when I saw that look in Henry's eyes directed toward you…fear set in, that you would take him away from me. That it would no longer be he and I. It would be you and him, and I would be cast aside."

"No," I told her vehemently, sitting up straighter in my chair. "That's not what I want. I would never allow that to happen. I want us to be a family. All three of us."

"Four." The word seemed to have escaped unintentionally, and Isabelle's eyes widened as she caught herself.

"What?" I asked quietly. I had a feeling I knew what she'd meant, but I wanted to nudge her gently toward her own realization. After a moment, it washed over her face as shock, but also awe and wonder.

"Four of us," Isabelle said with a small smile. "You, me, Henry, and Wren."

"Four of us then." I gave an answering smile, but it was fleeting, as the corners of my mouth turned down. I didn't know if Henry would still have me when he woke up.

"I can see what you're thinking, and you need to stop," Isabelle said sternly. "When Henry wakes up, he'll be overjoyed to see you here, and you two will be able to put the past few nights behind you."

"Do you truly believe that?"

"I do." Isabelle nodded. "That's what Vincent would have done for Rosalind, and we both know Henry is a lot like his father."

"You were going to tell me how you joined the Duval clan?" I prompted again.

I needed something to occupy my mind, so it didn't go to dark places, as dread threatened to swallow me whole. I hoped

Isabelle was right about how Henry would feel about me being here when he woke up, but I didn't know for certain that was how things would unfold. He might open his eyes and recoil in my presence, cursing the day I'd come into his life. He might banish me… My heart turned over with another wave of dread. I didn't know what I would do if he sent me away. I couldn't face eternity without him.

"I was twenty-three years old when I was turned," Isabelle's voice rang out in the quiet room, pulling me from my dreary thoughts. I latched on to her words, focusing on her story instead of the possible tragedy that was unfolding in my head. "The vampire that turned me…" She released a shaking breath. "Well, imagine Stern and Moreau combined into one despicable being, who fed on pain and suffering as well on blood." A shudder rolled through her. "I was an orphan, and never knew an easy life, becoming a lady of the night at an early age. The one who sired me was a client who liked me so much he wanted to keep me… for all eternity. Or until he got tired of me, I suppose. Either way, he wanted me to be less…breakable, to be able to endure all the twisted and depraved things he liked to do…"

Isabelle's eyes became glassy, as she stared into the distance as if lost in the terrible memories. Another shudder racked her as all color drained from her face. Her delicate throat worked on a swallow, and silence filled the room for a few seconds until Isabelle blinked, returning to the present. When she refocused on me, her eyes were glimmering with tears.

"Vincent knew my sire, and when he learned about what he was doing to me, he confronted him. The one who turned me lashed out, and Vincent killed him in self-defense. He then freed me from the cellar where I was being kept."

My throat closed up as I stared at Isabelle. She'd endured so much. I had the urge to go to her, to wrap my arms around her in a sign of support, but I knew the gesture would be unwelcome. If

I knew anything about Isabelle, it was that she didn't need or want my pity. Even after everything she'd been through, she was a fighter, not a victim. It didn't go unnoticed, though, that she'd never called her abuser by his name, but I didn't think it was out of fear. It was because she didn't want to give him that much importance. Because he wasn't important. He was a part of her past, but he was not the one who'd formed Isabelle's character. It was Vincent, when he'd shown her kindness.

"After he'd freed me, he tried to take me in. They were already a family: Vincent, Rosalind, Gerard, and Henry." A small, reminiscent smile graced her lips. "They opened their home to me, but I…" She swallowed again. "I was too scared to trust them, to trust Vincent. I feared I was exchanging one abuser for another, so I escaped. I was no better than a Ravager then, bringing pain and suffering everywhere I went. Henry found me and tried to convince me that Vincent was different from the one who'd sired me, that the Duvals were different from the other vampires, but I didn't believe him, not at first. I remained on the move, never lingering in one place, but Henry kept finding me and talking to me, until one day, I began looking forward to our conversations, to him finding me, because it was during those moments when I felt the most human, sane. He didn't give up on me, and eventually, he convinced me to join the clan because that's what he does. He finds the ones who are lost and saves them even when they don't realize that they need saving."

"Even if they don't deserve it," I said low, my voice hollow.

I didn't deserve it, I didn't need to add.

Isabelle's knowing brown eyes settled on me.

"When he comes to, you let him make that decision. Don't take the choice away from him," she said.

I just stared at her, unsure of how to respond. A part of me wanted to take the choice away from him, to flee like a coward before he woke up. Because then it would be me leaving him, and not the other way around. In the end, it didn't matter—my heart would still be shattered forever—but at least I wouldn't be here to see the loathing in Henry's eyes when he came to. I wouldn't be here to hear him say I was a monster and didn't deserve him.

"Sophie?" Isabelle said, snapping me from my thoughts.

"Thank you for sharing," I told her in a tone that I hoped conveyed how much her opening up meant to me.

She nodded and then rose to her feet.

"As much as I hate to admit it, telling you my story took a lot out of me. I need a little time to regain my composure," she told me.

"You're leaving?" I asked, my voice panicked as Isabelle left Henry's side and headed for the door.

I was terrified of being alone with Henry. What if he woke up while it was just me in the room? What if I saw hatred blazing in his eyes when he finally pried them open? My heartbeat sped up in my chest.

"Whatever it is you fear will not happen," Isabelle said, stopping by me on her way out. "You asked me if I had doubts about Wren and me. Well, you need to cast aside your own doubts about you and Henry. Your love is stronger than this. It will persevere."

She pressed my shoulder in a comforting gesture before slipping out of the room. My attention zeroed in on Henry the moment the door had closed behind her. Before I knew what I was doing, I was rising from my chair, my body moving of its own accord. I approached Henry's bedside as if pulled by an invisible string and sat down in the chair Isabelle had occupied.

I didn't deserve to be here, but I couldn't fight the pull. I wanted to be close to him, to soak up being in his proximity in case he sent me away when he woke up. My hands twitched, itching to reach up and touch him. I wanted to trace his chiseled features, which I could picture perfectly, even with my eyes closed. My lips tingled as I wanted to brush them over his brow, his cheeks, and the hard line of his jaw. But I didn't dare disturb him. And just as I didn't deserve to be in this room and by his bed, I especially didn't deserve to touch him, to feel the smooth skin under my fingertips. So, I folded my arms on top of the bed and laid my head down, my gaze fixed on his face so close yet out of my reach. Before long, sleep pulled me under.

31

In my dream, I was still in Henry's bedroom, standing before the window, the heavy gray curtains closed tightly. My brows wrinkled. Why was I inside? I'd gotten used to being outside in my dreams, with Henry all hard, lean muscles and sun-kissed skin by my side. He was here with me now, standing to the left of the window much like he'd stood when I'd watched my last sunrise before being turned. My gaze darted to him, and I flinched. His arms were folded over his bare chest where the wound I'd inflicted was still healing, and he glared at me from beneath the dark brows.

"How could you do this to me?" he snarled, disdain dripping from his voice.

My heart twisted in my chest as breathing became difficult. Tears rushed to the surface and spilled, rolling down my cheeks.

"I'm sorry," I rasped. "I wasn't myself. I was lost, just like you said. I wanted to destroy our enemies. I wanted to keep you safe. I was scared of losing you—"

Henry's laughter interrupted me, and it sounded all wrong—cold and dead. I'd never heard such a sound from him before, and it made a shiver of trepidation curl down my spine.

"You were scared of losing me?" he asked, his eyes blazing. His gaze was scathing, blistering my skin. "The things you did...how could you do them? You were scared of losing me? Well, now you've lost me anyway. How can I love someone who'd committed such atrocious cruelties? You are a monster, Sophie. I can't believe it has taken me this long to see it."

A keening sound escaped me as violent tremors began to shake my body. I couldn't breathe in this place, inside this room with Henry spewing words of hatred at me. Why were we here and not under the sun, where the air was clean and not filled with smoke and shadows of the darkness? Why were the curtains closed tight? It was daylight outside, I could feel it. I needed to open the drapes and let the light in, let it banish the darkness that had filled this space, suffocating me. Maybe then Henry would see that not all was lost, that there was still hope for me, for us. I reached for the curtains and pulled them apart, desperate to escape the darkness. The sunlight blinded me, and I screamed.

Sophie!

I screamed as the flames erupted, eating up my skin and incinerating my flesh and bones.

Sophie!!

My eyes flew open. I was staring at Henry. He was sitting up in the bed, clasping my shoulders.

"Are you okay?" he asked, his gaze searching my face.

"Yes, it was just a nightmare," I replied, my voice hoarse from screaming in my dream.

"I gathered that," he said, his hands gliding down my arms before sliding back up to my shoulders, then to my neck as if making sure I was really here and in one piece. "I mean, are you *okay*?" he asked, cupping my face.

My chest constricted as tears blurred my vision. I'd thought I'd see loathing in his eyes, but I saw potent relief instead, and the scattered bleeding pieces of my heart pulled closer to each other as if they might stitch themselves together one day.

"You're asking me if I'm okay? After what I did—"

He sealed his lips to mine, silencing me. The salt from my tears mixed with the taste of him, and a whimpering sound escaped as I kissed him back, my tongue stroking his. Relief rolled off him in waves. Relief, not the hatred I'd been dreading to find when he opened his eyes. There was almost a longing in the way he kissed me, longing for the one he'd fallen in love with. For who I used to be before I turned into this…monster.

I abruptly broke the kiss, rising from the chair.

"How can you ask me if I'm okay?" I said through the tears, as I began pacing the room. "How can you touch me? How can you kiss me after everything I've done?"

"Because I love you—"

"I'm a monster!" I shouted.

The words rang out in the otherwise quiet room, loud and condemning. Once they were out, there was no taking them back. They carved into my skin like lacerations, like a brand to mark me for all eternity.

Henry grunted, trying to leave the bed.

"Don't!" I stepped closer, throwing my hands up as if to stop him from a distance.

He winced in pain as he rested his back against the headboard.

"If you don't want me to come to you, then you need to come to me so we can talk."

"How can you even want me near you?" I asked low, the words difficult to get out.

Henry's eyes shuttered.

"Come here," he whispered—no, he *begged*.

I didn't deserve him. Funny how mere weeks ago, I'd thought him a monster. There was only one monster in this room, and it wasn't him. I didn't deserve him, yet my legs carried me to him, my body always pulled toward him as if I couldn't physically be more than a few feet away.

They moved in unison, Isabelle had said earlier about Vincent and Rosalind. Now I thought I knew what she'd meant. I might be a monster, and I might not deserve him, but I couldn't stay away from him, either. It was physically impossible. I would always come to him as long as he wanted me by his side. And if there ever came a day when he didn't…well, I would still be close, hiding in the shadows, watching from afar…longing, desperate for another touch. But that day was not today, so I would take what he would give for as long as he would give it.

Slowly, I approached the bed and perched on the edge, close to where he was sitting. When he reached for my hand, I flinched, trying to pull away, as if my touch would hurt him.

I did this, I thought with a shudder, my gaze dropping to his chest.

These hands that itched to touch him, to trace the defined muscles and beautiful features, had caused him severe pain and suffering. I'd been desperate to protect him from the others. In the end, I'd failed to protect him from myself. A ragged cry broke past my lips, and I clamped my free hand over my mouth.

"Shh." Henry reached out and pried my hand away, before clasping the back of my neck and resting his forehead against mine. "Breathe with me."

At first, I couldn't do as he'd instructed because I was shaking too much, but after a while, I focused on the beating of his heart and his controlled, measured inhales and exhales. I began to match the rhythm, filling up my lungs with air when he did and letting it out slowly when he exhaled. Being so close to him helped soothe me, too, his fresh and woodsy scent surrounding me, settling over me with the comfort of a blanket.

Once my breathing had evened out, Henry pulled away and let go of my neck. He didn't let go of my hand, though, as he settled back against the headboard.

His eyes were haunted, and he swallowed, his throat bobbing, before he opened his mouth to speak. My heart dropped. He was going to send me away. Any second now, he would utter the words that would undo me, sentencing me to an eternity of misery and pain. Of loneliness. Because I knew there would never be another. Not after him.

My heart and my breathing sped up again, but before I could succumb to a full-blown panic attack, Henry said, "I think it's time I tell you about my human family." He didn't say "my real family" because the Duval clan was his real family, too. Just in a different life. In the life after the almost-death that had made him a vampire. But he had a past life. A life before that moment when Vincent had decided to save him because he'd seen good in him. Gods, how grateful I was to Vincent for everything. For helping my grandmother, then my mother with the amulet, for giving me Henry.

I held my breath, waiting for him to continue. He didn't for a long time.

The look on his face was tortured and pained, and his voice was hoarse when he finally spoke. "My father, Bernard, was a doctor." A pause and a thick swallow as if it were difficult for him to force the words out, to speak about his family. "He was like a rock, unwavering and firm. My mother, Louise," the corners of his mouth lifted slightly as his voice became gentle, reverent, "She was a nurse. They were healers in a small village they grew up in before they moved to the city. My mother was the softness to my father's hardness, but she was strong. It was the kind of quiet strength that told you if my father, the rock, ever crumbled, she would be there to pick up the pieces, making him whole again." Deep-blue eyes locked on me, and he wasn't just looking *at* me, but also *into* me. Could he see the broken shards of my heart? "Your strength is not always quiet, but you do remind me of her."

"You mean me before…before I became this." I didn't deserve to be compared to her, to the one who'd brought him into this world.

Henry's lips thinned into a firm line, and he didn't acknowledge my comment before he continued, "They had me when they were young, and they wanted more children, but as the years went on, it became clear that wasn't going to happen for them. One day, when I was nineteen, apprenticing with my father, someone brought a little girl into the infirmary where he worked. They found her on the streets, gravely ill. She was an orphan. We nursed her back to health and took her in."

"What was her name?"

"Marceline…Marcy." A smile lit up his face, genuine and warm, the brightest one I'd ever seen. "It was almost strange how easily she fit in. One day, it was just the three of us. The next day, we were a family of four, and it felt like Marcy had been with us all along, as if she'd always occupied the spare bedroom by the stairs, and that place in our hearts we hadn't even known was empty until she came into our lives."

Now it made sense why Henry was so good at finding those who were lost—he'd done it before with Marcy. I wondered if he'd fought so hard for Isabelle because she reminded him of his little sister.

"What happened to them?"

Henry's smile fell, and his features became so hard I knew they would feel like stone under my fingertips if I were to touch him. And I wanted to touch him. I wanted to wrap myself around him to shield him from the oppressive darkness that had descended on him.

"I was twenty-five when Vincent turned me. Marcy had been with us for six years at that point. She had just turned twelve and was beginning to learn from my mother, hoping to become a nurse one day…" Henry closed his eyes and clenched his jaw, the muscles of his face contorting as if he were in excruciating pain. I hated seeing him like this, and I almost opened my mouth to tell him he didn't have to finish the story, but before I could, he continued, "I was confused, deranged, and…hungry."

My stomach dropped as Henry began to tremble, his hand shaking around mine.

"I felt so lost, and there was only one place I knew I would feel found again. I wanted to escape what I'd become, I wanted to go…home." His voice broke on the last word, and he was breaking, too, crumbling right before my eyes.

When a vampire is first turned, the bloodlust is nearly impossible to control. I had Vincent by my side to guide me through it, but he couldn't always be there to stop me when the hunger struck, Henry had told me before.

He'd wanted to go home, where his father could protect him from what he'd become, where his mother could offer a warm embrace and tell him he wasn't a monster, where his sister's light could banish the shadows. Even in his deranged state, he'd been drawn to the safety of his home, to his safe haven. But his family hadn't been able to save him from himself. The bloodlust had prevailed.

A harsh exhale left Henry as he opened his eyes. He didn't look at me, though. His black lashes swept down, and he lowered his gaze to the ground.

"I slaughtered them," he said so low I could barely discern the words, even with my supernatural hearing.

Shame and sorrow poured out of him, and I finally understood why he carried this weight around him, this guilt. His hand tightened around mine to the point of pain, as if I were his lifeline to this reality. He needed me to tether him to the present lest he'd be lost in the horrible memories of the past forever. I placed my other hand on top of his and pressed it in quiet support—*I'm here.*

"That's why you don't have portraits of them anywhere," I said quietly. I'd wondered before why his bedroom was so bare, not offering even a glimpse into his past or who he was.

"I don't need their portraits to remember them. Their faces are forever seared in my mind. For the longest time, I saw them every time I closed my eyes. They don't haunt me as much as they used to, but I wish they still did because I don't deserve a reprieve from the constant reminder."

My chest constricted at his words because I knew it would be his face contorted in agony that I would see every time I closed my eyes. I hoped the image would haunt me for years to come because I needed to suffer for the pain I'd inflicted on him. I deserved it.

"So, you see, Sophie." Henry lifted his gaze to mine. "If you are a monster, then I am one, too. In fact, I am worse than you. You slaughtered our enemies; I slaughtered innocent people. People I loved more than anything else in this world. People who trusted me."

"It's not the same," I interjected. "You were not yourself. You were a new vampire, overcome by bloodlust."

"And you are a new witch," he pointed out. "Perhaps when you become something new, something inhuman, the darkness is right there, hiding in the shadows, waiting to lure you to its side. It knows you're vulnerable. It can smell your fear, and it tries to sway you, testing you. So, you have to give it everything you've got to stay true to yourself."

I thought it over, angling my head.

"Celeste said there are realms alongside this one and that there is a constant war between good and evil."

"I believe it," Henry said without hesitation. "The darkness is treacherous, always waiting for you to falter, ready to sink its claws in."

"That's no excuse for what I've done. You should be disgusted by me, by the things I've done. I've hurt you..." I went to turn away, unable to look at him.

"And I forgive you." He cupped my face, holding me in place to make sure my gaze stayed on his. "Now, you just need to forgive yourself."

"I don't know if I can," I rasped, my voice raw. My insides were raw, too, as if my chest had been flayed open.

"You can and you will because it will make me happy. You want to make me happy, don't you?" His tone was serious, not teasing. He didn't need to ask—he already knew the answer. "Our love is bigger than what happened, than what you've done. It will overcome it, but only if you let it. Please...let it," he whispered. "Don't hold on to what happened. Because if you do, you will be holding on to the darkness, inadvertently letting it win."

32

"I have something that I think will help," Henry said, letting go of my face to reach into the top drawer of the bedside table.

My eyes widened when he pulled out the locket holding the portrait of my mother.

"My necklace!" I exclaimed, my hand flying to my chest.

I'd forgotten Camilla had ripped it off my neck back at Stern's lair. I hadn't missed it because I'd been so consumed by the darkness, but now that the haze had lifted, it felt like there was a void in my chest, in the spot where the locket usually rested.

"You went back there? After everything you endured in that place?" I stared at Henry in disbelief.

His face became ashen before he replied, "It wasn't easy. But for you, I would face my worst nightmares. Always. Turn around."

I shifted on the edge of the bed to give him my back.

"Where is the Tear?" he asked, gently moving my unbound hair to the side.

"I gave it to Amelie for safekeeping. I didn't think I deserved to wear it after…" *After the monstrous acts I'd committed.*

Henry didn't say anything as he clasped the delicate chain of the locket behind my neck. He didn't immediately pull away, placing a soft kiss on my nape, which elicited a soft gasp from me. As soon as the weight of the locket settled on my chest, I wrapped my fingers around it and took a steadying breath.

"She would be disappointed in me," I said in a shaking voice as I faced Henry again.

"No, she wouldn't," he replied, knowing that I'd meant my mother. "You stumbled and fell, but you will pick yourself up. I will help you."

"You will? Do you still want to be with me?" The words were difficult to get out, but I had to know. I couldn't take another breath in until I knew where we stood. With one word, he could grant me everlasting happiness or sentence me to eternal damnation.

"Do I still want to be with you?" Henry chuckled low as if he couldn't believe I'd asked that question. "Sophie, with you is where I belong. I told you that you were my heart, and it's the truth. My heart beats alongside yours in your chest. Can't you feel it? If your heart ever stops, mine will stop too, for I don't want this world without you in it. And I don't want this life if it's not with you."

My vision blurred as tears welled in my eyes.

"I love you," I breathed. "I love you, I love you, I love you," I whispered, planting soft kisses on his brow, his eyelids, his nose, and his cheeks.

I briefly pressed my lips to his before brushing kisses along his jaw and his neck. The tears fell, and a sob escaped as I buried my face in his chest. He held me as I cried, trembling in his embrace. I wept for what felt like hours until the sobs racking my body slowed, and I relaxed in his arms. We sat in silence for a while, with him stroking my hair and placing gentle kisses on my temple. When I felt ready, I lifted my face from his chest and looked into his eyes. The deep blue of his gaze washed over me like calming waters, soothing my battered heart.

"I love you," he said, cupping my cheek.

A shuddering exhale left me before my breathing evened out, along with my heartbeat. A feeling of peace descended on me, wrapping me in its warm embrace. Everything was as it should be. I was in Henry's arms, and we were in love. I was exactly where I belonged.

My pulse quickened as my gaze dropped to his mouth. Desire crashed into me, and I had to swallow to relieve the sudden dryness in my throat. Forcing my gaze back up to Henry's, I found him watching me, his eyes hooded.

"What are you thinking?" he asked, his voice thicker, richer.

"I'm thinking you need to rest," I forced myself to say, but the words came out low and husky.

"Liar," Henry whispered with a teasing smile.

"I can wait," I lied, squeezing my thighs to tame the throbbing ache between my legs.

"And what if I can't?" His daring smile grew. "Will you deny me?"

"No. Never. I will never deny you," I assured him.

"Prove it," he rasped, his eyes turning several shades darker.

"You're injured…"

"I can handle it."

He pulled me into the bed, and I planted my knees on either side of his hips to straddle him. A harsh groan left him when I did, the rough sound igniting my blood. I rolled my hips against him, gasping when I felt him hard against my core.

"You would never deny me?" he ground out, grasping my thighs to pull me closer to him. "Are you sure you want to be making a promise like that? We have a very long life ahead of us."

"And I can't wait to spend every moment of it with you," I said as I lowered my head to claim his mouth.

To my surprise, he stopped me before I could kiss him. Fisting my hair at the nape of my neck, he held me in place, moving away a few inches so he could peer at my face.

"Truly?" he asked, as a strange expression settled into his features.

"Yes," I told him, staring into his eyes. The raw vulnerability I'd witnessed before had returned.

"Then...will you marry me?" he asked, his voice hoarse with emotion.

"Yes." The word flew from my lips. I didn't need to think about it. I was as sure as I'd ever been of anything in my life. Saying yes felt natural, like breathing. The easiest answer I'd ever had to give.

"Yes?" he whispered, his eyes wide and glistening with tears.

"Yes!" I exclaimed, as a startled laugh burst out of me.

I couldn't believe I'd gone from having the lowest point of my life to this pure moment of utter happiness and bliss in a matter of a few hours. The feeling was surreal, but I didn't have time to dwell on it because Henry kissed me, stealing my breath away. His lips and tongue moved over mine with burning fervor as if he was trying to pour all his love into the kiss to show me how happy he was I'd said yes. Before long, he was tearing at my clothes while I fumbled with his pants. I was trying to be careful with his chest, but he didn't seem to care, his movements hungry and desperate. He wanted to claim, to take what was his, and I let him. For he was mine, too, and soon I would take him as my husband for all eternity.

After Henry had made love to me, wringing out every last drop of pleasure, he'd fallen into a deep sleep, his large body wrapped around mine as if he'd wanted to ensure I'd never leave the bed. I didn't want to leave, but there was something I needed to do, so I carefully untangled his heavy limbs from around me and slipped out of his hold. He stirred but didn't wake, which told me he was still on the long road to recovery. I left the bed and picked up my pants and tunic that Henry had cast to the floor a few hours earlier. I shrugged the clothes on and lingered by the bed, fighting the urge to crawl back into it to stay with Henry.

Exhaustion pulled at my bones. It wasn't just the physical exertion, but also the emotional one. All my resources were depleted, and it felt like I could sleep for days, wrapped in Henry's arms. Or perhaps I just wanted to sleep for a long time because I secretly hoped that once I woke up, the horrible acts I'd committed would be a thing of the past. That I, along with everyone else, would be able to forget what I'd done. I couldn't run away from it though. I would have to live with it, but I refused to let the shadows of the past hold me back from enjoying my future with Henry. My mind made up, I left the bedside and walked to the vanity, where I quickly dragged a brush through my tousled hair before slipping from the room.

Fighting the heaviness in my sore muscles, I set off to a run in the direction of the Black Forest. I only had an hour at most before sunrise, and glimmering would be faster, but I didn't dare use my magic, fearful that the darkness would latch on to me again and drag me back to its side. So, I ran, darting through the woods until I reached the clearing where Celeste's cottage sat, bathed in the glow of the moon.

"I've been expecting you," the witch said, when I skidded to a halt by the front porch, my chest rising and falling rapidly.

"Of course you have," I said simply, once my breathing evened out.

"Sit with me." Celeste pointed to the chair next to hers.

With a nod, I lowered into the rickety piece of furniture. We sat in silence for a few minutes as I let myself relax, my gaze gliding over the forest before me.

"I'm sorry," I finally said, without looking at Celeste. I could feel her intent stare on me.

"I'm sorry, too," she replied, surprising me. "I should have paid closer attention."

My gaze shot to hers.

"It's not your fault. You tried to warn me. I just…" I swallowed the lump that had formed in my throat. "You were right when you said that my love for Henry blinded me. The feeling…it scares me sometimes," I admitted.

Celeste's expression turned empathetic—something I'd never thought I'd witness on the witch's face. "There is no reason to fear it. Love is like magic—an incredibly powerful force. It can either save you or ruin you. It saved you this time."

"But not before it almost ruined me," I pointed out.

"In the end, what could have happened doesn't matter. It wasn't your first trial, nor will it be your last. Hold on to your love. It is a weapon, not a weakness."

My brows climbed my forehead as I studied Celeste's features. Was she speaking from experience?

"Did you ever have someone you loved and were desperate to save?" I asked.

The witch sighed, giving the impression she'd been expecting the question. She didn't seem irritated by it, though. If anything, she looked relieved I'd finally asked, so she could get it off her chest.

"What I know about love and loss is not about romantic love like yours, it's about family ties."

"You had a family? Someone you lost?" I asked in a hushed tone.

Celeste inclined her head. "My sister Antaris."

"The head priestess?!" I exclaimed, staring at her with wide eyes. Antaris had been Xanthus's main follower, and perished with the rest of the Dark Witches when I'd destroyed them.

Another nod. "She succumbed to the darkness years ago. I tried to bring her back to the light, but sometimes the ones you care about the most are beyond saving."

All words left me as I sat there, staring at the witch. Henry could have given up on me, but he hadn't. He'd kept coming for me, risking his own life to save me from myself. I would atone for what I'd done, even if it took me an eternity to do so. As long as it was an eternity by his side.

Silence stretched for a few minutes as Celeste and I were both lost in our thoughts. The witch broke it first by saying, "So, tell me, why did you run here instead of glimmering?"

I tilted my head to the side. Was she seriously asking me that question?

"I'm scared to use my magic. I don't want to make it easy for the darkness to sink its claws into me again. I don't know if I'll ever use my powers again." Admitting that was difficult. Even now, as I sat here, my skin tingled slightly from the magic humming just below the surface.

"You're a witch. Magic is a part of you. You can't deny its pull. It would be like denying your vampire side craving blood. You can only fight it for so long," Celeste said calmly.

"I know you're right, but I…" I trailed off, unsure how to put what I was feeling into words.

"Fear is good," Celeste continued, "You are finally learning respect for your magic."

"Do you think I could use it for good? Without going insane?" I asked, and held my breath. My magic was my legacy. I wanted to be able to use it so I could feel closer to my mother and my ancestors who'd come before her, but I would stifle my powers forever if it meant not making myself a danger to Henry and others.

"You're the girl who defeated the Dark Witches," Celeste said, matter-of-fact. "Surely if you put your mind to it, you can do anything."

A smile tugged at my lips. "Will you help me?"

"Are you going to listen this time?" She arched a white brow.

"I will," I promised as my smile grew. A heartbeat later, it faded. "What are we going to do about Damien?"

"Leave him up to me."

"Just you? You can't fight Xanthus alone."

"Xanthus?" The witch looked at me incredulously. "The one you have been dealing with is not Xanthus."

"He's not?" I asked, confused.

"No." Celeste shook her head. "Xanthus can't enter this realm. The one who has been tempting you with dark magic is one of the minions who serve Xanthus. A demon."

"A demon?" I tried the foreign word on my tongue. "And you can take him on by yourself?"

The witch nodded. "I have a plan."

A feeling of foreboding crept into my chest.

"Are you sure you don't need help? I learned the hard way that fighting the darkness alone is not a good idea."

"I'm sure. I have seen my fair share of darkness through the years. It hasn't prevailed over me yet. Besides, don't you have a wedding to plan?"

I couldn't fight another smile as it lit up my face. Of course she would know about Henry's proposal through the threads.

"I do, but we're not in a rush to get married," I told her. A thought occurred to me then, and I shifted in my seat, nervous but also excited. "Speaking of which...You said you would help me with my magic. Do you mind if we start soon? I have an idea for something, but it involves using my powers." Celeste gave me a skeptical look. "Using them for good," I assured her. "To create something beautiful."

33

"It's healed," I murmured, running my fingertips over Henry's smooth chest. "I was afraid it would scar."

Catching my hand in his, he brought it to his lips and kissed the pads of my fingers. He was still inside me, our chests rising and falling shallowly after what we'd just shared. My knees on either side of his hips, I was straddling him, and he was sitting upright, his back propped against the headboard.

"Of course, it's healed," he said low, turning my hand to brush his lips over my knuckles.

I couldn't take my gaze away from his chest, where I swore I could still see the wound I'd inflicted.

"Don't do that," Henry said quietly, gently guiding my chin up with his thumb and index finger. I knew my eyes were glistening when my gaze met his. "Don't think about that. It's in the past."

A ragged exhale left me, and I buried my face under his chin, trying to fend off the tears. His fingers threaded through my hair, and he held me there as our breathing and our heartbeats slowed. I managed not to cry this time, which was an improvement. During the last few days, I'd broken down many times, with Henry always there to help put me back together.

"We need to get ready," he said after a few minutes, untangling his fingers from my hair. He glided them down my bare back, massaging it in the process. "The clan leaders will be here soon."

His words instantly flung me to the past, as if I'd glimmered myself to the last time we'd met with the clans. Horrible memories of that night invaded my mind.

With a sigh, I lifted my head from Henry's chest and met his stormy blue gaze.

"Tonight feels a lot like that night weeks ago when everything went very, very wrong," I said in a hushed tone.

Henry's perfect features tautened. A muscle flexed along his jaw before he said, "I know, but we have to do this. We have to try. My hope is that tonight will go differently."

"It has to," I told him. "I can't go through that again."

His understanding gaze flicked over my features. "Come here."

He pushed on my lower back, and I gasped when his rigid length shifted inside me. He was ready to go again, but I knew we wouldn't when the kiss he gave me was tender and sweet, not hungry and demanding.

"I feel like we are so close to our new life," he whispered against my lips. "That's all I want. A new life. With you."

My heart squeezed in my chest.

"It's all I want as well."

"Then, let's go and make it happen. Together." He rested his forehead against mine. We shared a breath before I pulled away and eased off him.

We quickly showered and got dressed, debating whether or not to wear our armor.

"I don't want to send the wrong message," Henry said, clutching his leathers in his hand. "If the clan leaders get here and see us in our fighting gear, they will immediately go on the defensive."

I heaved a heavy sigh. He was right. We had to take the risk and hope that the meeting tonight would go differently, and we needed to do anything in our power to help ensure that. Tonight felt a lot like the night from a few weeks ago, but it also felt different. The pressure on my chest was not as tight and constricting as it had been then. The feeling inside was more of unease than foreboding. Perhaps the threads were telling me that everything would be okay.

"I think you're right," I told Henry, setting my own leathers aside.

Just my teal dress and leggings then, I thought, stepping closer to the vanity.

While I brushed my hair, Henry put away our fighting gear in the tall dresser behind me.

When he turned around and faced the vanity, I let my gaze roam over his reflection. Dressed in a plain white shirt and black breeches, he looked like he had on the night of the Selection. Even his hair looked like it had then, swept back to reveal his masculine features. I had the urge to run my fingers through the glossy mane to dishevel it, and one side of my mouth ticked up at the thought.

"What is it?" Henry asked, coming to stand directly behind me. When he wrapped his arms around my waist, I relaxed into his hold, reveling in the feel of his strong body against mine.

"You look so well put-together," I told him, setting the brush on the vanity. "I can't decide if I like this look more, or the unruly, wild one you wear sometimes."

Henry smirked but didn't say anything as I let my head fall back against his chest. We stood in silence for a few seconds, simply enjoying the moment of quiet peace.

"I think I love all your looks," I said, turning around to face him. I slid my hands up his powerful body and wrapped them around his neck. "I love you," I told him, staring into his eyes. I made sure to tell him every day now.

"I don't think I will ever tire of hearing you say it," he

murmured, as the black from his pupils began bleeding into the deep blue of his irises.

"I'll never get tired of saying it," I assured him with a soft smile.

Stark lust sharpened his features a moment before he brought his lips to mine. There was a hunger to the kiss that hadn't been there earlier, and I opened up for him, wondering if we had time to go again before the clans arrived. Henry was determined to make time, it seemed, because he lifted me off the floor and sat me on the edge of the vanity, parting my thighs to step between them. I wrapped my legs around his hips, and we both gasped as our bodies aligned. He ground into me, eliciting a breathy moan as tension began building inside me. His hands dove under my dress while mine went to his breeches. He yanked my leggings and undergarments down, and I almost freed him from his pants…when a knock sounded. We both froze, and Henry broke the kiss.

"The clans will be here any minute," came Isabelle's voice, causing Henry to growl in frustration. Isabelle huffed out a laugh on the other side of the door. "You'll have to finish what you started later. You'll be fine. You two have an eternity together, after all."

We'd told Isabelle days ago about our plan to get married, and she hadn't been surprised. Her big brown eyes had locked on me when we'd announced the news.

I told you his feelings for you wouldn't change, the look had conveyed.

"We'll be right there!" Henry snapped, and I stifled a laugh. Usually, he was the voice of reason, but it seemed right now his desire for me was stronger than his sense of duty.

"She's right, you know," I said, as I unwrapped my legs from around his hips. "If everything goes well tonight, we'll have an eternity together."

"It won't be long enough," he said with a heavy sigh.

A short laugh did burst out of me then.

"No?" I teased, arching a brow.

"No," he assured me, his expression serious. "Because when it comes to you, I'm ravenous. I will never get enough of you."

My heart sped up in my chest at his words. He was right—an eternity would not be enough, because when it came to him, I was insatiable. The more I got of him, the more I craved him.

"Ready?" he asked, seemingly having regained his composure.

When I nodded, he lowered me from the vanity and helped me pull up my leggings. While I rightened my dress, he straightened his breeches.

"I'm glad you got it back," he said, and I found him watching me, his gaze fastened on the Tear pulsing on my chest.

I'd gotten the amulet back from Amelie the other night after my training session with Celeste. I still felt unworthy of wearing it, but Henry had insisted the Tear belonged with me.

"I wanted to wear it tonight to remind the clans I still had the means to destroy them," I said, more to myself than to him.

"Great idea, though I doubt they need a reminder. I think everyone is acutely aware of what a powerful witch you are," Henry pointed out.

Good, I thought, *I want them to fear me.* I planned never to use my magic to hurt anyone ever again, but the clans didn't need to know that. I wanted them to believe that if I ever felt threatened again, I wouldn't hesitate to kill them in the most gruesome way possible.

Lifting his hand to my chest, Henry tucked the locket holding the portrait of my mother under the collar of my dress and righted the Tear atop it. When he was done, I turned away from him and quickly smoothed out my unbound hair before giving my reflection a nod of encouragement.

"I'm ready," I said, as I faced Henry again.

He clasped my hand, and together, we left the bedroom and walked to the study where Isabelle and Wren already waited.

"Are you sure he needs to be a part of this?" Isabelle asked after we'd joined them.

Her voice shook slightly, betraying her nervousness. She wanted Wren out of the house while it was teeming with vampires, and I didn't blame her, but he had to stay. We wanted to do everything right this time, which meant including a human in the conversation about the future of the Empire. Madam St. Clair, the human Governess of New Haven, would have been our first choice, but she still hadn't returned from up north. Waylon was the second choice, but after I'd saved Henry and set out on my quest for vengeance, he had left the White Witches' settlement and set out on his own mission to spread the word that the Dark Witches were no more. Once the news had reached those who'd traveled away before the war, they'd begun trickling back to their home regions. My father hadn't returned yet, but every day, more and more humans arrived in New Haven, so I hoped to see him soon.

A knock sounded on the front door of the mansion, snapping me out of my thoughts. Everyone stilled, instantly on edge. Henry's unease was palpable as his hand tightened around mine. I waited for him to pull me in the direction of the foyer, but he hesitated. When I gave him a questioning look, his deep-blue gaze fastened on me, and my breath hitched at what I saw in his eyes. Fear. All color had drained from his face, and his muscles had coiled so tight that I was afraid they might snap. Understanding washed over me then. He was hesitating because the last time we'd met with the clan leaders, days of torture had ensued for him.

Turning to face him fully, I placed my free hand over his racing heart. My chest was painfully tight as I stared at him. Moments like these were rare, when he let me glimpse how much what he'd endured truly affected him.

"Breathe with me," I said, looking into his eyes. "I won't let anything happen to you."

Gaze locked on mine, he covered my hand on his chest with his, and inhaled and exhaled deeply, matching my breathing. After a few seconds, when his heartbeat had evened out, he gave a small nod and lowered my hand from his chest. Together, we turned toward the study door and walked out into the foyer.

34

We returned to the study a few minutes later, with the five clan leaders and Celeste in tow. Just like the humans deserved a seat at the table during this meeting, the White Witches also needed to be included. Besides, Henry and I had a plan on how to enforce the new world order, and we needed Celeste's help to help carry it out.

Still holding my hand, Henry led me to stand in front of the oversized desk. My gaze briefly snapped to the Battle of New Haven painting on the wall behind it. The art piece was something I would be glad to leave behind when we moved out of the estate. Turning away from the canvas, I faced the other vampires in the room. Henry assumed a position to my right, with Isabelle and Wren standing beside him. Celeste flanked my other side, and I wondered if Henry had placed me closest to her in case things went very wrong again. Even if they did, I wouldn't leave him. Never again.

Henry glanced at me as if he knew what I was thinking, and I gave him a reassuring smile before I faced the clan leaders again. My gaze slid over all the perfect faces. Thanks to me, Yvonne was the only original clan leader left. She was also the only one who'd seen first-hand what I was capable of. Unease rolled off her in waves as she shifted from foot to foot, her gaze cast down to the floor. A young man with rich-brown skin and short, thickly curled hair stood to her right. I knew his name was Remy, and he was the new leader of the Stern clan. Thankfully, I didn't pick up on the same air of arrogance and entitlement his predecessors had displayed when his dark brown eyes met mine. His flawless face was open as he stared back at me, which I hoped was a good sign.

Shifting my gaze away from him, I looked at Dion Bouvier, who'd taken over after Lena. The male was tall and slim, with a narrow face that seemed to be permanently set in a snide expression. He stood to Yvonne's left, and his cold, nearly translucent eyes bored into me as he lifted his chin in defiance. I smirked at him and briefly glanced at the two remaining vampires in the room.

Adelaide had taken over after Camilla, and Delphine after Moreau. The former had long blonde hair and pale-blue eyes, while the latter had glossy, black locks that currently sat in a topknot. A few wispy strands were left down to frame her face, highlighting her unusual violet eyes with upswept corners. The two females were a striking contrast to each other, standing off and to the side between Dion and Isabelle. Their expressions were mostly neutral, if a little wary.

"Without further ado, thank you all for coming tonight," Henry's deep voice rang out in the study. Gone was the brief moment of weakness he'd let me witness earlier. Now, he was a cool, stoic presence by my side. "Your clans have chosen you all to replace the ones who perished." All eyes in the room darted to me. Even Yvonne finally dragged her gaze from the floor to focus on me. Henry's choice of words had been intentional—he'd wanted to establish dominance, to remind them who was in charge. "We hope that you are different from your predecessors, and that you will help us usher in a new era."

He looked around the room at the other vampires, but all the wide-eyed, wary gazes were still fastened on me.

"Everyone in this room knows what transpired a few nights ago," I spoke up, my voice loud and steady. It bounced off the walls in the otherwise quiet study. "Your former leaders crossed me, so I retaliated. The only reason you are all still standing here is because I chose to spare your lives." I gave Yvonne a pointed look. She swallowed thickly but held my gaze. "The past few days have proven I'm capable of great monstrosities, but I am not a monster. You don't have to be one, either," I paused, letting the words sink in. "We're offering you a chance. A chance at a future in a new world ruled by humans, not vampires. You can live alongside them or not live at all."

I could feel Henry's rapt attention on me like a physical touch. He was enjoying this—my shameless display of power.

"A new world ruled by humans? Where would we live?" Dion asked. Not surprising he would be the first one to speak up.

"How will we feed?" Adelaide chimed in, her glacial gaze darting around the room.

I noticed Yvonne's lips curve into an arrogant smile—she'd expected such resistance from the others. Moreover, she'd counted on it.

"You can keep some of the wealth you have accumulated," Henry took over like I'd known he would. After all, we'd discussed our plan of action beforehand. "But you will have to move out of your lavish estates and give them back to the humans. As for feeding, you can take the blood you have left in your cellars with you. When you run out, you can feed from humans but do so discreetly and without harming anyone. It's all about self-control. That was how we survived in the past, before the Red War. We would feed from humans, but then give them our blood to heal the bite marks and compel them to forget. We would return to that, to leading a quiet, discreet life in the shadows."

Delphine snarled and jerked her head to the side, fixing her gaze on the wall. She clearly hated what we were suggesting, but was choosing not to engage. *Smart.*

"The rules are simple," Henry continued. "We are not asking you to do something you haven't done before. Vampires had lived in the shadows before the Red War. We are simply going back to how it used to be. To how it should be."

"And what if we don't agree to your terms?" Dion challenged.

"Ask Yvonne if you should find out what happens then," I challenged back.

Dion's fish eyes darted to the female who paled, looking like she was about to be sick. "I buried Emeric's clan under a mountain. Do you want your family to meet the same fate?" I forged on. Henry and I were planning to dig them out eventually, but he didn't need to know that.

"No," Dion rasped, meeting my gaze again.

I wasn't proud of what I'd done when the darkness had consumed me, but the clans would never know I felt even a smidge of regret. All they would ever see would be the cold, menacing facade of a predator who was more powerful than them. I hoped that would be enough to deter any thoughts of rebellion in the future. And if it didn't, well...we would have to find a way to squash it, hopefully without resorting to me embracing the darkness again.

"We propose a pact forged in blood to seal the agreement," Henry said, and the clan leaders exchanged nervous glances at his words. This was where Celeste came in. In training with her, I'd been growing stronger with my light magic, but I wasn't powerful enough for such an intricate spell.

"A blood pact?" Yvonne asked, her dark brows climbing her forehead.

Henry nodded and glanced at Celeste—a cue for her to take over.

The witch let the suspense build for a few seconds as her gaze slowly traveled over all the vampires in the room. When her perusal was finally over, she reached into her cloak and retrieved a piece of parchment.

"All I need is a drop of blood from each of you," she said, as she walked around the desk and rolled the parchment out on top of it. I could recite the words on the paper by heart—after all, I was the one who'd written them down. They mirrored the terms Henry had laid out to the clan leaders.

Yvonne stepped closer to the desk first, peering down at the parchment atop it. Her eyes quickly scanned the paper before lifting to Celeste.

"How will this work?" she asked.

"Your blood will make it binding. If you ever break any of the rules outlined in this agreement, the spell I will place on it will alert me, and then…" She trailed off, turning her head to look at me.

"I'll take it from there," I said darkly, trying to infuse my voice with as much menacing energy as I could.

Yvonne paled and staggered back a step.

"We are not going to require that everyone in your clan signs the agreement," Henry said, drawing the attention to him. "But as the clan leaders, it will be your responsibility to keep your families in line."

"And what if we don't?" Dion asked.

"Then you are not fit to be their leader," Henry told him. The look he gave him spoke louder than words, making Dion curl into himself. "I'll go first," Henry said, letting go of my hand. "The Duval clan will be a part of this contract just like everyone else," he declared, in an attempt to show good faith.

He turned toward the desk and pricked his index finger with his claw, letting a drop of blood drip on the parchment.

"Who's next?" Celeste asked, as Henry's blood bloomed on the paper.

"I'll go next," Remy said, speaking up for the first time. "The sooner this meeting is adjourned, the sooner I can be on my way to begin making preparations for our new way of life." His boyish voice didn't carry even a hint of malice, and he sounded almost relieved by the decision. I angled my head, taking a closer look at him. It appeared not everyone in the Stern clan was a depraved psychopath.

After he'd stepped up to the table and added his blood to the parchment, silence stretched as everyone else in the room stood unmoving, their gazes cast down to the floor.

"You do realize that when Henry said we propose a blood pact, that wasn't really a suggestion?" I said, folding my arms over my chest.

I fixed my eyes on Yvonne standing in front of me, letting my gaze bore into her until she had no choice but to meet it. With a snarl, she moved to the table and added a drop of her blood.

After the remaining clan leaders had begrudgingly done the same, a sigh of relief almost left me. It appeared we'd won, but I knew I would never truly rest easy while other vampires were still in the world. I would always be on high alert, waiting for something to happen. In a way, it would be easier to kill them all, only leaving Henry, me, and Isabelle, but that would make me a monster, and I refused to be one.

"It's your turn," Celeste said, looking at me.

With a nod, I pricked my thumb and ran it across the parchment, smearing the six drops of blood.

"What are you doing?" Adelaide asked, scrunching her face up in concern.

"Binding your will to mine," I replied. "You will never be able to run or hide. I will always be able to track and summon you."

Shock splashed across the clan leaders' faces just as Celeste held out her hands above the parchment and uttered an incantation.

Potent magic filled the study, making it difficult to breathe. The others seemed impervious to it, but as a White Witch, I was experiencing the full effect of Celeste's powers. It clogged my throat and constricted my chest, suffocating me. When Henry noticed something was wrong, he placed a hand on my lower back for support. I gritted my teeth through the discomfort, as Celeste's chanting grew louder until it abruptly stopped. The oppressive waves of magic ceased at the same time, and I inhaled deeply just as the parchment under Celeste's hands flickered. The edges of the document burst into blue flames that rapidly spread, eating up the paper until they met in the middle, dissipating in a puff of white smoke. Even after it had burned, the parchment appeared perfectly intact, shimmering slightly.

"It is done," Celeste declared.

No one moved. Everyone barely breathed as the witch rolled up the parchment and handed it to Wren, who paled as he received it.

"There is one more matter we need to discuss," Henry said next to me. His deep voice jolted everyone out of their stupor, and all the eyes in the room fixed on him. "Are there any Ravagers left that we don't know about?"

My gaze slid to Yvonne, and her amber eyes widened in fear.

"The Ravagers you sicced on me at your estate. Where did they come from?" I asked her.

Yvonne squared her shoulders, standing tall as she met my gaze. She was terrified of me—I could smell her fear. Yet, she didn't cower before me. A part of me still admired that about her.

"I made them," she said loudly, but her voice trembled, betraying her terror. "I made them, hoping they would take you down when you came for me."

Henry tensed next to me. I knew how he felt about Ravagers. They were feral killers, but through no fault of their own. As new vampires, they needed guidance, but their makers refused to provide any, leaving them to the darkness and at the mercy of the sinister hunger that warped their minds.

"Are there still any left?" Henry asked quietly, his tone deadly.

"Yes," Yvonne replied, her voice catching. At least she had more sense than to lie about something we would eventually find out.

Her eyes filled with tears, and her forehead was slick with sweat. I was willing to bet she thought that with that one word, she'd just signed her death sentence.

"Anyone else?" Henry's deep-blue gaze swept over the faces in the room. The other clan leaders shook their heads in denial. Henry refocused on Yvonne, and she seemed to grow small under his scathing glare. "How many?" he asked low. I knew the quiet tone was not a true representation of the storm raging inside him. Yvonne knew it, too, and her gaze was begging when it shot to me before returning to Henry. "Four," she said in a soft whisper.

A muscle flexed along Henry's jaw, and his hand tightened on my lower back as if he were barely containing his rage.

"I can kill them if you wish..." Yvonne said.

"No," Henry cut her off. "You will take them with you wherever you decide to go, and they will become a part of your clan. You will work with them and guide them out of the frenzy of bloodlust. Do I make myself clear?"

"Yes," Yvonne breathed, staring at him in shock. I wasn't sure if she was shocked because Henry was sparing her life, or because of what he'd just asked her to do.

"We will help you," Henry told her. When he glanced at me, I nodded in agreement.

"Now, this meeting is adjourned," I declared.

The clan leaders swept from the room, with Yvonne lingering behind for a moment as if she couldn't believe she was leaving the study alive. After she was gone, a rough exhale of relief left me, and I sagged against the desk. His hand still on my back, Henry leaned in, resting his forehead against my temple.

A strange quiet settled over the study, interrupted only by the crinkling of parchment in Wren's trembling hand. Isabelle broke it first by saying, "Did that truly happen? Did we pull that off?"

Henry lifted his head from mine and looked at his sister.

"I think we did," he said with a hesitant smile.

A smile pulled at my lips as well, but it quickly faded as I turned to Celeste.

"We still need to do something about Damien," I said.

"I know," the witch replied. "I haven't been able to locate him. He is somewhere in the Black Forest. I can sense his malevolent presence, but anytime I try to ambush him, he's gone."

"Is it possible there is more than one of those...demons?" Henry asked, looking at the witch.

Celeste shook her head.

"Believe it or not, even gods have rules to obey. Dispatching too many demons into this realm would upset the delicate balance, so Xanthus only sends one of his minions at a time. That's why he can't send an entire army to take over this dimension. If he wants an army, his demon must build one here, on this plain, recruiting those susceptible to his dark influence."

An involuntary shudder rolled through me at her words. I had been one of those susceptible to the darkness.

Even though the thought of dealing with Damien again terrified me, I forced myself to say, "Let me know if you need my help with finding and fighting him."

Henry tensed next to me when I made the offer, but added, "If you need *our* help."

Celeste's knowing gaze drifted to his face before returning to me.

"I don't need your help. I told you I have a plan," she said. "Enjoy this moment of peace. Who knows how fleeting it will be."

With that, the witch turned and left the study.

Her parting words lingered long after the door had closed behind her.

Would our life always be like this? A desperate attempt to cherish transient moments of calm before the next storm?

When I looked at Henry, I found him watching me, making me wonder if he was thinking the same thing I was.

Even if our life would always be like this, I didn't care, I decided, as long as he was by my side.

35

Packing up my things felt strange but also liberating, because leaving the estate meant leaving the old world behind—the world where the vampires ruled over humans. Two nights had passed since we'd met with the clan leaders, and I still had to fight the urge to pinch myself when I thought about the outcome of that meeting. Even now, doubt crept in if this was truly my reality. Fear surged that maybe I was dreaming. Would I wake up and find I was still at Celeste's cottage and Henry was still in captivity? I quickly dismissed the thought. For the past two nights, I'd woken up next to Henry, to his hard, magnificent body wrapped around mine. I'd woken up in his bedroom at the Duval Estate, not at the witch's cottage in the Black Forest. It *was* my reality. We'd won.

Blinking rapidly, I shook my head to clear my thoughts and finished shoving my belongings into the small bag I'd brought with me when I'd first arrived at the estate. Thankfully, I didn't have that much to pack. I was leaving all of the expensive gowns behind, not anticipating I would need them once we'd found a simpler, less lavish dwelling. I'd also decided not to take any of my things from my father's home. Those knick-knacks belonged to the old Sophie, not the new Sophie I'd become. As much as I wished I could erase the past few weeks, a small part of me knew that I wouldn't, even if I could. They'd made me who I was today. Still broken, but healing. Flawless on the outside, but fractured on the inside.

My close brush with the darkness had revealed I was susceptible to it, probably more so than most because I was both, a vampire and a witch. But it had also proven that I could overcome it, albeit with Henry's help, but overcome it, nonetheless. I didn't see my dependence on him as a weakness. As much as I depended on him, he depended on me. We chose to depend on each other. It was us against the world. I hoped the new world would be kind to us. But even if it wasn't, we would face the challenges and persevere. Together, we were unstoppable.

Forcing myself out of my thoughts again, I looked around the bare bedroom. It had never gotten the "lived-in" look because of my short time here, but I knew I'd miss it all the same. A smile tugged at my lips as the memories from my first night here invaded my mind. I could see a phantom image of me propped against the low dresser with Henry towering over me. I'd held a wooden dagger to his chest then, threatening his life. Not even in my wildest dreams would I have imagined that his life would become the most precious to me.

Lifting my eyes to the ceiling, I listened to him move about in his bedroom upstairs. My smile grew as warmth blossomed in my chest. I was beyond excited to start the next chapter with him. The past few weeks had been nothing but a prologue. Our adventure was only just beginning, and knowing that filled me with nervous energy but also great anticipation. Beaming at the thought, I grabbed the bag I'd packed and left the room, closing the door behind me with a soft click.

I quickly walked down the long hallway, my steps easy and light. I couldn't remember the last time I'd felt so unburdened and carefree. Even after I'd defeated the Dark Witches, I hadn't let myself relax and revel in the victory because there had been so much uncertainty about the clans. The future was still uncertain, and Damien was still on the loose, but after I'd looked the darkness in the eye and had come out on the other side because Henry had fought for me, I knew there was nothing we wouldn't be able to face together. My mind was clear, and my heart was full of love and hope. I felt exhilarated and limitless, and it wasn't because of the black magic flowing through my veins, but because of Henry and his love for me and my love for him. Nothing had ever felt so right, and I was soaking up the feeling, floating through the empty hallway. When I reached the foyer, Wren was there, piling up bags by the front door.

"Let me guess—all Isabelle's clothes?" I arched a brow, my lips still stretched in a grin.

"Yes, and she's still packing." Wren huffed out a laugh.

"Henry's still packing, too. I'm going to check on him," I said, turning toward the grand staircase.

"Sophie," Wren said, stopping me in my tracks. "Can I speak with you?"

"Of course." I faced him again, meeting his pale-blue gaze.

He swallowed thickly, his throat bobbing. His nervous look told me to prepare for a serious conversation.

"What happened in the past—" he started.

"Is in the past," I cut him off.

His blond eyebrows flew up in surprise.

"I just want to make sure we're truly able to put it behind us. I'm sorry for what I did. So, so sorry." He cast his gaze to the ground and gave a small shake of his head. "The thing is," he looked back up at me. "I wish I could tell you if I could go back, I wouldn't do what I did, that I would choose death over working for the Dark Witches, but I can't tell you that because I'm still not sure that I would. I'm not yet the man that I aspire to be. What you did to defeat the Dark Witches…your selfless sacrifice… I admire it, truly, but I'm not as brave as you. I'm selfish, and that makes me a coward."

Speechless, I stared at Wren. Weeks ago, I would have called him weak and spineless, but I could no longer do that after what I'd been through. Perhaps the battle of good and evil Celeste had mentioned before did not only unfold on the realm level. The battle also took place on the individual level, in each and every one of us, regardless of the species. Human, witch, vampire—we all carried some darkness within us, some more than others. It was a constant battle to keep that darkness contained and not let it take over.

"I forgive you," I told him, and I meant it. "So you should forgive yourself and keep working on becoming the man you want to be."

A look of potent relief and appreciation washed over Wren's features because I'd set him free—as much as I could by forgiving him. The rest was up to him. He needed to let go of the guilt. "And the selfless part?" I said, searching his face. "I think you just didn't have anyone worth sacrificing for. But you do now, don't you?"

Wren paled slightly, as if what I was implying was a new and startling revelation.

"I do," he said low, as if to himself.

I walked away then, leaving him alone with his thoughts. As I climbed the stairs to the second story, another phantom image appeared before me. It was a memory of me from the night when I'd sneaked into Henry's bedroom to search for the Tear. I followed the sheer silhouette down the long hallway, lost in thought. That night I'd revealed to Henry the truth about my mother's death, and he'd learned that Vincent's death had been my fault. He could have chosen to loathe me, to hold the grudge forever, but he'd found it in his heart to forgive me. More than that, he'd fallen in love with me despite my role in Vincent's untimely demise. He'd chosen love over hatred. He'd chosen *me*.

He would keep choosing me for the rest of our everlasting nights. And I would keep choosing him. Always and forever.

I rapped my knuckles on the bedroom door and walked in. Henry was standing by the bed, a half-packed bag on top of the covers before him. His gaze cast down, he was looking at something he was holding in his hands. A picture, I realized when I approached. I stopped behind his back and peeked around him at the small portrait set in a simple black frame. His human family. My breath left me as I stared at the faded piece of parchment. Henry had gotten his raven-black locks from his father, who'd been tall and broad-shouldered like he was. His deep-blue eyes were his mother's. She'd been beautiful, with long, wavy blonde hair and a kind, round face. He and his sister, Marcy, were in the picture as well. The portrait must have been painted right before Henry had turned, because he looked like he did now, a twenty-five-year-old man, and Marcy appeared to be about twelve, six years after they'd taken her in. The girl looked innocent and sweet, with golden ringlets peeking out from under her bonnet, framing her heart-shaped face.

A ragged exhale left Henry, his large body heaving with it. The energy pouring out of him was heavy, full of sadness and regret, but it was also mixed with love and wistful longing. Gently, I wrapped my arms around his torso, resting my head on his back.

"Where have you been keeping the portrait?" I asked quietly, breathing him in.

"In the bedside table," he admitted.

"You shouldn't hide it anymore."

He placed the picture in the bag he was packing and carefully unwrapped my arms from around him.

"I dreaded telling you about them," he said low when he turned around to face me. "I was scared of losing you."

I put my hands on his arms and squeezed lightly.

"There is nothing you could ever say or do to lose me," I

assured him. "You don't need to hide that part of your past. We need to honor them. You're not a monster, and nothing could ever convince me otherwise."

"I don't deserve you."

"Funny, because I think I don't deserve you."

He chuckled low, wrapping his arms around me and pulling me to his hard chest. I rested my cheek against the steady rhythm of his heart.

"Where are we going to live?" I asked, knowing the answer didn't truly matter to me as long as I was with Henry.

"I don't know. Where would you like to go?"

"Maybe we can find a place by the Starling Sea… I love being by the water," I mused aloud.

"Wherever we go, I'll like it anywhere as long as I'm with you."

His words stirred a memory, and I lifted my head from his chest and looked into his eyes.

"You've said that to me before," I said. "In one of the dreams I had while you were…gone."

"Oh?" Henry's brows climbed his forehead. "A premonition, perhaps? You are a White Witch, after all."

"Maybe…" I trailed off, thinking about that dream in which Henry and I had been lounging in the meadow drenched in sunlight.

Silence stretched as Henry became lost in his own thoughts, his gaze sweeping over the room.

"I don't think I'm going to miss this place. It had always felt empty and cold. Until you moved in." A smile tugged at his lips.

A small laugh bubbled up. "I'm sure at first you cursed the day I showed up in your life."

Henry's gaze returned to me, and it was full of mild amusement. "I didn't expect a wooden dagger strapped to your thigh. But then again, I didn't expect many things. Like finding the love of my life."

My breath caught as my heart swelled with so much emotion, I thought it might burst.

"I love you," I breathed, my gaze dropping to the smirk on his perfect face.

His lips parted, and he leaned in for a kiss, his breath coasting over my mouth. My heart danced in my chest as if I hadn't kissed him countless times before.

A fist pounding on the mansion's front door snapped my attention from Henry's lips. He lifted his head and stilled, listening. Another knock sounded louder than the one before.

"Are we expecting someone?" My brows lifted.

"Not that I know of…unless—"

"My father is back!" I exclaimed, sprinting from the room.

36

*H*enry followed close behind, and by the time we'd arrived in the foyer, it was already teeming with people. Wren must have left them in. My father was here, with Waylon and Amelie. Madam St. Clair and Ezra were here as well, along with a few other humans who'd used to serve the Duvals.

"Father!" I exclaimed, crashing into him and enveloping him in a tight embrace. With a startled laugh, he hugged me back. I had to remind myself not to squeeze too hard as I held on for a few minutes. "You're back," I rasped, pulling away to look at him. His weathered features blurred as tears gathered in my eyes.

"It's good to be back," my father replied, his voice hoarse. His blue-gray eyes were also glistening with tears. "Waylon told me about what you've accomplished. You defeated the Dark Witches..." He trailed off, studying my features as if to make sure I was still me. "He also told me what happened after... Are you okay?"

Suddenly, I felt like a little girl in his presence; the weight of the past few days crashing into me, nearly sweeping me under. I managed to stay on my feet as I nodded.

"I'm okay," I assured him. *I will be.*

"I see you brought her back like you promised," I heard Waylon say to Henry.

"I did," was all Henry said.

He didn't add that bringing me back had almost cost him his life. My skin prickled at the thought. As if sensing my unease, Henry stepped closer to me, his proximity bringing instant comfort.

"What about the clans?" Waylon asked, his features tense.

"They live," Henry replied. "They appointed new clan leaders, with whom we met the other night. They have agreed to give up control over the Empire."

Waylon looked shocked but not relieved.

"How are you going to enforce that?" he asked, his tone apprehensive.

"We forged a magically-binding contract signed in blood. If the clans ever get out of line, Sophie and I will be there to put them back into their place. All we ask is that the humans leave us be and let us live peacefully alongside them," said Henry.

A heavy silence followed his words. Everyone turned to Waylon as if waiting for him to decide how they should feel about what had been revealed. It didn't go unnoticed that even though the Governess was among us, Waylon seemed to hold more authority than she did at the moment.

Finally, after another beat of silence, Waylon's shoulders sagged, and his features relaxed just a fraction.

"That's great news about the clans and the blood treaty. I believe you will help reinforce the new world order, but I still plan to recruit more men into the Order of Light and become more organized."

He turned his attention to me.

"I tried to spread the word about what you did for this country," he said. When I tensed, he added, "Without giving too much away."

The secret of the Tear is safe with me, I read in his eyes.

"I don't have a problem with the vampires living alongside us. Especially, if you can help keep them in check. But I can't guarantee the others will feel the same way. The border guards…" His throat worked on a swallow. "The ones that remained… They'll seek retribution for what the clans did. It will be safer for you to leave the region."

As if on cue, Isabelle strode into the foyer, loaded with bags. Wren rushed to her aid though she didn't need it.

"We know," I said to Waylon. "We are planning to leave as soon as possible."

We'd realized days ago that not all humans would see me as their liberator. They would see me only as a vampire—a predator whose protection they no longer needed. An animal that had to be put down so the humans could feel safe. Our family couldn't stay here. We needed to go away—to get lost in another region, enjoying a simple life without attracting attention to ourselves. The only reason we hadn't left yet was because I'd wanted to see my father to say goodbye.

"Lord Duval—" Madam St. Clair's husky voice rang out in the foyer, drawing everyone's attention to her.

"No need for formalities, Madam St. Clair," Henry interjected. "I am no longer Lord Duval, I am simply…Henry."

A look of wonder stole over his face as if this was the first time he realized that he no longer had the Lord's title attached to his name. He didn't seem upset by it. On the contrary, relief was etched into his striking features, and his deep-blue eyes danced as he glanced at me. Smiling, I stepped away from my father and closer to him. He smiled back, lovingly tucking me to his side.

"My Henry," I whispered, so low that only he could hear.

His smile grew.

"On behalf of the humans of the Empire, I would like to thank you for what you did for this country," Madam St. Clair said, looking at me. Her shrewd gray eyes scanned me from head to toe as if she was seeing me for the first time. "I should have known you were up to something when you volunteered to participate in the Selection the second time."

I lifted a shoulder in a non-committal gesture.

"I, for one, am glad you didn't suspect anything. When you let her participate in the Selection again, you brought her into my life," Henry said, affection pouring out of him as he stared down at me.

"I have a feeling even if I didn't, she would have found another way into your life," Madam St. Clair remarked.

Henry laughed, not taking his eyes off me. The sound was nice and deep, reverberating through me all the way down through the tips of my toes.

"I think you're right," he said.

"So, where will you go?" the Governess asked.

Henry tore his gaze away from me and looked at her.

"Wherever it is we end up, we will lead a quiet life without harming anyone. You have my word," he told her.

"I trust your word, Lord—" Madam St. Clair caught herself with a low chuckle. "Henry."

"What will happen to us?" Ezra spoke up, looking around at the other servants in the room.

His mahogany brown hair had gotten longer since I'd last seen him, and he was not as pale as he'd used to be.

"You all are free to go," Henry said, his deep voice carrying through the foyer. Ezra's brown eyes widened at his words. Apparently, that wasn't what he'd wanted to hear.

"We'll give you some funds to help you until you get on your feet," I said out of nowhere. Isabelle shot me a look of dismay while Henry squeezed me closer to him in a sign of approval.

The other servants lit up at my words and began chatting excitedly among themselves. Ezra still looked uncertain, though, shifting from foot to foot. Understanding washed over me as I realized that he didn't have any family left after Rory had died. Ezra wasn't from New Haven like most of the other servants, so he had no one to help him adjust to this new world where he was free and no longer had to serve the Duvals.

"You can stay with me until you find a job and a place of your own," my father offered, glancing at me. I gave him an appreciative smile. It would be good for my father to have company after I was gone, and he could help Ezra start a new life. I had no doubt that he would treat him like his own son. Warmth blossomed in my chest at the thought.

"Are you sure?" Ezra asked him. "It would be nice to stay in New Haven where Rory is buried..." he trailed off, looking down to the stone floor. I had to remind myself that only a short time had passed since her death. It only seemed like ages to me because of everything I'd been through. Ezra was still grieving, the shadows of his loss draped over him like a shroud.

"I'm sure." My father clasped his shoulder in assurance.

"Surely you're not going to leave until after the wedding?" Amelie asked, snapping my attention to her.

"The wedding? What wedding?" My father's gray brows shot up.

Henry stiffened next to me before he cleared his throat and said, "Thomas, I need to officially ask you for your daughter's hand in marriage."

My eyes pricked with tears as emotion swelled in my chest. Henry knew I didn't need my father's permission but wanted to ask for it regardless. Because he always wanted to do the right thing.

My father paled.

"You're getting married?" he asked, with something akin to sorrow in his voice.

My brows knitted. I didn't need his permission, but it would still break my heart if he didn't approve. Perhaps I just needed to convince him, to tell him how much Henry meant to me. "My little girl is getting married?" my father said, and my scowl smoothed out as understanding dawned on me. He wasn't against the marriage; he was just sad because his little girl was growing up. I'd grown up a long time ago when I'd found my mother dead and discovered her note about the Tear, but it seemed my father had still been harboring hope that I would return to him one day. And now that hope was slipping away because I would not be returning under my father's roof. I would be making my own life and future with my husband.

Untucking myself from Henry's side, I approached my father and took his weathered hands in mine. They trembled slightly as I held them.

"Yes." I smiled at him. "I love him, Father, and he loves me, and there is no doubt in my mind that he will make me the happiest girl in the world."

"I think he already does," my father said, his eyes glistening. "Of course you have my permission," he added low, pulling me into a tight embrace. "I know you didn't need it, but thank you for asking anyway," he murmured against the top of my head. "It means a lot," he added, and I knew the words were meant for Henry.

"Well then." Amelie clapped her hands in excitement. "Sounds like we have a wedding to plan."

I laughed softly, shaking my head as I let go of my father and walked back to Henry.

"It looks like we'll be getting married sooner than expected," I told him, watching for his reaction. With a soft smile, he wrapped his arms around my waist and looked into my eyes.

"Truly, it's perfect. I can't wait to call you my wife."

37

"Are you nervous?" Amelie met my gaze in the vanity mirror. I sat before it while she worked on my hair.

"No, I'm not," I told her with a small smile. I'd never been so sure about anything in my life.

"Of course, you're not—what a silly question. After everything you went through to get Henry back, why would you be nervous about marrying him?" The girl muttered as if to herself. "I have to admit, I didn't understand it at first. When Celeste told me you went…" Bright green eyes shot to mine in the mirror.

"Unhinged?" I prompted.

Amelie grimaced but nodded.

"I couldn't understand it at first, but I think I'm beginning to now…" she trailed off, her cheeks turning pink.

"You like Waylon," I said a moment later.

Amelie swallowed before words began spilling out of her. "I have these…feelings in my chest, in my heart, and mostly they bring me joy, but…sometimes they terrify me," she rambled, mindlessly worrying the loose strands of my hair. She'd pinned the top half up, leaving the bottom to cascade down my back. "I've never had feelings like these toward anyone. I've only ever read about them in books. It's so scary to fall..." she caught herself, releasing a shuddering breath.

When I went to turn away from the mirror, she realized what she was doing with my hair and let go of the silky locks.

"Did Waylon tell you about our history?" I asked, as I rose from the chair and faced her.

"He did, and I have to admit it made me a bit jealous at first when he told me," Amelie said, meeting my gaze. "But then I saw you with Henry, and seeing you two together erased any doubts from my mind. It's obvious you only have eyes for each other."

I inclined my head in confirmation she didn't need.

"I only asked if you knew about Waylon and me to tell you that we've known each other for a long time." I clasped her delicate hands. "Waylon is a good man, so if you fall, he will be there to catch you."

"Like Henry caught you?" she asked, and my lips curved into a smile.

"Yes." My gaze grew distant as I thought about it. "I think he was catching me even before I knew I was falling."

My breath hitched as my chest became too tight, struggling to contain the love I felt for him. I took a steadying inhale and refocused on Amelie. "But because Waylon is a good man, I need you to promise me something." My gaze fastened on hers to make sure she was listening and paying attention. "When you fall, and he catches you, you will have to catch him in return."

"I will," Amelie whispered as if making a vow.

I smiled at the young witch, and she smiled right back, her pretty face lighting up with girlish excitement.

"Isabelle's here," I said, letting go of Amelie's hands.

My vampire ears had picked up on her approach a few seconds before.

When she rapped her knuckles on my bedroom door and walked in, I turned toward her.

"Are you ready for your wedding dress?" she asked, holding up a long, ivory-hued gown with lace overlay.

My smile grew as I took in the gown. The flutter sleeves were short and made entirely of lace, while the neckline was in the shape of a V but didn't plunge too deep. The dress was simple and elegant and instantly felt like me.

"Did you select the gown yourself?" I asked Isabelle, my eyebrows raised.

"I did." She inclined her head, looking proud of the fact. "I would have picked something more revealing to flaunt your slender form, but I know your taste is different from mine."

"It's perfect," I breathed, reaching out to brush my fingers over the lace. "Thank you." I lifted my gaze to Isabelle's. "For everything."

I was grateful to her for so many things. For fighting with Henry against the clans after he'd sent me away, for rushing to his side to help him when I'd shown up at the estate with his limp body in my arms, for not tearing out my throat when she'd realized that I was the one who'd hurt him, but most of all for telling me not to give up on our love even when she'd been scared I would take him away from her.

Isabelle's stunning features softened as we stared at each other.

"Thank you for making Henry happy," she said. "And if you ever hurt him again, I *will* kill you," she added, but her mouth twitched as if she were fighting a smile.

I didn't hide my own smile as I said, "I wouldn't expect anything less from you."

When I turned back to Amelie, her eyes were wide as they darted between Isabelle and me.

"If that interaction was sweet by vampire standards, I don't want to know what you do when you're mad at each other," the girl said, and Isabelle and I both chuckled at the comment.

"Let's hope you never have to find out," Isabelle remarked,

taking the dress off the hanger. "Let's get you into this gown so my brother can marry you. He's practically bursting with anticipation."

"Actually, I'll get myself dressed," I told her. "I'd like a few minutes alone."

Isabelle's sharp gaze flicked over me, and she looked like she wanted to argue.

She must have decided against it because she said, "Of course. We'll be in the ballroom along with everyone else." She draped the dress over the chair by the vanity and headed for the door. "Sophie," she said, stopping on her way out. "Henry is waiting for you. Don't make him wait too long."

"I won't," I promised, with a small smile that I hoped would put her at ease.

It did, and with a nod, she swept from the room.

"Are you sure you don't need help?" Amelie asked, halting by the door after Isabelle had left.

"I'm sure," I assured her.

"What you said about Waylon…thank you for that," the witch said, her cheeks pink again as she turned to leave.

"You're welcome."

After she'd ducked her chin and slipped out of the door, I quickly changed into my wedding gown. My hands trembled slightly as I ran them down the lacy silk skirt. It wasn't nervousness that had invaded my senses—it was excitement and anticipation. I'd asked for a few minutes alone, but not because I needed to steel myself. I'd wanted this time to let what was happening truly sink in, so I could soak in this moment and revel in it.

I knew what Henry and I were about to do wouldn't change anything between us. I was already his, and he was mine, but this moment still felt special, and I wanted to lock it away in my heart as a happy memory, which I knew would be one of many to come.

I stepped into my low-heeled shoes and clasped the locket holding the portrait of my mother behind my neck. I decided to forgo wearing the Tear tonight, leaving it where it was stowed away in the vanity drawer. My gaze settled on the locket on my chest in the mirror's reflection. My mother couldn't be here with me on my special day, but she was here with me in spirit. As soon as the thought crossed my mind, I felt a hand land on my shoulder, making me suck in a sharp breath. No one else was in the room, but I felt my mother with me. Standing behind me, she was clasping my shoulder just like she'd done on the night I'd defeated the Dark Witches.

Peace and serenity washed over me…and love. My mother's love felt different from Henry's. His was powerful and smoky—a worship with a hint of spice. Hers was no less powerful but also radiant—the love of a mother for her child. I breathed in deeply, inhaling that love, filling my lungs and my heart with it. My mother was here with me, and she approved of my union with Henry, just like I knew she would.

A smile tugged at my lips and my eyes were bright when I cast one last look at myself in the mirror before walking out of my bedroom. My smile grew the closer I got to the ballroom. I couldn't wait to see Henry. I couldn't wait to make him mine in every definition of the word and declare in front of everyone that I was his forever. Before I knew it, my feet were carrying me with supernatural speed, and a few seconds later, I skidded to a stop in front of the closed ballroom door. I halted right by my father, who jumped when I appeared before him as if out of thin air.

"Sorry." I gave a small, apologetic smile.

"It's okay." He squared his shoulders. It was strange seeing him in the finely cut clothes Isabelle had picked for him, but he wore it well, looking like he could be a nobleman in another life. "Sophie," he said, his voice catching as he took me in. "You look beautiful."

"Thank you," I told him, smoothing out my hair that had gotten tousled from my sprint through the halls.

"Are you ready?" Ezra asked from where he stood by the door.

I nodded, curling my arm around my father's, and he straightened and lifted his chin as Ezra opened the double doors. Brightly lit ballroom greeted me, tastefully decorated for the occasion. Isabelle and Amelie must have worked on it together, because red roses and bold, gilded elements were carefully woven in with more subtle, delicate flowers and accents. I waited for my father to start walking, but he hesitated. When I glanced at him, I found him watching me with a mix of pride and awe on his aged face.

"I'm so proud of you," he said, his voice hoarse with emotion. "Of whom you've become and what you've accomplished."

My heart squeezed in my chest as I stared at him, at a loss for words.

"Your mother would be proud, too," he continued. "If only she could see you now..." he trailed off as tears filled his eyes.

"I think she can," I told him past the lump in my throat. "I feel like she's here with us."

My father glanced behind me as if he thought he'd see her standing there.

"I think you're right," he said a moment later, his gaze refocusing on me. "I love you, Sophie."

"I love you, Father."

He cleared his throat and smiled at me, patting my hand on his forearm.

"Let me take you to the one whose love will carry you through eternity, even after I'm gone."

He turned away from me then and faced the ballroom. I stared at him a moment longer before I also faced forward. We began moving, stepping into the ballroom, and my gaze immediately zeroed in on Henry. It was as if I always knew where he was in any room. I wasn't sure if it was because I was part witch and the world whispered things to me, or because he and I were one, linked by an invisible string, always pulling me to him, tugging me in his direction.

Relief washed over Henry's features as if he'd feared I wouldn't come, but then his eyes darkened with molten heat. My throat went dry, my skin tingling with awareness from his intense stare. I loved being on the receiving end of that look, but right now, I wished he would stop staring at me like that because it was making it difficult to concentrate. As if he'd read my mind, Henry's expression changed, becoming enraptured and reverent. Now he was looking at me as if I were the only thing he would ever want or need in this world. I'd seen that look on him before, and every time, it threatened to bring me to my knees. Tonight was no exception. My legs were weak as my father and I approached where Henry stood before a simple wooden arch overflowing with fresh flowers.

Madam St. Clair stood under it, looking formal and dignified. The last time I'd seen her look like that was during the Selection weeks ago when I'd come here planning to destroy the supernatural forces holding humanity captive, plotting to kill the vampires along with the Dark Witches. Now, I was a supernatural creature myself. I was also marrying one and planning to spend the rest of my life with him. I supposed one never knew where their happiness awaited. Mine was right in front of me now, his deep-blue gaze pulling me in. A pleasant shiver rolled through me as Henry took my hands in his. One side of his mouth turned up at the charge that passed between us.

"You look stunning," he said in his deep voice, his pupils dilating again.

"You look rather dashing yourself," I replied, low and husky.

Henry was wearing a fitted jacket with a white shirt underneath and black trousers, and I found it hard to keep my gaze from roaming over every powerful inch of him. Thankfully, Madam St. Clair cleared her throat, drawing my attention to her.

"Tonight, we are celebrating the love of Sophie and Henry. A love that blossomed despite the odds and persevered in spite of the trials. The world is changing, but their love will remain constant and unwavering." Henry gently pressed my hands as if in confirmation that the words were true. I knew they were—I felt it in my heart.

Ezra handed us the rings that I'd given to him earlier—two simple gold bands that gleamed in the light of the chandelier.

I was first to place the ring on Henry's finger and utter the words of my vow, "I, Sophie, take you, Henry, to be my wedded husband, to stand by your side for all eternity," my voice rang out in the hushed silence.

I heard Henry's sharp intake of breath as his gaze dropped to the ring on his finger before returning to my face. He looked almost dumbfounded, as if he couldn't believe this was happening and that I was choosing him. He thought he didn't deserve me, but in reality, I was the one unworthy of him. I couldn't stop my gaze from dropping to his chest, to the spot where I'd hurt him when I'd almost killed him. Tears welled in my eyes, blurring my vision. Touching my chin, Henry gently guided my gaze up to his like he'd done many times before when I'd gotten lost in the terrible memories.

His eyes held mine the entire time as he proclaimed, "I, Henry, take you, Sophie, to be my wedded wife," his voice caught on the word, and he swallowed before continuing, "to be your rock for the rest of our everlasting nights."

When he slipped the ring on my finger, the band's weight brought instant comfort as if I'd been destined to wear it. My vision cleared as Henry brought my hand to his mouth and skimmed his lips over my knuckles.

"By the power granted to me by the Empire of Seven," Madam St. Clair started but paused, realization washing over her wrinkled face. "Well, I suppose it can no longer be called that." She cleared her throat as a murmur swept through the room. It seemed now was the first time everyone was beginning to realize this country was no longer the Empire of Seven. "By the power granted to me by this land, whatever it is we choose to become as we move into the future," the Governess forged on. Her words resonated within me. *Whatever we choose to become.* The humans had that choice now, because Henry and I had ensured it. "I pronounce you husband and wife."

Time slowed as Henry and I stared at each other. Everything and everyone faded away until it was just he and I. We weren't in the ballroom anymore. We were outside, standing in the sun-drenched meadow from my dreams.

"You may kiss the bride," Madam St. Clair's voice barely registered, sounding far away.

Henry moved almost immediately, as if he'd been waiting for the signal ever since the ceremony had started. He sealed his lips to mine, and I melted into him, every stroke of his tongue sending sparks through my entire body. The kiss was passionate, but ended as abruptly as it had begun—only a taste of what would come later when we were alone.

"I love you," Henry murmured against my lips before he pulled away.

"I love you, too," I whispered back.

Cheers erupted, bringing us back to the ballroom, and I almost frowned, instantly missing the meadow. Henry pulled away but didn't let go of me, his hands on my waist, holding me close. He looked happy—genuinely happy—and content, letting out a rough exhale as if he'd been holding his breath. Then he smiled at me, his smile as warm and beautiful as the sun we'd just been standing under, and I found myself smiling back, unable to avert my gaze from his perfect face. He was perfect, and this moment was perfect, and I wanted to pinch myself to make sure I wasn't dreaming. Still smiling, Henry let go of my waist and took my hand in his before turning us away from the arch. He threaded his fingers through mine as we faced our guests.

My father sat in the front row, wiping away tears from his eyes. Isabelle and Wren sat next to him, cheering and applauding loudly. Amelie and Waylon were also here, as well as Celeste and a few other White Witches.

"Let's dance!" Isabelle exclaimed, rising from her seat.

The former servants who were also in attendance spurred into action at her words. Some began serving wine and champagne, while others set up in the corner of the ballroom with their musical instruments.

"I can't believe Amelie and Isabelle were able to put all this together in just a few days," I said, as soft music began drifting through the ballroom.

"It is impressive," Henry agreed, taking a flute of champagne from a passing servant.

He handed it to me before grabbing one for himself.

I took a sip of the bubbly drink as I watched Isabelle and Wren begin swaying to the music, their bodies nearly flush with each other.

"I still don't like him," Henry muttered, following my gaze.

Isabelle's head whipped in our direction as his words reached her vampire ears. She scowled at Henry before turning back to Wren, who was watching her with rapt attention.

"You need to give him a chance," I said low. "I have a feeling he'll be a part of our lives for a long time."

When Henry gave me a questioning look, I lifted a shoulder in a non-committal gesture. He opened his mouth to ask what I'd meant, but closed it when Celeste approached us.

"Congratulations," the witch said with a warm smile.

"Thank you," both Henry and I replied.

"And thank you for helping me with my magic," I added.

Celeste nodded.

"You're welcome. Keep working on it even after you leave. The demon was right about one thing—your magic is strong.

Your power will only grow, and with proper care, you can accomplish great things."

"Speaking of Damien...has he shown himself yet?" I asked her, and held my breath. I hoped he hadn't found another susceptible soul to corrupt in the White Witches settlement.

"Not that I'm aware," Celeste replied, drawing her mouth into a straight line. "I'm tired of waiting for him to reveal himself. Since searching for him hasn't worked, I'm going to try to summon him instead. Demons are drawn to power, and I have it in spades. Perhaps if I offer myself to him, he won't be able to resist."

My blood chilled in my veins at her words.

I glanced at Henry before I said, "When are you going to do it? If you can wait until tomorrow night, I'll help you. There isn't much I can do, but I still think you shouldn't do it alone."

The witch stared at me for a moment as if trying to decide if she wanted to take me up on my offer. I hoped she would—I couldn't leave without helping her. I couldn't let her battle the darkness alone.

"I will," she finally said. "We will try summoning him tomorrow night."

The cold feeling in my limbs hadn't lifted. If anything, it seemed to grow and spread, but I refused to let it. I knew that Damien needed to be dealt with as soon as possible. We'd already waited too long. But I was delaying it, trying to prolong the moment of peace, much like Henry had done after I'd defeated the Dark Witches. One night. Our wedding night. We deserved that much. Fighting the darkness could wait, if only for a few more hours.

After Celeste had left our side, I turned to Henry.

"We can't leave until I help her," I told him, hoping he would understand.

The look he gave me told me that he did, and truly, I hadn't expected anything less from him. I waited for him to say something about what tomorrow night might bring, but he didn't.

"Dance with me?" he asked instead, gently squeezing the hand he hadn't released after we'd exchanged our vows. In that moment, I knew that we wouldn't talk about tomorrow night. There would be no dread or uncertainty tonight; there would only be peace and joy.

"Of course. I would never deny you, remember?" I teased with a hint of a smile.

"I hope you remember that promise later tonight," he teased back, one side of his mouth turning up.

My blood heated at his words, and a wave of desire rolled through me. Dark lust flashed in Henry's eyes, but he quickly reined it in. We handed our champagne glasses back to the servant before Henry hauled me to him for a dance. The world faded away again, but this time, we didn't go to the meadow. We remained by the arch, the sweet scent of flowers wafting through the air around us. Still, I wasn't seeing the ballroom and the guests, just as I wasn't hearing the music. All I could see was him, and all I could hear was the steadfast rhythm of his heart, which beat in unison with mine. Time seemed to crawl as we danced, without saying a word, completely immersed in each other. We didn't need to speak. There was an understanding between us, a quiet confidence that came with knowing that I was his and he was mine, and nothing could ever come between us.

38

I wasn't sure how long our dance lasted. It could've been minutes or hours. I didn't care as long as I was in Henry's arms, swimming in the deep-blue waters of his eyes. They didn't stay blue for long, as his features became harsh with stark lust. He pulled me to him, flush with his powerful body, before he kissed me…deeply, hungrily. The scrape of his fangs on my lips was a demand, and I knew the time for revelry was over. He wanted me to himself, and I was more than happy to comply. Because I wanted him to myself, too.

In the back of my mind, I knew it was too early for us to leave our own celebration. Our guests expected a speech or at least a chance to congratulate us, but it was hard to care as Henry's mouth moved over mine. The guests, the party…it was all secondary. It occurred to me that even if Henry and I were the only ones left in this world, just the two of us, I would still have everything I needed. He was enough. Before, the thought would have terrified me, but now Celeste's words floated up in my mind, *Love is a weapon, not a weakness.*

My love for Henry was a weapon, a shield against the dangers of the world.

"Are you ready to go?" he murmured against my swollen lips.

His hold on me tightened, and he pressed my body more fully to him so that I could feel him, *all* of him, letting me know how ready he was to have me all to himself. The answering pulse between my thighs made my breath hitch, and Henry's nostrils flared as a low, rough sound rumbled from deep within his throat.

"Yes," I breathed, clutching his arms.

I didn't want to run upstairs to his bedroom. Even with our supernatural speed, it wouldn't be fast enough. I couldn't wait another second to be in his arms, skin to skin, with nothing between us. So, I called upon my magic, feeling it light up my veins along with my growing arousal.

"Sophie—" Henry sucked in a sharp breath.

"Trust me," I whispered against his lips.

"Always," he said without hesitation.

Tiny sparks lit up every part of my body as I felt myself moving through space, carrying Henry with me. In the blink of an eye, my feet left the ballroom floor, planting on the fur rug in his bedroom. The world tilted as he swept me off my feet, lowering me on the mattress.

"This dress," Henry growled, shrugging off his jacket and casting it aside. "You're staying in this dress. It does something to me."

"The dress?" I asked as he gathered my skirts, lifting them up to my waist.

He tore at the lace undergarments beneath, and the urgency, the desperate need rolling off him only intensified my desire. I was in awe of how much he wanted me despite having had me so many times before. I was his now for all eternity, but knowing that only seemed to spur him on. Being desired like that...madly, ravenously...was a thrilling sensation, and I reveled in it.

Once Henry had gained access to the throbbing point between my legs, I expected him to slam into me in one smooth motion to finally feed the insatiable need. I was ready for it, trembling beneath him. But he didn't tear at his pants to free himself like I'd expected. Instead, he slid down my body until his head settled between my thighs. There was no teasing, no building up anticipation before he unleashed himself on me, his tongue diving inside, skillful and fierce. I cried out, fisting the sheets as he devoured me, wrapping his arms around my thighs to hold me in place as I writhed on the bed.

My head fell back against the covers, and I squeezed my eyes shut as all my senses zeroed in on where his mouth was sealed to my heated flesh. Every swipe of his tongue, every plunge of it into my drenched core, dragged me closer to the edge. The sounds I made...I was being too loud, but I didn't care. I was lost in the intense pleasure, the curling sensation between my thighs intensifying to the point of pain. The graze of his fang over the sensitive bundle of nerves was my undoing, and I shattered with a sharp cry, my back arching off the bed.

Panting and trembling from the powerful release, I barely felt him let go of my thighs and slide up my body. When I pried my lashes apart, he was hovering over me, his dark, hungry gaze locked on mine. His lips glistened from what he'd done to me, and the sight made me feral for him. Fisting my hand in his hair, I drew his mouth to mine and kissed him deeply, tasting myself on his tongue. Henry broke the kiss, breathing heavily as he reached for where I was already fumbling with the buttons of his pants. He tore at them, freeing himself, and I moaned at the sight of his rigid length. Curling my fingers around the silky hardness, I drew my hand up and down, eliciting a harsh groan from him. His head kicked back, and the tendons in his neck stood out as I pumped him hard, just like I knew he liked it.

The noises he made sent a slick rush of desire through me, and another thready moan escaped because I couldn't wait to feel him inside me, filling me, bringing me to the edge. I knew he couldn't wait either when his black gaze fastened on me and his hand wrapped around mine to stop what I was doing. When my fingers around him relaxed and let go, he grabbed that wrist and brought my arm up and over my head. A second later, my other arm joined it as he pinned my wrists to the bed and settled between my thighs. He was right where I wanted him, where I *ached* for him, yet he didn't push in. He just stared down at me, breathing hard. I whimpered, staring up at him. What was he waiting for? Did he want me to beg? Because I would. I would do anything to feel the exquisite burn and the aching pleasure of having him inside me. I was on fire, every part of me hyper-aware, waiting to see what he would do next.

"I love you," he rasped, looking into my eyes.

Then he thrust in as deep as he could go.

My ragged cry got lost in his loud moan as he slammed in to the hilt. I finally got what I'd wanted, and the feeling was pure ecstasy. I'd expected him to set a quick pace, but once again, he defied my expectations. He took his time as he withdrew, almost leaving my body entirely before thrusting back in, deeper than before. Another cry tore from my lips as my eyes drifted closed from the pleasure. Henry kept moving in and out of me in long, luxurious slides that were both utter bliss and torment.

"So beautiful," I heard him rasp. "So fucking beautiful, and mine."

I forced my eyes open and looked at him. His gaze had left my face and was roaming over my body and the wedding dress. Understanding dawned on me then. He'd wanted to leave the gown on because it was a symbol—a symbol of our union.

"Release my wrists, I want to touch you," I breathed.

His gaze shot to mine, and he immediately did what I'd requested. As soon as my wrists were free, I reached for him, sliding my hands down his face, his neck, and his broad shoulders. He reveled in my touch, still moving in and out with me in slow, torturous thrusts. When my hands slid to his chest and lingered there, Henry's gaze swept down, his long, black lashes shielding his eyes. Bracing himself on one arm, he covered my left hand with his, touching the wedding band around my finger. When he lifted his eyes to mine again, a primal hunger had invaded his gaze. Suddenly, everything changed. He clasped the back of my neck with one hand as he began moving faster, thrusting in deeper. His other arm wrapped around my thigh to keep me in place as he drove into me. I took it all, gasping with pleasure while Henry snarled with it. The sounds of our bodies coming together filled the room, and soon, my inner muscles were quivering, clamping down on him as release threatened.

"Bite me," I begged, shaking with need.

With a growl, Henry threw his head back and bared his fangs.

So magnificent and mine, a thought flashed through my mind a second before he struck.

The world shattered, and I shattered along with it as release crashed into me. It whipped through me, scattering me into hundreds of bright, dazzling pieces. My vision dimmed before turning white, as wave after wave of impossible pleasure swept me under. Henry roared against my neck, his large body bucking as he followed me over the edge. He buried his face in the crook of my neck, holding me tight while the aftershocks of his release racked him.

"I love you," I whispered, holding him close to me while the spasms rocking his body slowed.

It was just the two of us left in the world, and I couldn't be happier.

39

HENRY

*M*y wife. The two words kept replaying in my lust-addled mind as I held her in my arms. My wife, my everything.

When she'd found her release, I'd seen stars as she'd dragged me over the edge along with her. She'd held me as bolts of intense pleasure darted through me. She'd held me even though she'd still been shaking from her own release. We were holding each other now, waiting for our heartbeats and breathing to slow. When my mind had cleared enough for me to form coherent thoughts, I lifted my head from her neck and rested my forehead on hers, breathing her in.

"Two hundred years," I said low.

"What?" she asked, even though she'd heard me.

"Two hundred years I have waited for you."

"Was it worth it?" she breathed.

I lifted my head and looked into her eyes. She stared back at me with a soft smile—she already knew the answer.

"Yes. A million times, yes," I told her anyway.

Her smile grew before it faded.

"Thank you," she rasped, her eyes wet with unshed tears.

"For what?" I asked, my brows knitting.

"For waiting for me. For choosing me. For fighting for me." A tear escaped, rolling down the side of her face and soaking into the covers.

I stared at her in astonishment. She was the strongest creature I had ever known, yet right now, she was allowing herself to be weak. She was baring her soul before me, and I knew that for her, doing so took greater strength than defeating the Dark Witches or the darkness within.

"Thank you," I whispered.

For saying that, for being vulnerable with me, for letting me be the only one to see that side of you, I wanted to add, but the words wouldn't come.

So, instead of speaking, I sealed my mouth to hers. When her perfect lips parted, I glided my tongue over hers, and she moaned, sinking her fingers in my hair. The soft sound ignited my blood, which still hadn't cooled from earlier. I grew hard and thick inside her, and she gasped, arching her back and tilting her hips.

"Fuck," I groaned, feeling another release tingling down my spine.

Not yet, I thought as I withdrew, chuckling low when she whimpered in protest.

I quickly shrugged off my shirt and reached to pull her wedding dress over her head.

"Get on your hands and knees," I said, casting it aside.

The heat in Sophie's eyes intensified, and the salacious look she gave me had me pumping myself while I waited for her to get in position. When she had, I grabbed her hips and thrust in, eliciting a moan from her that nearly undid me. My head fell back, my eyes drifting closed, as I moved inside her, not truly believing this was my life. Two hundred years I had waited for her and now I had her. She was mine, and I could never get enough.

SOPHIE

My skin prickled with awareness as it always did right before sunrise.

Hide, it's a new day, the tingling sensation warned.

It *was* a new day, but I no longer had to hide. Opening my eyes, I blinked away the remnants of my sleep and looked at Henry sleeping peacefully beside me. His left hand rested on his bare stomach, and when my gaze snagged on the golden band on his finger, my heartbeat sped up in my chest.

The ring was a promise, a declaration of love, but it was also more. So much more. Exhaling softly, I reached out and threaded my fingers through his. Henry shifted next to me, stirring from his slumber. His deep-blue eyes fastened on me as soon as they opened.

"What are you doing up?" he asked, his voice gruff from sleep.

"Good morning." I smiled at him instead of responding.

"Good morning..." he said, his brow furrowing.

Such a simple phrase. Yet, as vampires, we never uttered the two simple words. After all, morning was never good. It was the evil that brought painful death or banished us to the shadows. No more. Not for us.

"I need to show you something," I said, pulling my hand away from Henry's.

His grip on my fingers tightened a second before he let go.

I left the bed but didn't go far, standing by the edge, looking at him expectantly. His hooded eyes turned darker as he took in my naked form.

"I think I like where this is going," he teased, one side of his mouth turning up.

I rolled my eyes and shook my head, sending waves of my hair over my bare shoulders.

"Later," I said with a small smile, turning away from him.

A pulse of desire rippled through me, but I shoved it aside as I stepped closer to the window.

"What are you doing?" Henry asked, sitting up in the bed. His tone was wary and for a good reason. I stood before the window now. "Sophie…" he warned as I reached for the curtains.

When I turned my head to look at him, he was crouched on top of the covers, his muscles tense as if he were going to shoot off the bed at any moment to tackle me away from the window.

"Do you trust me?" I asked him, as I hooked my thumbs between the drapes that were still sealed tight.

Henry's gaze darted to my fingers before returning to my face.

"You're scaring me…"

I arched a brow instead of repeating my question.

Henry's gaze darted back to my hands on the curtains, then back to me. He searched my face for a few moments. Whatever he saw must have given him the confirmation he'd needed.

"Always," he finally said, with a heavy sigh.

With a nod, I turned back to the window.

"Sophie!" I heard Henry's panicked shout a second before I pulled open the drapes.

The night sky greeted me, but the sunrise was close. The clouds were already catching the first pink, orange, and red hues of the sun that was still below the horizon. We didn't have much time.

When I looked back at Henry, he was on the other side of the room, standing flat against the wall. He'd scrambled off the bed and thrown himself there when I'd opened the curtains. I'd never seen his eyes so wide as he stared at me. He didn't say anything for a few minutes.

"How is this possible?" he finally rasped. "Is it because of your magic?"

I walked over to him and extended my hand.

"Come with me," I said low as a smile pulled at my lips.

"Me?" His tone was guarded.

"Yes, you." I laughed softly. "You will always come with me. Wherever I go. If I will stand before the rising sun, then so will you."

Henry's lips parted slightly as he looked past me, toward the window. I could see impossible longing etched into his striking features. His expression became almost pained, as if he wanted to believe something so badly it hurt.

His stormy gaze returned to mine.

Trust me, I pleaded with my eyes.

Always, he gave a small nod as he put his hand in mine.

I led him to the window, and he followed slowly, hesitantly, his breathing speeding up the closer we got to our destination. When I stepped into the early morning light, Henry stopped abruptly on the other side of the line that separated where I stood from the shadowy part of the room. His eyes glistened with tears as he watched me, his gaze like a caress gliding down my body bathed in the glow of the lightening sky.

"One more step," I urged him, reaching for his other hand.

He let me take it and pull him gently toward me.

I heard a sharp intake of his breath as he willed his legs to move. Squeezing his eyes shut, he put one foot in front of the other and stepped closer to me. He stood frozen before me, and I didn't think he was breathing. Reaching up, I brushed my lips over the hard line of his jaw, which was clenched so tight that the tendons in his neck stood out.

"Open your eyes," I whispered against his lips. "You wouldn't want to miss it."

A few more moments passed before Henry unclenched his jaw and released a shuddering breath. Slowly, he pried his lashes apart and looked at me. Awe and confusion were carved into his features. Then he turned his head toward the window, and I watched him as he took in the sight before him. The sky at the horizon was a bright orange hue now, pouring a warm glow over the landscape.

"How is this possible?" he asked again, turning back to me. "Is it your magic? Are you projecting it onto me somehow?" His gaze dropped to our joint hands.

My gaze lowered to them as well before I lifted it back up to his face.

"It is my magic," I told him, smiling softly. "But I'm not projecting it onto you."

Slowly, I slid my hands from his, and Henry's fingers closed around thin air as he tried to hold on. He squeezed his eyes shut again and jerked his face away from the window, expecting to burst into flames. A few seconds later, when he didn't, he cracked open one eye, then the other and turned back to face me again.

"It's the rings," I whispered as we stared at each other. "I used my magic to create them." Henry scowled. "Light magic," I quickly added to put him at ease.

"Like your mother created the Tear?" he asked, his taut features smoothing out.

"Yes. Only the objects I created allow us to walk in daylight."

Henry didn't say anything for a long time. I'd expected his gaze to be glued to the horizon, to the first sunrise he'd experienced in almost two hundred years, but instead, he was staring at me.

"Sophie, this is incredible," he finally said, his voice hoarse with emotion.

"Consider it a wedding gift," I rasped, getting choked up.

"Thank you." He lifted his hands to cup my face. "This means so much. I am grateful beyond words, but you already gave me the best gift I could have ever asked for. You said yes," he whispered softly as a little smile graced his lips.

"Of course I said yes," I whispered back. "With you is where I belong," I repeated the words he'd spoken to me when he'd proposed. "If I have your heart, then you have mine. Or perhaps it's just one heart beating in both of us. Two halves of one whole, because only when I'm with you do I feel complete. I love you."

I didn't realize that tears were streaming down my face until Henry gently wiped them away. He kissed me then, and it was tender and sweet, but also raw and overwhelming, just like my feelings for him. When his lips left mine, he turned me toward the window and moved behind me, folding his arms around my waist.

"I love you," he whispered into my ear, as the sun finally crested the horizon, casting a rosy hue across the morning sky and lighting up the world with the glow of a new day.

EPILOGUE

CELESTE

LAST NIGHT

Demons. They prowled the earth, corrupting innocent souls. Xanthus had sent them to restore the delicate balance. When Sophie had defeated the Dark Witches, she'd tipped the scale, and demons were the counterweight. The girl had been so happy then. I hadn't had the heart to tell her that there would always be a constant battle, another evil threat to defeat. The good could never win, just like the darkness couldn't prevail. There couldn't be light without the dark.

"You summoned me, Witch?" the demon said, snapping me out of my thoughts.

Sophie had said he went by the name of Damien. He had claimed to be Agatha's son. No doubt in an attempt to make his deception more believable. I had sent a message out through the threads, standing by the creek where I'd found Sophie talking to this vile creature before, and he had answered my call. Sophie had wanted me to wait so we could confront the demon together, and I had told her I would. I'd lied. I knew that for my plan to work, I had to be alone.

A feeling of foreboding needled me deep inside. I ignored it. White Witches listened to the world around them, but fate was never sealed. It was still possible to change the course of events.

"I did summon you, demon. It's time to put a stop to this."

"To what? Me promising others what they truly desire?" Damien hissed, the black from his pupils bleeding into his eyes until no white remained.

"Your promises are laced with poison. You warp their minds, twisting their perception of reality," I said, staring into the glossy black depths.

"Or I simply uncover what they covet the most."

I smirked, rallying my power. This conversation needed to end. Nothing good could ever come from engaging with a demon.

"What about you, Witch?" the creature asked, cocking his head to the side, the movement rigid and unnatural. "Surely there are things you want for yourself? Your power is greater than most. You should have all the things you desire."

"The only thing I desire is to rid this world of your evil," I said, as I felt my magic thrumming under my skin.

The demon's features mottled in a deranged smile. "I won't make this easy for you."

"I know," I told him, my magic crackling at my fingertips. "I know that nothing in this life comes easy."

I thrust my hands out, and my power shot out of my fingers, latching on to the demon, digging like talons into his skin. It ripped the creature out of the shell that he used as his disguise, and the human body crumpled to the ground with a thud. The demon was now in his true form—a mass of churning shadows; a black, pulsing phantom of dark energy that thrashed in the ropes of my magic.

Do not be afraid, I whispered a reminder in my head a second before I yanked the threads back to me.

My power retreated into my fingers, hauling the screeching demon flush to me. *In* me. I sucked in a sharp breath, absorbing the darkness. Once it was inside me, there was no time to waste. I imagined a tiny obsidian box in my chest, made of the strongest metal. I shoved the pulsing shadows in it, slamming the lid and sealing the darkness away. A shuddering exhale left me, and I bent at the waist, bracing my hands on my knees for support. It was over. For now. I didn't know for how long I could store the demon inside me, but I wasn't delusional to think I could keep him inside forever. When you carried the darkness within you, eventually, it always broke out.

I stood unmoving for a few minutes, waiting for my heartbeat to slow and my breathing to become even. Once they had, I went to take a step, but didn't get far. Excruciating pain twisted my limbs, tearing a keening sound from my throat. My body spasmed and twitched as I heard a voice in my head, an eerie hiss made of the blackest shadows, "I told you I wasn't going to make this easy."

Abruptly, the pain stopped, and with it, everything else. I didn't feel anything, only numbness, as my body straightened, my limbs relaxed, and my facial features smoothed out. My body was a vessel now. It was not my own as it began moving, walking, leaving who I was behind in the woods. A piece of me still remained inside, but it was now confined to a tiny black box made of the strongest metal.

ALSO BY V.I. DAVIS

Crimson and Shadows

Josephine's Tear

Sophie's Ruin

ABOUT THE AUTHOR

V.I. is a chocolate-loving coffee enthusiast who enjoys a quiet life in a small town with her husband and two kids. She writes stories with fantasy, romance, and all your favorite tropes. Her journey as an author has only just begun, but she has a feeling it will be a great one. You can sign up for her newsletter or find her on social media platforms if you want to follow along. Happy reading!